# Deep Dire Harvest

Deep Lakes Cozy Mystery Series Book 4

## Joy Ann Ribar

Wine Glass Press

GENRE: *Cozy Mystery*

**Deep Dire Harvest**
Copyright ©2022 by Joy Ann Ribar
All rights reserved.
Published in the United States by Wine Glass Press.

This book is a work of fiction. Names, characters, places, and incidents are the product of the author's imagination or are used fictitiously. Characters in this book have no relation to anyone bearing the same name, and are not based on anyone known or unknown by the author. While some locations and locales are real, the author has added fictional touches to further the story. Any resemblance to actual events, locales, or persons, living or dead, is coincidental.

ISBN (paperback): 978-1-959078-00-5
ISBN (ebook): 978-1-959078-01-2

Edited by Kay Rettenmund
Copy Editors: Janelle Bailey, Katie David

Cover Design by Tom Heffron

First Edition: September 2022

Birds of a feather flock together... To my flock, scattered far and wide. You know who you are.

And especially to my brother, Daryl, who taught me everything I know about Purple Martins. He's a real bird-brain, and that's no insult!

## Deep Lakes Cozy Mystery Series

- *Deep Dark Secrets - Book One*

- *Deep Bitter Roots - Book Two*

- *Deep Green Envy - Book Three*

- *Deep Flakes Christmas-A Nisse Visit - Prequel*

Available at your favorite indie bookstore (if you don't see them, ask the store to order them!)

Available as an ebook in most formats.

Visit joyribar.com and subscribe to my quarterly newsletter. https://joyribar.com/signup

Your review, even a short one, is most welcome anywhere you and your friends visit and buy books - thank you, kindly!

# Chapter 1

*You and I once fancied ourselves birds, and we were happy even when we flapped our wings and fell down and bruised ourselves, but the truth is that we were birds without wings. You were a robin and I was a blackbird, and there were some who were eagles, or vultures, or pretty goldfinches, but none of us had wings.*

*For birds with wings nothing changes; they fly where they will and they know nothing about borders and their quarrels are very small.* — Louis De Bernieres

Shauna Champagne welcomed most mornings before sunup with a run in the countryside near her home on Blackbird Marsh. In fact, she'd been running more frequently of late due to a troubled mind that kept her awake at night.

It's not that Shauna didn't love managing her husband's construction company, Nothing but the Finest Champagne Builders; she just yearned for something more. Shauna's son was working on a law degree in Minnesota and fully independent. Marcus didn't need his mom to be, well, mommy-like any longer.

Shauna had majored in art and her roots were calling her back to a desire to use her creativity once again. She'd been dabbling lately, designing the apartment above the craft shop next to Bubble and Bake, in the historic downtown building owned by Shauna's sister-in-law, Frankie. She'd also redecorated the studio above the workshop at Lovely Lavender Farm, where Aunt CeCe lived, and was a consultant to Hannah and Ashley Turner in decorating Sunflowers and Cattails, an elegant country barn venue.

What would her husband James say if she wanted to venture off on her own, no longer part of the daily routine at Nothing but the Finest? The uncertainty of her quandary left a knot of nausea in her stomach, accompanied by sleepless nights and early morning runs, as circuitous as her thoughts.

Shauna's serpentine inner conversation occupied her to the point where the music from her earbuds no longer registered, and she was startled to find herself thrown roughly to the ground, nearly facedown, in the squishy grass on the edge of Blackbird Pond. She paused a moment to catch her breath and turned over gingerly on her bottom, checking to see if she'd sustained any injuries. She sat up and peered at the direction from which she'd come, glaring at the hummock a foot away that tripped her up. Groping around the wet grass for the earbuds and cell phone that vaulted from her body, her eyes captured a dead bird lying a foot away on the shore.

Shauna gathered the phone and earbuds and, limping a bit, made her way to the dark lifeless bird. Out of the corner of her eye, another dead bird appeared. She noticed both were wet, with shimmery heads and matted, short feathers in neutral shades. Something about their beaks made her surmise these were babies. She scanned the area and gasped. More dead birds littered the shoreline and she saw a few lapping the shallow water. Her body sank, instantly sad for the birds and their parents.

She looked around for a predator hunting the marsh. Maybe a bobcat or large hawk was nearby or even someone taking pot shots with a pellet gun. She didn't see anything in the dim dawn light except for a dark shape bobbing on one side of the pond near the shoreline. Shuddering, Shauna walked silently toward the shape. She was at the bottom of the sloping area by the public access point to the marsh, and she peered upward to see a car in the parking area.

Like a bird, she cautiously scanned the area, eyes darting every which way, just in case. In case of what, she couldn't be certain. She had to go into the water a couple of feet to reach the shape, knowing instinctively what she was about to uncover and trying to decide if she should touch the shape or flee.

She could see the field jacket billowing outward like a sail; attached below it were creamy legs and, further down, feet clad in hiking boots. Closing her eyes, she pulled the feet toward shore as if pulling a rope attached to an inner tube, but this was heavy and took a pained effort. She didn't look back until she thought the whole bundle was ashore.

No turning back now, she knew she must heft the body over and attempt to find life or, in its absence, breathe life as an offering. A gulp of acid rose in her throat when she came face-to-face with the lifeless woman, who most certainly had drowned. Old training kicked into gear as she turned the cold head to one side, simultaneously compressing the chest then blowing air into the woman's lungs. She counted ten times, ten times more, then surrendered to call 911 on her cell.

Frankie Champagne walked the vineyard rows around Bountiful Fruits, jotting row numbers and grape varieties in the logbook as she strolled. Every season in the vineyard held its own spotlight, but harvest was the culmination of each trip around the sun when all the nurturing and labor yielded a success story. A success, that is, if Mother Nature lent a helping hand.

This year, harvest would hit before summer was on the wane. An early summer brought the grapes on in full and the above-normal temperatures ripened them into fat clusters ready for picking. Frankie and Manny Vega, the vineyard manager and grape whisperer, had been tasting grapes for several weeks, anticipating a September reaping. At the same time, the two had placed nets over the ripening vines to keep the birds from harvesting before the humans. Flocks of robins and turkeys in particular were known for decimating vineyards, as were white-tailed deer.

Although it would be at least another three weeks before her precious Frontenac variety would be ready for its first wine harvest, the green-yellow Brianna were ready now, and plans for picking Monday morning were underway. A crew of volunteers would assemble at first sun to help Manny and his workers make short work of the picking process.

Frankie smiled, thinking of the crop of Briannas, some of which would be crushed for a new vintage, an apple mead conceived by Violet, Frankie's college-aged daughter majoring in microbiology. Violet attended

UW-Stevens Point, about an hour away, but would be home on and off to oversee her pet project to its fruition.

Frankie reached out to pluck a grape for tasting but was interrupted by the jingle of her cell phone. The icon of her sister-in-law, Shauna, appeared on the screen.

"Hi Shauna." The two were not famously close, and Frankie generally assumed the subject would be business-related, so she was taken aback to hear Shauna's panicked voice coming through.

"Frankie, I'm at Blackbird Pond. I was out for a run and, and...there were all these dead birds and... someone floating in the water!" Shauna gulped air and choked back an emerging sob.

"Whoa, slow down. Are you okay?" Frankie was unable to get a clear picture of the scenario in which she imagined a person floating on an inner tube, cocktail in hand, on the rustic pond, surrounded by dead birds.

Shauna took a deep breath. "I fell by the pond, and when I got up I saw a lot of dead baby birds, then a body, Frankie. I tried to save her, but I was too late." Now the tears were flowing as the sob broke free from her throat.

"Did you call 911?" She believed Shauna probably had called it in, but sometimes panic trumps logic.

"Yes, of course. After... after I tried to do CPR." Frankie heard Shauna making heaving noises, as her stomach finally gave way amid the shocking situation.

"I'll be right there. Hold tight. Sit down somewhere and put your head between your knees and take some deep breaths, okay?"

Frankie walked cross-country, a much quicker route than driving the roadways to Blackbird Pond. Blackbird Marsh and Pond adjoined the vineyard property, which was a parcel of land Frankie purchased from her brother, James. James owned a number of acres surrounding the marsh. Traversing the fire lanes and following the deer trails, Frankie managed to arrive at the pond within a few minutes.

Shauna sat with her head between her knees as instructed but looked up when Frankie called out to her. Frankie noticed her leggings were caked in dirt and her running shoes were covered in wet grass. Shauna's blond ponytail held in place, but her face conveyed her distraught state, puffy from crying. She wore perspiration on her brow partly from her run and partly from hefting the floating body to shore. She grabbed Frankie and hugged her tightly, explaining what she saw upon her arrival at the scene.

Frankie was glad Shauna had called 911 but knew there wouldn't be much time to look around before the police arrived and chased her away. Frankie had been an unwelcome addition at a few recent investigation sites and imagined a police perimeter would be immediately erected, and she would be on the other side of the tape.

"Sit here and don't move. The police are going to want to investigate this, and we can't disturb anything that might be evidence, or we'll be in big trouble," she instructed Shauna. She didn't mention that moving the body from the water could already be considered tampering with the investigation. Shauna had moved the body in an attempt to save the woman's life, so how upset could the police be?

Frankie had already taken in the big picture at the pond, perplexed by the dead baby birds that must have fledged from the purple martin house between the parking lot and the pond but were sadly too young to fly. That was her first mental note, which she instantly followed to the dreaded next conclusion. Frankie was certain she knew the identity of the drowned victim.

Carefully tiptoeing to the pond's edge, Frankie made sure not to walk over any footprints that may have been made by someone else, someone who wasn't her sister-in-law. Reaching the edge of the shoreline, Frankie peered down at the face of Fern Mallard, ornithologist and guest presenter for the weekend Fall Migration Days event. Frankie had just met Fern last night at a reception hosted by her own esteemed bird club, the Whitman Seekers.

In fact, club members and guests would be assembling soon at Blackbird Pond, where Fern's presentation about purple martins would begin with a demonstration of how the apartment house worked, and attendees would see her tagging baby martins to track them after they fledged. Frankie heaved a deep sigh.

If first impressions could be trusted, Frankie immediately liked Fern, who was a bird genius but didn't flaunt her expertise. Fern's enthusiasm for her science was expressed in terms everyone could understand, coated in humor and contagious passion.

Working swiftly, Frankie gingerly lifted and turned over Fern's right hand and arm, then the left one. Scratches on the left forearm revealed welts, and there were purplish marks around the left wrist. Handling birds could account for the scratches, but Frankie thought they likely indicated a skirmish. Had Fern been attacked? Her face was scratched up a little, but there were no welts or bruises, so maybe those scratches surfaced after she was already dead.

Like many field scientists, the ornithologist wore a jacket with multiple pockets for tools and specimens. A pair of binoculars hung from a thick strap around Fern's neck; caps still covered the lenses. The largest pockets on Fern's moss green jacket were bulging, so Frankie reached in, her fingers wrapped in a tissue. She closed her eyes, hoping she wasn't about to encounter a dead bird. Instead, she pulled out a rock the size of a bar of soap. Several more similar rocks followed. The other pocket carried the same contents. There was nothing remarkable about the rocks, in fact, Frankie was pretty sure they came from the parking lot boundary lines.

Frankie stared out toward the pond where she glimpsed a nylon explorer's hat floating on the surface. The color matched Fern's field jacket. A few shriveled-looking birds floated around the hat, doing a macabre synchronized water ballet. Frankie's stomach twitched, and she turned her attention elsewhere.

She scrambled up the path from the pond, ready to look around the Subaru Outback that most certainly belonged to Fern. Her heart beat rapidly as she noticed two long grooves in the dirt beside the path that led all the way to the pond from the martin house. She squinted to see if shoe prints were present but was in too much of a hurry to notice. Hopefully she could find out from the police detectives.

Frankie skirted around to peer through the Subaru's windshield. She could see a knapsack on the passenger seat. It was open, but she couldn't see its contents. A travel coffee mug was tipped over onto the driver's seat. The glovebox was hanging open. Either Fern was in a hurry this morning, or someone was looking for something in her car. Frankie wanted to press her face against the windows to see more, but she couldn't risk contaminating the scene. And she didn't dare try to open the doors, which would be dusted for prints, so she had to settle for the meager clues she could see.

Sirens wailed down Blackbird Marsh Lane, causing Frankie to scurry down the path to sit beside Shauna. Shauna gripped Frankie's arm, linking it through her own, and leaned on her shoulder. Frankie patted her arm.

"The police are going to take a statement from you, Shauna. I can stay with you if you'd like. Or I can call James, too." Frankie wanted to hear Shauna's statement since more details were sure to come forth, given the detective's keen questions. More so, she wanted to protect and comfort her sister-in-law, who was clearly in shock.

Two squads pulled onto the grass beside the parking area, so as not to disturb any evidence. Driving the brown SUV with the Whitman County insignia was Sheriff Alonzo Goodman, Frankie's lifelong friend, accompanied by Detective Shirley Lazaar.

Frankie couldn't have been happier to see the two officers until the muscular frame of Officer Donovan Pflug emerged from the other squad. Pflug looked as though someone ruined his Saturday breakfast by calling in a dead body. His scowl deepened considerably when he spied Frankie sitting next to Shauna. Frankie and Pflug had an unpleasant history, and though she managed to avoid him the past several months, her luck had run out.

Pflug marched purposefully over to Shauna and glared at Frankie. "I don't see any ovens or grape vines around, so I'm not sure what you're doing here," he spoke scornfully, jabbing a meaty finger at her chest. Pflug's military haircut was covered by a Smokey Bear hat, a last second grab from the passenger seat, that he used to look more intimidating. As if he wasn't already an imposing figure at almost six-and-a-half feet.

Frankie herself was a mere five feet in stature, which she made up for in a fierce brand of spunk. Because she was used to Pflug's surly demeanor, she didn't flinch. "I'm here because Shauna called me after discovering the victim. She is my sister-in-law, after all." Anticipating what would happen next, she added, "She's asked me to stay with her while she gives her statement."

Pflug frowned, looking like a bullfrog with a migraine. Stepping between the two seated women, he roughly pulled each one up by an arm and escorted them to a bench near the parked squad. Grimacing, he barked at Frankie: "You can stay, but say just one word, and you'll be baking in the back of my squad, got it?"

Question after question methodically flowed from Pflug in a stiff, detached tone. Frankie grudgingly admired his expertise as she tried to follow his line of logic and keep track of the details. She cursed herself for not having a notebook along, not that Pflug would have allowed her to write in it. After a few taps on her phone's note app, he snapped at her to stow it or lose it.

At least the bench served as a vantage point for Frankie to watch Shirley gather evidence from the scene. Shirley examined the scratches on Fern's left arm and swabbed them for possible DNA and checked all the jacket pockets, pulling out rock after rock with gloved hands. Each rock went into its own baggie and would be examined for prints. Frankie learned from Shirley that rocks can retain fingerprints, something criminals often fail to recognize.

Frankie made a mental note when Shirley turned the victim's head, took several photos of the back of it, and swabbed it. *I wonder if Fern has a head wound. Maybe she was hit from behind and then dragged to the pond.* Frankie recalled the grooves in the dirt, probably drag marks. She wondered what Alonzo was finding in the Subaru and whether or not she could coax any information out of him. The two were close friends, but Frankie's investigations in the capacity of news reporter crossed the line with the by-the-book sheriff.

Since Frankie began moonlighting for *Point Press* as a regional reporter, she'd investigated several suspicious deaths and developed a cautious friendship with Shirley. The female detective often traded information with Frankie. Maybe because they were both women in industries still dominated by men. Maybe because Frankie sweetened their exchanges with bags of Bubble & Bake pastries from the downtown shop she operated with her pal, Carmen.

Frankie's attention circled back to Pflug and Shauna as the questions turned to why she had moved the victim from the pond and what lifesaving maneuvers she had performed. Pflug wanted exact details. Frankie couldn't wait to see his expression when Shauna told him what she'd told Frankie.

Wide-eyed, mouth agape, Shauna informed Pflug that she had pulled several feathers from Fern's mouth before attempting resuscitation.

# Chapter 2

*Hold fast to dreams, for if dreams die, life
is a broken-winged bird that cannot fly." —
Langston Hughes*

*Everyone carries with them at least one piece to
someone else's puzzle. — Lawrence Kushner*

If Frankie was hoping Pflug would shudder at the idea
of a victim with a mouthful of bird feathers, he didn't
even have the decency to offer a twitch for her benefit.
Instead, Pflug commented dryly, "I've seen way worse.
This isn't cringeworthy by any stretch."

The questioning completed, Frankie turned Shauna
over to James, who had driven to the pond to pick up
his distraught wife. He thanked Frankie for her help,
and the two left as Frankie walked up the path again
to the parking area where a number of people were
clustered. She recognized several members of the bird
club, there for Fern's presentation that morning. They
flocked together with others who were probably there
for the same reason. Word spread quickly about the
victim's identity, and disbelief registered on their faces
and in their comments.

Frankie veered away from the group toward Alonzo, who was standing by his SUV, radio in hand, calling for extra officers to set up a roadblock at the end of Blackbird Marsh Road to keep away any more gawkers.

The morning sun promised another warm day as it reflected off the sheriff's glasses, which had slipped down the bridge of his nose from perspiration. "Wanna tell me how you happened to be here this morning, Frankie?" Alonzo's face was serious, not agitated.

Frankie reached up to squeeze her friend's shoulder. She cared for him like a brother. He'd been the best man at her wedding years ago and took Frankie's side when her husband left her for another woman and moved West. Alonzo was protective, another protector in the herd since Frankie had four brothers already at her service.

"Anything I can do to help, Lon?" she asked him, after explaining Shauna's call and encounter at the pond. She glanced over at the gawkers huddled together, who were decidedly curious about Frankie's presence on the other side of the police tape.

Alonzo nodded, kicking the dirt with one boot. "We're spread pretty thin this weekend. I had to call in the fire department to set up a roadblock. I've got an officer looking into a burglary on Lake Loki and another responding to a two-vehicle crash by Whitman's Bridge." He looked past her at the gathering crowd, then straightened to his full height, shoulders squared, as a man wearing a ball cap ducked under the yellow tape.

Prepared to block the man's path, Alonzo held up a warning hand for him to stop. The man faltered, then proceeded a couple steps forward. "Please, I must speak with you." He held up an ID with credentials of some sort, so Alonzo motioned him forward.

The man looked to be in his 60's with mostly gray windblown hair and weathered features, indicating a life spent outdoors. He held out one work-heavy hand toward Alonzo's.

"I'm Daryl George with the Midwest Wildlife Foundation. We sponsored Fern Mallard's study on these birds, so I'd like to get her field notes from her car and net the dead birds." George pointed at the pond below. He wore powerful binoculars around his neck and a grim expression on his face.

Alonzo shook his head at the official. "My team has to look through the victim's belongings before we can release them, I'm afraid, so I can't give you the field book until everything is processed. Once we're done gathering evidence by the pond, you can net your dead birds. Anything else?"

"Yeah. I need to assess the house." George pointed to the apartment-style birdhouse perched on a tall pole to the left of the parking area.

Alonzo nodded and handed him a pair of latex gloves. "It's been dusted for prints already, but you'll need to wear these in case we missed something. I don't want any extra fingerprints muddling up my investigation."

George took purposeful strides toward the birdhouse, and Lon leaned over to whisper to Frankie. "Go with him and keep an eye on him. Let me know if he says or does anything strange."

Frankie couldn't be sure if Lon was trying to keep her occupied for his own sake or if he was seriously suspicious about Daryl George. The wildlife official seemed harmless to Frankie. Soft-spoken and unassuming, the man was small but sturdy and had kind blue eyes that crinkled at the corners.

"Hello, Mr. George. I'm Frankie Champagne. I'd like to watch you assess the martin house if you don't mind." Frankie shook his hand.

He looked confused. "Are you with the police?"

Frankie pretended innocence. "Oh no. I'm a member of the bird club, and I'm actually here for Fern's presentation. I'm so sorry about what's happened."

George donned the latex gloves with effort, making a face at the smell and texture. "I hate these things. Call me Daryl, please. I'm not a government suit. I actually get my hands dirty all the time."

Frankie knew there were large differences of opinion between environmental scientists who worked in the office versus those who worked in the field. Being a doer herself, she respected Daryl's methods.

The purple martin houses in the area were officially erected as part of the Purple Martin Project, a government-sanctioned effort to restore the population of the species of swallow. "Martins eat tons of flying insects and rely solely on humans for nesting because their nesting habitat of old growth forest giants were logged out decades ago," Daryl told Frankie, slipping easily into his instructor mode.

Frankie had some knowledge of the species. She'd volunteered to monitor martins last summer at one of the five colony houses around Deep Lakes. Martins nest in colonies in a house with numerous compartments, usually enough for about 12 bird families. The house sits on top of a metal pole and is accessed by a crank and pulley system that lowers the house and allows a field scientist to open the compartments to count and tag the dwellers within.

The birds arrive in the spring and begin nesting almost immediately. The houses have to be monitored for invading species like European starlings. Frankie recalled birders reporting that discovered starlings were immediately evicted. Sometimes, tree swallows nest in the colony, too, and are allowed to remain since they are chiefly mosquito eaters, very beneficial to humans.

Frankie watched with interest while Daryl opened each compartment and made notes on a diagram in his logbook. He frowned. "Only two adults here and five young, total. What a shame."

He shaded his eyes and scanned the electrical wires where birds hang out to rest and watch for bugs. Frankie followed his gaze, seeing numerous birds on the wires, knowing they were likely swallows because of their small size. Daryl lifted the binoculars to get a closer look.

"Just what I thought. I see two martins up there, but the rest are tree swallows." He produced a disgusted sigh. "I'm going to need to look at Fern's field log to get a real count. And I need to get down there to round up those dead fledglings."

Frankie logged a quick note about Daryl's findings, then tucked her phone back in her pocket. "What do you think happened this morning, I mean, from a bird scientist point of view?"

One gray bushy brow rose in surprise, followed by a deep breath. Daryl looked from the Subaru to the martin house to the pond. "Fern Mallard was a seasoned ornithologist. She started working on this study almost two years ago, so she knows how to handle martins. I think she came out early, before the birds' breakfast, when they'd still be sleepy."

He paused to flip back through his logbook. "Young martins fledge by August, but this is a new house with a late-arriving colony, so these birds probably wouldn't fledge for another week or two. Fern would know that. She would never risk the young birds fledging before their time."

He paused several seconds, looked again regretfully toward the pond and waved a hand. "That's what can happen when young aren't ready to fledge. A martin's first flight is right over water. If they can't fly, well... you can see the results."

Frankie decided to press him further. "I see, so how do you account for all those dead babies down there?"

Daryl's lips twisted thoughtfully, and he measured his words cautiously. "I guess that's where the police come in. I'd say maybe Fern never opened the martin house today. Maybe she never had the chance."

Daryl wrote a few more notes in the official logbook, closed it with an angry slap against his thigh and made his way back toward Alonzo. Frankie snatched her phone from her pocket and began speaking into the notes app: "I get the feeling Daryl George has seen something like this before. I mean, dead bird babies or a botched field study. Either way, he's officially angry."

# Chapter 3

*If one bird foraging in a flock on the ground
suddenly takes off, all other birds will take off
immediately after, before they even know what's
going on. The one who stays behind may be prey.*
— *Frans de Waal*

*Pessimism of the spirit; optimism of the will.* —
*Antonio Gramsci*

*Some people would be discontented in Paradise,
others ... are cheerful in a graveyard.* — *Arthur
Lynch*

Alonzo gleaned a quick summary of Frankie's time spent
with Daryl George, then asked her to please find a place
for "your bird geek friends" to regroup. "You know I'm
a fan of wildlife, Frankie, but I've got bigger fish to fry
this weekend, pardon the expression."

It was Labor Day weekend, the official end to the
tourist summer season, and a police officer's nightmare
of patrolling crowds of people on both waterways
and highways. Besides Fall Migration Days in Deep
Lakes, the Chicken Chew barbecue with a mini carnival

attracted locals and visitors to Spurgeon Park, the center of Deep Lakes summer festivals.

Frankie made a beeline for Tasha Rivers, the Whitman Seekers president and organizer of Fall Migration Days. The event seemed likely to be a bust now that its main attraction was, well, incapacitated. Following the presentation and morning bird hike, Fern was supposed to be leading a how-to session in creating a backyard environment welcoming to birds, as well as crafting birdhouses with kids in the afternoon.

Frankie approached Tasha warily and tapped her on the shoulder. "Hi, Tasha. I'm so sorry about all this."

Tasha looked as wild-eyed as a hormonal chimp. "Oh Frankie. This is what you call a disaster. I don't even know what to do now." Tasha thumped her forehead, smashing her cowboy hat against it. Her long dark braids, twisted with colorful beads, hung down her front; one braid caught inside her large hammered hoop earrings.

Frankie admired Tasha's New Age-meets-country energy, and wanted to support the younger woman's first attempt in a leadership position. Tasha worked part-time as Whitman County's extension agent with duties varying from organizing 4-H clubs and events to agricultural activities like visits to the farm and the county fair. She and her husband, Ben, had moved to Deep Lakes from Milwaukee in hopes of a quieter life for their two young sons.

Frankie patted her hand gently. "Let's regroup. Why don't we all meet at Bubble & Bake to talk and get some goodies? It's time to create a Plan B."

The hubbub of the last couple of hours made Frankie forget what was waiting for her at Bubble & Bake. Thankfully she arrived before the birding group, who were deep in speculative conversations at Blackbird Pond before departing for town.

Saturdays were consistently busy for the bakery, but Labor Day weekend Saturday looked like the queue for a popular Disney ride. The line snaked down the front ramp along Granite Street past the alley where Frankie maneuvered around customers to park her SUV. The line continued to the next business on the block, Callahan Realty. Advance planning meant the B&B crew had plenty of baked goods on hand, after putting in extra hours Thursday and Friday, but it appeared the staff couldn't keep up.

Frankie grabbed a shop apron as soon as she set foot in the back door in order to dive into action behind the counter. In the kitchen, however, she was immediately face-to-face with a troubled Peggy Champagne, her mother. Not much can ruffle the unflappable Peggy, so Frankie grew pale and vaulted toward her mother.

"Thank goodness you're here, Frankie. It's just terrible. Poor Cherry, poor Pom." Peggy pulled a handkerchief from her apron and dabbed her nose.

Light dawned and hit Frankie's brain like glaring headlights. How could she forget that Fern Mallard was a cousin to her employees, Cherry and Pom Parker? Both were working this morning and must be hurting immensely. Frankie couldn't admit her forgetfulness to her mother, however.

"I got here as soon as I could, Mom. I stayed with Shauna while the police took her statement." Frankie's announcement was news to Peggy, so daughter hastily filled in mother, then trotted out front.

Pom and Cherry waited on customers; both women wore cheerful smiles despite the long line and their own shock. Aunt CeCe operated the register while the two younger women bagged and boxed kringle and butterhorns, famous favorites at the shop, among other treats. Frankie dashed to the office alcove, where a second money bag waited, then logged onto the other computer by the wine bar, the shop's second register. She caught the eyes of both of Fern's cousins and touched her hand over her heart with a sorrowful expression. Pom and Cherry acknowledged Frankie's sympathy, but the two pros went right back to serving customers.

The line dwindled to a point where Frankie could see the birders standing at the end of the shop's expansive picture windows. She excused herself momentarily, made her way out the back door, down the alley, and up to the bird group.

"Come with me. I'll take you in the back way and you can sit on the deck for a bit. I'll be out as soon as I finish up the rush." Frankie led the group down the alley and up the steps to the deck that overlooked Sterling Creek and a backyard dotted with bird feeders and flowerbeds designed to attract butterflies. "At least you can enjoy some bird watching," she said hopefully.

Frankie nimbly sped up the steps and through the kitchen, pausing to tell Peggy about the extra guests on the back deck.

"I'll bring them a pot of coffee and some treats from the kitchen," her mother called after her. Peggy had regained her composure and would capably handle the birders while Frankie assisted out front.

Less than a half hour later the shop was empty except for the loungers, who leisurely nibbled on pastries and sipped coffee in the café chairs scattered around the shop. Aunt CeCe lovingly embraced Pom and Cherry, insisting she would take over customer service for the rest of the morning, so they could go home. Frankie squeezed each of the Parkers as their tears flowed freely.

"I'm so sorry about Fern. I just don't know what to say. I hope you can tell me more about her later, but right now you should be home with your family." Frankie used her motherly voice.

Pom was first to shake her head, causing her bouncy blonde ponytail to swish back and forth. "I want you to help us find out who did this terrible thing to Fern. She didn't deserve it, Frankie. Fern was golden." Pom's hands were balled into upset fists.

Cherry nodded her agreement. "Fern was an amazing person. But Frankie's right, Pom. We should go home. Mom will want our help with arrangements.  And, someone needs to call the rest of the family to come...early." Cherry's voice broke on the last word. The Parkers had planned a family reunion for Monday, and most of the family would be arriving tomorrow.  It was rare for Fern to be in the area, since her ornithology projects kept her globe-trotting. The martin study that included the Deep Lakes colonies was expected to keep her in town for the next two weeks.

Frankie grabbed the two by the hand and led them into the kitchen. "I'll certainly do all I can to help you find out what happened to Fern," she promised as she packed up butterhorns, cinnamon streusel muffins, and lemon tarts in one box, while Peggy packed another with assorted scones. "Here, take these with you. You're going to have a lot of people to feed." She escorted Pom and Cherry out the front door to avoid an encounter with the inquiring minds of the birders waiting on the deck.

Peggy was already out front tending customers with Aunt CeCe when Frankie walked back through.

"You two are dears. Thank you for taking over for Cherry and Pom. I'll be out on the deck trying to salvage Fall Migration Days activities, if you need me."

The birders were happily munching baked goods and slurping coffee when Frankie grabbed a seat at the first picnic table. With the help of past-president Trish Oleson and her long-time birder husband Ed, Tasha had constructed new plans.

Trish and Ed were acquainted with Dominic Finchley, a notable ornithologist in his own right. Finchley was in town for a family event, so Ed called him, and Finchley agreed to take over the afternoon workshop on creating backyard spaces for birds.

The birdhouse building with kids seemed easy enough for the members of the bird club to handle. Tasha pointed out that the houses were basically kits with precut wood pieces that just needed to be nailed together. A few volunteers stepped forward to handle the activity.

WIth business out of the way and a little time to kill, the rumor mill wound up for another grinding discussion of what happened to Fern.

"I think it was her ex. I heard she just broke off their engagement," offered Dawn Richards. Dawn was a thirtyish receptionist at Triple Crown Marine, the foremost industry in Deep Lakes, producing boat motors for most of the country. New to the bird club, rumor had it Dawn was shopping for a boyfriend and dabbled in many activities the small town offered in hopes of finding someone.

"What about her assistant? Jealousy is a strong motive. I heard the assistant wanted to take the lead on the purple martin study." The nasally sharp speculation came from Howie Tucker, a perennial candidate for the Whitman County Board of Supervisors. Howie was a known complainer who attended government meetings just to hear himself talk.

"I met her assistant and she's very professional. Besides, it looked like she and Fern worked well together. But...," Tasha's voice trailed off a moment while she considered whether or not to add to the gossip. All ears were tuned toward Tasha. "Well, I heard Fern say something about another field biologist who wanted to be part of the study but was turned away. A Naomi someone."

"Let's not forget that Fern comes from a huge family. In my opinion, there's always a family secret, a black sheep or two in the woodwork." That comment flew from Bonnie Fleisner, the busybody former owner of the former hardware store around the corner from Bubble & Bake. For years, Bonnie had said they would move somewhere warm after they sold the store, yet here they were, still in Deep Lakes, much to Frankie's displeasure.

Frankie didn't appreciate ill talk of Fern's family and felt especially defensive about Cherry and Pom, so she cut off further conjecture. "Well, it looks like the police will have a lot of people to interview. Why don't we think of something we can offer the family to express our condolences from the bird club."

# Chapter 4

*Birds were created to record everything. They were not designed just to be beautiful jewels in the sky, but to serve as the eyes of heaven. — Suzy Kassem, Rise Up And Salute The Sun*

Bird club business aside, Frankie decided not to attend the afternoon Fall Migration Days activities. With all the pieces of information niggling around her noggin, she felt restless. Now that the chattering bird club members had departed, the silence was an echo chamber of bombarding theories about Fern Mallard's death.

Frankie chewed her bottom lip. There was no getting around it: she had promised Pom and Cherry to help find answers. She already had information only known to the police, thanks to Shauna's statement and Frankie's snooping venture at the scene.

Upstairs in her home above Bubble & Bake, Frankie dragged a cork board out of her bedroom closet. She'd cleared it free of photos, yarn, and sticky notes from the sheep farm case that had occupied her earlier that summer. She thought about that case, how she couldn't avoid being involved in that investigation since the crime centered around her best friend, Carmen, and Frankie's own daughter, Violet.

Here she was again in an unavoidable situation. This case resonated with her, too. Because of Pom and Cherry. Because she was a member of the Whitman Seekers Bird Club and because Fern was a kindred spirit. Because Shauna had discovered the victim and Shauna was family. Mostly, because Frankie couldn't just let it go. The empty board beckoned her to fill it.

She began simply. One sticky note in the center with Fern Mallard's name on it. Although she wasn't supposed to, she'd taken a photo of Fern so she could remember the details of her appearance and accessories. She sent the photo to her printer and tacked it to the middle of the board above the post-it note. The photo stabbed her with guilt. Was she becoming morbid?

An outer circle of sticky notes followed, one for each suspect thus far. The ex-fiancé; the assistant, whose name was Robyn, Frankie remembered from seeing her at the reception just last night; Field Biologist Naomi Someone; and family with a question mark. She was certain more suspects would emerge. On one side of the board, she added a note with the word "motive" in capital letters. On the other side, she posted a note with the word "means." Below "means" she tacked on three separate notes: rocks, head wound, drowning. Across the bottom she pinned separate notes with suspicious details: Fern's field journal, dead baby martins, drag marks at the scene, scratches on Fern's arm.

Frankie's process was interrupted by her cell phone. It was Magda Guzman, Frankie's contact and the regional editor from *Point Press*. She must have heard the news already.

"Hello, Magda. Slow news day, hmm?" Frankie greeted her brightly with a side of sarcasm, exactly in tune with Magda's personality.

"So, you got a dead bird nerd in a pond and it looks like foul play, huh?" Magda was chewing on something in Frankie's ear, probably multitasking as usual. Magda was a recipe of high energy stoked with ambition and a smidge of compassion here and there. She was looking beyond her role as regional editor, gunning for a power position in journalism, so she never missed a beat. Frankie figured the news wire buzzed a constant feed through Magda's earbuds, even when she went to bed for the night.

"Well, some people would say *ornithologist*, Magda. And her name is Fern Mallard, and she just happens to be the cousin of two of my Bubble & Bake crew." Frankie was feeling a little snappish toward Magda's typical flippant delivery.

The editor didn't bat an eyelash. "Fern Mallard! You couldn't make up a name like that. You mean Mallard—like a duck? That's too funny...but perfect for an ornithologist." Magda took a loud swig of some kind of beverage. "And her cousins work for you? That's perfect. You'll have access to all kinds of information."

Frankie wasn't in the mood for Magda's cocksure attitude at the moment. "I don't know if I want to work on this story, Magda. It hits pretty close to home." Frankie's glum voice disguised her eagerness. She knew she was playing with fire because Magda could find any number of live-wire reporters dying for a chance to pick up a coveted crime beat story.

"Oh just stop it, Frankie. You've got the nose for this story. If I know you, you've already started fact gathering."

Magda paused, considerately waiting for Frankie's response. The pause wasn't lost on Frankie. Magda was busy and didn't have time for games.

"Look, I'm sorry about your employees' cousin being the victim. All the more reason that you should work the story, right?" Magda was going the extra mile to be conciliatory.

"Yes," Frankie jumped in sharply before Magda changed her tone. "Of course I'll work the story. I owe it to Pom and Cherry, Fern's cousins." She measured each word and pronounced them succinctly in case Magda doubted her annoyance. "And you're right, Magda. I was actually at the scene. My sister-in-law discovered the body."

Magda's hoot on the other end and signature finish, "keep me posted" ended the call.

Frankie proceeded back downstairs to check on the afternoon wine lounge numbers. Peggy and Aunt CeCe were running tastings now that the bakery section was closed for the day, and the lounge was starting to fill. This was good news for Frankie. She'd been concerned about business since a new wine bar, Nearly Napa, had opened last month on Meriwether Street, a few blocks down from Bubble & Bake. Not that Deep Lakes couldn't support two wine bars. The touristy lake town boasted several bars and a taproom of regional craft beers, and they all appeared to manage well.

But Nearly Napa was a wine bar that marketed itself as upscale, a chic hangout spot for tourists heading north out of the cities, mostly Chicagoans who considered "upscale" the flavor of the day. And for that niche crowd they offered varieties from California, Washington, and Oregon; very different flavor profiles from Frankie's vintages at Bountiful Fruits. Wisconsin wines were typically sweeter and fruit-forward, although many dry, crisp, complex varieties were being crafted at Wisconsin wineries, too.

What concerned Frankie most were the rumors that Nearly Napa's owner was disparaging Bubble & Bake's wines and atmosphere. Frankie could accept competition but wanted a fair playing field. She didn't like playing hardball, but when push came to shove, she wouldn't back down either. It was high time to pay a visit to the new establishment, which would happen tomorrow as soon as the place opened. Frankie, along with Garrett, her beau and Whitman County coroner, and Carmen, her business partner, planned a reconnaissance mission at twelve-hundred.

Thinking about Garrett reminded Frankie that he would be preoccupied today examining the body of Fern Mallard. Instead of calling him, Frankie texted a brief message wishing him good luck on the exam and hoping he'd be able to get in some fishing in the evening.

A dead body wasn't part of his original weekend plan, which was to go fishing with Alonzo on Little Hopeless Lake. The lake's name was contrived by locals, since it deterred visitors from trying their luck, expecting a dismal fishing expedition. In reality, some of the best fishing happened regularly on Little Hopeless. She added a kissy face emoji to the text, pressed send, and smirked at her own shift into romantic juvenility. Oh, well.

In the B & B kitchen, Frankie readied four quiches, intending to take them to the Parker house later. One of the quiches, her latest concoction she'd christened Kiss My Acropolis, featured sun-dried tomatoes, feta cheese, olives, spinach, and oregano. Ingredients aside, the name brought a smile to every customer's face.

Aunt CeCe came through the doors, singing a melancholy tune about a weeping willow and someone buried beneath it. Typically a free spirit, Aunt CeCe channeled the emotions of everyone she cared about. Pom and Cherry's sadness stuck to her today like tree sap.

"How are you doing, Frankie? I can't imagine what a shock it was for you to be at the scene with Shauna, seeing all that death. Poor Fern. Poor baby birdies." Aunt CeCe draped both arms around Frankie in a warm hug, and she instantly felt better, inhaling CeCe's lavender and honeysuckle aroma.

"I'm okay. It hasn't all sunk in yet. That's why I'm in here doing what I do best—making food for comfort." Frankie donned one of Tess's colorful hair wraps made from material in a traditional Ethiopian pattern of blue, red, and green diamonds. Tess, Frankie and Carmen's prize baker, was in Madison for a couple of days, visiting friends she'd made at culinary school.

"Let me know if you need my help out there, Aunt CeCe. Carmen, Jovie, and I will relieve you and Mom at four, but I can jump in anytime."

Aunt CeCe grabbed two cheese and meat boards from the cooler, balanced them on one arm and reached back in to grab a large veggie tray to carry in her other hand. Aunt CeCe had been a carhop at a local drive-in in her teen years. Frankie scooted her direction to retrieve two dip containers from the cooler to carry out behind her aunt, following her to an alcove where eight people were pouring glasses of Persephone's Temptation, a pomegranate zinfandel style wine.

The lounge design made Frankie smile. Decorated in simple Scandinavian furniture with bright printed pillows, wooden two-and three-seater couches squatted low on the wooden plank floor. Scattered around the couches, mammoth floor cushions invited guests to perch in comfort around repurposed vintage flat-topped trunks that served as coffee tables. The lounge was lit with strings of mason jars filled with fairy lights that were programmable for color changes as the mood or holiday suggested. They hung from the beamed ceiling and wrapped themselves lovingly around posts that hugged the walls.

From the time she'd hatched the idea of a bakery and wine lounge, her intent was to create an atmosphere of hygge, a cozy space based on the Danish concept of comfort and contentment. *Stick that in your Nearly Napa upscale setting,* she thought.

By two o'clock the quiches had cooled enough for transport, so Frankie loaded up her trusty blue SUV. She ducked into the wine lounge to update her mother about her visit to the Parkers' and promised to be back by her 4 p.m. shift. Frankie and Peggy were closer now than anytime Frankie could remember, but the relationship was not without its difficulties.

Perfectionist Peggy was polished and poised, while Frankie considered herself to be more like a picnic, a come-as-you-are kind of woman. Peggy fussed with her appearance and possessed a regal beauty: tall and slender, complete with frosty silver hair and icy blue eyes, her clothes never had a wrinkle.

Frankie's five-foot frame didn't allow for willowy limbs, and she often harshly assessed her legs as stumpy even though she was well-toned from yoga and dance workouts. Her hair was a red-brown blunt cut bob, and her green eyes held fire. She dressed for comfort over style, so the latest fashions didn't even register.

The only daughter in the Champagne brood of five, Frankie was the light of her father Charlie's life. The two were famously tight, and she was heartbroken when he died more than five years ago now. Somehow for Frankie, she didn't feel she could quite measure up to the daughter her mother had dreamed about; at least that's the story Frankie told herself.

A casserole carrier in each hand, Frankie walked up the driveway to the Parkers' back door on Hickory Lane. The cheerful Dutch Colonial was painted white with sunny yellow shutters and brown gambrel roof. The driveway side wall featured a stone fireplace chimney from bottom to top. A large columned front porch greeted visitors and was bordered by a flourish of annuals: bright yellow and purple petunias, sweet alyssum, orange and pink dahlias, white cosmos, and blue bachelor buttons. Frankie could see sunflowers reaching for the sky at one corner, continuing around the west side of the house. Cherry and Pom's parents were avid gardeners.

Before she pressed the bell, the front door swung open, and Cherry took one of the carriers, thanking Frankie for the food. Frankie hesitated in the entry area, after noting the number of vehicles surrounding the house, but Cherry motioned her inside.

"Please come in, Frankie. I want you to meet some of my family. Besides, my mom and dad will want to thank you personally for all the food."

Frankie shook her head. Thanks were not necessary in her mind. But, she followed Cherry into a long kitchen bordered by a counter that split the room into a breakfast bar and dining area. The mission style dining table currently seated around eight people, and Frankie could see a sunroom to the right of the dining area where at least another six or so individuals sat talking. Frankie remembered the Parkers planned a family reunion for Monday, which must account for the numbers.

A rotund man with white slicked-back hair and sideburns that whirled into a mustache hoisted himself from a dining room chair and walked stiffly toward

Frankie and Cherry. His gait was punctuated by a little hop every couple of steps, since he dragged his left foot. His smile revealed large capped teeth. "What have we here?" the man inquired.

Frankie couldn't be certain if he meant her or the food, so she waited on Cherry to take the lead.

"This is Frankie Champagne, the owner of Bubble & Bake, where I work," Cherry beamed. "Frankie, I'd like you to meet my Uncle Drake. This is Mom's brother."

Frankie wished Cherry's grandparents were alive, so she could find out more about them. She only knew they were nature lovers to the nth degree, naming every one of their children after a bird or plant. Frankie imagined they were inspired by the Mallard surname. Fern's mother, Flora, was a sister to Cherry's mother, but the family took the Mallard name because Flora's husband was graced with the last name "Ailbhe," which almost nobody could spell, much less pronounce correctly. The nature naming continued into the next generation and maybe beyond.

"Uncle Drake and his wife are antique dealers in Chicago," Cherry continued.

"How interesting and very nice to meet you. I brought freshly baked quiches, so I hope you like them," Frankie shook the puffy hand offered by Uncle Drake, who possibly suffered from high blood pressure and overeating salty foods.

Cherry gestured past her uncle to a slightly less puffy woman wearing a colorful print caftan and ballet flats that strained to contain her feet. "That's Uncle Drake's wife, Auntie Carol."

Auntie Carol raised one cupcake-bearing hand toward Frankie, who waved in return.

Frankie was relieved when Cherry stopped the introductions, and instead motioned her through the

kitchen toward a door that led down several steps to
a lower-level living area. Frankie heard more voices
coming from a large family room, but Cherry skirted past
that room and out double glass doors to a patio, where
her parents sat with Pom and two other people.

Frankie could only imagine how overwhelmed the
Parkers were at this moment, even though they'd
expected house guests, but for a happy occasion, not a
death of one of their own. Frankie noticed Willow Parker
first, who was a weeping willow indeed. Seeing Frankie
brought fresh tears as Willow rose to greet her with a
hug, while Fred Parker waved a greeting over his wife's
shoulder.

"I'm so sorry about Fern, Willow. This must be such
a shock to all of you," Frankie murmured, while Willow
nodded and wept. Then she quickly sat back down and
asked Frankie to do the same, as she wiped her face with
a tissue. Fred put an arm around his wife, and Pom patted
her hand, looking a little helpless.

"Please let me know what you need in the next few days
and how I can help in any way," Frankie said, looking at
all the faces around the table.

She noticed one of the strangers was a man in a
wheelchair, probably in his 20's, with boyish good looks,
wavy toasted blonde hair, and blue eyes. Frankie recalled
that one of the cousins was in a wheelchair following a
snowboarding accident. As if reading her mind, Cherry
resumed her role as chief hostess.

"Frankie Champagne, this is my cousin Ash. Ash is
Fern's little brother. And this is my cousin Ivy. She's the
daughter of Uncle Drake and Auntie Carol."

Frankie waved across the table to the two cousins.
Frankie's first impression was that Ivy was much more
attractive than her parents, and she wondered which
parent she actually favored. The dark-haired beauty

merely whispered a disinterested hello. Ash produced
a disarming smile, however, causing Frankie to wonder
where such a charming smile came from under these
circumstances.

"It's wonderful to meet you, Frankie Champagne.
I've heard so much about you from Pom and Cherry.
Finally, they've let me out of the dungeon so I can
meet you in person." Ash delivered the statement with a
perfectly deadpan expression, and Frankie didn't know
what to make of him. Maybe Ash was accustomed
to communicating with strangers who noticed his
wheelchair first. Frankie didn't think she was staring at
the chair; it was impossible to bypass the handsome face
and penetrating eyes.

Pom reached over the table to give Ash a playful slap
on the arm. "Don't tease Frankie, Ash. She doesn't know
your sense of humor. Good grief!"

"Ouch, Pom. If you're going to hit me, at least aim for
my legs so I won't feel it," Ash didn't miss a beat.

The exchange prompted a disgusted grunt from Ivy,
who adjusted Ash's chair so the afternoon sunlight was
out of his face. "Ash, you're positively a pain in the butt,"
Ivy scolded. "Can I get you something else to drink?" she
asked him, lifting his empty glass.

"No thanks, Ivy. And stop fussing, please." Ash
directed a meaningful look at Ivy.

Frankie decided she'd endured enough family
introductions for one day. "I'm sorry, but I really need
to get back to Bubble & Bake. I'm working the rest of
the day at the wine lounge, and I expect it will be busy.
Saturday night, you know," she said awkwardly.

Frankie perused the family group seated around the
glass-topped patio table. It was easy to tell that the
Parkers comprised a family unit. Willow, as her name
suggested, was a tall willowy figure with ash blonde

hair, which she wore long, somewhat unconventional for women her age, who often preferred shorter styles. Her triangular face and aristocratic nose had been passed down to Pom along with the stormy gray eyes that currently brimmed with sorrow. Pom was the same height as Willow and must be the spitting image of a younger version of her mother except that Pom, like Cherry, had natural golden blonde hair people craved.

Cherry's features matched her father's. Fred's hair was a striking white now, but he looked like he could be a brother to comedian Steve Martin, if Steve Martin sported a medium-length beard and mustache, that is.

Then there were the two Mallards. Ash didn't look a smidge like Fern. Ash had wavy blonde hair, whereas Fern's oak-brown hair was— well, had been—a mass of springy curls. While his complexion was fair, hers was a much darker, rich amber tone. If memory served her correctly, they didn't share any similar facial features. The contrast made Frankie wonder what Flora and Stuart looked like. Then there was Ivy: raven black hair, porcelain skin, and dark saucer-shaped eyes. She seemed to resemble Drake more than Carol, but it was difficult to picture the couple in their younger days.

Willow, who was sniffling again, hugged Frankie a second time. Pom and Cherry walked Frankie out to the backyard from the patio and up to the driveway. She was thrilled not to be tracking back through the kitchen and dining area again.

"I'm sorry about Mom," Pom began. "Fern's mother was mom's only sister. She and Flora were almost like twins; they were so close. When Flora died, mom sort of adopted Fern and Ash as her own children."

"So you must have spent a lot of time together, too, then?" Frankie didn't know the family history well enough to make assumptions.

Cherry nodded. "Aunt Flora and her husband, Uncle Stu, raised horses in Kentucky for some high-end breeders and trainers. We exchanged visits a lot when we were growing up. Fern, Ash, and Ivy often spent weeks with us when their parents were traveling to horse shows and antique conventions. We formed our own little neighborhood club, the Sensational Six." Cherry laughed at the memory.

"Six?" Frankie counted five cousins. Was there another waiting in the wings she hadn't met?

"Oh, yes, Lars is number six. Lars Paulsen." Pom pointed across the street at the large Victorian house on Hickory Hill. "Lars was an only child, so we adopted him into our family, too. His parents were such fuddy-duddies; at least that's what Mom always said."

Frankie was well versed in Deep Lakes history, so she knew the familiar Hickory Hill House belonged to the Paulsens, one of the Deep Lakes founding families. She was older than the Sensational Six by almost ten years in some cases, more in other cases, like Ash's. She didn't know Lars Paulsen, but she knew of his parents. Lars, the senior version, served on the city council with her father, and Charlie Champagne spoke highly of him, which carried a great deal of weight in Frankie's mind.

"Will Lars be coming to the funeral?" Frankie didn't think funeral talk could be avoided forever.

Cherry and Pom nodded. "He's already in town, actually. He still owns a home on Lake Joy near Founder's Square. He called my mom as soon as he heard about Fern," Cherry said, adding, "Oh, I forgot to tell you, Frankie. The funeral will be Wednesday. Mom and most of us are meeting with the funeral director Monday. Not exactly the family reunion we'd hoped for."

"So, we'll be at Bountiful Monday morning to help with the first shift of the harvest," Pom jumped in.

"You two have enough on your plates. Forget the harvest for now," Frankie meant it.

"Nothing doing. By Monday, we're going to need an excuse to get away from this house for a while," Cherry said.

# Chapter 5

*Competition has been shown to be useful up to
a certain point and no further, but cooperation,
which is the thing we must strive for today,
begins where competition leaves off. — Franklin
D. Roosevelt*

Frankie had barely started the engine on the SUV when
her phone rang. Oh boy. It was Abe Arnold, the bulldog
editor of the local *Whitman Watch*, a county weekly
paper where Frankie often submitted features about
shop events and new wine releases.

She knew without a doubt this call was about Fern's
death. Frankie had scooped the paper three times in
her past investigative reporting stints with *Point Press*,
and Abe wanted a piece of Frankie's good fortune, as he
called it.

"Hello, Abe. How's everything at *The Watch*?"
Frankie's tone was cool but not antagonistic. She'd
been rejected years back when she interviewed for a
reporter's position at *The Watch*, even though she had
a communications degree. Abe Arnold still operated
under old school journalism, favoring men over women
in serious reporting jobs. He'd treated her like a silly

little girl, insisting her forte lay in crafting human interest pieces, like the local business articles she'd been submitting.

Once she had opened Bubble & Bake and Bountiful Fruits, she was too busy to consider news writing, but the rejection still stung. Then she was given her chance to cover a mysterious death for a much larger regional paper in Stevens Point. When she beat Abe to the finish line, he changed his mind and asked if they could collaborate on the next two investigations. Frankie said no.

Abe's tone was friendly but cautious. "Well, summer's winding down, so pretty soon news is going to circle back to school activities, I suppose." He paused momentarily to gear up for the purpose of his call. "Rumor has it you were at Blackbird Pond this morning when Fern Mallard's body was recovered."

"It's true. I was there." Frankie adopted her newsy persona, clipping information to the bare minimum. She'd learned that tactic from the county police, who carefully answered just the specific question asked, sometimes skirting their way around it if they didn't want to disclose any particulars.

Abe heaved a sigh that came out like the groan of a dog that had just been reprimanded. "I know we have a past, Frankie, but can't we put it behind us? Look, you've got a knack for getting to the bottom of things, murders especially. So, why don't we work together on this one?" Abe's voice was fatherly, but grudgingly admirable, too.

"Maybe. What's in it for me, Abe?" Frankie wondered how long she could string him along.

Abe chortled on the other end, sputtering like a boat motor. "Geez Frankie, I'm not exactly an amateur. Excuse me, Miss High and Mighty, but I've been in this biz for thirty years and you...you're, well..." He checked his commentary.

Frankie was glad he couldn't see her Cheshire cat grin. The truth of the matter was that Frankie respected him and his old-fashioned style of fact-checking. He was a pro and a well-respected member of the press, which is why he had vast resources at his disposal for information. Resources that would benefit Frankie's investigations, too.

"Relax, Mr. Arnold. It might be time to bury the hatchet. Let's share information on a trial basis. This is all new to me, Abe, but I'll try. You probably know everything I do right now, unless you've talked to the county cops since this morning?"

A quick conversation revealed Abe officially knew what Frankie did. She wasn't ready to share her knowledge of evidence found at the scene. It was all too precarious. And she certainly wasn't going to share the speculations from the birders at the shop. The two made a verbal agreement to talk when they had any good leads.

"Yes, we'll talk, after I've run those leads down first," Frankie said into the disconnected call. She knew full well that Abe would do the same.

Frankie waved to Carmen and Jovie when she arrived in the wine lounge after changing into a sleeveless turquoise wrap dress that was one of her new favorites. The freshwater pearl pendant hung perfectly in the vee of the neckline and was accompanied by dangling earrings to match; the whole ensemble was perfect summer wear and reflected wine lounge hostessing.

Thanks to Carmen and ironically, Aunt CeCe—a woman in her seventies—Frankie had updated her wardrobe. She'd always been nonchalant about her fashion decisions, choosing sloppy comfort over and over instead of varying her clothing styles to accentuate her good points. She admitted that she liked the results of the changes.

Frankie's mother and aunt were gone, and the lounge hummed with a steady stream of tasters and those who lingered over wine and appetizers in the various lounge alcoves. Jovie danced around the lounge, serving flatbread pizzas, quiche slices, cheese boards, and veggie platters, then gathering up the empty trays to stack in the kitchen.

Frankie and Carmen marveled at the change in Jovie since her mother had moved to Florida and stopped controlling her life. In her mid-thirties, Jovie navigated two part-time gigs that showcased her talents, baking at the Bubble & Bake and crafting floral arrangements at Shamrock Floral down the street. Happily for Frankie, Jovie had begun dating Alonzo a few months ago, which had the effect of brightening the sheriff's mood.

When Carmen and Frankie weren't ringing up sales or presenting tastings, they swept the lounge and back deck, and replaced empty wine bottles with full ones. Labor Day weekend sales would be the last hurrah of the season. The wine lounge would have plenty of good business during fall, but this weekend marked the end of the most profitable season of the year: summer.

Just before nine o'clock, the women were announcing last call to their guests, helping them choose wines to purchase, offering deals on full cases, and in some cases, toting customer purchases to their vehicles lest they stumble from their consumption.

Wisconsin laws dictate that wineries and wine bars must close by ten o'clock, as a favor to the business of traditional bars, thanks to the strong political presence of the state Tavern League. The upside of the law means very few patrons become intoxicated at a wine bar, creating less legal woes for wine bar owners. At Bubble & Bake, the crew watches for potential problems and nips them in the bud, offering coffee and food items as deterrents.

Carmen carried three glasses to one of the comfy alcoves that didn't face the street. Frankie followed with an open bottle of Sassy Pants, a lemon summer riesling, and Jovie carried two other varieties, Fiesta Alegria, a fruity red blend that mimicked sangria, and Summer Sundown, a full-bodied red blend. At the end of a busy wine lounge evening, the crew would habitually wind down with conversation and share opened bottles from tastings that were less than half-full, preferring to open fresh bottles the next business day.

Carmen kicked off her sandals and plonked her feet on top of the low table. "What a long day for you, Frankie. I mean, starting your day off with a dead body and all." Her tone suggested she might have been talking about finding a stray cat.

Frankie lifted both brows pointedly at her friend. "Really, Carmen? You make it sound like something that happens all the time. Geesh."

Carmen managed to still look fresh as a just-sliced cucumber. Her thick, dark hair always seemed to obey the braid, ponytail, or bun she wore to work, not a strand out of place. Still, she patted her hair back and offered a sly, curvy smile at her business partner. "You have to admit, Frankie: it happens to you more often than anyone else I know."

Carmen shifted her body into a more comfortable position, while Jovie stared off into the distance, lost in thought. "Come on, Frankie. Spill the beans. Tell us what you think about Fern's death."

An unusually reserved Frankie sunk deeper into the couch cushion and sipped a half-glass of Summer Sundown. "I'm not ready to talk about it yet, Carmen. I'm hoping I can find out something tomorrow, pick the brains of my two favorite county employees." She glanced warily at Jovie, unsure how her employee felt about Frankie's endeavors now that she was dating the sheriff.

Jovie snapped out of her reverie, swiveling first toward Carmen then toward Frankie. "Huh? Did you say something to me? I was thinking about poor Cherry and Pom. What a sad day for their family."

The two nodded their agreement. Carmen switched the topic to tomorrow. "Are we still on to scope out that Napa place?" When Frankie nodded, Carmen asked what their tactic would be. "Are we going to pretend we're wine snobs from somewhere foreign, or maybe fancy vineyard owners? Oh wait, we could pretend we're inspectors or even wine critics!" Carmen snorted, clearly relishing the idea of making the Napa owner squirm.

"All that sounds fun, but I was thinking we would just be honest. Introduce ourselves, talk about how much we enjoy sampling wines from other areas, welcome them to town." Frankie's smile was a bit too cagey.

Carmen offered an exaggerated nod. "Oh, I get it. Kill them with kindness. They won't know what to think."

"There's nothing wrong with being nice to strangers, you two," offered Jovie.

"Jovie's right. I want Napa to know we can play nice in the same sandbox." Frankie clinked her friend's glass.

"Until someone starts throwing sand," Carmen replied, under her breath.

# Chapter 6

*The vine bears three kinds of grapes: the first of*
*pleasure, the second of intoxication, the third of*
*disgust. — Diogenes*

Rina Madison announced herself as the proud owner of
Nearly Napa, offering a wilted handshake to Frankie,
Carmen, and Garrett and a smile that was best described
as a sneer. Rina had bleached-blonde hair, the blondest
hair this side of the Mississippi and north of the
Mason-Dixon, worn in long, shaggy waves that had seen
too much sun, a condition that was echoed by a tan just
south of the color of coral.

Frankie, Carmen, and Garrett introduced themselves
to Rina as soon as they were invited to sit at the tasting
bar. Frankie didn't want pretense of any sort that would
only serve to make her look unprofessional. A shadow
passed over Rina's expression, considerably depleting
her business smile.

Frankie noticed manicured hands that hadn't seen
much labor, a fact publicized by exotically painted
nails studded in rhinestones. Dressed in a black sheath
destined to be surgically removed at end of day, and

stiletto strappy sandals, Rina stood around five-and-a-half feet, minus the shoes, Frankie surmised.

A definite taboo in the food and drink industry, Rina wore a strong floral-scented perfume, or perhaps it wore her. It was impossible to tell. She plopped tasting menus in front of the three, promising to return in a few minutes after they made their selections.

"Is it okay to take a breath again?" Garrett whispered to Frankie, who stifled a laugh. Carmen made a production of taking a tissue from her purse and holding it to her nose with a dramatic flourish.

The three looked around the bar. The space was fairly small since it had been a hair salon prior to its remodel. The front window had just enough space for three small tables: glass-topped, antiqued wrought iron. Posed below each table were metal stools with round, upholstered seats. The stools looked like they were made for a powder room vanity. Atop each table stood a bronze-colored punched metal candle holder with a grape cluster design.

The walls were faux brick in various shades of cream and tan, decorated with Napa Valley vintage-themed art in splashy colors. A narrow walkway bordered the right side near the entrance, leading to one unisex restroom and possibly a back office and storeroom. The other wall was framed by a floor-to-ceiling wine rack with a backdrop made in an artsy design from wine corks.

The u-shaped tasting bar could seat twelve on its black metal saddle seat stools. Etched mirror panels in gold crackle designs hung behind the bar and reflected the entirety of the lounge in watery light, the light descending from individual amber globes above the bar. The globes dipped downward from dark metal stems, having the appearance of upside-down wine glasses hanging above the granite bartop of sepia tones.

Frankie, Carmen, and Garrett each made their own mental notes of the setting and would discuss them later. Their attention turned now to choosing wines from those offered for sampling: five tastes for twenty dollars. While this was probably the going price in Napa Valley, maybe even on the bargain end, Frankie could imagine some customers would balk at paying that much when Bubble & Bake offered tastings for free.

The menu was classically divided into reds, whites, and rosés, each with a pretty description of notes, aromas, and variety of grape used in the wine. Some touted a specific estate where the wine was produced. All were from California, Oregon, or Washington.

They made their selections in the most efficient manner: Garrett chose whites; Frankie chose reds; Carmen chose rosés. This method would eliminate dickering over multiple options and also expedite the process.

Although they were presently the only customers, Rina returned with a young brunette, Daria, according to her name tag, and reported that she would be doing the tasting. "I have to prepare for the onslaught that will be coming within the hour," Rina pronounced with a theatrical flourish of her hands, then disappeared into the back room.

Daria spoke precise English with an eastern European accent that she apologized for in advance. She told us she was from Romania, here through next year on a student visa. She arrived in May, first waitressing in a Wisconsin Dells restaurant and living in housing provided for J-1 laborers, that was "not so good" in her words. Frankie wasn't sure if Daria was referring to the restaurant or the housing.

She brought three different styles of wine glasses: a wide bowl with a long stem for Frankie, a narrow bowl with a longer stem for Garrett, and a fluted bowl with a medium length stem for Carmen. Daria explained that the longer stem would keep chilled wines from warming too quickly and was appropriate for whites and rosés. The wide bowl for the room temperature reds made for greater aeration to experience the aromas and complex flavors offered by many red varieties.

When the tasting ended almost an hour later, all three complimented Daria on her excellent speaking skills and wine knowledge, tipped her over and above the requisite gratuity to make a point, and left, never seeing hide nor hair of Rina Madison again. A young couple arrived just before the tasting was finished, and Daria set them up at the other end of the bar. So much for the expected onslaught.

The three reconvened at The Hat Trick, a local hangout on Dodge Street, where Carmen's husband, Ryan, waited at a table with a pitcher of Spotted Cow and four tall glasses.

Frankie ducked into Bubble & Bake, first, to check on business. Doing some quick math, she saw Tess was conducting two tastings on one end of the expansive walnut bar with Peggy on the other end managing three different groups, for a total of 15 customers. Pretending to be in a hurry, Frankie breezed through the lounge with a quick wave to Jovie and counted another 14 customers noshing on appetizers and sharing multiple bottles of her wine. A satisfied smile gripped her face as she left out the back door.

Garrett was halfway through his first beer at The Hat Trick when Frankie trotted through the afternoon crowd of locals, who were whooping it up because it was a three-day weekend. The handsome coroner pounced on Frankie, swooped her into a dip, and kissed her cheerfully. "Now that we're out of Napa, we can dispense

with the hoity-toity decorum," he teased, caramel brown
eyes twinkling, mesmerizing Frankie's green ones.

Ryan greeted Frankie impatiently. "Now that you're
here, I want to hear all about it. These two wouldn't
say anything until you got here." The spirited Irishman
made a mock scowl, but his pronounced dimple belied
any irritation.

Frankie motioned for Carmen, who was ready to burst,
to begin. "Twenty dollars for what? Not even three
ounces of wine, total. Those were less than half-ounce
samples." Carmen stuck out her tongue in disgust.

Frankie nodded. "But the wine itself was a strong
representation of the types enjoyed on the west coast.
They were good but not very affordable."

"And, Deep Lakes is not Napa Valley. I don't think
we attract that many tourists here looking for high-end
wines." Garrett made a good point.

"What did you think of the decor? Was it trying too
hard to look like a Napa winery?" Carmen wondered.

Frankie shrugged. "I guess we need to go to Napa and
find out. Pack your bags, Carmen. The quiet season will
be here before we know it." Looking from Garrett to
Ryan, she added, "You can live without us for a week or
two, right?"

Neither man responded, and Ryan changed the
subject. "Did you meet the owner?"

They nodded, and the three began talking at once,
laughing at the clamor of their own
anticipated assessments. Ryan pointed to Frankie.
"You should go first. She's your competitor."

"She didn't spend almost any time with us, so it's hard
to get a read on her. First impression: she's never worked
in a vineyard, at least not for a very long time." Frankie
described Rina's soft hands and polished long nails, two

things a vineyard worker would have to forego, even if they wore work gloves.

Carmen added, "Yeah, well I can spot a phony a mile away. I think she stumbled into the business and probably doesn't know much about wines. Somebody must have set her up. I heard she's the niece of some Napa wine tycoon."

Garrett nodded for Carmen's benefit. "I don't know for sure if Rina Madison is a phony, but she certainly didn't make any effort to be a collegial business associate. In other words, don't expect her to play nice."

Following an early evening hike along the lake trail by Founders Square, Garrett and Frankie strolled around downtown Deep Lakes, arm in arm. Garrett paused to look at her face, now illuminated by the throwback Victorian street lamp next to Bubble & Bake. His wavy, salt and pepper hair hung just below his ears. The couple simultaneously reached out to tuck windblown locks behind each other's ears, smiling deeply as they did this simple intimate task. Garrett stared several inches downward to Frankie's sparkling green eyes, then tilted her chin upward for a kiss.

"Want to sit on the back deck and talk for a while?" he asked, taking her hand to lead her down the alleyway behind the shop.

The warm temperatures remained into the night, but moisture clung in the air, a reminder of the shorter days and impending autumn season. They sat side by side on the rattan loveseat, their favorite spot on the shop's deck, and momentarily looked up at the starry sky. Cygnus or the Northern Cross shone down from overhead, blessing them with brilliance, and Cassiopeia, the easily recognized "W" constellation, tilted precariously to one side.

"So, you didn't tell me how fishing went last night with Alonzo." It was more of a question than a statement.

Garrett kissed Frankie's hand and chuckled. "I think you're the one doing the fishing, Miss Champagne. Why don't you ask me what you really want to know."

Frankie pulled her hand away in mock offense. "Okaaaay. Care to share any details about your exam of Fern Mallard?"

In the hopes of restoring the romantic mood, Garrett cut to the chase. "I think the scratches on Fern's left arm were from a struggle. She suffered two head wounds before she ended up in the pond. I won't know for certain until Tuesday if the head injury or drowning caused her death, but since there were drag marks from the birdhouse to the pond, she may have been dead and dragged to the pond afterwards."

Frankie shuddered. "Any idea what made the head wounds? One of the rocks from the parking lot, maybe?"

Garrett shrugged. "It's possible. One wound produced a lump near the temple, while the other was made with greater force, creating a deep laceration, and I pulled some particles from that wound that need to be evaluated. Of course, there are several scrapes on the body, further indications she was dragged to the pond."

Frankie let the information sink in, her shuttered eyes indicated she had more questions. "Maybe you can't tell me: Did Alonzo say anything about the car? Did they find any prints that were not Fern's? Did they find her field notes? What about..."

Garrett held up both hands in surrender. "We didn't talk in great detail, but I do know they found several fingerprints that have to be processed. If the prints aren't in the database, they'll have to print persons of interest as they're interviewed, which won't start until tomorrow sometime. And, the famous field journal is missing."

Frankie gasped, her mind at work spinning theories. "I bet the missing journal holds the key to finding the killer. There must be something in it that someone doesn't want revealed. But what could it be?" She began brainstorming a list of people to talk to, starting with Robyn and Daryl George. Plans were underway for cornering Fern's colleagues at her funeral.

Garrett slid his arm around Frankie, distracting her thoughts. "Can I please get off the stand for now, Counselor?" Frankie traced one deep dimple from the corner of Garrett's mouth to his chin, lost in his velvety, toffee eyes. Enough interrogation for one night.

# Chapter 7

*Grapes are among the most desirable and the best fruits known on earth, prized for their beauty, their place in classical legend and mythology, their succulence and varied flavors as luxury table fruits, their noble metamorphosis into wine, and their more utilitarian roles as sources of fresh juice and tasty jellies. — Annie E. Proulx*

Labor Day dawned with hazy pink skies and dewy grasses. Frankie met Manny Vega, her vineyard manager, and two other hired hands as the light grazed the eastern horizon. The group started up the two small field tractors, trailers attached and loaded with grape bins.

Frankie carried snips and gloves in a canvas tote up from the pole shed to the section labeled "Brianna," 18 rows for the picking. She began undoing the nets that covered the fruit, as her hired hands pulled back the nets on subsequent rows like fishermen dragging nets out of the sea, except these nets billowed upward toward the sky, only catching grape leaves in their wake.

Volunteers would be arriving anytime now, meeting in the parking area at the top of the vineyard to hear instructions, then grab their weapons of choice. The scissor shears operated exactly as expected by their name, but Frankie preferred the razor snips, a tool with a two-prong, wide, fork-like head with sharp blades between the prongs. Razor snips were easier on the hands, requiring a brisk upward or downward thrust after the forked head meets the cluster stem.

By 6:15 most of the volunteers were assembled. Violet and Sophie, Frankie's daughters, could always be counted on for the harvest. Violet greeted her mom and sister with tight hugs. Sophie gathered her long blonde hair into a ponytail holder and pulled it through an Audubon Society ball cap that proclaimed, "The forest is calling and I must go."

Sophie took a swig from her coffee travel mug. "Sorry Max couldn't come, Mom. He's studying on his day off." Sophie's fiancé, also a nurse at UW Hospital in Madison, had returned to college to become a physician assistant. Since Max had begun the program last year, the two had precious little free time together.

"I'm sorry that he has to study, Honey, but it's all good. Max will make a wonderful PA. How are you doing?" Frankie wanted to be sure Sophie was well. With her exhausting hospital schedule, the two managed only short conversations most of the time.

Sophie gave her mom a thumbs-up. "We can chat later. There's grapes to pick," she smiled brightly, then turned her attention to Pom and Cherry, who had just walked over from their car.

Frankie's daughters met them en route to offer hugs and condolences. Alonzo and Garrett arrived just behind the sisters, together in Lon's official county Jeep, indicating he was on call.

Aunt CeCe came with Peggy, choosing the early morning shift in the coolest part of the day. Vineyards

were notoriously sunny and offered little to no shady
respite. Grapes needed heat and sun along with adequate
rain to produce the best fruit.

Aunt CeCe threw her arms around Violet and Sophie
in giant bear hugs reminiscent of Charlie Champagne.
Frankie missed her father's hugs the most because they
created a sense of comfort and security that could
not be replicated. In Peggy fashion, she gave each
granddaughter a shoulder squeeze and bussed their
cheeks with a quick smooch. Peggy never offered much
physical affection, preferring to show her love in other
ways, mostly by fussing over the tiny details of life.

Harvesters worked in tandem on opposite sides of the
same row of vines. Grape clusters hung on both sides and
often in the midst of a tangle of vines and leaves, so each
cutter had a different view on the row, ensuring all the
grapes were cut. Long plastic bins squatted below the
row so clusters could easily fall once clipped.

The volunteers scooted the bins down the rows as they
went and placed mounded overfull bins between rows,
where the field tractors picked them up as they cruised
along. The filled bins were next dumped into large vats
on wheels parked by the end of the Brianna section. A
large tractor hauled the large vats to the crushing shed
to begin the wine-making process.

It was still early when Aunt CeCe and Peggy stopped
their work to bring water, lemonade, muffins, and scones
to the field workers, walking row after row and pulling a
garden wagon behind them. Frankie pushed the brim of
her garden hat upward as they headed in her direction
and was surprised to see her sister-in-law, Shauna,
manning the wagon beside her mother.

"Shauna," Frankie waved a friendly greeting. "I'm
sorry I haven't called, but you've been on my mind. How
are you?"

Outwardly, Shauna didn't look worse for wear. She was dressed in work clothes, her hair pulled back into a tight ponytail and through her ball cap. She gave Frankie a hug, catching her off guard.

"I wanted to come over to help today to thank you. I really appreciate it that you were there for me when I needed you."

Frankie was accustomed to Shauna separating herself from vineyard activity. She and James visited the shop, but she rarely participated in bottling wine and never came for harvest. Frankie warmly hugged her back.

"You're welcome, Shauna. We're family. I'll help out any time you need anything."

"Show me where to start picking grapes." Shauna said, simply.

She joined Carmen, Ryan, and their twins, Carlos and Kyle, who just arrived too after finishing sheep chores for the day. The twins were almost 15 now, and Kyle shared his dad's passion for all things on the farm, while Carlos tolerated the farm work for the time being, hoping he could work at one of the area restaurants once he turned 16.

Along with Peggy and CeCe, Pom and Cherry said their goodbyes for the day to help their parents make funeral arrangements for Fern. Frankie thanked them all for their help and wished the two sisters well, knowing the daunting task they faced in planning the funeral for a loved one.

Jovie arrived at noon toting carriers loaded with pizzas from Anton's Food Truck, a summer hot spot at Founders Square by Lake Joy.

"You're a sight for sore eyes," exclaimed Alonzo, who lifted Jovie off the ground, twirling her around in a little jig.

All harvesting ceased while hungry pickers devoured pizza slices and chugged water and iced tea. *No alcohol until all harvesting was finished for the day* was Frankie's policy. Amid discussion of the expected weight of the Brianna harvest, how much wine could be made from it, and plans for new vintages, Alonzo's pager sounded off, and he stepped away.

"Looks like I've got to go to work, people. Sorry, but thanks for lunch." The sheriff pecked Jovie on the lips, and gestured for Garrett to follow him, and surprisingly, Frankie, too.

"We've got a lead on a suspect in Fern's death. The Swansons saw a bright orange jeep barreling down the marsh road that fits in the time of the murder, and they can identify the driver. I'm going to take their statement, and then I'm going to pick up Dominic Finchley for questioning." Alonzo pushed his hat onto his head matter-of-factly.

"Dominic Finchley, the bird scientist?" Frankie recalled the name of the man who agreed to lead the "backyards for birds" workshop Saturday. Her perplexed expression wasn't lost on Alonzo, who was ready with his next bombshell.

"Dominic Finchley is Fern Mallard's ex-fiancé." He watched Frankie's eyes widen into saucers. "I don't have to remind you that this is not for public consumption. You have to keep this under wraps, Frankie. I'm trusting you." Lon wagged a finger in front of her nose before lowering his frame into the Jeep and driving away.

Frankie was pleased with the timing of the Brianna harvest. Bubble & Bake always closed on Mondays; Labor

Day was no exception since most people headed back home early, while many locals were nursing hangovers or enjoying the shortened work week with time on the lake or backyard cookouts.

Violet and Sophie departed in the afternoon before traffic reached a fever pitch and clogged the interstate that led north to Violet's and south to Sophie's. Sophie promised to return for the next picking, which Frankie estimated was three weeks away.

"You're going to be seeing a lot of me this fall," Violet reminded her mom, brimming with enthusiasm. "I'll be down Friday or Saturday to recheck the mash for the mead."

Violet had just completed a summer internship for her microbiology program at none other than Bountiful Fruits, where she hatched an idea to make an apple mead, the first mead to wear the Bountiful label, if it turned out. Violet's recipe received full endorsement from Nelson and Zane, the two scientists at Bountiful's lab.

Nelson, who had graduated in May, would begin a professional gig at a pharmaceutical research lab in Madison. His departure created mixed emotions in Frankie. While she was thrilled for Nelson, she considered him irreplaceable and wished she could afford to pay him a competitive salary and benefits. Now, she was relying on Zane and the microbiology department at UW-Stevens Point to send another lab scientist her way.

Shauna managed to glisten prettily when she sweated, just another thing Frankie found unfair about life, but she was truly grateful for the gesture her sister-in-law made and wouldn't forget it.

"Thanks so much for your help today, Shauna. Every hand was needed, and I'm glad you were here."

"It actually was fun doing something that wasn't construction-related. Next time you have a bottling party, I'm there." Shauna spoke sincerely, then walked up to the parking area.

Frankie and Garrett went their separate ways to clean up after a sticky harvesting session, promising to reconnect for an evening movie at Deep Six Cinema. The two had caught previews for the new, and perhaps final, James Bond movie, which was certain to provide chills and thrills aplenty.

Frankie had plans before the movie, having turned down her mother's suggested pontoon ride on Dan Fitzpatrick's boat. Dan began dating Peggy several months ago; the two had spent many happy times together in the past when Dan's wife and Peggy's husband were still alive. Charlie Champagne had been gone more than five years, and Dan's wife had died two years ago, so both seemed ready to move forward. Frankie had always liked Dan and wanted her mother to do whatever made her happy.

What was making Frankie happy at the moment was slipping back into her detective husk. Somehow, she had developed an alternate persona when she nosed her way through an investigation, making her fiercely confident and competitive.

She loved baking and was passionate about wine-making. Both made her see herself as the herald of comfort and joy. But solving a crime puzzle pushed her boundaries and made her the harbinger of justice. She laughed at her own self-proclamation. Maybe her head was getting a little too inflated after her recent successes.

Now she paused her trip down self-awareness avenue to look at fire numbers along County K near Blackbird Marsh. She knew Paul and Marcy Swanson lived somewhere nearby and believed they were the Swansons who had called the sheriff about the suspicious jeep speeding away from the scene of the crime.

She pulled into a paved driveway on the left where a new log-style home sat with a large screened-in porch out front. A rap on the door brought a cacophony of barking from at least two different canines, based on the pitch and cadence of the yaps.

The door opened to reveal the friendly face of Paul Swanson, who recognized Frankie from Bubble & Bake and a few bird outings he'd attended with Marcy. Nosing their way around the door to greet or gobble up the visitor were two dogs: the bigger one, a wire-haired terrier, and its underling, a sweet-faced Westie. Marcy was behind the black and brown terrier, tugging it away from the door by the collar. The Westie followed like a good little minion.

"Hi, Frankie. Come on in. Don't mind these two. They're noisy but friendly." Paul opened the door wide now and led Frankie to the kitchen table, which sat facing the front porch, and notably, the county road.

"Can I meet your two dog buddies? It always makes me feel better to get acquainted." Frankie sat at the oak chair in the center of the table. She shook the paw of Chewy, the wire-haired male who then laid his head lovingly on her leg for an ear scratch. Chewy's approval signaled the little Westie, Maybelline, to jump into Frankie's lap, where she stayed until the end of her visit.

Frankie took out a notebook and pen and set them on the table. "You may or may not know, but I work part-time as a crime reporter for *Point Press* out of Stevens Point. I heard you reported a jeep speeding down the road away from the Blackbird Marsh area. Would you tell me about that?"

Neither Paul nor Marcy appeared unsettled by Frankie's recitation. Marcy, a sturdy woman somewhere around 60, rose from her seat to procure a pitcher of iced tea from the refrigerator and a bowl of snack mix. She poured three glasses and set paper towel pieces in front of each chair to serve as snack plates.

Paul was already explaining what he'd told the police. "Marcy and I were having breakfast. Early, you know, because we planned on heading out to the flea market in Gibson before it got too crowded." Paul was a little man, proportionately smaller and thinner than Marcy's stout stature, and Frankie marveled that he'd been a steer rancher for decades, a profession requiring lots of muscle.

Marcy entered the conversation with a rich contralto voice that contrasted her husband's high-pitched one. "We couldn't miss that bright orange jeep racing down the road. You don't see many vehicles that color. I says to Paul, where'd ya s'pose that fool's going in such a big hurry?"

Paul nodded. "We finished breakfast and were having another cup of coffee when that orange jeep showed up right across the road!"

Frankie's pen paused midair. "Wait. The jeep turned around and came back to park across the road after it had been speeding away?"

Paul nodded, and Marcy shook her head simultaneously, leaving Frankie's brow furrowed. Marcy took over, hoping to clear things up. "No, ya see, the jeep was coming back down the road the other way. It was speeding up toward the marsh and the second time, it was speeding back again but the driver slammed his brakes and parked right there." Marcy pointed out the window at a flat spot on the shoulder. The picture window provided a clear view of anyone who chose to park there.

"Did you go out to check on the driver?" Frankie wondered, doubtfully. Most people around Deep Lakes minded their own business unless someone looked like they were having trouble.

Paul again. "We were about to because we could see he was having a time of it. But by the time we got to the door, he pulled away and left."

"What do you mean you could see he was having a time of it?" Frankie asked.

"He was slumped over the steering wheel," Marcy informed her. "I says to Paul, I think that man's having a heart attack or something. But Paul didn't think so. Anyway, the man was holding his head in his hands, crying maybe."

Frankie recorded every word verbatim. "What time was this?"

Paul and Marcy agreed it was before six when they saw the jeep the first time and after six the second time. They couldn't be sure how many minutes passed between the two sightings.

"And when did you call the county?" she asked, remembering Alonzo's pager had gone off sometime after noon today, two days after the incident.

Marcy's face colored. "We didn't know it might be important until after we went to the backyard bird workshop Saturday afternoon. Both Paul and I thought the man teaching it looked familiar, but we couldn't place him."

Paul continued. "He was such a nice fella. We talked to him afterwards about feeding the birds and all. Nice as pie."

"But then we saw the orange jeep in the parking lot when we left, and that man went right to it and drove away." Marcy seemed surprised by this even in the recounting, and she looked at Paul, who also shook his head in disbelief.

"Okay," Frankie said. "I'm missing something. You saw the jeep. You knew the man's name who taught the workshop. What made you suspect something?"

Marcy threw up her hands as light dawned. "Oh, that. We'd heard about the bird lady drowning at the pond, o'course. But, then we saw the Olesons at the feed mill this morning, on account that Dave Harris likes to open the mill five days a week, even on a holiday. Seemed like they had the same idea - the Olesons ya know - like us, to stock up on some new kinds of bird seed to attract more birds to our yard. We always have sunflower and thistle, but safflower was new to us, so I asked Dave at the mill..."

Frankie didn't want to follow Marcy Swanson down the rabbit hole she'd just dived into about bird seed, so she kicked the chair leg, causing Chewy to elicit a startled bark. "Sorry about that. Had a foot cramp."

She steered the conversation back on course. "What did the Olesons say? Something that made you decide to call the sheriff?" Frankie's interest piqued. She knew it was Ed's idea to contact Dominic Finchley for the workshop in the first place.

Paul continued the narrative. "Right. Ed told us, real quiet-like, that Dominic Finchley was that dead ornithologist's ex-boyfriend. Well, Marcy and I just stared at Ed, then looked at each other..."

"And scooted right out the door to home. Soon as we got here, we called the sheriff to leave a message. Didn't suppose he'd get to it today with the holiday, though, but I guess it must have been important," Marcy sat a little straighter and puffed out her chest.

After thanking them for the information and assuring Marcy she would give them credit as a source in any article she wrote, she was on her way back to town. She wondered what the Parkers thought about Fern's former fiancé and whether or not they knew he'd become the prime suspect in her demise.

She checked the time and wondered if the Parkers were done meeting with the funeral home and if she should call Cherry or Pom to see if she could come over for a chat.

Frankie thought about her crime board. The feathers found in Fern's mouth loomed large and ominous. The murder was highly personal, Frankie decided, and what was more personal than an ex-lover?

# Chapter 8

*Suddenly she realized that what she was regretting was not the lost past but the lost future, not what had not been but what would never be. — F. Scott Fitzgerald*

Cherry picked up Frankie's phone call immediately. Her voice sounded weary, and Frankie felt like an intruder.

"I'm sorry to call, Cherry. You sound tired. How did the funeral arrangements go?"

"I think the shock is wearing off, Frankie. Everything is in place for the funeral. Mom picked out the perfect hymns that Fern would love, and now we're going through photos to make a couple of displays for the visitation."

Cherry suddenly sounded very mature compared to the flighty girlish individual Frankie knew. You years ago at 33, Cherry had moved back home after a bad breakup with her live-in boyfriend. Since then, she had a relationship of convenience with Frankie's playboy brother, the charming Nick Champagne. Frankie adored Nick, and the two relied on each other often, but Frankie didn't necessarily approve of Nick's love-them-and-leave-them way with women. She thought that maybe Cherry hoped for more from Nick than he was willing to offer, and that idea made her pity Cherry and sometimes think less of her than the woman deserved.

"I think you're doing a good job of holding the family together," Frankie shared. She had witnessed Cherry's careful handling of Willow and managing the relatives staying at the Parker house.

"I suppose you have a house full, and now wouldn't be a good time for me to stop by to ask some questions?" Frankie's voice rose at the end, indicating she was hoping for permission.

"You must know something about Fern's case, or you wouldn't be asking. I know Pom's going to want to hear your information, Frankie. You should come to the house," Cherry spoke firmly, making Frankie respect her all the more.

Again, Frankie pulled up to the Dutch Colonial on Hickory Lane, this time finding an easy parking spot in front of the house. Only Pom's car and one other were in the driveway, and Frankie wondered where the remaining relatives were stashed. Pom, a middle school English teacher, lived across town in an apartment, and Frankie wondered why Cherry had chosen to move home instead of moving in with her sister.

Pom met Frankie at the front door. "Let's talk on the patio, if you don't mind. Mom and Dad are sorting photos with Ivy and Ash, sharing a lot of memories. I'd rather not talk in front of them just now."

Frankie couldn't resist asking, "Where are all your relatives?"

"Thankfully, rooms opened up around town starting today, so they've all relocated elsewhere. Only Ash and Ivy are staying with us now." Pom looked relieved.

"There were too many people for Mom to have around 24/7." Frankie nodded, reassuringly,

Cherry waited at the patio table. A thermal pitcher and three ceramic mugs waited, too. Cherry looked ten years older. Dark circles below both eyes indicated she wasn't getting enough sleep. She poured three cups of coffee from the carafe after Frankie nodded at her to pour her one, too.

Pom's expectant look communicated to Frankie she should cut to the chase.

"What do you two and the rest of the family think of Fern's ex, Dominic Finchley?"

Frankie expected categorically negative responses from both women, who instead surprised her with shrugs. Pom began.

"Dom and Fern were happy for a long time. I mean, they had a lot in common. Their passion for the bird world and love of nature, for starters. Maybe they were just too much alike to make it work in the end."

"Who broke it off?" Frankie wondered, her notebook laid out on the table, turned to a fresh page.

"It was Fern," Cherry said. "And it was news to all of us. She only told us when she arrived at the house a couple of weeks ago."

"Did she say when and why?" Frankie hoped to jog their memories of Fern's pronouncement.

"Yes. Mom asked when Dom would be coming. You know, we expected him for the family reunion wed planned. That's when Fern said she had broken it off with him, right Pom?" Cherry rubbed her temples, trying to recall the exact conversation.

Pom added to the story. "Fern said they hadn't been getting along well ever since she started the martin project. I think she said they were living in two different worlds. Does that sound right, Cherry?"

Cherry nodded. "Fern worked at Riverwood in Chicago when she wasn't traveling around for research. Dom accepted a research scientist position at University of Minnesota in Minneapolis right after Fern was awarded the martin study. That's a long distance relationship for sure. I don't think they could make it work."

Frankie imagined that Fern's time was largely occupied with research, followed by teaching a course or two at Riverwood. That would leave little room for a serious relationship to flourish. "How did Fern and Dom make it work before he took the Minnesota post?"

"Dom worked at Riverwood, too. That's where they met," Pom pointed out. "In fact, they worked together on a bluebird study a few years ago where they spent most of their time in the Midwest. We got to see them pretty often during that time."

It was time for the tough question, and Frankie prepared for a defensive assault where Dom was concerned. "Do you think Dom could have killed Fern?"

Pom and Cherry exchanged looks of disbelief, then steeled themselves for whatever Frankie was about to tell them.

"I think he's a prime suspect. Reliable witnesses saw his jeep speeding toward Blackbird Pond then back again, all within the time frame of Fern's death. If his fingerprints are on any of Fern's belongings or in her car, that will only add to his troubles."

Frankie stopped short of speculating that the jeep was already being combed over for DNA and other evidence. The murder weapons, namely the rocks found in Fern's pocket, were being checked for DNA, too. She also wondered if Dom had something to gain from stealing Fern's field journal.

Pom gasped as something surfaced in her memory.
"Dom came over yesterday afternoon. He asked if he
could look through Fern's room for something of his."

"Fern's room? You mean, Fern was staying here this
whole time?" Frankie's mind was awash with possible
things Dom might be searching for in Fern's belongings.

Cherry nodded. "She always favored the room in the
attic. It was like her secret hideaway, so when she visited,
Mom asked her if she wanted to stay with us in her
old room. She was ecstatic." Cherry's expression shifted
from the blissful memory to suspicion about Dom.

"Pom, didn't you go with him to the attic?" she asked.

Pom assured them that she had. "He looked incredibly
sad, I mean for real. I don't think he was faking. Anyway,
he looked on Fern's dresser, on the shelves around the
room, and asked if I would open the dresser drawers,
where he felt around her clothes. Whatever he was
looking for, he didn't find it. He left empty-handed."

"Why didn't you ask him what he was looking for,
Pom?" Cherry's tone had grown antagonistic with the
news that Dom was a suspect and had been searching
through her cousin's room.

Pom looked bemused. "I might have, but he didn't
answer me. Then he just looked so lost... I didn't push it,
especially since he didn't find whatever it was."

Frankie placed one hand over Pom's, reassuringly, then
addressed Cherry for permission on the next move. "Can
you take me upstairs to look in Fern's room? Maybe we'll
notice something important, even the tiniest detail."

An hour later, the search had yielded nothing but
a promise from the sisters they would keep both eyes
open for anything that surfaced, specifically the missing
field journal that Frankie confessed Garrett had told her
about.

"And I promise to keep you posted after I talk officially to Alonzo, Shirley, or anyone else in the department about Fern's case," Frankie said, not mentioning Officer Pflug by name. Somehow, she hoped he wouldn't be too involved.

Frankie rose particularly early Tuesday morning, dabbing her eyes with a cool face cloth as she squinted at her undesirable image in the mirror. She'd spent the night being chased through her vineyard by bad guys dressed in black feathers carrying assault rifles, a jumbled nightmare of James Bond meets Blackbird Pond.

There was no point in returning to her bed and a shower seemed pointless, too. She planned an early outing to Bountiful to run a test on the Edelweiss grapes. Day to day changes were taking place in the fruits as harvest season approached. The vineyard distracted Frankie. It would be good to get her hands dirty doing countless small tasks, so showering after her morning expedition made the most sense.

There would be enough time for Frankie to proof some dough for bakery orders, so she scampered off to the kitchen downstairs, not bothering to change into regular clothes. The leggings and T-shirt she wore to bed would do, with a shop apron topping the ensemble.

But first, coffee. Frankie wholeheartedly adopted the motto she saw donning shirts, coasters, and mugs at many shops. She woke up the machine with a tamped-down shot of Italian espresso grounds, whirring it into action to chug into a mug of heated oat milk. The aroma alone began working on her nerve endings before the first sip.

Now it was time to wake up a yeast cake with warmed milk. Frankie wondered if it was too early to call Alonzo or Shirley to inquire about Dominic Finchley, the questions gnawing at her insides. Maybe Abe Arnold had information she didn't have. That thought only worsened the gnawing.

She carefully measured sugar, butter, eggs, almond extract, and more milk into the yeasty mix, then added large amounts of flour and some salt. She could make butterhorns in her sleep, which was fortunate, since she relied on her reflexes and mechanical memory. Fern's case was a distraction.

Frankie had enough time to make two jumbo batches of cookie dough, too. Her classic peanut butter cookies with chocolate and butterscotch chunks were popular in every season. Since she was winding up summer, she made her first fall cookie dough of the year, cranberry white chocolate walnut, which produced a semi-soft, semi-chewy delight.

Although it was nice to have dough chilling for orders, Fern's murder kept turning forward and backward sommersaults in her brain with no place to go. Frankie needed information only the police could provide.

Frankie hung up her apron and climbed the stairs to change into vineyard clothes. The sun wasn't up yet, and the temperature registered 54 degrees, so she dressed in her favorite steel gray Eddie Bauer hiking pants, durable and comfortable, and a long-sleeved tee. A sweatshirt would quickly prove too warm once the sun rose.

Downstairs, she jammed on the extra pair of garden shoes she kept by the basement entrance, and was on her way. A quick glance at the SUV dashboard clock, and

Frankie made the hasty decision to punch in Alonzo's cell number before she could think about it again.

"I wondered when you'd get around to calling, Frankie. I can't believe you waited this long. Let me guess. You talked to the Swansons about Dominic Finchley. And maybe the Parkers, too." She could hear Alonzo's mocking tone partially covered by the fatigue of a long holiday weekend.

"Sorry, Lon. I just couldn't wait any longer. I know it's a little before business hours, but I was hoping you could give me information about Finchley. Do you think he killed Fern? Do you have any hard evidence?"

"All I can tell you at the moment is that Finchley's our prime suspect. After we questioned him, he called a lawyer. We have evidence to process and should get a few answers from that today. We took Finchley's fingerprints. I expect it's going to be a long day at the office, which includes your sweetheart, Frankie, in case you had plans." Alonzo yawned loudly, then tried to stifle it.

"Thank you for letting me know that much. I do appreciate the way you do your job. You're an excellent sheriff, Lon." Frankie sometimes forgot that Alonzo had a professional job to do and a public he had to answer to. He couldn't just give her details on a case because she was a lifelong friend.

"Save the butter for your pastries, Frankie. I know you're hoping for details I can't give you. And by the way, business hours start two hours from now." Alonzo's voice held no animosity, but he enjoyed getting the red-headed baker riled up.

The call ended as Frankie found herself at the Bountiful Fruits driveway. It was a packed dirt lane, bordered by white pines ascending upward gently, then flattening again as the concrete block winery came into view. Beyond the building, the vineyards were a sight to behold in the September sunrise. The lime green vines glistened, resembling polished leather. Hanging clusters of grapes in hues of greens, reds, and deep blue hung like giant pearls from the stems.

Frankie pulled her cloth garden hat around her disobedient bobbed hair-do and trotted down the slope to the red pole shed, where the Brianna grape clusters were undergoing separation of stems and fruits, then pressed. The juice would pour out into a tank of its own, leaving behind pounds of grape skins, also known as must or pomace.

Instead of tossing away the must, Manny Vega loaded the skins into an empty wagon and spread them under and around the berry bushes that grew on the southeast fence line. The pomace was a perfect pH leveler for soils that had too much or too little acidity, enhancing the yield of Bountiful's blueberries and raspberries that Frankie used for wine and pastries.

Before snow covered the pomace fertilizer, many ground feeding birds picked around the must for grape seeds and juicy bits, another bonus to using the leftover mash.

Frankie's eyes adjusted to the lower light inside the pole shed, which was empty save for the churning crusher. She peeked into the tank where liquid gold juice flowed and bubbled. She inhaled deeply the satisfying earthy scent of grape stems in tandem with the fermenting tropical notes emitted from the golden Briannas.

Since the crusher was running, Manny couldn't be too far away. Frankie walked over to the counter where various wine equipment and tools were stored. She opened one drawer labeled "testing tools" and retrieved a refractometer, used to measure the Brix or sugar content of the grapes in question, and a digital pH meter with calibration solutions nearby. She found the mini hand-held press and a glass pint jar in the dish rack by the sink, next to a box of disposable gloves. She retrieved a pair of gloves and exited the pole shed.

When Frankie began making her own wines, she started with a kit, then graduated to working with other vintners to learn the tools and terms of the trade, along with the methodology. She'd only managed a C in high school chemistry, so she marveled at the fact she understood the science behind growing and fermenting grapes. Her wine education hadn't stopped and likely never would.

When she neared the top of the vineyard, Frankie spied Manny bent over near the Frontenac vines, examining something on the ground. Those Frontenacs, which were beginning to turn from red to blue, were Bountiful's babies, having been nurtured by Manny and Frankie since they were planted six seasons ago. Now mature enough, this would be their debut harvest for winemaking, their long-awaited arrival expected mid-September.

Frankie ambled past the Edelweiss variety she planned to test this morning to see what garnered Manny's attention. He straightened before she had a chance to pounce on him from behind, which was typical of their familiarity. The two made a habit of scaring one another in both common and creative ways around the vineyard.

Manny raised both brows at Frankie and pointed to tracks in the dirt just outside the net-covered Frontenacs. "Looks like deer and probably turkeys are playing grape inspectors. I wonder if I should spray some repellent around the rows."

Frankie examined the easily recognizable hoof prints of white-tailed deer. The three prong prints of wild turkeys always reminded her of a prehistoric creature, and she didn't underestimate their ability to decimate grape vines. This time of year, turkey flocks included a throng of young. All were gobblers in more ways than one.

Before vines began to fruit, Manny and Frankie sprayed a natural water-based cayenne pepper concoction that turned away deer and rabbits from Bountiful's flora. After fruiting, neither one wanted to risk ruining the taste, so nets were the best deterrent. However, Manny thought an extra dose of pepper spray in the grass around the rows might be worthwhile, and Frankie concurred.

"The Frontenacs have come too far to take any chances now." Frankie beamed. "We're so close, and you've done an amazing job with these vines."

Manny turned on a dazzling smile but looked humbly at the ground. "It won't be long now," he said. "I'll go get the spray. Are you testing the Edelweiss? I think they might be ready early this year, too. They're looking full and frosty."

Frankie nodded and proceeded back several rows to the green trailing Edelweiss that provided the tropical flavor for Bountiful's Crown Me Pineapple table wine. The full grape clusters looked like the giant bunches found at the grocery store, and the "frosty" description Manny mentioned referred to the dusty silver color, translucent over the pear-green thin slipskins covering the round baubles.

Weaving her way in and out of the vine leaves, Frankie randomly chose a representation of single grape berries. She picked a few of each from clusters that received different amounts of sunlight, located at varying levels from top to bottom on the vine, and collected them in the pint jar.

She brought the jar over to an outdoor table where she'd left the other accouterments and dumped the grapes into a basket that fit inside the small hand press. She pulled down the long handle with the flat metal disk over the basket, gave it a mighty squeeze, and was pleased to hear the juices flowing into the pot below. She opened the press a few more times, shifted around the grapes, and squeezed again.

A few drops of the Edelweiss poured from the press onto the round hold on the refractometer. The device had two buttons: one to measure the temperature of the juice and one to measure the Brix in degrees, which indicated the amount of sugar available for fermentation. Typically, when the Brix registered between 14 and 20, the grapes were ready. Higher Brix levels would transform the sweet Edelweiss into something foxy and undesirable.

The rest of the juice went into a long tube, and Frankie inserted the digital pH meter, hoping to see a level between 3.0 and 3.4. Manny, sprayer in hand, sidled over to the table to hear the test results.

"The Brix is 13 and the pH is 3.0. We'll have to test every day now and alert the volunteers. What's the weather report?" Frankie recorded the findings in a logbook as she talked.

Manny, a walking weather expert, made an okay sign with his free hand, grinning. "Steady as she goes for the rest of the week. We're not looking at any rain chances until late Monday or Tuesday. I think these vines can sit tight until Monday, but you never know."

The nice thing about Edelweiss grapes is that a little rain won't harm them. Hardy and resilient, they make a great start-up variety, and that's why they were the oldest vines on the property. But it was a well-known fact that grapes could be unpredictable from year to year.

"Agreed, and that's why we'll test every day, just in case," she replied.

Manny continued to spray around the Frontenacs, and Frankie took the testing tools back to the pole shed, pausing to duck away from a group of wasps gathered around a fallen apple. With the warm weather, she was glad Violet and her college friends had picked the majority of the apples last weekend during an early cool spell. This year, all of the Bountiful apples were slated for Violet's mead project and had been trucked to the nearest orchard in Gibson for pressing.

As if responding to the droning wasps, Frankie's phone buzzed in her pocket, revealing a text from Cherry to call when she had a minute. Frankie first washed the testing tools and containers in hot water with a sanitizing solution and set them on the rack to dry.

She punched in Cherry's number, and Cherry answered immediately, breathless. "Frankie, Pom and I found something in Fern's room. It's strange, but we're sure it's important. Can you come over?"

"Sure," she said with a bit of uncertainty, wondering why Cherry couldn't just tell her what they'd discovered. "But let me check in with the bakery first, just to see if things are going well." Frankie was supposed to be on her way there even now, and she was struck with a pang of guilt for calling the shop to see if she could be late. It seemed that every business in town was holding some sort of meeting, and Bubble & Bake had the bakery orders to prove it.

Tess answered, and Frankie could hear the mournful sounds of a corrido, or Mexican ballad, which could only mean Tia Pepita was there, and the sky was falling in her world. The music faded, so Tess must have exited the kitchen to talk to her boss privately.

"Good morning, Tess. How's everything going in the kitchen?" Frankie opened.

"We're holding our own. Are you out at the vineyard?" Tess's lilt had an anxious quality she couldn't disguise. After two years of working together, Frankie recognized the baker's state of mind.

Frankie and Carmen had hired Tess from the Madison College culinary program as an intern for a one-year stint. But Tess fit into the rhythm at Bubble & Bake like a hand in a potholder mitt, so the owners converted her internship into regular employment, which was supposed to end this past June. Unfortunately, Tess's home country of Ethiopia wasn't allowing certain designated students to return until a government transition was in place.

Since she'd graduated in May, Tess lost her student housing and had no affordable place to live. The space above Rachel Engebretsen's shop next door to the bakery was ripe for remodeling. Frankie had purchased the historic cream city brick building that occupied one corner of Meriwether and Granite, the main downtown streets. She rented out the Meriwether side for Rachel's craft store, Bead Me, I'm Yours, but the upstairs served as storage, which wasn't needed.

Within two months, Nothing But the Finest Champagne Builders, courtesy of Frankie's brother James, with extra help from siblings Nick and Will, transformed the upstairs into a cute studio apartment where Tess resided for a tiny sum. Of course, Shauna had done a masterful job designing the apartment's interior.

"Why don't you tell me what's happening at the shop, Tess. What's up with Tia Pepita?" Frankie didn't have time to take the roundabout trail today to get to the crux of things.

"How did you know...ah, you heard the wailing music." Tess spoke better English than many Americans, but she sometimes used atypical descriptors, which made Frankie cheer at their cleverness. "Wailing music" was an appropriate label for the classical Mexican ballads about all sorts of loss.

"Tia Pepita is having a day. She is saying her life is pointless. God never gave her children to love. Her husbands—all gone. And now she is losing her eyes, too," Tess recited Tia's woes du jour.

Frankie tried not to laugh at Tia's moods. True, she was a drama queen who told some of the best exaggerated stories Frankie had ever heard, but she was big-hearted, a talented baker and cook; plus she was Carmen's aunt, visiting from Texas for experimental eye treatments. "Let me guess, she's making Sad Tomato Pie." Tia usually baked items which corresponded to her moods.

"Weeping empanadas," Tess reported. "Before you ask, we're about to change the music to Aunt CeCe's sunshine bop from her convertible days," Tess chuckled. "That always cheers her up, so she won't have to chop onions all morning."

At Frankie's request to be a little late, Tess said everything would be fine. Aunt CeCe had taken out the cookie dough and already had several trays in the commercial oven. Scone dough would be resting for a half hour, and Tess said she'd start butterhorns using the dough in the cooler, with Frankie's permission. With the fall festival on the horizon, the shop needed large quantities of butterhorns and kringle on hand, so there was no option but to bake ahead and freeze them.

"What is Carmen up to?" Frankie had expected her business partner to answer the phone rather than Tess.

Tess laughed loudly, and Frankie could picture her tilting her head back in all-out joy, although she had no idea what was so funny. "Carmen's on her way to the Madison market. You don't even know what day it is, do you?" She laughed again.

Frankie admitted that holiday weekends left her muddled. Holiday weekends with a murder, even more so. "Oh, right. Today's Tuesday. Alright, I'll see you as soon as I can, Tess. Hold down the fort."

Bubble & Bake's fall hours officially began this week, meaning the shop was closed on Mondays and Tuesdays. The bakery proper was always closed Sundays, but the wine lounge opened for business from noon until five. Frankie had mixed emotions every year when it was time to change the schedule. It meant an official end to summer with its high volume of tourists and good money coming in most days of the week. The song "Turn, Turn, Turn" played in her head. "To everything there is a season..." she said aloud.

One more left turn and there she was, back on Hickory Lane again. The Parker house still looked quiet, so most of the relatives must be preoccupied with other activities. There were two extra vehicles in the driveway, so Frankie parked on the street.

Cherry met Frankie at the door, looking a little fresher than the day before. The dark circles had faded, and her deep blue eyes sparkled with anticipation. "Come this way," she said, pulling on Frankie's hand.

They paraded past the kitchen, where Frankie noticed Willow was sitting at the dining table next to a woman Frankie assumed was a relative she hadn't met. The two women were huddled over a notebook, quietly exchanging ideas.

Cherry peered back over her shoulder at Frankie. "That's cousin Dahlia. She's the writer in the family. Dahlia's helping Mom write Fern's eulogy."

Dahlia wore zebra print reading glasses, hanging from a long beaded chain. The glasses rested on the tip of Dahlia's nose as she swiveled her head back and forth between an oversized red book on the table beside her and the notebook. Dahlia wore a decidedly determined expression that dredged up memories of Frankie's English teacher standing over her shoulder as she wrote, judging every word on the page.

Frankie followed Cherry past the living room and up the steps to the attic room recently occupied by Fern, where Pom was sitting on the bed, waiting.

Pom looked even more excited than Cherry. She held up a stuffed animal of a robin and waved it in front of Frankie.

"I found it this morning when I was changing the bed sheets. It was stuffed inside Fern's pillow," Pom spoke as if she'd found buried treasure.

"Tell me more," Frankie said.

"I was taking the pillowcase off the bed pillow, when I felt something lumpy inside the pillow itself. So, I cut the pillow open along the seam and found this inside."

Frankie continued to stare blankly at Pom, then gazed at Cherry, hoping for clarity. Obviously, the stuffed robin indicated something to the cousins, who knew Fern best.

Pom continued and passed the robin to Frankie. "I'm sure someone gave this to Fern, knowing her love for birds. It's one of those Audubon birds that sings the call of the bird it's supposed to be."

Frankie pressed its sides, belly, and breast, but the robin wasn't singing. She shrugged and set it on the bed.

Cherry jumped into the conversation. "We think Fern left us a message. Why else would she bother sewing this bird into her pillow? We think Fern knew she was in danger, and probably wrote about it in her field journal, which is why it's missing."

Frankie considered this. It made sense. Maybe Fern suspected someone was coming after her. But why? "So, what do you think the bird is trying to tell us?" *After all, it wouldn't even sing*, Frankie's internal monologue snarked.

Pom's eyes lit up. "Well, her field assistant is Robyn. Maybe Fern thought Robyn was a threat."

Frankie scoffed until Cherry pulled a plastic tub out of the closet that contained at least twenty other Audubon stuffed birds. "You see, Fern had a collection of them. She chose the robin on purpose."

Frankie wondered why Fern would bring her bird collection with her when she was here to do a field study, then remembered she was supposed to make birdhouses with kids at Fall Migration Days, so the little birds would be great teaching tools.

Frankie retrieved a few birds from the tub and squeezed each one. They all sang out in various tweets and whistles. She picked up the robin again and felt around its insides more carefully, gasping when she felt a hard lump. Maybe it was the soundbox? She turned the bird over and noticed tiny stitches that had been quickly sewed along the seam.

"This bird looks like it has something to tell us. Let's open him up," Frankie said as she showed the stitches to Pom and Cherry. "Do you have sewing scissors? We need to be careful in case something fragile is in here."

Cherry returned with a pair of sharp, small snips, perfect for cutting the threads along the robin's belly. Frankie handed the robin to Pom after making the cut. "You should do the honors, Pom. After all, the bird is your discovery."

Pom dug her fingers into the plush robin, pulling out fluffy stuffing and something else: a brass key. On one side, the number 256 was engraved. On the other side, 1NB.

"It's a safe deposit box key," Frankie was certain.
"And possibly the 1NB stands for First National Bank?"
First National was the biggest bank in Deep Lakes and
likely represented more than half the town's business
accounts, including Bubble & Bake.

"Let's go down there, right now!" Pom and Cherry
vaulted off the bed and headed down the attic steps.

As much as Frankie wanted to accompany them, she
felt the pull of duty to be at the shop. Besides, Pom and
Cherry were family, and the safe deposit box might be
personal or at least family business. "I can't come with
you, I'm afraid. I need to get to B & B and start filling
orders."

Pom and Cherry flushed with guilt. They were
Frankie's employees after all but had taken time off to
help their family. Frankie saw their expressions.

"Hey, you two! You are right where you belong. Bubble
& Bake will be waiting for your return next week." She
gave them each a shoulder squeeze. "Promise me you'll
tell me if something important shows up in the safe
deposit box."

They promised.

# Chapter 9

*And if the whole wide world stops singing, and all the stars go dark, I'll keep a light on in my soul. Keep a bluebird in my heart. — Miranda Lambert*

The Bubble & Bake kitchen weather had changed since Frankie's call with Tess. A jaunty version of "Rockin' Robin" sang out from the speakers, and both Aunt CeCe and Tia Pepita were tapping their toes to the tune, while Tess whistled merrily with the refrain. Tess was a champion whistler, something Frankie admired since she always claimed her own whistler was broken.

Slanted sunlight poured across the black and white tiled floor, and open windows pushed a welcoming breeze into the hot kitchen. Frankie inhaled deeply, basking in the scents of peanut butter, warm sugar, and cinnamon. When she greeted Tia with a gentle hug, she caught the carmelized onion smell wafting off the weeping empanadas on the tray next to her station.

"Good morning, Frankie. How are things at the vineyard? Are the grapes happy now?" Tia Pepita had a way of assigning human emotions to everything, a quality Frankie found delightful.

"Well, they're getting there," she said. "I think we'll be harvesting Edelweiss on either Sunday or Monday."

"Maybe I'll help, if I don't have a headache." Tia Pepita often suffered headaches in the morning hours.

Aunt CeCe raised a concerned eyebrow from her station where she was making blueberry and raspberry scones. The season of berries in Wisconsin was nearing its curtain call, so the bakery used fresh berries as much as possible while they lasted.

"Are you using the lavender pillow and drinking the lavender tea that Coral made especially for headaches?" CeCe asked Tia, who nodded in response.

"Of course, CeCe. And they both help, but I hope all the headaches will stop after the surgery." Tia sucked in a worried breath of air. The UW doctors determined she would be a good candidate for an experimental surgery that could save her eyesight. The surgery would be performed on her worst eye, first, to measure results.

Frankie knew Tia worried about everything, and her belief that she was cursed certainly didn't help matters. "Everything's going to be okay, Tia. It's worth it to have the surgery. You've tried everything else, after all."

Tia dabbed her eyes and face with her apron and nodded tearfully, prompting CeCe to scamper over and give her friend one of her soulful hugs. CeCe and the universe were tuned to the same frequency. Everything she encountered was blessed by her brand of magic.

The rest of the morning passed pleasantly, as music from The Four Seasons, The Dave Clark Five, and The Temptations bounced around the kitchen, mingling with the commercial mixers working cookie dough and muffin batters.

Carmen arrived before noon from the Madison market, and the cheerful unloading began. It was often like Christmas morning when the shop van brought back surprises from the market. Tess and Frankie exclaimed over a flat of fresh autumn mushrooms and the first squash of the season—the delicious cream-colored, green-striped delicata, shaped like a pudgy acorn squash and with the flavor of sweet potatoes.

Bags of fresh herbs, the last of the garden cauliflower, and fingerling potatoes were carried out next, followed by two five-gallon pails of tomatoes. Plump, tasty tomatoes still appeared in abundance in Wisconsin well into September. Nothing could compare with garden-grown local tomatoes, or any local fruits and vegetables for that matter.

"I see Sad Tomato Pie in our immediate future," Frankie laughed, as she hauled one of the huge pails up the backstairs, struggling with each step. It wasn't because she didn't have the muscle, but Frankie was only five feet tall, so getting leverage put her at a disadvantage in tasks like this.

"And probably Tia's Cha Cha Cha Quiche, too," Carmen added as she toted the other pail a couple steps below Frankie.

Since Tia's name came up, Tess informed Carmen about her aunt's difficulties that morning, along with the mood change that followed. Carmen sighed. Tia's habits were nothing new.

"I hope the eye surgery will be a success. Maybe then she'll think her luck has changed." Carmen set the tomatoes on the back deck and came face to face with a furry feline perched in the back window. Startled, Carmen stepped backwards, fortunately into the deck railing that kept her upright.

"Did we get a new cat, Frankie?" Carmen twisted her lips and batted her eyes accusingly at her business partner, who usually kept her informed when a new orphan was coming to roost at the shop.

Since there were so many strays available to adopt, the B & B partners had decided to help Dr. Sadie Chastain, the local vet, by hosting guest cats until they were adopted. Most of the time, the cat visitors were there a few weeks at most before a customer adopted them into a forever home.

The newest arrival hadn't come from Dr. Sadie's clinic, though. "Carmen, meet Piper. I just brought him from the Parker house. It seems that Fern found him roaming the Lake Michigan shoreline, half starved, a couple of months back, ." Frankie had encountered the fluffy furball that morning, hiding under Fern's bed in the attic.

Carmen raised a pointed brow. "So the Parkers don't want him?"

Frankie shook her head. "Willow is allergic."

"What about Fern's brother?" Carmen wasn't going to let Frankie off the hook so easily.

"Ivy offered to take the cat, but Ash hates cats, and since she lives with Ash, well, that's out." Frankie repeated what Pom and Cherry had told her.

Carmen shook her head as if bugs had landed in her hair. "Wait, what? Catch me up. Why does Ivy live with Ash?"

Frankie smiled. She'd planned to give a full report on all she knew surrounding Fern's case and family, but Piper's appearance at the shop disrupted her sharing of the revelations.

"I asked Pom and Cherry the same thing. Here's the history. When Fern's parents died in a car accident, Ash was still in high school. Since Fern was an adult, she became her brother's guardian, and they lived together near Northwestern University, where Fern was getting her graduate degree."

The three women continued carrying the contents of the van up the backstairs to sort out on the deck.

Frankie stopped to catch her breath, halting their progress.

"Ash took up snowboarding and was a natural. Then he had a terrible snowboarding accident when he was 18, which left him paralyzed. Fern had just completed her first field study assisting an ornithologist at Northwestern. She used the money to put a downpayment on a house designed specifically for someone in a wheelchair. But Fern was completing her doctorate and couldn't give Ash the care he needed. Ivy was working as a practical nurse, so Fern hired her as his full-time caregiver and suggested that she move into the house with them. It seemed like a logical solution."

Carmen's expression darkened to sadness. "Poor Ash. He's had a lot of loss to deal with for someone so young—his family and his mobility."

"Maybe that's why he's so sarcastic. It's probably a cover," Frankie explained Ash's comments when she'd met him at the Parkers'.

'Back to Piper. He looks like a bobcat. Has he been to Dr. Sadie's for a going-over?"

The feline stood regally in the window as if he owned the place. His face and coat indeed resembled a bobcat's in coloring but was fluffier. Piper had large erect ears with tufts at the tips. His paws had tufts of hair sticking out between the claws.

"I just brought him to the shop this morning. Dr. Sadie will check him out later today," Frankie conveyed. "He's a beauty, so I'm hoping he likes people. Pom and Cherry were relieved when I offered to take him off their hands."

"I'm sure they've got a lot on their plates right now. It's all good." Carmen gave up being upset about Frankie's impulsive decision. "You better fill me in on the rest of the case, though. While we work, that is."

Carmen was gifted at working and talking. Frankie, however, was prone to storytelling with various hand gestures, which slowed her progress at either the task she worked on or the story she recounted.

Frankie iced butterhorns, boxing up orders of her signature pastries, as she filled in Carmen about the most recent details surrounding Fern's death, and the rest of the women tuned in as well. "I'm waiting to hear from Alonzo about the case evidence and whether or not Dominic Finchley's prints are on Fern's car, or worse: the rocks in her jacket pocket."

Carmen interjected, not bothering to look up from the sugar cookie dough she scooped onto a large tray. "Dominic was Fern's fiancé until very recently. Doesn't it seem likely his prints will be in her car and on the door handles?"

Frankie, who had switched gears to batching dough for Twisted Potato Chip cookies, couldn't disagree. "That's why we'll have to see if they're on anything else, like the rocks or maybe her binoculars. It's possible Fern was hit with the binoculars. Garrett said the head injury looked like it was made by something other than a stone. So I was thinking maybe..."

Carmen smirked. "So, you're just guessing about the binoculars for now."

Frankie shrugged off her friend's skepticism. "I'm just as curious about the safe deposit box. It's been a long time. I should be hearing from Pom and Cherry." She poked one finger into the eggless cookie batter, tasted it, closed her eyes, and smiled in satisfaction. The toffee-laced cookies were made with cupfuls of crushed potato chips, just the right combination of sweet and salty.

Aunt CeCe and Tia Pepita iced sugar cookies as they cooled, adding sprinkles in autumn colors. Tess had finished a big batch of green-tea honey cakes and was frosting special order birthday cookies cut into zoo animal shapes. The kitchen had quieted during Frankie and Carmen's exchanges, and everyone was growing weary from the warmth emanating around the room.

Tess paused to adjust her colorfully printed head wrap, now coated in sweat. She'd whizzed through several cookie elephants, moving the decorating bag like a street artist spray painting a sidewalk. "I made some lemonade tea this morning." She pointed to the walk-in cooler. "Anyone else want a glass?"

It was well past the time the crew usually stopped to munch on something together for lunch. Frankie felt guilty for losing track of time. "Please get glasses for everyone, Tess. I'll look for something in the cooler to eat."

Wiping her face on a tea towel, Frankie gratefully entered the walk-in, enjoying the cool respite. She fetched San Marzano tomatoes, fresh mozzarella pearls, basil, and a large jar of mixed Greek olives. Scooting to the pantry, she grabbed five plates and a squirt bottle of balsamic reduction, then quickly made caprese salad and dumped the olives into a bowl. Carmen produced a loaf of chewy ciabatta from her market bag and sliced it thinly for dipping into one of the herbal oils they kept in stock.

Glasses of the iced lemonade tea were consumed and refilled more than once, as the women ate and drank in silence, smiling at each other and the pastry-laden countertops. None could deny the satisfaction from the work done by caring hands in a sea swell of sweet and zesty aromas.

Aunt CeCe and Tia were told to go home for the rest of the day. A full morning in a hot kitchen was enough for women of their age. CeCe was happy to oblige Carmen by driving Tia home to the O'Connor farm, so the others could complete orders for pick-up tomorrow.

CeCe picked up her large straw bag trimmed in three-dimensional butterflies and stopped at Frankie's station to whisper in her ear. "Keep looking for more details about Fern's death, Dear Heart. I had a dream last night that a large flock of birds were flying in a lovely formation, then suddenly dropped to the earth, dead. There were many different kinds of birds in the flock that fell and died. Strange."

Frankie felt chilled as CeCe's words swept over her. She didn't know if the dream had anything to do with Fern, but she knew Aunt CeCe had a penchant for receiving messages from the universe. Most of the time her dreams were trivial in nature or offered generalizations that could be found in a fortune cookie, but she didn't underestimate them just the same.

Frankie's absorbed trance was interrupted by her ringing phone, but she waved the aunts out the back door before picking up Cherry's call. What she heard were stereo voices on speaker.

"The deposit box had another key and a note inside," Cherry chirped, interrupted by Pom's apologetic vocal, "Sorry for not calling sooner. Mom needed some things from the store."

"The note said 'Ent circle,' then 'fireman's day,'" Cherry continued, struck by a long space of silence from Frankie, which Cherry countered with, "You're just going to have to see it in person, I guess."

By now, Frankie was certain the cousins spoke a coded language only known to them, so she'd have to settle for their interpretation again. "Okay, so can you explain her message to me?" she asked.

Pom again. "It's not going to make any sense unless we show you, Frankie. Besides, we shouldn't talk about this on the phone. You never know who may be listening."

Pom had a point if she feared that someone in their inner circle had harmed Fern, which might be the reason she'd left behind the coded messages.

"I need to finish up here first. Give me a couple of hours?"

"Meet us at Pine Avenue Park at three-thirty?," Cherry whispered. "Do you know where that is?"

Frankie affirmed, bewildered. Maybe the Ent Circle was there?

No sooner had she ended the call with the two sisters, when the phone rang again. This time Officer Shirley Lazaar's voice crowed in her ear.

"Helloo, Frankie. Are you up for trading stories?"

This was Shirley's way of saying she had information on Fern's case she was willing to share, and was hopeful Frankie had something that would help the investigation, too. Or maybe Shirley just wanted butterhorns in exchange.

"Hi, Shirley. I sure am. But I have to finish up my day at the bakery first, then I have an appointment at three-thirty." Frankie wasn't willing to give up too much on the phone.

Shirley chomped on something crunchy. "Oops, sorry about that. It's been a long day. How about a hike up Blackbird Hill, say at five o'clock?"

Frankie relished the long summer days and weather that allowed her to be outdoors getting extra exercise. "Sure, see you then. Meet you at the parking area."

Pine Avenue Park was a small wooded plot of green
space south of downtown. A small formal flower garden
greeted visitors, who parked along a cobblestone wall.
In the center of the garden, a statue of Hans Christian
Andersen sat reading a book to a group of children
gathered around him. The park had been a gift to the
city from two of the founding families, the Paulsens and
the Andersens. Peder Andersen claimed Hans Christian
as an ancestor, so the statue literally cemented that
relationship.

The park was a seldom-used sanctuary with plenty of
shade and was a great spot for bird watching or a respite
from a hot summer day. There was no playground and no
picnic area, just a few stone benches scattered along the
brick path.

Pom and Cherry sat on the stone wall, waiting for
Frankie. Barely able to contain their excitement, they
sprinted to the brick path, which was still recognizable.

"I guess someone must be taking care of this place,"
Frankie said. "I didn't think the city maintenance crew
had time to handle any of the small green spaces around
here."

Cherry affirmed Frankie's remark. "No, the city
doesn't take care of this. Lars Paulsen hires someone
to mow the grass, kill the weeds between the bricks on
the path, and plant and water the flower garden. The
Andersens don't help at all anymore."

If memory served, the only Andersens left in Deep
Lakes were Peder the third, who was now well past
80 years old, and his granddaughter, Ava, an esteemed
member of the Whitman County Historical Society and a
local realtor. Ava was probably too busy competing with
real estate mogul Bram Callahan to be concerned about
the welfare of Pine Avenue Park. Frankie was impressed

that Lars Paulsen would bother with such a little-known wooded dot on the map.

Frankie closed her memory file and followed the sisters. "Where are we going anyway? Is someone going to give me a clue?"

The bricks ended, and the sisters continued walking further into a wooded area of large white oaks and white pines. Pom pointed off to the left at a jagged, red boulder about the size of a piece of luggage. "Right there!"

Cherry and Pom stopped at the boulder and began pointing at imaginary things, counting. Frankie only saw bare earth and a few tree stumps. The counting ceased, and the two sisters carefully walked around the stumps toward several copses of trees growing together.

"That third section of trees there," Pom pointed ahead. "That's the Ent Circle."

"When the Sensational Six played together, we sometimes rode our bikes down here, since the park belonged to Lars's family. Fern had the best imagination. She loved Tolkien and read to us from *The Lord of the Rings*. We found this copse of trees, and well, you'll understand when we go inside." Cherry pulled Frankie by the hand.

Cherry parted a small curtain of some vining shrub that served as an entrance to a perfectly lovely fairy circle of soft moss surrounded by tall linden trees. The circle was large enough to accommodate several children. Two rotting logs sat on opposite edges of the circle, and two somewhat flat stones occupied the outer edge as well.

"This was our secret spot. Look up at these two trees," Pom instructed, and Frankie could make out the formation of faces on the old linden trunks, reminiscent of Tolkien's description of the Ents or Tree Shepherds from *The Two Towers*. Tolkien's Ents looked like old trees with human faces and could move about their Middle Earth forest home.

Frankie nodded and smiled broadly. "I see why you called this the Ent Circle. What a terrific spot to have secret meetings!"

"Yes, and we'd leave notes here for each other inside Penny Loafer's trunk." Cherry pointed to one of the trees that had a face, then downward to the bottom of its trunk. There was a hollow space there and the tree did look like it was wearing a pair of loafers.

Frankie giggled like a child. "Marvelous. What about that one? Does he have a name?" She pointed upward at the tree that appeared to have one large ear and a bulbous nose.

"Ash named that one Uncle Wart. He said it resembled Uncle Drake, which we thought wasn't very nice, but the name stuck anyway." Pom laughed at the memory.

Frankie needed to get back to business since she had one more appointment to keep. "Okay, we're at the Ent Circle. What's next?" She had no idea what "fireman's day" meant.

Pom pointed to the piece of paper containing Fern's note with a small steel key taped to it. "Ash's dream was to become a fireman, even into his teen years. So, Ash is the fireman and his day must be his birthdate."

Cherry reached up into the hollow insides of Penny Loafer. She found nothing, but Pom wasn't about to give up so quickly. She left the circle and reentered with a long thick branch. Poking upward into the hollow caused a few things to fall out. What looked like an old woodpecker's nest tumbled down along with many dried leaves. Another poke brought down a woven wild grapevine basket with a box in the center.

All three gasped in wonder. Pom brushed leaves out of her hair, then forced the box out of the grapevine contraption. The metal box was locked but had a tiny combination padlock and a keyhole behind it. Pom was shaking now.

"One of you try the combination, please. I'm too nervous."

Frankie gestured to Cherry. "You know the numbers. Go ahead."

Cherry turned clockwise first to the number 11 for November, then counterclockwise to the number 5, then stopped abruptly. "I don't know what to do now. The numbers on the lock only go to 30. Ash was born in 1996."

Pom suggested she try 26 since it was Ash's age. It didn't work.

"Maybe the lock is set up with more than three numbers to open it. Start over, but after the 5, go clockwise to 19, then counterclockwise to 9, then clockwise to 6. You know, to break up the 1996 year." Frankie felt pretty confident that she was on to the solution, but it didn't work, even after a few tries.

Cherry went back to a three-number solution and tried 19, but it didn't work, then 9 the second time, then 6 the third time. None of these combinations opened the lock.

Frankie pulled out her phone. "Fern was extraordinarily clever, so there has to be something else we're missing." She looked up the date for international firefighter's day, which is May 4th. "Try the number 4."

Cherry repeated the previous 11 and 5 followed by 4 to the right and the padlock sprung. "Good thinking, Frankie!" Pom cheered.

Cherry inserted the tiny key and the metal lid lifted freely. Cherry pulled out folded paper copies and sucked in a huge breath of air. "These are photocopies from Fern's field journal!"

It seemed Frankie was right about the missing journal being important to the case. Unfortunately, much of the important information was coded, and on the first reading, Pom and Cherry couldn't make sense of it.

"Did you use a secret language when you were kids that Fern is using in her journal?" Frankie asked hopefully.

Pom and Cherry nodded. "We did, but it was very simple, like Pig Latin, and that's not what this is at all," Pom said.

Frankie sighed heavily. "Well, take this home and keep the pages inside the box and lock it. Can you hide it somewhere safe? I mean really safe, too, because you have no idea who might want this."

The sisters looked worried. "I think we should give it to Alonzo for the investigation," Cherry said. "It's the right thing to do."

"But first, we're going to make copies of the pages for each of us," Pom said, a sly smile curving her face.

Frankie nodded. "Atta girl, Pom. Let's take them to the shop, and I'll scan them on my printer." Never mind Whitman County's finest, this trio was all in to continue their side investigation into Fern's demise.

# Chapter 10

*Climb the mountains and get their good tidings.*
*— John Muir*

At Bubble & Bake, Frankie handed a set of Fern's copied notes to each cousin and promised to give the copies found in the box to Shirley Lazaar.

"I'm meeting Shirley at five to hike Blackbird Hill and trade information," Frankie said, tucking her set of the copied journal pages into a file folder. She passed the wooden box, padlock, and key to Cherry.

"Will you two be showing the journal notes to Ash and Ivy, so they can help decipher them?" Frankie was curious if the cousins were still as close as they were as children.

Pom and Cherry exchanged questioning looks, and it was apparent to Frankie the two were not on the same page about the cousins.

Cherry, the older sister, took on the role of spokesperson. "Pom's worried the journal pages might upset Ash and Ivy, but I think we need their help to break the code. Not only do we have different memories of Fern, but we process things differently."

Pom twirled one long lock of hair thoughtfully. "Those two have been through so much emotionally. I just get a funny feeling around them, like they're not being straight with us. Ash isn't the happy-go-lucky kid he used to be before his accident, and Ivy has become like a mother. She acts like a bitter old maid sometimes."

That remark made Cherry laugh. "It's true. Ivy acts older than the rest of us, even though she's not even 30. She's always bossing Ash around. She used to be so carefree. I guess we've all changed, though."

Frankie turned the conversation back to the secret language in the journal. "What's your plan for these notes?" She tapped on the sheaf of papers in her hand.

Again the sisters exchanged questioning looks and shrugged simultaneously. "I guess we'll look at them together first and see if we can translate anything valuable. If we hit a dead end, we'll have to decide what to do next." Cherry, at least, was willing to give Pom's intuition the benefit of the doubt.

Frankie followed the two out after stopping in the kitchen to grab a bakery bag containing four butterhorns, an offering to Shirley. She also stuffed the sheaf of journal notes into a file folder to hand over as evidence. She wondered if Whitman County had access to any code-breaking experts. Probably not, but maybe they had a contact in a major metro like Chicago or Minneapolis.

The day was picture perfect with a few clouds helping to keep the sun at bay. The Blackbird Hill public access point was off County K on Fawn Avenue. On the drive, Frankie slowed when she spied a red-shouldered hawk circling above a field, then suddenly swooping to ground level to pounce on its dinner. It rose upward again carrying something in its talons, either a mouse or chipmunk by the looks of it.

The SUV sped up again, rounded a curve and made a left onto Fawn. In a couple of minutes, the parking lot, which was little more than leveled ground with a brown information sign on a post, emerged on the right. Shirley's personal vehicle, a big black Buick, was already parked with Shirley standing next to it, leaning on the hood.

When not in uniform, Shirley was likely found in jeans or denim capris, a T-shirt, hiking sandals, and a ball cap. Today's cap was from her former Chicago police unit, faded blue with the historical landmark building of the old 7th precinct.

Shirley grinned conspicuously at the bakery bag, and reached out greedily to take it from Frankie. "Butterhorns, I hope? I know they're a hot commodity, Frankie." She winked and laughed heartily as she opened the car door to set the bag on the floor out of the sun.

Shirley was the first county officer to take Frankie seriously as an investigating news reporter. Maybe because they were both women, or maybe because Shirley respected Frankie's observations, or maybe because Frankie claimed extensive knowledge of Deep Lakes and its citizenry. Shirley could see an advantage in listening to Frankie and sharing case details that could be easily discovered anyway.

Frankie felt relaxed with Shirley; they had an easy back and forth with one another and a level of trust that increased case by case. Frankie believed it didn't hurt her position that she dated the highly respected county coroner either.

"Shall we?" Frankie pointed to the trailhead, eager to make the hike after a day that mostly consisted of standing at her kitchen station. Blackbird Hill's trail started out level through a prairie of wildflowers and milkweed, where butterflies and skippers flitted around, feeding and laying eggs. Monarchs danced around the remaining blooms. It wouldn't be long now before they would make their landmark flight to Mexico for the winter.

The path made walking side by side easy for the time being, so Shirley began a recitation of their case findings so far.

"I'm sure you're interested in hearing about Dominic Finchley's status as a suspect," Shirley intoned, as if speaking at a press conference.

Frankie nodded emphatically. If Dominic's prints were on the murder weapon, he was a dead duck.

"Finchley's prints were all over the Mallard woman's vehicle. On the inside and outside passenger door handle, on the console, the glove compartment, and on the clasp of her knapsack."

Frankie's eyes widened as she took in the information. "It doesn't look good for Fern's ex then," she commented.

Shirley held up one hand meaningfully. "Right, except that there were no prints on the stones found in the jacket pocket, and no prints on the field glasses either."

Frankie's excitement was growing. "So, the binoculars were a factor in Fern's death?" Somehow, she knew she'd been right about that.

Shirley nodded. "The right lens and the tripod connector both had blood and skin particles matching the victim. The head wound she suffered was consistent with the field glasses as the weapon."

"But you didn't find prints on the field glasses?"

Shirley again. "The only prints anywhere on the field glasses belonged to the Mallard woman."

The two nodded knowingly at one another, "The killer wore gloves," they both said.

Shirley continued. "I imagine Garrett already told you that the victim died from the head wounds, then was dragged to the pond to make it look like she drowned."

Frankie shook her head. "I haven't had time to connect with him today, so thanks for sharing that."

"Is Finchley still a suspect, and who else is on your radar?" Frankie's sense was that someone connected to Fern's field work was the culprit.

Shirley's tanned face held determination, echoed in her dark steely eyes. Frankie imagined the former Chicago detective was a force to be reckoned with in her heyday. She could still outrun Alonzo in a foot chase, and her mind was calculating, sharpened from urban experiences Frankie couldn't fathom.

"We've got our work cut out for us, since Mallard had a number of contacts related to her field studies and her university work." Shirley's expression became hawkish as she assumed the role of the predator on the hunt. "Luckily, many of them are in town for her funeral tomorrow, which is where we'll be on the lookout."

Frankie smiled, too. She planned to do her own brand of prowling at the funeral as well.

The trail began to climb upward, narrowing to a footpath embedded with partially buried rocks and thick tree roots. The two continued in single file and talk subsided.

Frankie registered the information Shirley provided, but wondered about the scratches on Fern's arm. She bounded a few steps ahead of the officer, so she could turn around without startling her. "Shirley, what about the scratches on Fern's arm? Any DNA news to speak of?"

Shirley stopped, holding onto a pine branch for stability. "We swabbed Finchley's fingers per his consent. That was before he lawyered up. We're waiting on those results. We swabbed under the victim's nails, too, in case she was able to fight off the assailant."

"The ex was pretty cooperative? What kind of vibe did you get from him?" Frankie trusted Shirley's instincts as much as she trusted facts and science.

"Finchley's hard to read. He's a cool cucumber, but he freely offered up information, answered all our questions, and allowed us to take his prints and DNA samples. For my part, it's a waiting game. Maybe Finchley was smart enough to wear gloves to kill the woman, then go through her car without gloves, knowing we'd expect to find his prints there. They only broke up a couple weeks ago."

Frankie's eyes narrowed. "Did you ask him about Fern's field journal?"

"Naturally," Shirley offered. "Finchley said he was looking for it in her car but didn't find it. Apparently, the jilted fiancé planned to use it to finish her work. Pretty noble, eh?" She scoffed, snorting.

"So he admitted to being there, at the scene? Did he say why he was there or if Fern was alive when he saw her?" Frankie knew she was reaching too far with her questions, but it was worth a shot.

"Can't say exactly." Shirley spoke tightly, mouth drawn into one thin line. She knew she'd already said too much.

Frankie switched topics. "Any leads on tire impressions or footprints?"

"I don't think footprints are going to help. We have a couple partials near the drag marks, but the grassy area didn't yield much. Then the shoreline had footprints from your sister-in-law and from you, right? There were two sets of shoe prints in the parking lot, probably the victim's and the ex's. One set appears to match the bird lady's hiking boots."

That didn't add up in Frankie's mind, unless Finchley *was* the killer. Or the second set of prints belonged to someone else? Or the killer covered their tracks? Her mind was racing with ideas. "Tire tracks?"

Shirley weighed the question over, considering whether or not she should answer. "Tire tracks in the lot match the jeep, but that wasn't a surprise." She let the comment hang in the air without further detail.

"Let's finish our walk, huh?" Frankie rarely pressed Shirley for additional information she wasn't entitled to have, and their conversation had come to a stopping point for now.

They resumed climbing, pulling themselves up over giant gray boulders to the limestone outcropping that overlooked evergreens to hardwoods to farm fields to the Blackbird River. The sight was breathtaking in every season. The women had the view all to themselves. Soon, the arrival of fall colors would make it a popular place to take in the view.

Frankie clicked a couple of photos with her phone. "Should we take a selfie? What do you think, Shirley? This could be the first of many hikes we take together." Frankie meant it. She didn't take time out for hiking, but she knew Shirley was a regular. If hiking was a common denominator for them, it would be a good way for Frankie to learn more about the detective biz.

Shirley threw her head back in laughter. "A selfie, huh? Well, this will be a first for me. Sure, why not?" The shot captured two thoughtful people with their heads together as if in cahoots. Behind them, the sun illuminated the evergreens, turning them into something ethereal.

They marveled at the photo, satisfied. "Send that to me, would you, Frankie?"

106106
106106
106106
106106
106106

"Of course, and I've got something for you in my SUV that's sure to keep you busy." Fern's cryptic journal pages waited on the SUV's floor, concealing her secrets for better or worse.

# Chapter 11

*Night brings out stars as sorrow shows us truths.*
*— Philip James Bailey*

The Bubble & Bake kitchen was a scene of serenity Wednesday morning, awash in the pink glow of dawn and the comforting fragrance of vanilla sugar, cinnamon, and pastries. Frankie, who had padded quietly down and into the kitchen from upstairs, inhaled deeply before greeting her mother, Aunt CeCe, and Tia Pepita.

Her thoughts went to Pom and Cherry, the weight of their loss, and the difficult day ahead of them as they said their goodbyes to Fern. Feeling grateful for her family and the cozy gathering place of her shop, Frankie wanted a few moments to enjoy the peace that accompanied a new day.

Peggy read her daughter's emotions and turned to give her a warm hug, an infrequent display of affection between the two. Frankie greedily accepted the hug and gave Peggy an extra squeeze.

"What time are you going to the visitation, Dear?" Peggy asked, as she smoothed the front of her shop apron.

The visitation would be taking place during the morning hours until the one o'clock funeral. The entire event was being held at the Hardison Funeral Home, one of two funeral homes in Deep Lakes. Since Fern didn't have any religious affiliations, and the Hardisons had an excellent reputation for their services, the Parkers made the choice to use the father-and-son business.

"I'm going to meet Carmen and Jovie at Hardisons' at eight. The Parkers said it was okay for us to come early, since they know we're working in shifts. The three of us will come here afterwards, so you can all go to pay your respects."

Frankie and Carmen were invited to the funeral dinner at five o'clock, which was when Carmen agreed to help Frankie scope out suspects, as they each worked the room. Today would present the best opportunity to gather information. With many key players in Fern's life gathered in one spot under unsettling circumstances, it was an opportunity to people-watch. After snooping around at a few other funerals, Frankie and Carmen were becoming adept at reading people.

After exchanging pleasantries with the aunties and steaming oat milk to pour into a double shot of espresso, Frankie tied on a purple Bubble & Bake apron printed with donuts and wine glasses and headed to a station at the counter.

Fresh cranberry maple scones were on the menu for the next few days. While Frankie fetched ingredients for an extra large batch, her mind drifted into sleuthdom. She wanted to bring her A-game to the visitation.

As she warmed whole milk in a heavy pot, glancing periodically at the thermometer, she ticked off a mental list of people she needed to meet. Dominic Finchley was at the top of the list, followed by field assistant Robyn, and then every bird colleague in attendance. Since she didn't know their names, the mental list was stalled for now.

Frankie transferred the milk to the floor mixer where a yeast cake waited in the stainless steel bowl. She returned to her station to send bags of ruby red cranberries through one food processor while chopping up walnuts with a second processor. Deep in thought, she chewed her bottom lip.

Peggy walked past her daughter, making her way out to the front with the pastry case to open the shop to customers. She paused. "What's going on up there, Honey?" Peggy pointed at Frankie's forehead.

"Oh, you know, just wondering how many of Fern's colleagues will be at the visitation this morning? I want to talk to all of them. Well, I actually want to watch them first, see how they act around the family and interact. Then, I want to talk to them." Frankie had a plan.

Peggy's eyes widened. "That could take a long time. You should plan on staying awhile. What happens if you don't see everyone at the visitation?" Peggy lifted her chin and stood taller. "I'm good at observing people. I can pick up where you leave off if you wish."

Since the sheep farm investigation earlier that summer, everyone in Frankie's orbit seemed interested in sleuthing. She wasn't sure how she felt about that, although she had relied on her mother's observation skills on more than one occasion.

She offered her a promising smile. "I'll keep you posted, Mom."

Frankie relished in her now-empty kitchen since Aunt CeCe and Peggy were out front to run sales, and Tia Pepita was taking a break. Carmen's aunt had disappeared through the swinging doors with kitty food in one hand and a plate of breakfast empanadas in the other. Frankie could think without distraction.

Her short-lived solitude evaporated as the kitchen doors swung inward announcing Alonzo in uniform, accompanied by Donovan Pflug. Alonzo carried a manila file folder and waved it in Frankie's direction.

"I got this from Officer Shirley a few minutes ago and thought I'd better stop in before you head over to Hardisons'. What do you know about this?" Alonzo looked at her accusingly.

Frankie stopped kneading scone dough and raised two floured hands in mock surrender. "I assume those are the pages from Fern Mallard's journal. We just found them yesterday, and I gave them to Shirley right afterwards."

The sheriff, arms crossed, failed to look convinced. "So, you're saying you haven't figured out any of the stuff in here? You didn't powwow last night with the Parker sisters to try to decode this?"

Frankie shook her head in earnest. "Pom and Cherry could use some space, so I'm not pushing them. They'll reach out when they need me. Meanwhile, today's a big day for the family, and they probably will work on decoding the journal when the funeral is over." Frankie marveled at how much she sounded like her matter-of-fact mother.

Pflug, dressed in a suit made for funerals, cleared his throat. "So, you admit that you kept a copy of the journal then?" He was soft spoken and sounded oddly sympathetic. He must be playing "good cop" today, Frankie thought.

Frankie stood up a little straighter. "Of course *they* kept a copy of the pages." She wiped her hands quickly on her apron, using her quasi-clean fingers to tick off her points. "Number one: Fern is their cousin. They have a right to her things. Number two: if anyone can break the code, it's probably going to be one of them." She almost said "one of the Sensational Six," but would then have to explain her meaning, including the Ent Circle at Pine Avenue Park.

Alonzo changed the subject. "You might as well tell me your plan for today, because I know you're not going to leave this case alone."

"I'm going to watch and listen. And, meet as many people as I can," she smiled. "Probably the same as you."

Alonzo laughed, throwing back his head. "I've seen you in action at funerals before, Frankie Champagne. That's why Officer Pflug will be your escort today."

Frankie couldn't refrain from scowling at Pflug. "Thanks, but I already have a date," she quipped. Frankie was satisfied that Pflug looked about as happy as someone with stomach flu about his assignment.

An hour later, Frankie changed into a pair of dark pants and a gray dress shirt, made sure she had her cell phone and a small notepad in her purse, then drove down the alleyway between Bubble & Bake and Callahan Realty Office, and proceeded left onto Granite Street. Peering out the rearview mirror, she saw the dark blue unmarked squad pull out behind her, making her cringe as she pictured the arrogant face of Donovan Pflug behind the wheel.

Hardison Funeral Home was a sprawling red brick-faced structure on Dodge Street, built around twenty years ago, after the original home, an old three-story Victorian house/funeral parlor, was renovated and turned into a bed and breakfast. Harold Hardison was the third generation mortician to run the business, which he would eventually pass along to his current business partner, son Michael.

Frankie pulled into the lot to park beside Carmen, who was waiting for her outside the front door with Jovie next to her. Pflug had to park further away from Frankie, so he had to trot briskly to catch up to his quarry.

Carmen looked sharp in a black skirt and print blouse, her dark hair nestled in a French twist at the back of her neck. She spotted Pflug, and her eyes narrowed as she whispered sharply, "What does he want? Is he following you?"

Frankie grabbed Jovie by one arm and Carmen by the other. Perched in the middle, she spoke quietly. "Pflug's been assigned to watch me, so we need to be covert. Text me with information and we can meet up in the ladies room."

Harold and Michael Hardison greeted the women inside the foyer. Harold, a tall gray-haired man with kind eyes, smiled gently at them.

"Good morning. I'm afraid the visitation doesn't begin until nine. Right now just the family and close friends are in the viewing room." Since Jovie was closest to Harold, he took her arm to quietly lead all three back toward the door, but Officer Pflug was blocking their path.

Unflappable, Harold spoke calmly to Pflug: "As I was just saying to these ladies, the visitation begins at nine. If you'd be so kind as to return then..." He left the sentence unfinished.

A small tick was pulsing in Pflug's jaw, but he didn't have the chance to respond because Cherry was whispering something to Michael, who stepped forward and placed a hand on his father's arm.

"These women are close friends of the family and were told to come early, Dad." Michael bowed toward the three. "Come right this way, please."

Pflug was momentarily left behind to speak to the elder Hardison. Frankie had the momentary satisfaction that he'd probably have to show his badge to gain admittance. Cherry and Michael escorted the women through a set of double French doors into the main viewing parlor.

The front of the room was heavily laden with floral arrangements in all colors and sizes; many of them included ornamental nests with wooden and velvet birds perched on them. The flowers ensconced a simple casket of recyclable materials per Fern's request. She had no intention of taking up precious land space but would be cremated following the funeral.

Rows and rows of cushioned folding chairs occupied the carpeted room where many people were already seated. Frankie recognized members of Fern's family in the rows. Ornate sofas sat regally against three sides of the room but were currently serving no purpose. Frankie knew the lay of the land.  She herself had stood around the perimeter of this very room with her family during the visitation for her beloved father, Charlie. The memory caught her off guard, and she inhaled sharply to swallow a sob that emerged, as if she'd just lost her father all over again. Soon, a line of Fern's family members would form, as they waited to be greeted and consoled, a chain of woe.

Cherry pulled Frankie by the hand toward Fern's casket before she could object.

"Here, I want you to see the photo boards we put together. The one on the left is her professional board. It includes photos with her colleagues. I knew you'd want to study them, and this is a good time to take a photo. You know, incognito-like." Cherry motioned toward Pom, and she joined them near the casket. The sisters huddled around the photo board while Frankie quickly snapped a couple shots with her phone.

"Are any of Fern's colleagues here yet?" Frankie asked.

Pom's golden blonde head tilted toward the back of
the room, where a man in a black suit stood talking
to Ash and Ivy. From a distance, he looked disheveled
with tousled tawny brown hair that hung limply over his
forehead. His darker mustache was unkempt, and the
scruffy beginnings of a beard sprouted along his jawline
and chin. He wore smart black-framed glasses and spoke
with one hand stuffed in his pants pocket as he gestured
wearily with the other hand.

"That's Dom, Fern's ex." Pom swiveled the other
direction and walked toward one of the  arrangements,
a substantial Norfolk Island pine, its boughs sporting
feathered red birds meant to resemble cardinals. Staring
at the pine, she indicated for Frankie to look to her right.
"That's Robyn Munson, Fern's assistant."

Robyn's sorrowful expression couldn't be missed.
Frankie walked over to the field biologist, who was
sitting in a chair away from others, dabbing her eyes
with a tissue. She stood up, either to greet Frankie or
to walk away from her—-Frankie wasn't sure—but she
didn't allow Robyn to make the choice. Frankie thrust
her hand forward in greeting.

"Hello. I'm Frankie Champagne. Pom and Cherry
work for me at Bubble & Bake downtown. I'm a member
of the Whitman Seekers Bird Club, so I had the good
fortune of meeting Fern Friday night at a reception."

Robyn shook Frankie's hand firmly, and it was easy to
gauge Robyn's strength in that handshake. Even though
she wore a dress, Frankie could discern her muscular
frame. She was used to seeing bodybuilders at the
Wellness Center, where she participated in yoga and
aerobics, and wondered how much Robyn could bench
press.

"I'm glad you had the chance to meet Fern. She was one of a kind," Robyn said. "It was a privilege to work with her." She choked on the last few words.

"Yes, I've heard good things about Fern's work. Maybe after the funeral you can tell me about the work you did together." Frankie hoped Robyn would open up. Maybe she knew something about Fern or others in their field she could share. Maybe she had insights about Dominic Finchley.

"Can I speak with you in the ladies room?" Robyn gestured toward the double doors, and Frankie followed.

A couple of older women from the Parker family were in there but exited quickly. Robyn looked under the stalls to be sure they were empty. Still, she spoke softly, leaning toward Frankie.

"I've heard you solve crimes, Ms. Champagne. I feel like what happened to Fern is partly my fault." Robyn's gray eyes filled with tears.

"Why would it be your fault?" Frankie asked, trying to look relaxed, although she pictured Robyn dragging Fern's lifeless body down the embankment to the pond.

"I overheard an argument between Ivy and Dom."

Frankie felt a hot flash coming in light of this revelation. "Ivy? You mean Fern's cousin? And Dom, the ex-fiancé? Tell me what you heard, Robyn, and when you heard it."

"It was two or three weeks ago. Fern and I were working in her home office, making plans for dividing up the field study locations we'd be doing here. I went downstairs to get some ice water when I overheard Ivy and Dom arguing in the kitchen. Dom said Ivy complained too much about Fern. He said Fern was overcompensating her for taking care of Ash. He called her a gold digger. Ivy argued Dom only wanted to marry

Fern so he could ride her famous coattails and get ahead in his career."

Frankie raised one hand to stop Robyn. "Just give me a second. Can I please write down what you just said?" She reached into her purse for her notepad and began scribbling what Robyn had relayed, then asked her what happened next.

"They swore at each other, and Dom walked out the back door, so I quickly went back upstairs before Ivy could see me standing near the doorway."

Frankie looked Robyn in the eyes, hoping to see honesty or deceit. "How does this relate to what happened to Fern?"

Robyn blinked hard, and tears began to flow. "I never told Fern what I heard. I think one of them might have killed her. Please try to find out." Robyn stood over the sink and splashed water on her face, then stood up. "I'm going outside for some fresh air before I go back in there."

Robyn went out the door, just as Carmen came in. "I wondered what happened to you, Frankie. You should see Pflug. He looks like a kid who lost his new puppy." Carmen snorted. "He just headed out to the parking lot."

Frankie grabbed Carmen's arm. "I just got an earful from Robyn Munson, Fern's assistant. I'll fill you in later. Have you talked to anyone, heard anything juicy?"

"Not exactly. Cherry's been introducing me and Jovie to the whole family. I thought I had a lot of relatives. I need a roster to keep everyone straight, not that I'm trying. By the way, Jovie thinks Ash is a charmer. And after dating your brother Nick a time or two, Jovie should know."

Carmen's comment about Ash hit a nerve with Frankie. "Do you think Ash is acting too cool about his sister's death? Almost like he doesn't really care?"

Frankie didn't want to make a snap judgment, but Ash's rakish behavior was gnawing at her.

Carmen shrugged. "Everyone handles grief in their own way. You should get back in there and talk to him. Turn on your Frankie Champagne listening face. You know, the one that makes perfect strangers spill their guts." Carmen snorted and headed into a bathroom stall. "Don't forget to tell me everything later."

Frankie saw Pom in the hallway outside the viewing room, watching Ash leave out the back door with Ivy close behind. Pom's face was a mask of sorrow.

"What's happened?" Frankie asked as she tried to console her.

"I think Fern's death is starting to sink in with Ash. He was looking at the family photo boards and made a fast exit." Pom appeared uncertain whether to follow him. "I guess I'll give him a few minutes."

Frankie squeezed Pom's hand and scooted down the hallway to the back door. Maybe Pom was willing to give Ash some privacy, but Ivy wasn't, so Frankie decided to assess the situation for herself.

She pushed open the glass door and immediately noticed Ash vomiting into the bushes on the far side of the fenced-in lot. Ivy stood over him like a mother, wiped his face with a tissue while handing him another. Ash took the offered tissue but pushed away Ivy's hand.

Surveying the fenced-in area, Frankie decided the large storage shed might be close enough to the pair for her to hear their conversation. Her insides felt shaky as guilt poured in, especially since she wasn't sure if she was more concerned about invading their privacy or about getting caught listening behind the shed.

Frankie pulled her phone from her purse and put it up to her face as if engaged in a call and crept toward the shed. She couldn't see Ash or Ivy, but she could hear them.

Ivy offered consolation. "At least we'll both be taken care of, Ash. Fern was able to pay off the house. I knew she wouldn't let you down."

Ash's voice was a mixture of grief and something Frankie thought was serious determination. "Look, Ivy, when all this is settled, we need to talk about what happens next."

"What do you mean by that?" Ivy's voice was uncertain and edgy. "Nothing's going to change. I'll take care of you just like always."

"Just stop, Ivy. It's time for things to change. We both need to get a life. You know it as much as I do." Ash's voice was quiet but forceful. "And please don't look at me like that. You're not my mother, and neither was Fern."

Ivy's voice broke into a sob that held sorrow and pity. "Don't talk to me like that. We did the best we could, Ash. For you." Ivy's voice trailed off, as she ran past the shed toward the back door.

Frankie ducked behind the corner of the shed, her heart doing a two-step. She walked purposefully in front of the shed, cell phone in hand, toward Ash, who was staring down at the grass, eyes closed.

"I'm sorry to disturb you, Ash, but I overheard your conversation with Ivy. I can't imagine how you must be feeling right now." Frankie knew she had no right to bother Ash at that moment, so she hoped she at least conveyed the sincerity she felt about his loss.

Ash looked up at Frankie, spinning his chair around so his eyes were out of the sun. Frankie moved with him for a better angle.

"No, you can't imagine how I'm feeling, that's true. You have no idea what a trio of tragic characters we've been playing for the past ten years. Now that one of the trio is gone, I think it's time to bring the curtain down on the tragedy." Ash's eyes were red from crying and throwing up.

"Are you talking about your accident? I know I'm a stranger, but you seem quite strong and capable. And you're young. Is there something I'm missing?" Frankie figured she might as well ask the question. She didn't see Ash as a helpless invalid and had to wonder why Ivy treated him as such.

"The accident was the worst day of my life, the worst day of Fern's life, and the worst day of Ivy's life." Ash's face contorted into something bitter and ugly. "The three of us were together on a snowboarding trip. Fern and Ivy knew I was a serious snowboarder. They knew I wanted to compete, so this trip was about finding a trainer. Fern set up a couple of trainers to watch me do a run with some tricks. What I didn't know was that Ivy had my board sharpened just before the trip and bought an experimental wax designed for speed."

Ash swallowed hard and looked at the sky's horizon, lost in memory. "I wasn't ready. I didn't have time to practice. The trainers came early, and weather was moving in, so it was a now-or-never moment. Between the sharp edge and the new wax, my timing was off. I crashed, and here we are."

"Fern and Ivy blamed themselves," Frankie spoke quietly, carefully weighing the new information. "What about you, Ash? Do you blame them?"

"No, never. Well, it might have seemed like it at first. I blamed everything I could—the bad weather, the trainers coming early, maybe even Fern and Ivy." Ash's face hardened into soberness, and his eyes looked directly into Frankie's. "I blamed myself, too, and felt worthless for a while. But physical therapy, meditation, and counseling helped me, Ms. Champagne. And for the last couple of years, I've wanted to make a life for myself."

"It doesn't seem that Ivy agrees with you?" Frankie asked.

"No. It's the guilt. She feels responsible no matter what I say. We've been over it so many times." Ash was getting agitated again. "My sister wanted to pay for everything, including a salary for Ivy and a place for all of us to live. She worked all the time, so we barely saw her. She applied for every study available because the house and my medical care was expensive."

Frankie knelt down and dared to place her hand over Ash's quivering one. "Tell me what you'd like to do with your life, Ash."

"I want to be a counselor for kids in wheelchairs," he said matter-of-factly. "I already have some college credits, so in three or four years I'd have my degree. And, we live near Chicago, so there's all kinds of options for programs." Ash's passion was evident in his voice and smile.

"Then you absolutely must find a way to do it, Ash. The world needs people like you. You could help a lot of kids." Frankie rose to leave, wondering if she should speak to Ivy directly or maybe to the Parkers about Ash's wishes. She was navigating uncharted waters.

When she reached the back door to the funeral home, something else bombarded her brain. Pom and Cherry said that Fern was at school when Ash had his accident. The two versions of the story didn't add up, making Frankie wonder if the Sensational Six had kept other secrets from each other.

She was surprised that Ivy wasn't lurking around the back entrance watching for Ash. When Frankie resumed her post in the viewing room, she was even more surprised to see Ivy engaged in a light-hearted conversation with a man Frankie didn't recognize. Cherry was standing in the back corner with the two, smiling and chatting.

Ivy reached out a few times to grasp the man's arm or hand amiably. He didn't seem to mind. Frankie decided he enjoyed the attention by the way he tossed his head back, allowing his luxurious blonde waves to dance playfully through one hand.

She needed to know more about this man, but her trek to the back corner was stymied when Daryl George flagged her down. Dressed in khakis and a plaid button-down shirt—short sleeved, no less—Frankie determined that Daryl was a man without pretense. He might be head of a wildlife foundation, but he wasn't going to suit up to please anybody.

Daryl stood near the far wall, across from the door, with two women who were probably Fern's colleagues.

When Frankie entered their conversation circle, Daryl turned away from the two women and spoke quietly. "I need to ask you something before you leave, but not here. Flag me down, and we'll talk in the parking lot."

Frankie was intrigued, turned her attention once again to the cozy corner conversation between Ivy and her Romeo, but was waylaid when Daryl guided her toward the two women by the far wall.

"This is Francine Champagne. She owns Bubble & Bake downtown, where the Parker sisters work. Frankie, these are two of Fern's associates: Naomi Travers and Dr. Sarah Fredrich."

Frankie shook each woman's hand, noting their indifference as she did so. "Good to meet you. Did you work on any of Fern's field studies?" She addressed both simultaneously. Her interest was genuine, a fishing expedition probably, but at least it was polite small talk.

Sarah Fredrich audibly sniffed, and not because she'd been crying. She looked at Frankie as if she were an insect she'd prefer to squash into oblivion. This was funny since Sarah, dressed in a form-fitting black and yellow maxi dress, looked like a long emaciated caterpillar. She addressed Frankie's question, ready to school her on the subject.

"No, I did not work with Dr. Mallard on her field studies. I was her *supervisor* on the studies. You see, I'm the department chair at Riverwood." Dr. Sarah looked down her aristocratic nose at Frankie, then turned toward Daryl as if to banish her from the conversation.

Naomi Travers offered Dr. Sarah a compliant smile but addressed Frankie. "Dr. Fredrich is one of the most published ornithologists in the world. She's a recognized authority on several species of birds. Dr. Mallard was honored to work with her at Riverwood."

Unlike Dr. Sarah, Naomi was dressed in an unassuming black shift, but her glamor girl looks were undeniable. When she spoke, her blue-green eyes lit with admiration for her superior. Her skin glowed, and she was one of those people who could wear makeup without looking like she wore makeup. Her thick brown tresses with golden highlights were clipped back from her face and cascaded down her back like a river of honey.

Dr. Sarah acknowledged the compliment with a tight smile. Older than Naomi by almost two decades, Dr. Sarah's makeup was obviously trying too hard to bring back younger days. Her skin was losing its tone, and the sagging cheeks and chin accentuated a bony face and beaky nose. Her short dark hair spiked all over in uneven lengths made her look even more like a caterpillar, Frankie thought.

"Ms. Travers, did you work with Dr. Mallard on any of her field studies?" Frankie decided Naomi deserved the same question.

Naomi bristled momentarily then recovered to look serenely at her audience of three. "I did have the pleasure of working with Dr. Mallard on a Townsend's warbler study a couple of years ago."

She didn't expound further, and Frankie couldn't come up with a follow-up question or comment. Thankfully, Daryl George entered the conversation.

"Ms. Travers will be Doctor Travers very soon. She's finishing up her graduate work in Iowa in May, and then I'm sure we will see her heading field studies of her own." Daryl nodded at Naomi and Dr. Sarah, but Frankie sensed the foundation chief wasn't being complimentary, just civil.

Frankie made a mental note of the conversation and excused herself to pursue Ivy, Cherry, and the mystery man at the back of the room. They were still there and seemed to be in their own world, enjoying each other's company amidst the heavy atmosphere of the viewing room.

Frankie glanced quickly at the time, decided she could spare just a little more of it at Hardisons', then sat down on an unoccupied sofa directly behind Ivy, where Cherry could see her. She took out her phone and made quick notes, highlights of the exchange with Daryl, Naomi, and Dr. Sarah.

Cherry directed Frankie's attention toward Ivy and the handsome stranger, possibly so they could meet, or maybe Ivy's flirtation was causing some discomfort.

"Is everything okay, Frankie?" she asked, startling Ivy and the mystery man back to reality.

Frankie rose immediately and joined their circle. "Yes, I just had to check a message." She looked meaningfully at Ivy. "Is everything okay with you?" She imagined Ivy had seen her walk toward Ash to talk with him in the backyard.

Ivy nodded but wouldn't meet Frankie's eyes. Cherry jumped into hostess mode again.

"Frankie, this is Lars Paulsen. I don't know if the two of you know one another..."

Lars nodded while Frankie shook her head. "I'm sorry, Mr. Paulsen. If we've met, I don't remember. I know the Paulsen name, and I know my father knew your father and grandfather quite well."

Lars nodded again as he firmly shook Frankie's hand. "I think you're right that we haven't formally met, but I've been to your bakery, and of course, you're well known around Deep Lakes, too. You and your family."

Lars was handsome and self-assured. Frankie was certain his suit hadn't come from a discount chain by a long shot. No wonder Ivy looked smitten. Lars made it difficult to notice there was anyone else in the room. She could picture him posing on a movie poster for *The Vikings* series.

"Well, it's nice to meet the final member of the Sensational Six," Frankie said, before realizing that they were six no longer until she saw the sadness written on every face. "Oh gosh, I'm so sorry. I have a way of sticking my foot in my big mouth. I can't imagine how all of you must be feeling about losing Fern."

Cherry patted Frankie's shoulder as Ivy produced fresh tears, signaling Lars to put a protective arm around her. Ivy looked grateful and took the opportunity to lay her head on Lars's shoulder in consolation. The moment evaporated quickly, however, when Lars dropped his arm and took a few steps backward.

"We were reminiscing when you came over, Ms. Champagne. We will miss Fern dearly, but we have fond memories to look back on about our time together in Deep Lakes. Now, of course, everyone has a life of their own." Lars seemed suddenly distant from Ivy and Cherry.

Frankie didn't know how to fill the awkward chasm that had opened among the three. She swept the room, noticed Ash was back wearing a fresh shirt, talking with Pom's father and Uncle Drake near the front of the room. She saw Jovie talking to Alonzo, who must have recently arrived, and saw Carmen talking to one of the townspeople. She didn't see Donovan Pflug anywhere, though. Then the double doors opened, and a stream of people entered the viewing room and formed a line.

Cherry took Ivy's hand. "Come on, it's showtime," Cherry said. Frankie imagined it was going to be a very long day.

"It was nice to officially meet you, Lars. I hope to see you at Bubble & Bake sometime when you're in town." She tried to sound kind but was put off by Lars's change in demeanor, something she intended to log in her notes. For now, it was time for Frankie to return to the shop and regroup with Carmen and Jovie.

Lars nodded coolly. "I'm sure we will see each other. I still live here part-time in the family bungalow on Lake Joy. When I'm not in Chicago, I prefer the peace and quiet of Deep Lakes."

Frankie nodded in return and made a beeline for Jovie and Alonzo. "Good morning, Sheriff. What happened to your watchdog?" Frankie raised both eyebrows sharply, stifling a giggle.

Lon grimaced. "I relieved him of his duties. But you and me: we're going to have a conversation later. I want the 411 on everything you learned here." Lon tipped her a two-finger salute.

Frankie was already in her SUV when Daryl George rapped on her passenger window, startling her. If she hadn't been short in stature, she would have hit her head on the ceiling. She'd completely forgotten that the wildlife foundation director wanted to speak to her privately. She waved him inside the car.

Daryl sat down quickly, shut the door, and peered around the parking lot. Clearly, he didn't want to be seen. Frankie anticipated receiving some good intel.

"Word's out you found part of Fern's missing field journal. Is it true?"

Frankie was taken aback. She hadn't expected the question. "I did, but I turned it over to the investigators. How do you think it will help the foundation? So much of it was written in code." Frankie wondered if Daryl knew Fern's secret code. Maybe he was the key to unscrambling the journal.

"Oh really? Code? What do you mean?" he asked, looking directly at her.

"Well, there are some doodles and numbers interspersed among the words. You've worked with Fern. Did she communicate like that in her journals regularly?" Frankie sighed, uncertain if she was giving away vital information to someone she shouldn't be sharing it with.

Daryl shook his head, peering out the side window toward the funeral home door. "No, at least I don't think so. She kept her field journals and turned in typed summaries of her findings. So, I haven't seen her handwritten notes."

He paused to turn around and look out the back window. His antics were making Frankie jumpy and curious. He looked at Frankie again with piercing blue eyes that held serious concern about something. "This time, I need those handwritten notes in order to finish the study." He frowned, looked like he might say more but didn't.

She heaved a deep sigh. "Why do I get the feeling there's more to this?" Frankie jabbed her finger toward his chest and drew her lips together into a skeptical pucker. "I might regret this, but I made a copy of the journal pages. I'll get you a copy, but you have to promise me that you'll tell me if you figure out what any of it means."

Daryl didn't look pleased at her revelation, nor relieved either, just grim. "Maybe we can help each other. This isn't the first problematic study Fern was involved in. I think someone let the purple martin babies fledge on purpose, knowing if they weren't ready to fly, they would land in the water and drown."

Frankie gasped. She hated the idea of anyone who would purposely hurt a living creature. "What other studies were a problem?"

Daryl stared straight ahead. "Her last study of hummingbirds in a Costa Rican habitat. All of the nests were abandoned by the females except two. It didn't make sense. All of the conditions were right for these birds to have a quality nesting season. It hurt the population big time."

"Did anyone come to a conclusion about what happened?" Frankie felt sad about the tiny birds and their potential dwindling numbers. As a birder, she knew the importance of stable populations and the delicate balances in play between nature and humans.

"We're still trying to figure it out using Fern's and Robyn's evidence and notes. But, no, we don't know what happened. And now, the martin study. This is the second colony in our area where the house was opened and the young martins died because they couldn't fly." Daryl's face was calm, but his features reflected serious displeasure.

Frankie made a mental note that Robyn assisted in both of the problematic studies. "Did Fern and Robyn work together on any other studies?" She recalled Ash saying Fern worked on numerous studies in the past several years.

Daryl shook his head. "But Robyn's a great field researcher. Once she gets her doctorate, she's going to be an important ornithologist leading her own studies."

She had a few more questions for the director. "What's your take on Dr. Sarah Fredrich?" She spoke noncommittally, hoping he'd give an honest response.

"She's ambitious and she likes to be in charge—of everything." Daryl's eyes popped, and he jerked his head around animatedly. "She has the best-funded animal science department in the country. She schmoozes with rich donors to fund her pet projects. And she explodes when studies don't go as expected."

"Like the last two studies Fern led?" Frankie figured she already knew the answer.

"Exactly. You can bet she's fuming over the mess, and Fern's death is going to create negative publicity she doesn't want. The woman's a viper." Daryl laughed quietly, nervously.

"And what about Naomi Travers? She seemed eager to be in Dr. Fredrich's good graces." Naomi projected spinelessness or maybe someone with a motive, Frankie couldn't tell.

"Naomi's hoping to climb the ladder, maybe get a position at Riverwood. She wants what every field scientist wants: studies of their own." Daryl spoke matter-of-factly.

"And she worked with Fern on past studies?" Frankie was jotting down notes in her phone, making no pretense that Daryl was a source in her investigation.

"The Townsend's warbler project in California a few years ago," he paused to jog his memory. "I've read the study, but it wasn't sponsored by the foundation."

Frankie looked up from her notes. "I got the impression that Naomi may not have worked well with Fern." She had sensed something in the way Naomi bristled when asked about her work as Fern's assistant.

Daryl sighed and drummed his fingers on the armrest. "I know from talking to Fern that she didn't want Naomi involved in her studies. She thought Naomi was sloppy, so she chose Robyn, and that was a good fit."

Frankie pursed her lips, thinking. "So, Fern gave up on Naomi without giving her a second chance?" Frankie found that odd, knowing the nature of Fern's aunt and cousins, rooting for the underdog and being lenient toward the faults of others.

"Fern worked with Naomi before the Townsend project. They were both assistants on a bluebird study before Fern earned her doctorate. So you see, Fern had already given her a second chance."

Frankie nodded. "Who led the bluebird study?"

Daryl snorted. "Dominic Finchley."

Frankie frowned. Daryl had thrown a few shovelfuls of dirt her way, and now she needed to spread that dirt on her crime board and see where it landed.

# Chapter 12

*Birds of a feather flock together; So do pigs and swine. Rats and mice shall have their choice, and so shall I have mine. — English proverb and nursery rhyme*

Frankie promised Daryl George she'd deliver the journal pages to him at the funeral dinner. Even though she'd been upset at herself for not cornering Dominic Finchley for conversation at the funeral home, she now had more ammunition to hit him with at the dinner.

She couldn't wait to get back to the shop to exchange stories with Carmen and Jovie. Breathless, she breezed through the back door, where she was immediately greeted by her mother's disapproving glare. Arms folded across her chest, Peggy was tapping one foot impatiently.

"What's happened?" Frankie figured the day would come when something terrible would happen at the shop while she was away.

Peggy smirked and tilted her head toward the swinging kitchen doors. "Officer Pflug is waiting to see you. He's flustered as a cornered badger."

Frankie grinned suspiciously. "Did he say what he wants?"

Peggy failed to look amused but uncrossed her arms to place her hands on her hips. The foot still tapped irritably. "No, he didn't say, but he's been here a while. He seemed certain you were here, hiding from him. What did you do to make him so testy this time?"

"Geesh, Mother, you make it sound like irritating Pflug is part of my daily routine." Frankie smiled upward at her mother's stern countenance and confided, "I may have given him the slip at Hardisons'. He was assigned to keep tabs on me."

Peggy threw her head back and laughed quietly. "Good job...I think." Then her gentility returned. "Anyway, better go face the music. I plied him with coffee and a butterhorn."

Aunt CeCe and Tia Pepita were tending the pastry case and cash register but flashed warning looks at Frankie as she paraded past them, smiling widely.

"Carmen and Jovie should be here any minute now. Then you can go to the visitation at Hardisons.'"

Tia pointed ominously around the corner and made a slashing motion across her throat as if the Grim Reaper himself waited there. That made Frankie's smile even broader. A natural actress, Tia Pepita had missed her calling.

Frankie rounded the corner where Pflug was sitting at a café table in a straight backed chair, scrolling through his cell phone. He looked Frankie over from head to toe as if she were an item at a rummage sale. In front of him sat an empty plate and empty coffee mug.

"How can I help you?" Frankie purposely used a Stepford wife voice.

Pflug pointed to the chair opposite him. "Sit."

"Sorry, I'm not a trained dog. I think I'll stand unless your manners improve." She still used the calm contrite voice. At least Frankie had learned something valuable from her mother's genteel ways.

Pflug stared out the window, looking bored. "Ms. Champagne," he began. "I didn't want to babysit you this morning, at a funeral home of all places, but that wasn't my decision. He rapped his hand on the table. The chunky insignia ring he wore issued a loud tattoo, which was meant to annoy Frankie, and it worked. "So you see, neither of us got what we wanted."

Pflug sounded tired, and Frankie wondered if his role as antagonist in her life was coming to a close. She sat down. "Did you like your coffee and pastry?" She wasn't sure what he wanted from her.

The officer swiveled his head to look directly at her. "They were fine."

He abruptly changed the subject. "Do you have a permit to house a bobcat in a wine lounge?" He blinked at her several times during the utterance, lips twisted.

Frankie feared that one day someone would pitch a fit about the animal orphans camping out at the shop. She knew a state inspector could put an end to that practice since her business sold food. But she couldn't be sure if Pflug was taunting her or if he was serious.

Dr. Sadie had established that Piper, the cat Fern had found, was a Maine Coon. He weighed 14 pounds, and his features certainly resembled a bobcat's. Could this be Pflug's attempt at a joke? Frankie figured her best course of action was to play nice.

"Oh, I see you've met Piper. He's new, but I think he's friendly. He's a Maine Coon. They're a popular breed, so I'm sure he'll find a permanent home in no time." She hoped her answer sufficed.

A small tick formed in Pflug's jaw. The officer always had a starched appearance from top to bottom. From his square head with its military cut, to his perfectly squared shoulders, to his polished black leather shoes, they didn't come any stiffer than Pflug.

"Alright. Have it your way. There's just one thing I want to know." His face was a smooth hard stare. "Did you try to give me the slip? Did you do it so I'd look bad in front of people?"

The questions rattled Frankie. Had she hit a nerve in the unflappable officer? She never considered that he actually cared what Alonzo or other people thought of him. In fact, she imagined he considered himself superior to everyone else.

When she spoke, her voice was absent of sarcasm or pretense. "I'm sorry if I gave you that impression. I was just trying to find out information, as a member of the press. There were many people I wanted to talk to. I honestly wasn't paying attention to where you were in the crowd."

All of those things were true, except that Frankie was resolute in her desire to help Pom and Cherry find answers. She didn't think Pflug would understand that, and she began to feel a little sorry for him, thinking he may not have friends.

Pflug grunted and vaulted to his feet, looking offended. "Make sure that cat doesn't attack anyone. Better get rid of it ASAP." Then he was gone in a huff.

Frankie returned to the kitchen where Jovie and Carmen were idly chatting with Peggy. The banter ceased when Frankie walked in, and all three faces turned towards her.

"Well?" The three spoke at once.

"I kind of feel sorry for Officer Pflug. I don't think he has any friends, and he might even have a self-esteem problem." Frankie shook her head at the three, who wore confused and alarmed expressions. "I think he's afraid of cats, too."

Peggy humphed loudly and untied her apron. "Sometimes you don't make any sense, Francine. But I don't have time for your folderol right now. I'm going to freshen up and go to Hardisons.'"

Frankie traveled back and forth to the kitchen between shop customers and chatted with Camen about the conversation with Daryl George.

"Dominic Finchley worked with Naomi Travers and Fern on a bluebird study. After that, Fern hired Naomi as an assistant, but it didn't work out, and she never hired Naomi again." Frankie paused to let that sink in.

"So, you think Naomi had something to do with Fern's death?" Carmen supposed.

"Daryl says she is a ladder climber, and I watched her grovel around the department chair from Riverwood. Maybe Naomi hopes to get Fern's job. That's motivation for murder."

Carmen reported her conversation with Ash and Ivy, which was mostly background chit-chat and their mutual love of the outdoors. "Did you know it was Ash that got Fern interested in birding? Apparently he's been a good bird spotter since he was a kid, and he learned bird calls early on, too."

Frankie grew thoughtful. "I wonder if Fern ever planned for a different career."

Carmen brightened again—she knew the answer. "You'll never believe it, but Fern wanted to work for the FBI."

The revelation surprised Frankie. "I looked at their family photos. Fern and Ash don't look anything like their parents. I noticed that their father, Stuart, looked like a jolly man, always smiling or laughing in every photo. Flora looked happy, too." Thinking about the photos made her feel sorry for Ash all over again. His whole family was gone.

Carmen jumped in, happy to fill in more blanks in Frankie's investigation. "I guess you didn't know Fern and Ash were adopted by Flora and Stuart. Ash told me that when I was chatting about how our twins look completely different from each other."

Frankie knew that people often remarked Kyle resembled Carmen, while Carlos was a younger version of his dad, Ryan.

"I don't know if that's important, but I'm adding it to my notes, because you never know."

Carmen expressed a theory. "I wonder if Ivy has feelings for Ash that go beyond familial. It could explain her doting behavior."

"Maybe. It's worth noting, too," Frankie shrugged. "But I saw her talking to Lars Paulsen, the nonfamily member of the Sensational Six. Ivy's whole being gravitated toward Lars."

Jovie was preparing tarts and muffins for Thursday, while Tess made quiches. Jovie had stuck by Carmen most of the time at the funeral home, so she didn't have anything to add to Carmen's findings. Now that Jovie was in a relationship with Lon, she had the tendency to stay tight-lipped about the citizenry of Deep Lakes.

Carmen sighed. "Sleuthing is tiring, Frankie. Can't say I'm looking forward to the funeral dinner tonight. What's the game plan, anyway?"

"I hope to make a beeline for Dominic Finchley. I haven't met him yet. I think you should take a turn talking to him, too. Two perspectives are better than one. Second, I want you to chat up Robyn. Third, go meet Lars Paulsen. I want to talk to Robyn again. I need more details about Naomi Travers and Dr. Sarah." Frankie yawned. "Guess I better make us both a double shot. It's going to be a long night."

"And how's it going working with Abe Arnold? Have you traded any information yet?" Carmen snorted, certain Frankie wasn't opening up to the local editor.

She colored in response. "Oh shoot. I'm supposed to be giving Abe a chance, aren't I? Guess I better give him a call. Maybe tomorrow."

The community center was set up for 150 with long tables laden with Wisconsin comfort food arranged in an L-shape at the front near the kitchen. The photo boards were relocated from the funeral home next to the food line, and a couple of the more ornate floral arrangements were placed on each end of the food tables.

Community volunteers from the bird club worked the kitchen and placed a line up of crock pots and casserole dishes on the serving tables. An assortment of cakes and bars donned the end table next to the coffee urn and water pitchers.

Frankie studied the room before choosing her first quarry. She was surprised her mother and the aunts hadn't stopped back at the shop following their funeral home visit. She had hoped to be armed with the most information available.

Fortune smiled upon Frankie, as she spied Dominic Finchley talking to Willow Parker. Frankie wanted to check on Willow to see how she was holding up, and now was the perfect time to do so.

"Hi, Willow. How are you doing?" Frankie smiled warmly and placed one arm around the woman's shoulders. Willow responded with a sigh and rested her head on Frankie's shoulder momentarily.

"It's been a long day, Frankie. Thank you for coming to the dinner. It means so much to my family." Willow dabbed her eyes with a crumpled tissue she held in one hand. "Oh, where are my manners? Frankie, have you met Fern's young man, Dr. Dominic Finchley?"

Dominic smiled weakly at Frankie and shook her hand. He still looked unkempt with the dark chin stubble and mustache that begged for a trim. His hair was playfully messy, and Frankie imagined he was more at home in jeans and T-shirt than the tailored suit he was wearing. She thought Dominic could be handsome if he could shake off his apparent angst.

"It's nice to finally meet you, Dr. Finchley. I've heard so much about you." Frankie was in fawning mode. It piqued her curiosity that Willow still referred to the doctor as 'Fern's young man,' but she supposed it was simpler that way. Did it matter that they had broken up less than a month ago?

Dominic wasn't in the mood to be lauded over and turned away to peruse the room. Frankie lightly touched his arm. "I'm a fan of Fern's work. I'd like to hear about the studies you worked on together, like the bluebird project."

Dominic raised both eyebrows in surprise. "That was the only study we worked on together, I'm afraid. But, it's also how I met Fern." The comment sparked a memory, and his thoughts turned inward, while a warm smile settled on his face. Frankie felt like an intruder.

Their conversation was interrupted when Naomi Travers pounced on Dominic from behind and embraced him tightly. Naomi had changed into a plum maxi dress trimmed in a peach and cream floral fabric. Her shimmery cinnamon lips parted, breathless, as if she'd just emerged from a long swim. Frankie blushed at the intimate smile she presented to Dominic.

"How are you, my darling?" Naomi gushed as if attending a party. She hooked her arm through Dominic's and turned him toward her. "Let's get something to eat and catch up." Frankie felt like a piece of litter that had just been kicked by Naomi's shiny high heels. She looked over at Willow and wondered if she felt the same, but Willow was chatting across the table with one of the bird club members.

Undaunted, Frankie would catch up with Dr. Finchley later. She resumed surveillance of the room, saw Carmen talking near the kitchen entrance to Robyn, who looked relaxed and tired. Ash, Ivy, Pom, and Cherry were in the food line behind other family members, and Frankie thought it would be nice to offer to get something to eat for Willow.

When she turned toward the woman, she noticed Lars standing a few feet away with a garishly blonde woman on his arm. Something about her seemed familiar, but Frankie could only see her back.

She tapped Willow on the shoulder. "Would you like me to get you a plate of food?" It was common for grieving people to forget to eat, especially when surrounded by the many visitors who wanted to pay their respects. She wondered if Willow had eaten anything since breakfast.

"That would be so sweet of you, Frankie. Just get me anything. I'm not fussy." Willow turned back to her conversation partner, and Frankie made her way toward the food line, just a couple of people away from Lars and the blonde. She glanced toward Ivy, who was seated with her plate now. Ivy was staring into space, the space occupied by Lars and another woman.

*Poor Ivy,* Frankie thought, remembering that Ash had called her part of the tragic triangle. Was Ivy longing for Lars while bound to Ash? The idea sounded like the premise for a romance novel.

The blonde ahead of her turned around and locked eyes with Frankie. It was Rina Madison, the owner of Nearly Napa. Frankie smiled, believing it was the right thing to do, but was met by Rina's look of discomfort. Frankie reminded herself that Rina was new in town, so it's possible she felt out of place, or maybe she didn't want to run into Frankie—it was hard to know. Frankie wondered how Lars had come to meet Rina. Small towns made it easy for people to connect, she supposed. The moment quickly dissolved as Rina turned back toward Lars and took the empty plate he offered her.

Frankie doubled up on plates, figuring she could deliver one to Willow as promised, then snag a seat near Rina and Lars with her own plate. She managed to catch Carmen in line en route toward Willow.

"Hungry?" Carmen asked her friend.

Frankie angled toward Carmen, stood on tiptoe to eyeball her, and spoke quietly. "I'm delivering one plate to Willow. Meet me at the table over there." She gestured with her head cocked toward the table where Lars and Rina were just setting up camp.

Carmen scowled in Rina's direction but nodded, grudgingly.

Willow gave Frankie a half-hug and an approving look at the plate. The Parker table was filled to overflowing with Fern's relatives. Fred, Willow's husband, was sitting at an adjacent table with Parker family members. It made it easy for Frankie to excuse herself with her own plate of food.

Pasting on a pleasant smile, Frankie sauntered to
the table occupied by Lars and Rina, where there were
several open places.

"Mind if I sit here?" Frankie asked, looking at both for
approval or at least acknowledgement.

Rina pretended not to hear Frankie, but Lars had the
decency to gesture toward the chair opposite him where
Frankie stood. "Please."

"Ms. Champagne, correct?" Lars fussed a moment
with his napkin, as he raised his eyes to meet Frankie's.

"Right, but please call me Frankie." She wondered at
Lars's memory. He seemed to know exactly who she was
that morning, so why act like he wasn't certain now?
She engaged Rina on purpose. "It's nice to see you again,
Rina. We barely had a chance to get acquainted the first
time we met."

Carmen arrived, taking the seat next to Frankie. "In
case you don't remember, I'm Carmen. I know you've
met a lot of people today." Frankie knew Carmen's
impersonation of Miss Manners when she heard it.

"Of course I remember you, too. You and Ms.
Champagne, I mean Frankie, are business partners. I've
been to the bakery. Marvelous kringle." Lars sounded
sincere, despite being presented with batting eyelashes
and a sour expression from Rina.

"Frankie, you said you've met Rina?" Either Lars
was the spokesperson for the two of them or at least
understood social decorum.

"Yes. Carmen and I visited Nearly Napa last week for
a wine tasting. We enjoyed ourselves." Frankie was only
partially lying. They found some pleasure in checking
out the competition and finding it lacking. She hoped
Lars wouldn't press her for details.

Lars placed one hand over Rina's and smiled
appreciatively. "Rina's been working day and night to

make the wine lounge a success, haven't you?" Frankie
noticed Lars squeezed her hand on the last two words,
as if he could push a button to make her speak.

Rina raised her head and produced a curt nod. "Nearly
Napa hasn't been open long, but we're making great
strides in public approval." Suddenly, Rina turned into a
commercial. "With our award winning wines, it's only a
matter of time before people will come here from all over
just to get their fix of Pacific coast vintages," she gushed.

Frankie and Carmen exchanged blank expressions, but
Carmen nudged Frankie's foot with her own. There was
a considerable pause while Frankie gathered her words
for an appropriate response.

"Isn't it wonderful there are so many wine varieties
to please everyone's taste?" Frankie spoke amicably.
Carmen echoed Frankie's words, nodding her agreement
and pasting on a sugary smile.

"I hope to see both of you at Bubble & Bake for a wine
tasting, that is, if you haven't already done so." Frankie
figured she could bait the pair. It was only fair, after all.

Rina's lemony expression returned. "Lars is certainly
welcome to try your wines. I just don't think I'll have the
time, at least not any time soon. We're just too busy, and
with the fall festival coming up in October, I'm going to
need every spare minute."

Frankie impulsively tried another tack. "You know, we
could share a booth at the festival, Rina. Bountiful will
have a couple of new vintages to launch, and I'm sure
you'll have new offerings, too. Why not kill two birds
with one stone?"

Carmen stomped Frankie's foot under the table at
the offer, causing her to cry out in surprise. Lars's
half-smile seemed to indicate he understood Frankie's
lack of sincerity and Carmen's outright disapproval, but
he waited for Rina's reaction.

"Thank you for the kind offer, but I don't think our two businesses pair well. I mean, you'll have baked goods as well as your wines, and well: we're from two different cultures, I'm afraid."

Rina's words, punctuated with regret, left Frankie wondering if she'd miscalculated Rina's motivation. Or had her Wisconsin enterprises just been insulted? Frankie relied on Carmen's judgment as the final verdict on Rina's response. Carmen was grinning a salty, calculated grin of contempt. Yes, her business had just received a fake "bless your heart."

"Come on, Frankie, let's go find some desserts together." Carmen pulled on Frankie's arm as she spoke.

Unfortunately, the linen tablecloth was caught in Frankie's lacy margarita chain bracelet. Carmen's pull threw Frankie off balance, and she grabbed the table with her other hand to keep herself upright, but the bracelet countered her attempt. The opposing forces toppled Rina's coffee cup and plate, both of which somersaulted into her lap. Rina stood, her mouth a cavernous hollow of disbelief and disgust.

Frankie was certain the woman would shriek, blow a gasket, maybe even punch Frankie for her gaffe. Instead, Rina threw her napkin on the table and stormed off toward the restroom.

Frankie wanted to laugh in the worst way, especially since she heard Carmen gasping for air as she attempted to keep from bursting out herself. Frankie sat down, collected herself, and unclasped the bracelet to free it from the tablecloth. Channeling her best version of Peggy Champagne, Frankie whispered demurely, "Lars, I am so sorry. Please tell Rina how embarrassed I am. And of course, I'll pay for her dry cleaning."

Frankie and Carmen didn't wait around for Lars to reply. They quickly excused themselves and disappeared into the community center kitchen, where they laughed until tears ran down their cheeks.

When they could once again form words, Carmen gave Frankie's arm a friendly punch. "I don't think you and Rina Madison are going to become good friends any time soon. If anything, she's going to bad mouth our business even more."

Funeral dinner guests dwindled until only family and some of Fern's colleagues remained in the community center. Most were pitching in to help clean up the dining area, including Frankie and Carmen, who had managed small conversations with persons of interest after the mishap with Rina.

After exiting the restroom, Rina gathered her things and hurriedly left with Lars, but Lars had returned again and was sitting with Pom, Cherry, Ash and Ivy, catching up on old times or news. Lars was gentlemanly enough to tell Frankie that both he and Rina knew the earlier mishap was an accident, and there was nothing to worry about.

Frankie wanted to dive into Fern's journal with Pom and Cherry, especially after talking to Officer Shirley, who indicated the investigators were likely to hand it off to specialists in decoding. "We don't have the manpower to waste time on guessing games," Shirley had said.

It would be out of line to ask Pom and Cherry to study the journal that night, after the long emotional day they'd experienced. Instead, Frankie announced she would gladly open Bubble & Bake for wine and beer if anyone wanted to gather there to unwind.

Pom and Cherry gave enthusiastic approval and asked the few remaining bird club volunteers if they'd like to come along and pack up a few of the remaining desserts to snack on at the lounge.

Daryl George, Naomi Travers, Robyn Munson, and Dominic Finchley said they would appreciate a change of scenery that included adult beverages and made their way to the parking lot. Carmen and Frankie trailed after them to open up the shop.

Fern's older relatives, along with the Parker parents, were ready to call it a day. Willow and Fred thanked Frankie for the offer and asked her to kindly look out for their daughters, especially if they drank too much. Frankie promised, hugging them tightly.

Cherry and Pom arrived with Frankie's brother, Nick. He'd been spending more time with Cherry this week when she needed a strong shoulder to cry on, something Frankie found thoughtful and troubling at once. If she had her way, they would both find new partners and develop meaningful relationships. But, for now, she was pleased to see Nick giving aid and comfort to Cherry.

Frankie waved as they entered the wine lounge and pointed to a large alcove that would comfortably accommodate all the members of the mourning party. Bird club president Tasha was already there, chatting with the ever-hopeful-for-attention, Dawn, and the faithful former club president, Trish.

Frankie followed Pom, Cherry, and Nick to the alcove and noticed all chatting ceased upon their arrival. Frankie supposed the birders were once again speculating on suspects in Fern's demise.

"We're expecting a few more people, but I wanted to give you a big enough space for everyone. Feel free to roam around, though." Frankie surveyed the group. "I think you're all familiar with our wines, but there's a list on the table in front of you."

Pom raised a finger, eager to get the evening going. "Frankie, would you mind bringing bottles of Persephone's Temptation, Spring Fever Riesling, and Endless Summer to get us started?"

Frankie nodded, uncorked the bottles, placed each one in a stainless steel wine cooler, and grabbed six stemmed glasses. Carmen trotted along behind her with a cheese and cracker tray in one hand and a veggie and dip tray in the other. The partners didn't want people drinking without some snacks to break up the alcohol absorption.

While they delivered food and drink, the door opened to the obnoxious twitter of Naomi on the arm of Dominic. Robyn, a step behind them, stared daggers into their backs, and Daryl George was right behind her.

Frankie turned to greet the new arrivals and gestured toward the alcove behind her. "Come on in. Feel free to join the others. I'll bring four more glasses."

Naomi looked at the group gathered there and frowned. Maybe she didn't feel like mingling, but Dominic briskly walked over to take a seat next to Pom. Naomi would have to follow or detach herself from him. She followed, sitting beside him on a low sofa. Daryl and Robyn sat next to the birders on chairs across from Pom, Cherry, and Nick.

Frankie returned with four more glasses, another cheese and cracker board, and leftover funeral desserts. "Let me know if you need anything."

Dominic pointed to the wine menu. "Do you have anything stronger than wine and beer, Ms. Champagne?"

Frankie smiled. It had been a long day for everyone. "As a matter of fact, I do. We don't put this on the menu because we only make a limited quantity. I'll bring you a bottle of Bountiful Blackbird Port, our wine fortified with Wisconsin brandy."

Frankie opened the half-liter bottle and left it on the table with four small stemless glasses, then went back to the kitchen where Carmen was cutting up veggies for another tray.

She raised her head when Frankied walked in. "What now? Do you think we should join them, or are we going to hang back and serve instead?"

"Oh, I think we should join them. There's room, and it's our place. We're not open for business, after all." Frankie was adamant.

"Oh, I get it. You want to pick up nibbles from their conversations." Carmen giggled and leaned toward Frankie to whisper, "We should have separated them into smaller groups. I bet they'd talk more."

Frankie nodded. "I think they'll separate themselves if we give them a little time. That way, we can see who wants to talk to whom." Her eyebrows danced up and down, conspiratorially.

The two spent several minutes finishing the veggie tray and another cheese tray to place in the cooler for the next day. When they emerged from the kitchen, they saw Dominic and Naomi had already left the gathering. They sat cozily in a small corner, sipping port, their heads together while looking at one of the books from the shop shelves. Carmen elbowed Frankie, and they exchanged suspicious grins.

Frankie boldly walked over to interrupt the tête-à-tête. The pair was perusing a coffee table book of Wisconsin state parks boasting showy photos of nature in every season.

"I love that book," Frankie commented. "I'm happy to say we've sent plenty of customers off to explore our state parks based on those photos."

Dominic looked weary but smiled approvingly, while Naomi's half-hearted grin was wilted at best.

"I bet. Naomi and I were just tallying up the number of these parks we've been to just for birding purposes." Dominic spoke vacantly, lost in memory. Naomi squeezed his knee in a familiar way, and a soft expression highlighted her beauty.

"Remember when we surveyed bluebirds at Horicon Marsh?" Naomi giggled. "It never stopped raining, and we both looked like drowned rats by the end of the day."

Dominic moved away from Naomi and looked up at Frankie. "All three of us were soaked to the skin," he amended Naomi's remembrance. "Fern was there, too."

Fern's presence managed to dampen Naomi's moment. Dominic shifted topics and raised his glass. "Mighty fine port. You should be proud of it, Ms. Champagne."

Frankie was glad she scored a point with the amber liquid. She was even happier she'd interrupted the duo's intimate chat. "Thank you for the kind praise, and please: everyone calls me Frankie."

"Well, Frankie," Naomi intoned in a churlish fashion, "I'm afraid I have to disagree with Dom." She offered her glass, which still contained port, to Frankie. "Could you bring me something else? Something more *sophisticated*." She said the word doubtfully.

Dominic intercepted the glass before it reached Frankie's hand. "I'll take that, please. I'm not about to waste this divine spirit."

Frankie grinned, Cheshire cat-like. "Of course, Ms. Travers. Do you prefer reds or whites?" She assumed she had nothing in the lounge that would pass muster with Naomi and wondered at her snobbery. How did a woman like that wade into marsh water to study birds?

Carmen brought Naomi a glass of Two Pear Chardonnay, while Frankie answered a call from Garrett.

"Miss Francine! How's everything going? It's been days, hasn't it?" Garrett's yearning to catch up with Frankie warmed her heart.

"It does feel like days, true. I thought I might see you at Hardisons' this morning. But I was stuck being watched over by Pflug instead." Frankie snorted.

Garrett had been burning the midnight oil to help the county. Officially, he was the county coroner, but his years of past medical examiner experience were invaluable, especially in cases like Fern's death.

"I just wanted to get my reports finalized as quickly as possible so Alonzo and the department could proceed. I did stop by Hardisons' before the funeral and had a short but lovely chat with your mother and CeCe." Garrett knew how to stay on Peggy's good side.

"What are you doing now, Frankie?" Garrett had logged enough time for the day and was hoping to see his favorite baker.

"Believe it or not, Carmen and I opened up the wine lounge for Cherry, Pom, and anyone else at the funeral dinner to come unwind a while. You're welcome to come hang out, too. I've got a bottle of Two Pear Chardonnay with your name on it." As much as Frankie enjoyed time spent with Garrett, he was quickly becoming her main accomplice in figuring out unsolved crimes, and she relished in their common bond.

"First tell me how the funeral dinner went, so I can know what I'm walking into," he chuckled.

Frankie relayed her suspicions regarding Naomi Travers, her sympathy for Ash and Ivy, including Ash's desire to go to college, and the potential one-sided romance between Ivy and Lars.

"Speaking of Lars, get ready for it. He's dating Rina from the Napa wine lounge. And I didn't score any points with her during dinner."

Frankie told Garrett how she'd invited Rina for a wine tasting and to share a booth at the fall festival. "But my graceful ways struck again! I hope she gets the coffee and food stains out of her clothes." Frankie explained the mishap with her bracelet and tablecloth.

Garrett laughed loudly. "I don't think you and Rina were destined to become close friends anyway, Frankie. But, I'll give you a gold star for trying."

"Anyone else I should keep my eye on when I get there?" Garrett asked.

"I'm going to let you work the room. I don't want to lead you astray, G."

Frankie stepped out of the office alcove to find Dominic and Naomi donning their jackets. She quickly ended her call. A light rain was making its way across the area, bringing temperatures down to around 50 and creating a fall feeling.

Standing near the door, Dominic waved across the room at Frankie, who decided to chase them down before they left.

"I hope you come in again. Next time under better circumstances." Frankie was sincere. "And I meant it when I told you I would be interested in hearing about the bluebird study. I've been trying to get bluebirds to nest in the houses along the creek behind the shop for years." Frankie meant that as well, but she gave the side-eye to Naomi when she mentioned the bluebird study. She registered Naomi's flared nostrils.

"Your shop is delightful, Frankie, and so are your wines. I'll stop in before I leave town if you save a bottle of port for me to purchase?" Dominic clasped Frankie's hand.

She planned to say goodbye to Naomi, but she was already out the door waiting on the street for Dominic. Frankie watched out the window, noted a brief exchange that included a clingy embrace instigated by Naomi, and then they climbed into separate cars and left. Dominic was driving a sports car, not the bright orange jeep that was likely sitting in the Whitman County shop being combed for evidence.

Frankie jumped when Carmen tapped her on the shoulder. "Sorry, Frankie. Boy, that Naomi is a piece of work. Who would ever pin a science badge on her? She acts like a red carpet celebrity."

Frankie couldn't agree more. "Did she comment on the chardonnay?" The competitive side of Frankie wanted customer approval, even from customers she may not like.

Carmen snorted, hands on her hips. "Ha! She said it was too sweet for her, but she finished her glass and purchased a bottle to go."

Garrett trotted up the steps, opened the door where Frankie was still standing, and folded her into a long tight embrace. "Man, I've missed you these past couple days," he whispered into her hair.

She stepped back to look up into the melted caramel eyes of the man she'd come to admire and trust. "Me, too. Come on, let's go sit with the group." She stopped at the bar to retrieve a chilled bottle of Two Pear, Garrett's favorite.

Frankie introduced Garrett to Robyn and Daryl George, figuring the bird club knew him from past outings.

Dawn Richards perked up when Garrett entered their circle and sat down. "Hi, I'm Dawn. I don't think we've met. It's so nice to know who the local coroner is," Dawn chirped, trying to find an entry point to further engage Garrett.

Everyone stared at her quizzically. Dawn stammered. "I mean, in a pinch. It's always good to know who's in charge around the county. Just in case." She trailed off, embarrassed.

Garrett laughed kindheartedly. "I'm flattered. Usually people don't need me around until it's too late. I can't say I'm very popular."

His remark made everyone relax once more. But, Dawn wasn't finished with her performance.

"What do you think of the ex-fiancé? He seemed pretty cozy with that other bird scientist." Dawn spoke without a filter, forgetting to consider Pom's and Cherry's feelings. Frankie noticed her brother Nick placed a protective arm around Cherry, who stiffened at Dawn's comment.

Trish, who was sitting next to her, narrowed her eyes. "Well, let's remember they are colleagues and both worked with Fern. They probably had things to discuss—professionally." Trish's voice warned Dawn not to continue down that road.

Robyn sneered at the mention of Naomi as the other bird scientist, and couldn't resist adding her own spin on their behavior. 'I think Dom is grieving, so he's looking for a willing shoulder to cry on. Considering the circumstances..." Robyn let the comment hang unfinished.

"Well, I'd say Naomi has shoulders to spare," Pom sputtered. It was clear she didn't think much of Naomi falling all over Dominic Finchley.

Robyn was about to broach a new topic, when the door flew open revealing Abe Arnold, editor of the *Whitman Watch*. He surveyed the group with curiosity.

"I was driving by and saw the lights on and people inside, so thought I'd stop in." Abe tested the temperature of the atmosphere and found it friendly enough.

"Pull up a chair. The wine is on the house tonight," Frankie said, certain Abe had an ulterior motive for being there. Frankie grudgingly introduced him to the group. The tall lean editor looked sideways at Frankie with a smirk. The gathering of suspects wasn't lost on him.

"Frankie, can we talk for a minute?" Abe gestured toward the bar area around the corner, where they wouldn't be seen or heard.

Frankie dashed behind the bar to retrieve two bottles of port, one for now and the other one for Dominic Finchley. She intended to call him tomorrow, entice him to the shop alone with the offering, and hopefully ask him some tough questions about the day Fern was killed.

"What's up, Abe?" Frankie opened the port, took two small tumblers from below the bar, and poured one for each of them. "I don't know if you've tried the Bountiful Blackbird, but last year's vintage is a marvel."

He thanked her and raised his glass to hers. "How about doing some old-fashioned research with me tomorrow? Can you spare a couple hours?"

Frankie had promised they would work together investigating Fern's death, yet she was hesitant. Something in her enjoyed the competition to be first to the finish line. "Thursday is usually a long day for me. I have to run some tests on grapes in the morning, then work in the shop kitchen. And, the wine lounge will be open for the next four days." She chewed her bottom lip.

"You make it sound like you're doing everything. Don't you have people to cover the shop and wine lounge?" Abe wasn't in the mood to take no for an answer. "This kind of work is slow going, and having two people going through information cuts the time in half. It's a win-win for both of us."

Frankie opened her phone to the calendar and looked at the shop schedule. Tess, Jovie, Tia Pepita, and Carmen were scheduled for the morning shift until the bakery closed. Peggy, Aunt CeCe, and Cherry were working the wine lounge from noon until five. Since it was after Labor Day, Thursday would be quiet, and the wine lounge closed at five, so she knew the place could manage without her.

"You win. It looks like I can spare a couple of hours. Where are we meeting and what time?"

"Meet me outside the public library at, let's say, nine?" Abe's eyes crinkled when he got something he wanted. Frankie admired the man. He may be pushing sixty or so, but he was sharp and limber.

"Oh wow, the library," she replied with sarcasm, "I can't wait." She clicked her glass against Abe's, and they both downed the drink.

"Thanks for the port. I'm heading home. See you tomorrow."

Frankie corked the bottle and placed it back on the shelf. She poured herself a beer glass full of cold water to combat the effects of the port and previous glass of wine, then returned to the gathering. The group looked relaxed, settled into their spots on cushy couches and the weightless wooden and leather chairs Frankie had purchased from a Scandinavian company.

Garrett smiled warmly and patted the empty spot beside him. "Everything okay?"

Frankie leaned in and whispered in his ear. "You're not going to believe this, but I'm working with Abe tomorrow on the investigation." Garrett just smiled.

Robyn, who had been waiting for the right moment, stood to address everyone. "I'm going to hold a farewell ritual for Fern, and I'd like you all to be there." She'd finished a third glass of wine, which made her talkative, so she shared her beliefs in the power of nature and spiritual connection to the earth and universe. "I know we took part in a traditional funeral today, but I also know that Fern was deeply connected to the natural world. So, I'd like to honor that."

The group decided they would hold the ceremony at the vineyard, in the gathering space below the vines and orchards, where Frankie had a firepit and picnic area.

Robyn's face glowed. "Wonderful. Let's meet there Sunday at six after the wine lounge closes. If you wish, you may bring something personally connected to Fern or something from nature to place on the altar."

Although Frankie thought Robyn's idea was a sweet one that would help Fern's assistant move forward, she couldn't help thinking about all the fact-finding she needed to accomplish before the bird specialists flew the coop, out of Deep Lakes, into parts unknown.

# Chapter 13

*I have read His righteous sentence by the dim and flaring lamps. His truth is marching on. —*
Julia Ward Howe

Thursday morning dawned with clear skies and the promise of sunshine. Last night's rain clung to the grass in the cool morning air as Frankie traversed from her parked car to the sloping vineyard rows. Pink fingers spread across the horizon, pulling the light of day upward.

It was still early, nearly an hour before full light announced the day, but Frankie wanted to test the Edelweiss, which were next in the harvest lineup, and check on the LaCrescents, the final white variety she grew.

Of course, her day would begin with a close look at her coveted Frontenacs, the only red varietal Bountiful cultivated. She and Manny had invested their time and dedication for the past five years, coaxing and caring for the Frontenacs, so they could have their debut pressing this season.

Frankie saw a bobbing light heading her direction, which must mean that Manny was already hard at work.

She turned on her own flashlight, which was embedded in her knit beanie, very handy for someone klutzy.

Frankie's good morning evaporated at the sight of Manny's grim expression. "Good, I'm glad you're here. I was just about to call you. It's the Frontenacs."

Frankie trotted to keep pace with Manny, her heart pounding in her throat. Knowing that something was amiss with her beloved Frontenacs made her feel like she was about to check on an injured child.

The two passed the rows of Briannas and Edelweiss, then stopped at the Frontenac section, where Manny pointed to the first row. The rows were open, and they were greeted by robins feasting on nearly ripened grapes.

Frankie and Manny ran down the rows, making loud noises and waving their arms to scare off the flock. The robins flew to the orchard trees, then returned a few at a time to resume their breakfast.

Frankie and Manny located the net lying on the ground four rows down, and each lifted a section, carefully moving it over their heads to re-cover the exposed rows. It took quite some time to maneuver the sturdy mesh over segments of each row. They had to pause to scare off the robins during their task so as not to capture any birds below the nets. The sun was emerging brightly as they staked the net down over the Frontenac section.

Manny and Frankie shined their lights over the net and stakes, looking for holes or other signs of destruction.

"Someone did this on purpose, Frankie. Look, the net's been cut along the stakes." The stakes positioned between the two sections of grape varieties held pieces of netting in place.

Frankie sighed heavily, willed herself not to cry, and stooped to shine her light along the rows to see if she could assess the damage. "I guess we should check the trail cameras and see if our culprit shows up."

The two walked down toward the shed that served as Manny's office, then stopped, mouths agape. Now that it was daylight, the spray-painted message on the shed's front was clearly visible: "Grapes of Wrath." Below the message was a cartoon cat face, a signature perhaps?

The two went inside the office where Manny reawakened the computer and clicked on the trail camera program. The Wednesday footage went from recording light rain on the vines to a black blur. Puzzled, Manny went to the other trail cameras along the orchard which showed a couple of swooping bats, a lumbering raccoon family, and a possum gnawing on a fallen apple. The cameras along the fence line also transitioned from rainfall to blurry darkness.

"Let's go take a look at the cameras," Frankie said.

The two started back up the hill to the vineyard. "You should call this in, Boss. Call the sheriff."

Frankie dialed dispatch rather than Lon's cell phone because she wanted to follow protocol like any other victim of a crime. She broke the rules often enough and felt better about reporting this crime by the book. She relayed the vandalism to Meg, the Whitman County dispatcher, stating they were still looking for more. Meg said she'd send an officer out right away, and Frankie prayed it wasn't Donovan Pflug.

Manny was already glaring at the first trail camera, and he snapped a photo of its lens, which had been spray painted. He pointed to the lens to show Frankie. "I expect we'll find more of the same around the vineyard and down by the fence."

Frankie nodded. "I guess our vandal must have used the firelane along the fence line to enter the property. I just don't understand why someone would do this." She was close to tears.

"It must be someone who knows you're looking into the murder of that ornithologist." Manny resumed walking, pausing to photograph the damaged camera lenses as he walked.

Frankie stopped to let Manny's words sink in. She shook them off. "I don't have any idea who killed Fern. I haven't even talked to all the suspects except to make small talk. If I've stumbled onto something, I haven't figured out what it means."

Manny turned and placed both hands on Frankie's shoulders. "Maybe this is a warning to stop trying to figure things out."

Frankie was grateful to see Alonzo's brown SUV with the sheriff insignia pull onto the cement slab by the winery. This case was small stuff compared to a murder investigation, so Frankie felt privileged to have her friend respond to her call.

Lon's look of concern made Frankie blink back tears. "So, what have we got, Frankie? Walk me through it."

He took photos of the cut net, spray-painted camera lenses, and graffiti on the shed wall. He scratched his chin methodically, reading and rereading the message.

"Any ideas what this could possibly mean, Frankie?"

Frankie shook her head. "I'll think about it, but off the top of my head, no idea. I mean, it's a literary quote signed with a cat face. Manny thinks it's a warning to stay away from Fern's case." The words caught in her throat, and she immediately regretted saying them.

"I think Manny's right. You should definitely stay away from the case." Alonzo looked sideways at her, one eye squinted shut and a half-frown on his face. "But, we both know you're not going to leave it alone, so..."

Lon traipsed down the hill to the fence line and examined the fire lane before returning to the shed where Frankie was staring trancelike at the message, turning it over in her mind. She spoke to the sheriff without looking at him.

"Did you find anything useful? Footprints? Tire tracks? Maybe tire tracks that match Dominic Finchely's jeep?"

"Any footprints that might be in the vineyard area have been muddled from you and Manny getting the nets back in place. And the fire lane has multiple tire tracks since the field workers use it as a shortcut from their mobile homes down the road."

Frankie relied on migrant workers each year for maintenance of the orchard and vineyard in the growing season. Manny had several contacts among the migrants, many who returned each year before following warmer weather to work in the agricultural industry. Most of them stayed in the mobile homes owned by Frankie's brother, James. He hired several of them to work seasonal construction jobs for him.

The late summer sun was at work cooking up a warm day, and Lon was sweating from his jaunt around the property. He took off his heavy mountie-style hat, produced a bandana from his pants pocket, and wiped his forehead. "Speaking of the ex-boyfriend, what's your take on him?"

"He seems to genuinely miss Fern. I don't know that the breakup was his idea. I think he's too cozy with Naomi Travers for his own good." Frankie paused to scan the rest of the Finchley knowledge lodged in her brain.

"I don't always get a good read on emotions, especially from men, but Shirley agrees that Finchley acted like a man grieving a loved one. Still, the guy admitted he was at the scene and had gone through her car. But he clammed up when we asked him why he didn't call 911 when he discovered her body. He lawyered up on the spot."

Frankie jumped in. "Right, but why would he admit going through Fern's car if he had killed her? And why were his prints in her car, but not anywhere on her body or the murder weapon? More importantly, why didn't he call 911? And..."

"Whoa there. A smart killer could wear gloves to commit the crime and not wear gloves to go through her vehicle just to throw us off. And, we're taking a closer look at Naomi Travers along with some others. Fern's colleagues might have motives to get rid of her. Professional jealousy, for starters."

"According to Robyn and Daryl George, ornithology is highly competitive. There are only so many studies to lead and only so many professorships open for hire," Frankie shared her limited knowledge of the field.

Frankie chanced asking about other possible suspects not in the colleague category. "Are you interested in any of Fern's friends or family?"

Alonzo grinned, weighing what he should share. He knew Frankie called the department because of the vandalism, and now she would be more absorbed in unraveling the vineyard crime and Fern's death, whether they were connected or not. "Well, of course we have to look at family and friends. But, Pom and Cherry have been cleared from that list with rock solid alibis."

It wasn't Pom and Cherry she'd been thinking about. "What about Ash and Ivy?"

Lon scrutinized Frankie's expression, saw that she was serious. "Why are you asking? Do you know something about Ash or Ivy that we should look into?"

Frankie shared the hearsay from Robyn about the argument between Dominic and Ivy, along with a brief comment on her own conversation with Ash. "Ash called himself, Ivy, and Fern a tragic trio, said both the women felt guilty about Ash's accident, and both the women felt beholden for his lifelong care."

"So Ivy's motive might be money? Or eliminate her guilt by getting rid of one of the players?" Alonzo speculated freely.

Frankie inhaled sharply, eyes widening. "Oh crud, Alonzo, do you think Ash's life is in danger? If Ivy's trying to get rid of her guilt, maybe Ash is next. If Ivy is motivated by money, she's likely to get everything if Ash dies. Who else would he leave anything to? His whole family is dead."

Alonzo patted her shoulder reassuringly. "We'll look into the Ivy angle, I promise. Meanwhile, are Ash and Ivy staying with the Parkers?"

Frankie nodded. "They're only staying through the weekend, then returning to Chicago on Monday. I don't think Ivy would try anything here. Too many people would suspect her if something happened to Ash. But, back in Chicago. Well, any number of accidents could happen to Ash there."

"Hell, your thinking like a cold-blooded killer is just a little disturbing. Where's that sweet baker I used to hang out with?"

Frankie laughed bravely, even though she'd just given herself goose bumps. "Before I forget, Robyn is hosting a farewell ceremony here on Sunday at six. Fern's family and friends will create a spirit circle and give her a send-off into the natural world. Jovie's coming, and I'm sure she'll invite you, so plan on it."

Obviously a skeptic, Alonzo snorted at the idea, rolling his eyes. Frankie wasn't about to let him off easily. "Oh come on, Lon. You're in tune with nature. You fish, you hunt, you camp." She couldn't help but laugh out loud at his withering expression.

Before leaving, Alonzo stepped back into law enforcement mode. "Get new trail cameras today, Frankie, and some kind of alarm that makes a painful sound when it's tripped. Put one by the vineyard and another on the fence line.  Manny will know what to get. If you figure out the message or the cat face sign, call the department."

Frankie promised they would get on it, but she had another idea in mind, one she intended to execute that evening.

She needed to stop at Bubble & Bake before meeting Abe Arnold at the library, so she left Manny in charge of securing the property as best he could. Manny had run brix tests on the Edelweiss and said they would be ready to pick soon, most likely on Monday. He also promised he would assess the Frontenacs and determine their losses.

Frankie didn't want to think about the Frontenacs or the message painted on the vineyard shed. She was getting a headache and knew the weight of the damage done at her beloved property would keep her from concentrating on the investigative work ahead of her.

Instead, she looked out the window as the SUV rolled along the country road. She spied the bright tangerine of an oriole flitting through the branches of a large maple, a cheerful sight that always brought a smile to her face. She imagined the bright orange birds were already making plans to split for the southern citrus groves, as the coming autumn temperatures and dwindling food supply would push them instinctively away from the North.

The upcoming weekend weather would offer abundant warmth, creating opportunities for the die-hard fans of summer: one last camping trip north, one last boat ride around the lake, one last picnic, one last swim. By the end of September, the Wisconsin highways would be clogged with vehicles pulling buttoned-up pontoons or jet skis or campers, all bound for winter storage or southern climates.

Frankie didn't have time to enjoy the dregs of summer. Her mind was preoccupied with harvesting grapes. Fickle Wisconsin weather offered little wiggle room for miscalculating the time of harvest. As each grape variety differed in its hour of optimum sweetness, vineyard owners had to be vigilant every day lest the grapes would be past their peak.

Now, she wondered if there was anyone who could supply her with Frontenac grapes or pressed juice to combine with her own lower yield harvest. Frankie's hope was to craft her own "estate wine" from the Frontenacs. According to industry standards, an "estate wine" must be made solely from one's own grapes, and the vintage would wear the coveted wine of origin label. She wanted that batch to be all her own.

Her anger flared, and she smacked the steering wheel. How dare someone violate her precious vines? Biting a trembling lip, she returned her attention to the road, where she spied a doe tentatively looking around on the shoulder. Frankie slowed, knowing the unpredictability of deer, who frequently moseyed into traffic without a thought. Then she glimpsed twin fawns hanging back in the wooded shrubs nearby. The fawns had lost their spots but were still smaller and friskier than their mother. The sight of the trio replaced her anger with determination. She would find out who was behind the Frontenac fiasco.

All systems were go at the bakery, so Frankie changed from vineyard grubby into unpretentious casual to meet Abe at the library. She decided to skip telling her bakery crew about the vineyard vandalism, knowing it would take too much time and potentially throw the shop into an unwanted tailspin.

Seeing Abe's old Wagoneer parked in the library lot, she chose a spot next to it, then trotted up the steps to the brick building on Pine Avenue. She barely glanced at the garden trail alongside the parking area that included favorite literary statues like Alice in Wonderland, the Cat in the Hat, and the Little Mermaid. Benches nestled between flower beds and statues, inviting people to sit and read. The first frost was probably a few weeks away now. It would turn the lovely petunias, zinnias, and marigolds to the same drab burnt brown hue. Nevermind; she didn't have time to stop and admire the colorful blooms that still persisted on the stems just now.

Sue Pringle, veteran city librarian, was seated at the reference desk, poised over her computer. She looked up as Frankie approached, smiled, and pointed toward a set of stairs leading downward.

"You must be Abe's date today. He's in the dungeon." Sue laughed.

Embarrassed, Frankie realized she'd never been to the library archives in the basement, not once in her long residency in Deep Lakes. *What kind of journalist are you?* She berated herself.

"Thanks, Sue," was all she managed, not wanting to get into a chat session with the amiable librarian today. Instead, Frankie adjusted her backpack over her shoulders, a recurring habit since she was short and the straps didn't quite accommodate her stature. She brought along her laptop, notebook, pens, and cell phone, of course. She wanted to show Abe she was ready for the investigative work ahead.

The library's basement was a long hallway that split off into rooms on the right and left. The first room on the right opened into a break room with a kitchen. Across from the break room was a decent-sized space set up for programs and activities. It appeared to be newly remodeled. Frankie remembered taking her daughters to many summer programs at the library, but they were held on the main floor back then.

She wore sneakers, so her footsteps barely registered on the tiled floor, but Abe's radar picked up on her presence. He called out from the next room down the hall.

"That you, Champagne?" Abe sounded impatient, even though Frankie was better than on time—she was five minutes early.

"Coming." Frankie entered the next door on the right. Her eyes widened at the so-called archives and could hear her grandmother's voice in her ear calling it "Fibber McGee's Closet," from the old radio comedy show.

File boxes lined two of the four walls and were stacked five high. An old puppet theater stage leaned against another wall; the puppets themselves hung on hooks, some looking out menacingly at visitors. Next to the puppets and stage, a variety of decor squatted, remnants of past summer programs, no doubt. Hawaiian leis adorned cowboy hats. A pile of maracas encircled an artificial campfire. Paper-mache boulders were scattered hither and yon.

Lining the final wall was a pair of long banquet tables book-ended by shorter desks. Wooden or folding chairs were lined up for seating. Abe sat at one of the computer stations. The desk nearest the back corner was fully occupied by an ancient monstrosity—the microfilm reader.

Frankie plopped her pack on the floor next to a folding chair on the other side of Abe. "What's the plan?"

"We're going to look up Fern Mallard and all of the studies she's participated in. Maybe we can find a common denominator that adds up to someone wanting her dead." Abe sipped from his super-sized travel mug.

Frankie began unpacking her laptop, slid over the computer attached to the library system, and plugged into the power strip. The library internet password was taped to the wall facing them. Abe looked at her laptop, questioning.

"I'd rather use my own equipment. Then I can save information as we find it. Plus, none of the information and search history will be left behind," she stated matter-of-factly, as if this was the obvious course of action. But for an old-school guy like Abe, it wasn't obvious.

He scratched his head and scrunched up his lips. "I guess I should enter the new millennium and buy one of those things, huh?" He gestured at the laptop. Frankie just smiled. Abe was a cheapskate. Why buy a laptop when he could use the library computers for free?

He turned his attention back to the screen. "I've started reading Fern's study on hummingbirds in Costa Rica, which was the last study she completed before starting the purple martin study. Can you go back and review the study before the hummingbird one?"

Abe pointed to Frankie's search screen. "If you search under her name plus studies, it should bring up a site with a list and then you can..."

Frankie smirked at Abe. Before he finished his sentence, she'd already found the site with the archived studies associated with Fern Mallard. Frankie might be new at investigative work, but being almost twenty years Abe's junior, she was light years ahead of him when it came to technology.

"Here's the Townsend's warbler project she worked on with Naomi Travers. I'll check it out." She couldn't help but smile when photos of the tiny insect-eating bird popped up on the screen. Its sunny yellow face was partly covered by a black mask, as if it were a superhero. The birds only nested in the Pacific Northwest, but a colony of them had found their way to northern California, which is where the study took place.

She and Abe exchanged few words as they continued the process of searching, reading, and making notes over and over again. They checked in with each other before moving on to new studies or sites, making sure they weren't doing the same work. The only sounds were the hum of the central air conditioning and occasional clunk of the ice machine from the break room.

Frankie began yawning repeatedly and wished she had included her own travel mug of coffee in her investigation repertoire. When her stomach sent up warning flares of hunger, and the computer screen started to blur, she stopped reading and looked at Abe. He had the audacity to look fresh as a daisy, while she rubbed her temples with tented fingers.

"So this is what seasoned investigators do, Abe." It was the decidedly unglamorous side of the profession. Still, she understood how necessary it was and useful to boot.

"This is it, Champagne. Now you know why my skin's so pale. I don't get to spend much time in the sun." Abe was stone-faced, his manner of delivering a witty quip.

Frankie looked at her fitness tracker. They'd been at it for over three hours without a break. Her 5 a.m. shredded wheat with blueberries and morning brew were a distant memory. "Sorry, Abe. I'm like a hummingbird. I need to eat frequently to stay alert. If you want to resume after some lunch, I can meet you back here in, say, a half hour?"

Abe barely nodded, engrossed in something on the screen. He finished reading and swiveled her direction. "Sorry. I hear you. I'm going over to Dixie's for lunch myself. I think we need to compare notes before things get stale. But, I have to switch hats for the afternoon and put this edition to bed." The *Watch* offered two editions weekly, one on Tuesday and one on Friday, so Thursday was a printing day.

Frankie thought maybe Abe had invited her to join him for lunch at the diner. He had been dating Dixie, the owner, for a few years now. "I'll pass on lunch at Dixie's, but maybe you'd like a change of scenery later? I'm planning to do a stakeout tonight at the vineyard, if you'd like to join me." She briefly recounted her morning discovery of the vandalism.

"Whoa, Frankie. I'm sorry. That's tough to swallow. Let me think about it. Can I stop by Bubble & Bake after lunch so we can debrief on what we found here?" He pointed at their computers and notebooks.

"Sure. The first drink is on the house." Frankie unplugged, packed up, and headed back out into the warm September sunshine. On her way to the SUV, she helped herself to large breaths of fresh air and paused to soak in the late summer colors of the flowers.

Frankie missed a call from Garrett, who also sent a text to her indicating she should call when she could. The short drive from the library to Bubble & Bake seemed like as good a time as any.

"Frankie, there you are." Garrett's voice held concern. "I heard about the vandalism at Bountiful. You okay?"

Frankie didn't want to dwell on the vandalism at the moment. She had compartmentalized her tasks for the day and was currently rooted in her fact-finding expedition with Abe.

"I'm okay. I've been working in the library basement with Abe Arnold all morning, looking at Fern's past studies for clues." Her mind jumped off there as she contemplated her evening plans.

"I mean, I'm upset about the Frontenacs more than anything. You know how I am about plans, counting my chickens in advance, and all. But don't worry. Manny is working on security today, and I'm going to watch the property tonight."

"Just what do you mean by 'watch the property tonight,' Miss Francine?" Garrett's voice had an accusatory tone.

"I'm doing an old-fashioned police-style stakeout. I won't be alone. I asked Abe to join me." Frankie sounded like a kid caught red-handed with stolen candy.

Garrett laughed heartily. "Abe?" He was incredulous but recovered and recalculated his approach. "Okay. Please try to stay out of trouble and danger." Garrett softened, and his tone returned to its usual good humor.

"Garrett, I'm at the shop and have a long to-do list. Can we get together to catch up soon? By the way, the Edelweiss will likely need picking Monday. Oh, and don't forget about Fern's farewell Sunday night." Garrett chuckled, blew her a buzzy air kiss, and wished her good luck.

A twinge of guilt struck Frankie as she bounded up the back steps to the kitchen. She wondered if she should have asked Garrett to join her in the stakeout. The impulsive idea had entered her brain at the vineyard during her discussion with Alonzo, then again at the library. She thought Abe would appreciate the old tactic and wanted to show him she was on board with their newfound collaboration.

She brushed off the guilt to focus on grabbing lunch and filling in her B & B crew about the vineyard before they got wind of it elsewhere. Bad news travels fast in small towns.

Nobody was in the kitchen. A swath of fresh-baked scents greeted her as she stepped inside. Carmen, Tia, Tess, and Jovie had completed the baking for Friday and into Saturday from the look of things. She poked her head into the cooler, where several quiches lined the shelves, ready for the weekend winery crowd. Her eyes lit up when she spotted a dish covered in foil with her name etched on it in black marker. Underneath the foil was a chef salad. Freshly made vinaigrette sat next to the dish. She sent up some gratitude for her wonderful friends at the bakery and dug in.

A few minutes later, Peggy popped into the kitchen, smiling brightly.

"I didn't know you'd returned, Dear. I just came to grab the Under The Stars order for Hannah Turner. She loaded a cart with bakery boxes filled to the brim. Besides Frankie's classic butterhorns, the order included two autumn favorites: Wisconsin Cranberry Delight muffins and Dairyland Harvest quiche made with cheddar cheese and apples. The new quiche was dubbed a "must have" by every customer who tried it.

"Thanks, Mom. When you're not busy, could you stop back? I need to tell you something."

Immediate concern overtook Peggy's expression. "Let me just run this out, and I'll be right back. Cherry and CeCe can handle the wine lounge."

Peggy was back in a flash, and Frankie relayed the vandalism she and Manny had found that morning. She made certain to let her mother know that it was reported to the police immediately.

Frankie was sure her mother's sharp inhalation would be followed by a lecture, but she was wrong. Her brow wrinkled with worry.

"What is it, Mother?" Frankie knew she was holding something back.

She regained her composure. "Oh, it's probably nothing. Just Aunt CeCe, well...being herself I suppose." She turned to look at her daughter. "She told me she dreamed last night that Big Bird and a mammoth alley cat were running amok in your vineyard, stomping all the grapes. I mean, I laughed at how silly it sounded."

"Until now," Frankie said. This was Aunt CeCe's second strange dream this week. She knew better than to discount her aunt's connection to the universe, but she didn't want to get into an argument with her mother about the logical side of dreams.

Peggy moved back to the issue at hand. "I'm going to look up 'grapes of wrath' and see if there are any symbolic references to consider. It sounds like a clue to me. And, I don't think it's a warning to stay out of Fern's case."

Lately, Peggy never ceased to surprise her daughter, which was good news for Frankie, who didn't divulge her plan for a late night stakeout.

"Thanks, Mom. I don't have time to look into the quote, so if you're willing to do that, it will help me out." She couldn't resist wrapping her arms around Peggy's shoulders for a tight squeeze.

Peggy squeezed back momentarily. "I am sorry about the Frontenacs, however. I know you were looking forward to using your own grapes in the new vintage this fall. I hope you have enough or can get your hands on some."

Peggy's tenderness touched Frankie, almost bringing her to tears, but Frankie had work to do. She wanted to update her crime board with some of the discoveries she'd unearthed at the library. "I'm going upstairs to do some work. Would you call me when Abe Arnold arrives? We're sharing discovery."

Peggy couldn't resist a light jab. "You and Abe Arnold—sharing? Does this mean you've reached a truce, or will you need a referee in the wine lounge?"

Frankie spent time updating the crime board, adding sticky notes with questions to the list of suspects and motives. Then she worked through the stack of mail she'd carted upstairs from her office and printed email orders from Bubble & Bake's website. A nagging voice reminded her she was supposed to teach Tess or Jovie to do some of these tasks, especially with grape harvest in full swing.

Her phone jingled with Peggy on the other end announcing Abe's arrival. Frankie grabbed the printed orders, hustled downstairs, and set them on the order board in the kitchen.

She found Abe seated in one of the corner alcoves in the shadows, a Spotted Cow already in his hand. She was about to return to the kitchen for iced tea, when her mother handed her a tall glass, a lemon wedge prettily perched on its rim.

"You're a mind reader, Mother. Thank you." Frankie joined Abe in the corner, notebook and pen tucked in one hand.

Abe raised his glass, scoffing. "What, you're not imbibing after all our hard work?"

Frankie took a sip of iced tea, then set the glass on a coaster next to her seat. "Afraid not, Abe. I've got to be on my A-game, or I'll never stay awake tonight. Wine goes right to my head."

"Fair enough. I guess I have more practice than you. Beer and I are good friends." Abe winked, sipped, and picked up his steno pad and a pencil, the old reliable tools of the trade.

"Let's start with the hummingbird study in Costa Rica," he moved his reading glasses downward to look at the hen-scratching he called writing. "The study ended two years ago on a nature preserve in Guanacaste, a rural mountain area." Abe mumbled through some other details regarding the land, trailing his finger along each line of scribbles.

"Aha! Here's the meat and potatoes. Purpose of the study was to establish a breeding habitat for hummingbirds. They logged fifteen species and 102 nests, confirming 96 nests with eggs. Approximately nine days into the incubation, they discovered numerous abandoned nests. Within 18 days, all but two of the nests had been abandoned, and the hummingbirds had vacated the area."

Frankie sighed in sadness. "Is there anything in their study that explains what happened? Speculation?"

Abe shook his head, still examining his notes. "Not really. There are anecdotal notes that question the presence of predators, although no predators were found outside the usual suspects birds always deal with. Most importantly, Fern and Robyn both adamantly argue they did not interfere with the birds or their nests."

"How were they able to determine if the nests had eggs, then?" Frankie wondered what type of technology was used in the study to obtain accurate data.

Abe shrugged. "I'm thinking  they set up cameras. We'll have to check with Robyn. Bottom line is that the study's conclusion indicates there is insufficient evidence to label the area successful for hummingbird breeding."

"There's more to it, Abe. That land was under the protection of the Costa Rica land bureau until a year ago when it lost its protective status." Frankie flipped a page in her notebook.  "It was sold in its entirety to a large coffee producer."

Abe jotted notes in the margins on the pages he'd just read from. "Hmm. Could be a coincidence. Might mean something. But, there's lots of dots to connect there."

"That's not the only problem study Fern worked on. Four years ago, she and Naomi Travers studied Townsend's warblers in California."

She turned a few pages ahead until she found what she wanted. "Long story short, the warblers were nesting on protected lands. Then, the breeding grounds suffered contamination of some sort from an unknown source. A lot of finger pointing ensued between Fern and Naomi. Naomi even filed a formal complaint against Fern, but nothing came of it. However, the land lost its status as a nature preserve and was sold to Imperial Farms, a corporate almond grower."  Frankie raised her brows sharply at Abe.

He groaned. "Okay, so maybe a few dots are connecting. But, it makes Fern look guilty. She's the common denominator in the two studies. Not to mention the purple martin one, a third study sabotaged in some way with Fern in charge."

Frankie frowned. "We need more information. I'm going to talk to Daryl George about the martin study again.  There may be answers in Fern's missing field journal, but Daryl must know more than he's told me before. I mean, Fern must have filed some reports along the way."

Abe nodded. "Good idea. You talk to George. I'll talk to Robyn. There's another study I want to read up on, too. Something Naomi Travers worked on, but Fern did not."

Frankie shifted in her seat and uncrossed her legs. "Any hot gossip from Dixie at the diner?" It was common knowledge that Dixie was Abe's frequent source on newsworthy tips about town.

Abe chuckled. "You know Dixie. She always has her ear to the ground."

Not to be deterred, Frankie went on. "What's the ground have to say today?"

"Nothing useful, I'm afraid. She went on a while about Fern's gang, the six kids who hung out on weekends and summers. They used to bring their allowances to the diner for ice cream sundaes. Dixie said they were thick as thieves, always cooking up an adventure of some sort."

Frankie smiled wistfully, thinking how nice it was to have bosom friends, especially during the innocent days of childhood. She and Carmen lived one street apart and spent summers together on bike rides and exploring the outdoors to get away from their brothers. She could see the two of them in her mind's eye, chasing stray cats, helping turtles cross the road, braiding grass, and sharing snacks they took turns sneaking out of their respective kitchens.

"Are we still on for eleven tonight?" Frankie double-checked.

"That's the plan." The editor swigged the rest of his beer and gathered up his notes.

He didn't know that Frankie would be poring over the coded pages of Fern's journal with Cherry and Pom that evening. Frankie wasn't ready to divulge all her secrets to the man, which made her curious. What was Abe Arnold keeping tucked away in his back pocket?

# Chapter 14

*When my love swears that she is made of truth, I do believe her though I know she lies.* — *William Shakespeare*

Frankie plodded back to the wine lounge to close out the computers for the day and say goodnight to her crew. After Abe left, she intended to reread the various bird studies again and make more notes, but she woke up hours later to find her face planted on her laptop keyboard, so she opted for a walk along Sterling Creek to enjoy the fresh air.

Peggy was placing clean tasting glasses under the long black walnut bar, and Cherry was corking sample bottles and putting them away for tomorrow.

"Hi, Frankie. It's been a pretty quiet day, so I sent CeCe home about an hour ago. We're just finishing up here." Peggy smiled uneasily, thinking of the vineyard trouble.

"Thanks, Mom. I just came down to say goodnight and close out the computers, but I see you've already taken care of that part."

"Any plans for the night, Dear?" Peggy wondered. "It would do you good to relax a little. Maybe have dinner with Garrett." That was classic Peggy Champagne, worried her daughter would settle into a life of solitude. Peggy may be independent but certainly hoped her daughter would find a life partner.

Before Frankie had to lie to her mother about her evening plans, the shop door opened, revealing Dominic Finchley wheeling a carry-on sized roller bag. He looked around the empty lounge, noticed most of the lights were off, and frowned.

"Sorry, it looks like you're closed. I was hoping to purchase a bottle of that wonderful port of yours, Frankie." He looked apologetic and in a hurry.

Frankie crossed the room toward the door, hoping Peggy and Cherry were out of earshot.

"No problem. We just closed. I'll be happy to grab a bottle for you. You look like you're on your way out of town?" Frankie still had questions she wanted to ask Dominic.

"Right. I'm due back in Minneapolis at the university." Dominic looked over at Cherry, clearly uncomfortable or embarrassed about something.

Frankie lowered her voice. "Do you have a couple minutes? I've been meaning to ask you something." When Dominic reluctantly agreed, she directed him to a small table near the bakery case area, further away from the bar.

"What is it you want to ask me?" He sounded weary. Here was another local asking questions he might not want to answer.

"I'm not going to beat around the bush with you. I know that you went through Fern's car out at Blackbird Pond. What were you hoping to find?"

Dominic looked down at the table, his hands folded tightly together. "If you know that, you probably know I was looking for Fern's field journal. I hoped I could take over the martin study, finish what she started."

"Don't you trust Robyn to finish the study?" Frankie was working her way toward questions she really wanted answers to.

"Of course I trust Robyn. But she doesn't have her PhD yet, so someone else has to take the lead. That study meant a lot to Fern, and I wanted to see it through." He clenched his jaw, fighting to stay composed.

"Look, Dominic. I don't believe you hurt Fern, but it's confusing why you would go out to the pond that morning, find her lifeless body, rummage through her car, and leave without calling 911." Frankie spoke softly and sympathetically, inviting his confidence.

"Ms. Champagne, I have a lawyer, and I'm not supposed to say anything to anyone." He hesitated momentarily, looked over both shoulders and then at the door. Frankie thought he might make a quick exit, no longer caring if he had the port or not.

"I couldn't believe it when I saw Fern's body floating in the pond. I ran to her, turned her over, and I could see it was too late to do anything. I figured whoever killed her probably wanted her field journal, so I went through her car. I didn't find it." His voice broke.

Frankie assumed her best investigating officer mode she'd heard on TV cop shows. "When you turned Fern's body over in the water, did you try to give her CPR or mouth-to-mouth resuscitation?"

Dominic nodded and continued looking at his clenched hands. "I knew it was too late already. She was blue when I found her." He closed his eyes and rubbed one hand through his hair.

"Do you remember what time it was when you went out to the pond?" Frankie knew Shauna had discovered Fern's body around 6 a.m.. because Frankie's cell phone log showed Shauna's frantic call coming in at 5:56 a.m. Fern was murdered before that, maybe around 5:30 a.m., meaning Dominic arrived on the scene after 5:30 and before 5:56, not much turnaround time before Shauna's fateful jog.

She smiled thoughtfully at the idea of the typically quiet Blackbird Pond seeing so much activity in less than an hour of time.

Dominic scratched one ear, trying to remember his timeline. "It was before six a.m. I don't remember exactly. I'd been up since four o'clock, thinking about what I was going to say to Fern." His voice broke again.

"You went through her car very quickly, from the looks of it, and then left. Is there a reason you left so fast?" Frankie wondered if he spotted Shauna jogging at a distance or maybe even heard the killer, if that person was still lurking.

"I didn't know what to do, and I wasn't thinking clearly. I mean, I was soaked with pond water from the waist down. So I just left. By the time I decided to call the police, they were already on their way."

"How do you know that?" Frankie spoke more sharply than planned.

Dominic looked defeated. "I had pulled off the road and was sitting on the shoulder. I think I was in shock. I sat there awhile, decided I better call the police. But I saw them drive past, along with an ambulance. I saw them turn down the marsh road."

Frankie softened again. What Dominic said was plausible. "I'm sorry, but I have to ask. Why did you and Fern break your engagement?"

His jaw tightened again, and he moved one hand to grasp the handle of his roller bag. "It wasn't my idea. Fern thought there was too much physical distance between us. I went out to the pond that day to convince her to give us another chance. I'd just applied for a professorship at Northwestern, so I could move to Chicago, and I wanted to tell her."

Frankie nodded sympathetically and placed her hand over Dominic's. "Thank you for talking to me. I'll be right back with the port."

Dominic rose and waited by the door, looking out the shop window until Frankie returned with the port in a wine bag. It was clear he didn't want to talk to Cherry.

"Here you go. It's my gift to you. Stop back in next time you're in town."

Dominic tried to protest, but Frankie insisted. He wished her well. Frankie decided that if the police didn't have enough evidence to hold Dominic or at least keep him in town, she would move him down the list of suspects, at least for the time being.

Cherry had been watching from behind the bar, where she kept busy wiping down bottles and sanitizing the bar top. Now she looked at Frankie suspiciously.

"Dom just stopped in for port? Nothing more?" Cherry's tone was apprehensive.

"Yes, just for the port. But I wanted to ask him some questions about the day Fern died. Is there something I should know, Cherry?"

Cherry shrugged. "He looked at me like he was guilty, and he avoided making eye contact with me. Don't you think that's a little strange? I thought he'd at least say goodbye since it looks like he's leaving town."

"Yes, I thought he was looking uncomfortable, too, but I didn't know if he'd already talked to your family about leaving. But Cherry, I don't think he killed your cousin. Do you?" Frankie sought reassurance that she was on the right track with the suspect list. Cherry shook her head. "None of us Parkers think Dom would hurt Fern. It has to be someone else. And, while we're on that subject, do you have time to go over Fern's coded journal tonight with me and Pom?"

Frankie didn't think Dom had killed Fern, but something about his story bothered her. She forced her mind to focus on the journal pages for now. "Absolutely. Where and when?"

Thursday was turning into an exhausting day of multitasking, Frankie thought, knowing that after her upcoming powwow with Cherry and Pom, she might be pulling an all-nighter at the vineyard, huddled in her SUV, watching and waiting.

In need of immediate sustenance, she grabbed her purse and made the short walk down Meriwether to The Mud Puppy for a basket of chicken tenders and sweet potato fries. The bar looked much like the rest of Deep Lakes on a Thursday night after Labor Day: nearly empty. Music sounded loudly, echoing through the bar area, with few customers in the way to absorb the noise.

Steffie was running the bar and serving table customers, too, while her boyfriend Harv manned the grill. She looked up from scrolling her cell phone when Frankie walked over.

"I've got your order right here," Steffie said. "Unless it's a weekend, you probably won't need to call in your order until pool and dart leagues start up again. It's pretty dead this week. You, too?"

"It's quiet, typical of the week after Labor Day. It's fine with me, though. I need to focus on harvesting grapes." Frankie laughed, always on the lookout for new recruits. "If you're bored, I'm happy to have extra pickers. We'll be harvesting Monday morning."

Steffie grimaced. "I'm not the outdoorsy type. I hate bugs, for one thing." Her milky white skin was proof enough that she didn't spend much time in the sun.

Frankie paid for her supper, hurried back to Bubble & Bake, and lit into the comfort food before the Parker sisters arrived at seven.

The sisters came the back way through the kitchen and into the wine lounge. Looking like twin Barbies, long blonde hair pulled back into swinging pony tails, Pom and Cherry sported the same sleeveless flared top, but in different colors. They both wore denim walking shorts and two-toned huaraches. The only thing not matching were their facial expressions. Pom looked particularly distressed.

Frankie motioned them to sit in the quiet corner alcove furthest from the windows to the outside world. Only the fairy lights were on in that section of the lounge, and it was quiet without the usual ambient music playing.

"What's wrong, Pom? You look stressed." Frankie wondered if a new travail had landed on the Parker doorstep.

Pom sunk heavily into the lime green cushions of the loveseat. "I'm starting school on Monday, and I feel like I'm way behind." Pom taught middle school English in town, which had begun on Tuesday. With Fern's funeral, the principal found a sub to start the school year, so Pom could take the full week off. But now she had to pay the piper for her absence.

"I stopped at school today to pick up assignments and start grading them. I don't even know who my students are yet, and I'm trying to figure out what I've missed." She sighed audibly.

Piper, the Maine Coon, crept out of the shadows behind the love seat, produced a full body stretch with his back arched like a Halloween graphic, yawned, and

launched himself onto Pom's lap. Pom smiled in spite
of herself and gave the kitty a snuggle. Piper responded
with a loud purr and rubbed his face against her hand for
more.

"I guess Piper sensed my anxiety. Cats always seem
to know what you need, even if you have to accept their
love on their terms." Pom chucked the cat under the chin.
Piper made a space for himself next to Pom and settled
in.

Cherry reached into the tote she carried with her and
pulled out the journal pages. She set them across from
Frankie's copies, so they faced her and Pom on the old
army trunk that served as a coffee table.

Cherry was all business. "Let's get started, so Pom can
go to bed early and get some rest. I'll tell you the parts
we've already figured out."

Frankie was only too happy to oblige. She couldn't
make heads or tails out of most of the picture symbols
scrawled in the journal. There were words in places, but
they didn't mean much out of context.

"Fern wrote this knowing that the people she trusted
would be able to figure it out. You see, each of the
Sensational Six had their own symbol." She pointed to
a scrap of unlined paper, a cheat sheet she'd created for
Frankie.

"I'm the cherries, of course. This vine with the
heart-shaped leaves is Ivy. Ash is the fire symbol. This
circle sectioned into wedges is Pom, you know, like
a pomelo, and the feathery frond is Fern's symbol.
The crown belongs to Lars. His name literally means
'crowned with laurel.' "

Frankie appreciated having a key, even if it was just
anecdotal. She hadn't noticed any of the Sensational Six
on these particular pages. "Okay, what's this next list?"

Pom giggled. "Fern wanted to be a spy. That's why she had the idea for us to use a secret code in the first place. She said that spies had to ask questions, so she made a code for each type of question."

Frankie giggled, too, thinking about her basic college journalism class that instituted the five W's—who, what, when, where, and why—and H for how as an outline for news articles. A child's imagination was clearly at work, as the owl face meant *who*; a hat meant *what*; a hen meant *when*; a head of hair meant *where*; an open eye meant *why*; and a Band-Aid meant *how*, since Band-Aids cover owies.

"Okay, got it. What's with the math problems? I'm not seeing anything on this key you made that helps with this." Frankie pointed to simple addition and subtraction equations on the pages.

Cherry explained. "You see, we used the letters from Bingo and the letters from Battleship games as code for letters. By using addition and subtraction, we knew we would have references to the whole alphabet. But, it's partly trial and error, because we used different methods to make the same letters."

Frankie knitted her brows together. It seemed like a lot of extra work to figure out a message. Then again, it was probably entertaining for kids with a lot of time on their hands.

Pom pointed to the first pictionary-type message. "See this sketch of a robin wearing glasses. We're pretty sure that's a reference to Fern's assistant, Robyn, since she wears glasses."

Frankie reluctantly went along with the idea. "What does this mean next to the bird? B1. J5. J1."

Cherry and Pom spoke at the same time. "It means Robyn is A-OK. That was Fern's way of saying she trusted someone." They smiled, sharing common memories.

"And just exactly how did you arrive at those letters? Show me." Frankie was clearly an outsider in this secret language.

Pom began. "The B is just that, the letter B. But, then you have to either add or subtract one letter, because of the number one next to it. If you add, you get a C. If you subtract, you get an A."

"And how did you know it was an A and not a C?" Frankie was still confused.

Cherry laughed. "You actually don't know until you look at all the possible combinations. So you write down each combination until you get something that makes sense."

Frankie stood up. "I think I'm going to need that glass of wine afterall. Sorry for saying this, but figuring out this code is like being a guest at the Mad Hatter's tea party. Anyone else like something to drink?"

She returned with three glasses and a bottle of Sweet Tias, the apricot chardonnay Bountiful had created the previous spring. "Have you deciphered this page? I mean, in the interest of saving time, why don't you two tell me what you think it means."

Pom took a luxurious sip of the golden orange liquid. "Sure. Let's see. This set of letters and numbers right here. You can see the same A-OK code here that we saw by Robyn. But, instead of a sketch, Fern gave us two more letter-number combinations. We think it means the initials DF. We're pretty sure Fern is saying she trusts Dom."

"Whoa. Let's back up a bit," Frankie was a bit riled. "Just exactly why would Fern indicate in her journal that she trusts Robyn and Dom? Can you figure out what the heading means?" Frankie pointed to a sketch with an animal's face and a wrench with a plus sign between them. The next connected doodles were something that looked like a bullet, then a ship broken in half, then what might be a clothes hamper.

The sisters shook their heads. "We're hoping we can decode that part together. So let's get back to what we think we know."

Cherry took up the tutorial. "We're fairly sure the next cluster refers to Daryl George, the wildlife foundation chief. We think this drawing is a Chinese takeout box and the question mark next to it means Fern is asking if Daryl George is doing something illegal."

"Huh? How did you decide that?" Frankie asked, skeptically.

"Well, a takeout box could mean he's on the take, or it could mean he's taking something. Maybe grant money?" Cherry spoke with authority to sound convincing.

"Okay, let's keep an open mind for now and move on."

Pom pointed to the next line. "Well, we think the drawing of the shovel and spy glass means Fern needs to look for more information on this person: NT."

Frankie gasped. "Naomi Travers. Of course." Naomi had moved up Frankie's list of suspects, and now it appeared that Fern didn't trust her either. Maybe. It was all a little too muddled for Frankie's liking.

Still, she plodded onward with the few remaining sections of text.

"I see here that Fern marked the top of the first page with one date, then left a gap after the shovel, spyglass, and NT code. See, here's a new date, just a couple days before her death."

Right below the date was a drawing of two bees. One was plain. The other wore a crown, and two arrows connected the bees. All three women wore puzzled expressions.

"I'm not sure how bees could be connected to Fern's work, unless it's an environmental issue. Are there any beehives near Blackbird Pond?" Cherry posed.

Frankie nodded. "There are a couple of beekeepers in the marsh area. Bountiful actually got its honey from one of them to use in the mead Violet is crafting."

Pom shrugged. "But what does it mean? Could there be a connection between the martins and the bees? Could it explain why the babies fledged early and drowned?"

Another conundrum. Frankie highlighted the drawing.

"Maybe the bees aren't related to the martin study at all, but I guess the dates on the journal correspond to the martin study and, of course, this journal was probably kept just for the study." She was thinking out loud.

"I'm curious about this final sketch below the bees. It's a flying bird. That bird looks like a robin, too. But this robin isn't wearing glasses." Next to the flying bird were the words 'No No' in capital letters, made bold by drawing over the letters repeatedly, followed by an exclamation point. "Any thoughts on that?"

Pom and Cherry both shook their heads, so Frankie took a highlighter and marked the drawing as something to figure out.

"Back to the top. We need to figure out this heading, ladies. Let's try brainstorming everything that comes to mind from these drawings. She pointed to the animal face, the wrench, the bullet, the broken ship, and the laundry hamper.

Frankie was fixated on the animal face, wondering if it was connected to the spray-painted cat face on her shed. Shouting commenced like a game of Outburst, listing possible animals: fox, cat, weasel, dog, lion...

"Somebody's a weasel and can't be trusted," Pom suggested.

"Or they're tricky, like a fox." Cherry said.

Suddenly Pom spouted, "Wait. It's a monkey. See, monkey plus wrench. Monkey wrench." They wrote it down in the margin.

"Okay, genius: figure out the bullet and the broken ship." Frankie decided to acquiesce to the sisters, who were much more adept at secret codes than she was, or maybe simply more in tune with Fern.

It was Cherry's turn to have an epiphany. "Duh. We should get this one. We played Battleship all the time. This isn't a bullet. It's a torpedo, and it's sinking the ship." Pom agreed, and they made another note.

"Extra points if you figure out the laundry hamper." Frankie felt disgraced—she was typically good at puzzles.

They stared at the connected drawings for some time. The little owl face at the end of the line was asking *who*. Frankie launched an idea. "A hamper can literally mean the word *hamper* as in who interfered with Fern's study? Who torpedoed the study? Who put the monkey wrench into the study?"

Running with the idea, Frankie launched from her seat and started pacing back and forth in the alcove. "Pom, you said Fern loved playing spy games. Maybe that's what she was doing. Maybe Fern was investigating the studies that went wrong, and maybe that's why she was killed." Although Frankie was excited by her insightful commentary, it was a painful reminder for Cherry and Pom.

"Let's put this away for tonight," Frankie suggested, "and tell me some more of your childhood memories about Fern."

Pom and Cherry departed around ten o'clock, leaving
just enough time for Frankie to change into dark clothes
and the denim bucket hat she kept by the back door for
gardening.

"Let's see. What does one need for a good stakeout?"
she spoke out loud, relishing the idea of participating in
a new investigative practice, something else she could
check off her list of experiences investigators must do.
She boxed up a few tarts and cookies from the shop
kitchen and made two double-shot lattes in ceramic
travel mugs to stay hot.

Finally, Frankie grabbed a flashlight she knew was
working, afraid the one she kept in the SUV might
be drained of battery life. She decided to wear her
butt-kicking boots, the description Carmen used for the
tall hikers with the hard rubber sole. The boots were
functional for anything Mother Nature could dole out
but would also be useful in chasing down a culprit and
dealing a harsh body blow if necessary.

Close to the vineyard driveway, she saw a car parked
off the shoulder and surmised that Abe was waiting
nearby to join her in the SUV. Frankie headed past the
driveway and turned into the fire lane that separated
her property from the wooded area where public trails
crisscrossed, some leading to Blackbird Pond, others to
the protected wetlands area.

She immediately switched off the SUV lights and
slowly navigated down the fire lane, creeping into a
shadowy spot closest to the tree line, where she could
observe access points to her vineyard and orchard. It
seemed like the logical spot to watch.

She gasped sharply and sprang forward when she saw a shadowy figure in a hooded sweatshirt appear in her rearview mirror. The figure rapped quietly on her window with a hand wrapped inside the sweatshirt cuff so as not to make noise. It wasn't Abe Arnold.

Before cracking the window, Frankie grabbed the flashlight, shined it toward the figure's face and thought she might be able to use it as a weapon in a pinch, although it was pretty small.

"What do you want?" Frankie stage whispered through the tiny opening.

"Sorry, Ms. Champagne. Abe couldn't make it, so he sent me to watch with you. It's Rance Musgrove."

Rance was one of Abe's young reporters at *The Watch*. Frankie didn't have much respect for the guy, who still appeared to be in the throes of puberty with his high nasally voice and *Leave It To Beaver* boyish hairstyle. She couldn't believe that Abe had ditched her and sent Rance in his place. Obviously, Abe still didn't take Frankie seriously, and she was steamed.

Still, she motioned for Rance to go to the passenger door, which she unlocked for him.

"Have you ever been on a stakeout, Rance?" Frankie's voice held an unwarranted tightness, barely holding her irritation in check.

Rance slunk closer to the passenger door and turned away from Frankie's accusatory expression. "No, I haven't. But, I'm excited to be here and to get some experience, and I'm good at observing, Ms. Champagne."

*Ah, there was the Rance she'd seen in action—the hyper chihuahua was back.* Inwardly, she admonished herself for her behavior. It wasn't his fault that Abe ditched her. Besides, she'd never been on a stakeout either, so who was she to judge?

Frankie indicated the latte in the nearby cup holder. "I hope you like a hardcore latte. I made it a double," she joked. When he didn't respond, she laid out the plan for the night.

"I don't know what Abe told you, but I'm on the lookout for any intruders. Someone sabotaged my vineyard last night, and it looks like they may have come in the back way along the property line here." She pointed through the windshield toward the fence.

"Since we have limited visibility, we have to watch for anyone with a flashlight on your side. Over there, beyond the fence, is the orchard and vineyard. We should be able to see big movements and lights of any kind from here."

Rance nodded, pulled down his hood and took a gulp of coffee that was much too hot. "Crap, are you trying to kill me, Ms. Champagne?"

Frankie laughed, not because of Rance's possible burnt mouth, but because it was the first time she heard him exercise some attitude other than the eager-beaver. "I'm sorry, Rance. I should have warned you. Please call me Frankie, by the way. Ms. Champagne makes me sound too old."

Wanting to make the best of an awkward meeting, Frankie instituted quiet small talk while they continued to survey the area. She was surprised to discover that Rance was witty and worldly, having grown up in a military family that moved around a lot. He had even spent part of his childhood in Germany.

"If you don't mind me asking, Rance, how did a smart guy like you end up being an errand boy for Abe Arnold?" The dark atmosphere of a still night made Frankie more brash than usual.

Rance sputtered into his coffee mug. "Is that how it looks to everyone in town? That I'm just a lapdog? I've heard the term before." Frankie was about to apologize, but Rance continued. "Look, Abe Arnold is a tough editor, but he's a pro, and I have a lot to learn. I don't plan to stay in Deep Lakes, not for long anyway. But as my grandma used to say, a little sugar sweetens the pot."

"Just remember: flattery only goes so far. Abe is savvy enough to know if he's being played, so you might not want to lay it on too thick, Rance. I think he'd appreciate you more if you showed a little backbone." Frankie spoke from experience. Then again, why had Abe ditched her tonight? Was it a professional slight?

Rance cringed at the word *backbone*. His military father used it constantly when Rance had difficulties in grade school with a beefy bully. In fact, Rance was certain his father was ashamed of the son who would rather read a book than go to the shooting range. He remembered his father laughing at his choice to major in journalism. "That's not a career for a real man," the elder Musgrove had said.

Rance stared out the window, withdrawing from the conversation. Several minutes later, out of the corner of his eye, he saw movement low to the ground. Probably just a raccoon foraging for food. He turned toward the front to scan the view again. A small ray of light drew his attention. Someone or something was coming toward them down the fire lane. The light was moving slowly, indicating the person was on foot.

Rance reached over and touched Frankie's arm, causing her to jolt awake. She bumped the steering wheel, letting out a small toot from the horn, and swore under her breath. Rance froze, never taking his eyes off the light. He pointed straight ahead, as Frankie cursed her clumsiness. The light was moving away from them now.

They both rolled down their windows, hoping to hear something identifiable. Seconds later, there it was, the unmistakable revving of a four-wheeler. The sound consumed the darkness, then faded into an indistinct hum.

"Shoot. I'm sorry, Rance. I scared him or them off, and now we have nothing to go on." Frankie disparaged herself for dozing off.

Rance actually laughed. "Just exactly what was your plan if someone showed up on the property?"

Frankie admitted she hadn't thought that part through. Calling the police might be useless since they were far enough away that the culprit could be gone before they'd arrive. She was wearing her butt-kicking boots, though. Furthermore, she was mad. *How dare someone come into her vineyard and ruin her hard work?* "Well, I guess my plan was to chase them down and kick some butt." She looked sideways at Rance, whose expression was inscrutable. She braced herself to be laughed at again.

"Well, I wouldn't mess with you, Frankie. I've seen you when you're determined." Rance spoke with respect.

Frankie smiled and patted his arm. "Thank you for the vote of confidence. I guess we're done here. I'll drive you back to your vehicle. That was your car parked down the road on the shoulder?"

Rance nodded. "Sorry it didn't pan out the way you hoped. But maybe we scared off the intruders for good. Now that he or they know someone's watching, they might not take the chance of coming back. At least you might be able to get your grapes harvested."

"Did you see more than one light beam? I'm trying to decide if my vandal is flying solo or not."

"I only saw one light. At most, an ATV will hold two people, and I'm sure we only heard one ATV riding away."

Frankie agreed. She dropped Rance off by his small gray Chevy and bid him goodnight. "Thank you for coming tonight. You know, you were much better company than Abe. Just don't tell him I said that."

# Chapter 15

*No one should ever go hungry, what with chewing ourselves out, eating crow and swallowing pride. — Chris Brady*

After a fitful sleep, thanks to the double shot of espresso and visions of an ATV riding rampant through her vineyard, Frankie surrendered at 3 a.m., dressed in comfortable drawstring cotton pants and a Bubble & Bake tee, and crept to the kitchen.

With the kitchen dark and too quiet, she immediately turned on a 60's station followed by every light in the kitchen. The Monkees merrily sang out "Cheer up, sleepy Jean," connecting with the equally sleepy Frankie. She wondered how long she'd survive the day on three hours of lousy sleep and a full agenda in front of her.

Determined to get a head start on kringles for the fall festival, she entered the walk-in cooler with a metal cart and pulled out rolled butter and milk. Kringle making was not for the faint of heart. The delectable coffee cake consisted of thin sheets of butter rolled into thin sheets of pastry, over and over again, until there were many layers laden with butter, a staple in Denmark for sweet-eaters.

Last year, Frankie buckled under Carmen's repeated suggestion to purchase a dough sheeter, which was much like a pasta maker, but specifically helpful in rolling out thin layers for pastries. The machine was a lifesaver, what with having to make hundreds of kringles for festivals and holiday orders. The sheeter could kick out 200 sheets in an hour! Frankie had found it on an auction site that sold used bakery and restaurant equipment so paid half-price for the stainless steel marvel that had seen minimal use. She figured it would give her shoulders another ten years before they'd be blown out from repetitive stirring and rolling dough.

Before she could think about using the sheeter, she had to warm milk and combine it with yeast to prepare the dough and had to watch the butter, which might sound silly, but butter is quite temperamental. It must be at a precise temperature for rolling, and even though the butter came in rolls, it was too thick for kringles, so there was work to be done.

By 5 a.m., Frankie had multiple dough balls chilling in the cooler, resting beside thin sheets of butter lying between waxed paper. Since the dough needed a good rest, she wouldn't be sheeting it with the butter until Monday. Such was the life of a kringle. Frankie wished she could crawl between two blankets and rest until Monday like the butter.

She walked past the espresso machine for the third time that morning, looking longingly at the red enamel, smelling the remnants of ground beans. But her stomach nixed the idea of accepting coffee. It was too early after having that heavy double-shot at eleven the night before.

She'd been drinking water the past couple of hours to stave off a headache and was ready to switch to tea before heading out to Bountiful to check the grapes and talk to Manny about last night's stakeout.

Frankie ran into Carmen and Tia Pepita on her way out and briefly gave them the current status of the kitchen, which was just about kringles in progress. They were free to begin anywhere on the agenda that suited them.

"You look terrible this morning. How long have you been up?" Carmen didn't mince words.

"I didn't get much sleep, so I gave up and started in the kitchen around three."

Carmen looked suspiciously at Frankie's travel mug. "How many of those have you had so far?" Carmen drank coffee, too, but not as much as Frankie, and she often nagged Frankie to stop drinking coffee in the afternoon so she could sleep unhindered from caffeine.

Frankie sniffed and jutted her chin forward. "This is tea, Carmen, herbal tea, as a matter of fact. I haven't had any coffee yet today." She turned away and trotted down the steps to her SUV.

It wasn't yet 5:30 when she drove up to Bountiful and parked on the slab outside the wine lab. Nobody else was around as far as she could tell, and daylight was still out of sight. She knew Violet would be coming to the lab tomorrow to continue her work in progress: the caramel apple mead she planned to debut sometime in October. Thankfully, mead didn't have a long fermentation process.

The two had a lunch date at Bistro on the Lake, a chic restaurant near Founders Square on Lake Joy. Frankie was excited to hear how Violet's new classes were going as well as receive a report on the progress of the mead.

Frankie pulled the bucket hat over her head and reached over the passenger seat to retrieve her hoodie. Cool mornings in the countryside were the harbinger of autumn and reminded Frankie of the waiting harvest, a smaller harvest now.

Her flashlight beam bounced along the sloping path toward the vineyard. She maneuvered straight for the Frontenac section and breathed a sigh of relief when she saw the net was intact, protecting what remained of the deep blue grapes. Robins scolded her from the trees edging the orchard.

"Too bad, birdies. No more grapes for you for a while." Once the harvest was completed, the nets would be removed. and the birds would be on the ready to glean the remaining fruits.

"Talking to the enemy, I see." Manny's soft voice sailed in from the opposite end of the Frontenacs.

Frankie waved the flashlight in his direction after jumping out of her skin at the unexpected interruption. "Where's your truck, Manny? I thought I was the only one here."

In the half-light of dawn, he gestured toward the main pole building that housed the grape crusher, tractor, and other equipment. "I drove down the fire lane and parked in the back lot."

"Speaking of the fire lane, I've got a story for you." Frankie relayed last night's escapade with Rance Musgrove, how he'd spotted the light beam, how she'd scared off the intruder with the car horn, and how they'd heard the departing ATV.

Manny met her by the Frontenacs, scratching his head. "I'm surprised they decided to come back. They must have thought we wouldn't have time to set up new surveillance. I guess I'm glad you disrupted their plans." He shook a finger at her in a scolding fashion.

"Did you call the sheriff?" Manny added.

Frankie shook her head. "No, but I texted Shirley this morning before I came out here to stop by the shop this morning. I'll let her know."

"You and Alonzo on the outs again? Is that why you don't want to call him?" Manny looked deeply into Frankie's eyes for confirmation.

She was taken aback. "No, not at all. I just have a long to-do list this morning, so might as well tell Shirley since I have to talk to her about other things." She was being evasive on purpose.

Manny could see right through her tactic and laughed. "Whatever you say, Boss. I think you're circumventing the sheriff because you can get what you want from Shirley with just a few butterhorns."

Frankie smacked his shoulder, but a smile planted itself on her face just the same. "Tell me about the Frontenacs. What's the bad news?" Frankie had been bracing herself to hear the report.

Manny's expression turned serious again. "We lost about a third of the crop, I'm afraid. The birds decimated the uncovered rows where the thickest clusters were. They were able to get into the next couple of rows as well. I'm sorry. Can you supplement with Frontenac juice from somewhere else?"

Frankie shrugged and frowned. "I really want to use just Wisconsin grapes, so it's going to be difficult, if not impossible, to locate grapes now that haven't already been spoken for months ago." Wineries knew from year to year how much juice or fresh grapes to order from area growers. They often had a standing annual order.

"Would you like me to call around? I can do it today. That is, after I finish installing the motion detectors. You're going to love them. They set off a blaring alarm with movements that are higher than four feet off the ground."

Frankie was impressed. She didn't want to have alarms going off with every raccoon and possum that lumbered around the property. But scaring away the deer would keep her orchard intact, and scaring off human intruders was exactly what she hoped for.

"Yes, you know the area wineries and growers. See if we can get lucky." Frankie wasn't optimistic, though. "And thank you, Manny, for making security a priority. Only a few more weeks before we have everything harvested."

The two reviewed the Edelweiss brix test and did a taste test on the LaCrescent, determined Monday was good for harvesting the former, while they wouldn't be testing the latter for another week or so.

A short time later, she rolled down the alley behind Bubble & Bake and saw Officer Shirley waiting on the back deck, a coffee mug in front of her on the picnic table.

"Mornin' Ace. What's doing?" Shirley looked chipper as always. Frankie wondered what the secret was behind all that vitality.

"Let's go inside. I have to work while we talk. How long have you been here?" She was surprised Shirley hadn't gone in and wondered if Tia, who didn't like outsiders in the kitchen, had booted her outside.

"Just got here. The coffee's from home." Shirley made a face. "It's not the best. Tony's a great short order cook, and his pasta and sauce is unbeatable, but the man can't make a simple cup of coffee."

"I'll hook you right up with a latte, Shirley." Frankie brushed past her and motioned her to come inside. Carmen was cutting out circles of dough for empanadas, while Tia was fussing with conchas— pan dulces/sweet breads— as they were called in Mexico. Traditionally, the decorative shell-shaped pastry was formed with two types of dough: the bottom is like a brioche bun, and the top is a streusel-type dough in a different color, laid over the bottom and cut into a shell pattern.

Tia looked up and glared at Shirley, who smiled cutely in her direction, pulled a stool up to the counter, and made herself comfortable. Frankie intercepted the coming storm.

"Officer Shirley and I have business to take care of, so I invited her here. I'm too busy today to make a trip to the sheriff's department." Frankie looked meaningfully at Tia, as Carmen smirked at the dough she was rolling.

Frankie headed to the espresso maker, missing the childish exchange between Tia and Shirley. Shirley raised the coffee mug high in the air as a mock toast. Tia responded by flinging a small dough ball at the officer. Tia didn't trust the police, insisting she had a lot of stories to back up her opinions.

Frankie handed the fresh mug to Shirley and excused herself to get her notebook from the office. She returned and pulled over a stool to sit opposite Shirley, her back toward Tia. Shirley was chomping on a fresh cheese empanada, right out of the oven, a peace offering from Carmen. Shirley winced in pain, showing a mouth wide open with steam billowing out.

Frankie retrieved a glass of water, then pulled a cranberry-cherry twist from the pastry case. "Here. Munch on this until those empanadas cool off."

"I don't have much time, but I want to ask you a couple questions about Fern's case." Frankie took another quick look at her notes from yesterday's conversation with Dominic Finchley."

"You processed Fern's vehicle, right?"

Shirley nodded, chewing on a large bite of sweet roll.

"I'm curious. Was it wet inside? The seats, the floor? Did it smell like Blackbird Pond?" Marsh ponds had a distinctive earthy, almost mildew-like scent to them. If Dominic was waist deep in pond water, some of it should have been in Fern's vehicle.

Shirley's expression was a mix of wariness and curiosity. "I think we would have noted that, and I know I would remember that. So, that's a no on all questions. Mind telling me why?"

Frankie didn't know if she should spill the contents of her conversation with Dominic. After all, he stopped talking to the police and had a lawyer on retainer. She would be betraying a source, deeming her untrustworthy.

"Just a hunch, based on the fact Fern's body was in the pond." She would leave it up to the astute Shirley to reason through the case details. After all, Finchley told the police he tried to revive Fern.

Shirley grunted, not exactly pleased with Frankie's reticence to talk. "What else, Frankie?"

"Can you tell me the prime suspects—as far as the police are concerned?" Frankie doubted she would get a straight answer since her past relationship with Shirley had always been an equal exchange of information.

Shirley finished the cran-cherry twist, picking up the crumbs with one finger to consume every morsel. "Tell you what, Detective Frankie: you name someone, and I'll tell you if they're cleared or not. This case has more suspects than a house with termites." She resumed nibbling the empanada.

Frankie ticked off her list, counting on her fingers as she named them. Between bites and sips, Shirley conveyed that Ash, Ivy, Dominic, Daryl George, Robyn, and Naomi Travers couldn't be cleared as persons of interest. Frankie expressed surprise that the list hadn't been whittled down.

"They were all in town the day Fern was killed. They all have alibis but not ironclad alibis," Shirley stated.

Frankie scoffed. "You mean Ash doesn't have an ironclad alibi? He doesn't drive, Shirley. You think he wheeled out to Blackbird Pond in his chair?"

Shirley let the remark roll off. "Ash is Ivy's alibi, and Ivy is Ash's alibi. So, you see how that doesn't work, right?"

Frankie did see, and she was glad that neither Cherry nor Pom were here to listen to the conversation. She wondered if they suspected their cousins.

"Wait a second. Did you say Naomi Travers was here the day Fern was killed? What would she be doing here? I thought she came for the funeral." There was one more reason to suspect Naomi.

Shirley chuckled, licking some dripping cheese from her fingers. "Glad you picked up on that. She says she came to town to visit with Dominic Finchley. Isn't that convenient and curious?"

"Curiouser and curiouser," Frankie mumbled.

"So in this case, it's all about motive. Finding motive takes a lot more time than talking to suspects or coming up with a murder weapon, at least in this case. Old-fashioned, long-haul investigation is what this case calls for." Shirley knew her way around cases of all types, so she spoke from experience.

Frankie agreed. She had a taste of the painstaking side of investigative work with Abe Arnold at the Deep Lakes library. It was tedious and frequently led the investigation down one rabbit hole after another. "Have you been looking at Fern's studies, I mean, all of her studies?"

Shirley nodded. "I've been working with Officer Green on that, in piecemeal. I mean, we have other cases we're handling, too. Pflug is mostly interviewing suspects."

She stopped mid-thought and stared at Frankie. "Why? Have you been looking at the studies?" She already knew the answer. "Find anything interesting?"

"I'm still working on them, trying to put two and two together. But Shirley, we did decipher some of Fern's journal pages." Frankie's excitement was obvious.

"Who's 'we'?"

Frankie decided it was up to Cherry and Pom if they wanted to help the police with the journal code. "Cherry and Pom Parker. They are Fern's next of kin, so I think they should help you with the journal, not me."

"Good one, Ace. You're getting better at this investigative reporter gig. You're learning to be cagey. The day might come when I don't like you anymore." Shirley offered her a sly grin. It was no secret she didn't like the press, having numerous bad experiences with reporters in her days on the Chicago police force.

"Before you go, I need to tell you that there was at least one intruder at the vineyard last night." Frankie's statement caused Carmen and Tia to quit their projects full stop, their faces showing fear and concern.

"So, what happened?" Shirley was impassive, waiting to hear more.

"Wellll...I saw someone, or I guess I should say Rance saw a moving light beam near the fence line at the vineyard. When he poked me to look up, I jolted and accidentally hit the car horn, scaring off whomever it was. We heard an ATV drive off." Frankie accelerated the story as she told it, then prepared for the incoming volley.

Carmen was loudest. "What were you thinking? And, wait a minute, Rance who?" she pointed the pastry cutter at Frankie.

"Dios mío!" Tia made the sign of the cross, then wiped her forehead with her apron hem.

Shirley chortled at the story and the women's reactions. "So you were on a stakeout, huh? First time?"

Frankie nodded. "I was supposed to be there with Abe Arnold, but he sent his reporter Rance Musgrove instead." She was ready to move on without offering further explanation. "I talked to Manny, and we think the intruder came back because they figured we wouldn't have any new security up and running. We looked over the property this morning, and all is well. Manny is installing new motion sensors connected to noisy alarms today."

Shirley said she would add the information to Frankie's file and let Alonzo know of the new development. "Any plans for another stakeout, Frankie?" Shirley's negative tone was meant as a warning.

"No," Frankie spoke flatly, not wanting to elaborate. She doubted it was necessary to do another stakeout at this point.

Shirley produced a satisfied nod and looked longingly in the direction of the pastry case, which Tia was ready to wheel out front. Her brightly printed muumuu swung around to face Shirley before Tia's head joined the assault.

"Oh no, no, no.  No more pastries for you today." Tia twirled her hand into the air as if casting a spell on the officer. "These are for paying customers. Go mooch off someone else." Tia spun around and heaved the full force of her weight into the pastry case, nearly losing her balance in the process.

Shirley laughed wickedly at Tia's expense and received a sharp look from Frankie.  Shirley was someone she admired, and she enjoyed their collaborative discussions, but nobody outside the Bubble & Bake crew was allowed to disparage any member of her work family.

Carmen raised her eyebrows into points and took a purposeful step toward Shirley. "Don't make me regret sharing my empanadas with you. Tia Pepita is a sensitive soul, and she's been through a lot in her life. So, lay off."

Shirley saluted both women. "I didn't mean anything by it. We've got a good rivalry going. I think we both enjoy sparring, you know?"

Carmen and Frankie thought they understood. It was easy to get Tia riled up, and she was quite entertaining at that, but they still felt protective of the older woman.

"Frankie, if you decide you want to divulge any more details on the case, well." Shirley paused a long time, weighing her words. "The department could use any leads; even the smallest detail might matter."

As soon as the back door closed on Shirley, Carmen burst. "Rance? You mean that little lapdog reporter at *The Watch*? Why didn't you run the stakeout with Garret? Or maybe your best friend?" She punctuated the words as if they were shot from a nail gun.

"It wasn't my idea. I impulsively asked Abe to meet me at the vineyard. You know, while we were looking at bird studies. He said he would join me, then Rance showed up." Frankie faltered. "Oh, and I didn't ask you or Garrett because it wasn't a party, Carmen. I thought Abe would have expertise, you know?"

Carmen backed down. "Still, Rance the muskrat? Yikes."

Frankie's expression softened. "Rance has his issues, but we've misjudged him. He's smart and hasn't had such an easy life. I'm going to be nice to him from now on."

Before Carmen could reply, Jovie came in the back door and scurried into a shop apron so she could join Tia at front of house, running sales and boxing up baked goods. The swinging kitchen doors were still in motion

when Jovie popped back in, less than a minute later,
announcing Abe was there to speak with Frankie.

"I'm destined to get nothing done today," Frankie
sighed dramatically.

"Ha, you love this, Frankie Champagne," Carmen
called out to Frankie's backside.

Abe had settled into a small table away from the front
door and prying customers. Frankie smiled approvingly,
seeing a bakery box stuffed with assorted pastries sitting
on the table. At least he was trying to make amends for
standing her up last night.

He smiled thoughtfully and raised his coffee mug in
greeting. He started talking before she had the chance
to sit down and lay into him.

"Oh man, do I have a lot to tell you. You should
grab your notebook, Champagne." Abe looked like the
proverbial cat with a mouthful of canary.

Undaunted, Frankie summoned a prickly reply.
"Before I grab anything, how about you tell me why you
didn't show last night?" She was still standing, hands on
hips.

Abe lowered his voice so she had to lean in to hear him.
"Because I wanted time to look at some other studies.
Sue let me into the library and locked up behind me. I
was there half the night, and I think it paid off."

Frankie folded her arms across her chest. "Okay, I'll go
get that notebook. But I haven't got all day, so this better
be good."

Abe was polishing off a cranberry walnut muffin and
brushing crumbs off his shirt when Frankie returned,
taking a seat across from him. She noticed he was
wearing the same shirt as yesterday and had dark circles
under his typically alert eyes. Maybe he had pulled an
all-nighter at the library.

"I decided to look at the Eastern Bluebirds in the Midwest Project from several years ago. The ex, Finchley, was the lead on that study, assisted by Fern and Naomi Travers."

Frankie remembered the conversation at the funeral home, when Naomi noted that she'd worked with Fern and Dom on the study. She nodded for Abe to proceed.

"There was nothing unusual about the study. In fact, it was a great success, as it was instrumental in bringing back the bluebird population in the region. But the writing style bothered me." His lips twitched.

"In what way?" Frankie wanted to propel this conversation forward.

"It seemed strangely familiar. I didn't think I'd read anything by Finchley before, so, I went back to the Townsend's warbler and Costa Rica hummingbird studies. The writing styles were very similar."

Frankie was intrigued. "What are you saying? The studies were written by the same scientist?"

Abe nodded enthusiastically. "Just wait. I decided to look at two other Finchley studies. The writing style was the same as the other three. And, get this: Fern wasn't an assistant on either of those studies."

"But you think Fern was writing the studies for Dom?" Frankie confirmed.

"I'm sure of it. I may not know beans about birds, but I know writing, Frankie. Even in technical writing, individuals have their own style, turn of phrase, word choice, methods of organizing information, and presenting their arguments."

Frankie scribbled more notes, chewing her bottom lip as she mulled over the new development. "Doesn't this help to clear Dom's name in the case? If Fern had the writing chops between the two of them and was willing to give Dom the credit for the published works, why would he want to get rid of her?  It makes sense that he wanted them to remain a couple, which is why he went out to the pond that morning to convince her to take him back."

Abe shook his head. "Maybe so, maybe not. I agree that he'd want to keep cashing in on Fern's skills, but what if he tried to convince her for a second chance and she turned him down? Then, he kills her in a fit of anger."

Frankie couldn't disagree that the scenario was plausible. "Did you find anything else helpful?"

"I found another study where Naomi was the assistant. This one took place in Arizona, where they're trying to reestablish the thick-billed parrot. But it's a long, complicated study with a lot of players involved. I skimmed it and sent a link to your email."

Frankie snorted. "Wait, what? You sent a link to my email?  You are making progress for a 20th century guy."

Abe smirked and waved a hand in dismissal. "You should look at it when you can. There's a lot to unpack, but what bothered me is that most of the scientists, except the ornithologists, determined that preserving the bird habitat was the most viable option for Arizona's wildlife management organization."

"Except the ornithologists?" Frankie's jaw dropped. "Wouldn't you think the bird experts would want to give the parrots a chance in a protected environment?"

Here again was another recent study where it appeared the birds were the losers and wouldn't be given time or opportunity to repopulate. She wondered if the plan to restore the parrot population was still operable or if it had been discontinued, the lands instead being sold to some industry. Would the opinion of the ornithologists carry the most weight, or would the other scientists be able to sway the outcome?

"I'll look at the study as soon as I can. But this is another strike against Naomi in my eyes. It seems she's involved in two studies that didn't end favorably for the birds."

Abe raised a hand in caution. "Don't jump to any conclusions yet. You have to remember that Robyn has also been part of two studies that were botched. You can't discount her as a suspect. After all, she could finish Fern's study and take credit for it, publish it under her own name. That would be a feather in her cap."

"What's your next move, Abe? I think you should let me talk to Robyn. She trusts me."

Abe nodded. "I'm going to poke around some other rabbit holes." He stood and grabbed the bakery box. "Hey, how did the stakeout go?" He looked amused.

To his surprise, Frankie planted a serene smile on her face. "Actually, it was a mixed bag. Someone did show up on my property, but I scared the intruder away before we could see anything identifiable. Rance was a good stakeout partner, though. I'm glad you gave him the chance."

Arching one bushy eyebrow, Abe mumbled, "You never cease to surprise me, Champagne. I've underestimated you—again."

# Chapter 16

*Always be nice to the person who is holding*
*scissors next to your head. — Anon*

Frankie darted back to the kitchen and immediately began scurrying around like a squirrel, grabbing ingredients from memory to make pumpkin scones. The season dictated the return of pumpkins and the perennial popular pumpkin spice flavor. From candles to coffee to bakery, people couldn't get enough pumpkin spice in their lives.

Carmen's eyes followed her business partner's frantic maneuvers around the kitchen space, reminding her of the *Family Circus* comic with footsteps that crisscrossed repeatedly over each other.

In her effort to make up lost time, Frankie's jig about the kitchen created a soiree of small calamities. Carrying too many eggs in her bunched-up apron, she lost two and had to retrace her steps to mop up the sticky mess. Then she miscalculated while dumping the bag of flour into the bowl of the floor mixer, instead creating a small snowstorm that spread across the floor. Coughing, she retrieved the broom but not before Piper determined now was a good time for a stroll.

"Shoo, kitty, out of the kitchen." Frankie gritted her teeth and pushed the broom in the direction of Piper, who didn't need any more encouragement to leave.

Carmen couldn't stand to watch any longer. "Hey, Calamity Jane, why don't you slow down a second and tell me what the heck is bothering you?"

Sweeping up the flour, Frankie told Carmen about her conversation with Abe. "Every time I think I can eliminate a suspect, new information comes up. This case just keeps going around in circles, Carmie."

Carmen grunted. "Just like you, obviously." She snickered at her quip. "Now you know how the cops feel. It's not always going to come easy. Give your brain a break, and let's talk about something else."

Frankie marveled at how fast Carmen's fingers flew over the empanadas, filling them, folding them, and twisting the edges into a beautiful rope design to seal in the delicious fillings. Carmen was an efficient bake,r no matter what she made, and Frankie admired that about her friend.

"Tia Pepita's in a better mood now that Shirley left. She's out front chatting away with customers, enticing them to buy more goodies than they originally planned." Frankie giggled.

Carmen kept a steady rhythm between dough and fillings. "The distraction of working here is good for her. She's worried about her eye condition."

Frankie cut cold butter into small chunks to blend with the flour and spices in the mixer. "When do you expect her to have the surgery?"

"We think it will be in November." Carmen laughed lightly to herself. "It can't come soon enough. You should

see her and Sonny. It's like a competition to see how
many times a day one stumbles into the other."

Sonny was a premier herding dog at the O'Connor
sheep farm in his heyday, but he was losing his eyesight
and had been relegated to the house for his remaining
days. The sheltie had been Frankie's protector earlier
that summer. Canine and baker had become lifelong
friends.

"Poor Sonny. I need to come out and take him for
a walk. I haven't seen him since before Labor Day
weekend." It was Frankie's routine to walk Sonny every
couple of days, but the grape harvest and Fern's death
meant the dog had taken a back seat.

"Oh sure, add one more thing to that unending list of
yours, Frankie." Carmen huffed as she walked to the oven
with another sheet of perfectly formed empanadas.

Carmen's assessment of Frankie's list was right on
the money, but that didn't stop her from skipping
lunch, driving out to the O'Connors', and picking up
the happy sheltie. Sonny nuzzled against Frankie's hand,
scampered to a set of hooks next to the door, and
clamped his teeth over the leash to pull it down.

Ryan, Carmen's husband, laughed. "Yep, looks like he's
missed you. I hope you planned on taking him for a
walk."

"That's why I'm here. I'm going to take him over to
Blackbird Pond, though, if that's okay. I want to have
another look at the crime scene."

Ryan folded his arms, grim-faced. "I'm glad you had
the sense to tell me that's where you're going, Frankie. It
could be dangerous, you know."

Frankie had more big brothers in her life than anyone
else she knew. "Thanks for worrying about me. I'll have
my guard dog with me." She patted the sheltie's mane,
and Sonny raised devoted eyes upward to meet hers.

Frankie slid the SUV into the dirt parking area a short distance from another vehicle. She was taken aback to see another car in the lot and hoped it was someone she knew. Ryan's warning rang in her ears, causing her heart to thump a little quicker.

She surveyed the area, which was open from the lot to the pond and its prairie-like surroundings. The tree line circled the prairie, which is where the trails began before snaking into the woods.

She'd wanted this vantage point to test her newest theory about the killer. Since tire tracks from Dom's jeep and Fern's Outback were the only ones in the lot, she wondered if the killer could easily enter the area another way. Last night's ATV intruder at Bountiful was a revelation. An ATV would have access from the public trails on both sides of the pond. She shivered. Could her intruder and the killer be the same person?

A voice calling over the breeze broke her reverie and stirred Sonny into a panicked bark. Suddenly chilled, Frankie turned toward the sound and immediately blew out a long exhale at the sight of Robyn standing by the purple martin house. Frankie couldn't conceive how she hadn't seen her when she surveyed her surroundings.

At ease now, Sonny trotted over toward the house by Frankie's side.

"What are you doing out here? I thought you'd be busy today at the bakery." Robyn was dressed in field gear, sunglasses perched on her head, notebook and pen in hand.

"This guy needed a walk, and I guess I did, too. There's a lot on my mind. You, too?" Sonny lifted a paw to Robyn in greeting.

Robyn gave the sheltie a friendly pat and sighed. "Since Fern's journal is missing, I thought I should try to record anything useful in my own notes. But, as you can see, the birds are gone." Robyn gazed upward at the wires where the birds usually perched when hunting for insects. The lines were bare.

"Did you find anything helpful at all? Any clues as to what might have happened?"

"I was looking to see if the house had been tampered with. I can't find any evidence to suggest it was."

Frankie took Robyn at her word. "At the visitation you talked to me about Ivy and Dom, but I have to say, I don't think either of them killed Fern. I've been looking at Fern's studies. It seems more likely to me that someone had it out for her. First, they ruined her studies and then they took her life."

The realization gripped Robyn, and tears began to fall. "I'm afraid you might be right. First the hummingbirds, and now the martins."

"I think there's more than just those studies. The Townsend's warbler study that Fern did with Naomi didn't turn out well for the birds either. And there might be others we haven't found yet."

Robyn pulled her sunglasses back down and looked at Frankie. "Who is 'we'?"

Frankie wondered if this was a bad blunder on her part. Now that she couldn't see Robyn's eyes, she couldn't gauge her reactions. She soldiered on. "I'm working with our local newspaper editor to sort through information." She hoped her general response would suffice.

"What do you think will happen to the martin study now?" Frankie broached the subject, hoping Robyn would speculate freely.

More tears dripped onto Robyn's cheeks. "It's not up to me. It's up to Dr. Fredrich. We were at the end of the study with this last colony count. I'm hoping the first year, which was successful and without incident, will carry the most weight in Dr. Fredrich's decision."

Frankie's radar detected something intriguing. "You mean the study could proceed or be quashed by Dr. Fredrich? So, if the study is canceled, what happens next?"

Robyn choked back a sob. "Nothing happens. All the hard work, all the data is shelved. I'm sorry to sound selfish, but this could be the second unpublished study I've worked on. And that puts me back to square one in my career."

Frankie understood the professional disappointment. All of her effort went into making her bakery and vineyard successful operations. That was why the vandalism at Bountiful was so upsetting. "But if this is the only snag in the martin study, you must have enough other data to validate your findings?"

Robyn bit her lip, pushed her sunglasses back to the top of her head again, and confided in Frankie. "It's not the only snag," she said quietly. Looking out toward the pond, she revealed an earlier incident. "In July, Fern and I traveled to Buena Vista grasslands, where there are five sizeable colonies of martins we've been tracking in the study." Robyn swallowed hard. "When we got there, the majority of the young had fledged. The ground was littered with dead birds."

Frankie gasped. "What happened?"

Robyn shrugged. "Fern and I literally bent over and cried our eyes out. So many dead young. There was no apparent reason for them to fledge early. No strange weather. No detectable predators. We were there when they arrived and built nests. We counted eggs. We watched them feed babies about a week earlier."

Frankie breathed heavily, carrying forth one word. "Sabotage."

Robyn nodded. "We thought that, too. But why?"

"Fern didn't suggest any ideas?" Frankie figured Fern was smart enough to have some inkling why the sabotage happened. After all, she'd left the coded journal. The journal that seemed to indicate she trusted her field assistant. So, why didn't Fern confide in Robyn? Was it to protect her?

Robyn interrupted her thoughts. "I know Fern was working on something, but she kept me in the dark. She was working closely with Daryl George. They had a lot of meetings anyway."

"Have you ever worked with Naomi? Or Dom?" Robyn's professional insights could aid the investigation.

"The police asked me that same question. I haven't worked with either of them professionally. I only knew Dom as Fern's fiancé, other than attending some of the same bird conferences. Same with Naomi. We didn't socialize. And Fern never said anything about Naomi. She was too discreet, too professional for gossip."

Frankie pressed her further. "What about others? Was there gossip about Naomi or Dom that you heard?"

"Sure there was. The bird science world isn't as big as you may think. There was gossip that Naomi was after Dom, romantically. That she was responsible for breaking up Dom and Fern." Robyn didn't seem to mind sharing that morsel with Frankie.

Frankie didn't add to the gossip, despite seeing Dom and Naomi cozied up at Bubble & Bake. Of course, Robyn had been there to witness their behavior for herself.

"Just be careful, Robyn. If you're pushing to keep this study alive, you might be in danger and have to keep yourself alive, too." Frankie's remark made them both shudder.

Frankie trotted Sonny around the perimeter of the pond, feeling it was the least she could do since she promised him a walk. She removed his leash briefly, so he could run a few sprints along the shady tree line and scare up a couple of chipmunks. Frankie watched Robyn drive away, which put her mind at ease. If Robyn had any bad intentions, this would have been the perfect spot to act on them.

Gazing at the pond, she noticed its emptiness. All the dead birds had been removed and taken to some science lab, where they would be studied to determine if they died from disease or something unnatural.

Frankie had returned to her mental checklist for the remainder of the day. As if on cue, Sonny bounded out of the tree line, brought a chunky stick to Frankie and dropped it at her feet. He gave her leg a nudge and lowered his front legs and chest into a play posture.

"Okay, mind reader. Let's play." Frankie threw the stick a few times, checked her fitness tracker, and determined it was past time for them to leave. Sonny obediently stayed while Frankie reattached the leash, and they walked the tree line together back toward the parking lot. Was it her imagination, or did she hear the rattle of an ATV nearby? She raced to the parking lot, Sonny keeping pace as if reading her mind.

"How was your walk?" Carmen sat at the Bubble & Bake counter, looking at a couple of new recipes to try. She'd just returned from taking Tia back to the house. "We must have just missed each other. I bet Sonny was thrilled to get all that attention."

"Yeah, well, Sonny got short-changed on this walk, so I'll have to make it up to him next time." Frankie shared the details of her encounter with Robyn, omitting the possibility of an ATV spying on them.

"Maybe there's something I can do to help the investigation." Having been backup to Frankie in the past, Carmen felt like she was missing out on this sleuthing venture. "Tasha Rivers stopped by right after you left. She's hosting a bird walk tomorrow morning in honor of Fern. Everyone's meeting at six-thirty at Spurgeon Park to walk the quarry trail, looking for fall migrators."

"So you want to go on the bird walk tomorrow morning? That's not quite your style, is it, Carmie?" Frankie was surprised.

Carmen shrugged. "Why not? Maybe some of those birds will open their beaks and spill some juicy details." They both giggled.

"Okay, let's plan on it. The shop will be covered. It's probably not going to be a busy Saturday anyway." Frankie's thoughts turned toward dwindling sales but were cut off at the pass by Carmen.

"By the way, Tasha bought out the rest of the bakery case for refreshments."

"What's your plan for the afternoon?" Frankie looked at the shop list, saw check marks next to almost everything, and teetered between batching more scones or going upstairs to shower after her sweaty romp around Blackbird Pond.

Carmen glanced up from the recipes. "I'm in the mood to make these cherry-rhubarb butter bars. The recipe makes a giant sheet, and they can be frozen for our own use if they don't sell out." Carmen pointed to a hand-printed index card that had come her way via Ryan's Aunt Sally. The recipe featured tart cherries, rhubarb chunks, a shortbread crust, and streusel topping.

"That sounds scrumptious. Would you mind if I went upstairs for a shower? I could use one after playing with Sonny."

"Oh shoot, I forgot. Kris from Bloom Studio stopped by. She said she can squeeze you in this afternoon if you still want a haircut. She had a cancellation."

"Okay, quick shower for me and off to the hair salon. Cherry's coming in soon to prepare pizza ingredients and cut up veggies." The three women were staffing the wine lounge for the evening with Jovie on standby if needed. "You never know; it could be busy tonight."

Still in bustling squirrel mode, Frankie arrived at Bloom Studio shower-fresh in thirty minutes. "Hey, Kris. Sorry, I didn't get here sooner. I had a playdate with my favorite dog."

Kris motioned Frankie into the black and chrome swiveling chair and snapped a plastic smock over her head.

"No worries. I actually had time to work on paying bills this afternoon, what with a couple cancellations. The week after Labor Day is a real snore, even in the hair business." Kris spritzed Frankie's bob, framed it with both hands to assess its needs, and retrieved a comb to smooth it down.

"Your bangs are getting long. Do you want to keep them, or are we going to try something new?" Kris was hopeful her client would trade the tried and true for something more adventurous.

"Keep it the same. I don't have time to experiment or fuss with something I have to style." Frankie fell in love with the straight bob cut that turned under when it behaved. She was a wash-and-go kind of gal.

"Can't blame me for trying. It's my job." Kris said, laughing, then changed the subject.

"How's business at the wine lounge?" Kris was fishing, Frankie could tell. "I know the bakery is always steady, but how's the wine biz these days?"

"Are you referring to the fact I have competition in town from the new wine bar?"

Kris nodded. "I'm the newly elected secretary for the Chamber, so I like to keep tabs on the businesses in town."

Frankie laughed inwardly. If she wanted to know any of the hot gossip about anybody's *business*, she only needed a cut, style, and shampoo to find out. If the shop was busy with customers, she could leave the salon with enough gossip to fill a tabloid.

"My wine business is doing just fine, better than ever." What she said was true. As far as she could tell, the new wine bar hadn't affected her sales, but she couldn't resist knowing the latest scuttlebutt. "Why, what have you heard?"

Kris frowned, mouth agape, momentarily caught off guard. "Oh, I don't know." She pulled some of Frankie's hair through the comb and resumed snipping. "I guess I heard that the new place was doing very well, boatloads of customers, both tourists and locals."

Uncertain if Kris would divulge her source, she still needed to ask the question. "And just who told you that?"

Kris clapped her mouth closed, but Heidi, her salon partner, piped up. "We heard it from the owner, Rina." Heidi's skepticism couldn't be disguised.

"Is she a client?" Frankie really wanted to ask if she was a natural blonde but knew better.

Heidi nodded, ignored a warning look from Kris, and pointed toward the back of the salon where the tanning beds were located.

"I thought she was from California," Frankie protested.

"She is, but everyone knows you can't maintain a California tan in Wisconsin without a little help." Kris took over before Heidi had a chance to say more.

"She actually used to live in the area before she moved to California. That's probably why she came back here to live." Heidi offered.

Frankie pretended not to care too much. "Did she say where in the area she used to live?"

"Actually, Rina didn't tell us that. Someone else did, so I really can't say anymore about it." Kris appeared to want to move on. "Turn this way. I'm just going to get those bangs back in shape and then you're all set."

Frankie pressed. "Did she say anything about how she met Lars Paulsen?"

Kris paused, the shears hung in midair. She wrinkled her nose as if she had just stepped in something unpleasant. "She doesn't talk much about him," the word "him" came out like a large bite from a jalapeño. "Rina said something about the two meeting through her brother."

Frankie picked up on Kris's obvious dislike toward Lars. "It doesn't sound like you care for Lars Paulsen."

Kris snorted. "He's a picky one. He didn't like the way I cut his hair, so he only sees Heidi now." She threw a pretend punch at her salon partner, who laughed.

"Matter of fact, he's coming in tomorrow morning," Heidi said, glancing at the schedule. "I'm coming in just to cut his hair early, too, because he requested a seven a.m."

Frankie marveled at that kind of customer service, while she mentally noted that Lars's appointment meant he wouldn't be coming to Fern's honorary bird walk in the morning.

Heidi had nothing more to offer about Lars, while Kris wrapped up and thanked Frankie for the tip. For the first time, Frankie left the salon with little more than a fresh haircut.

Walking back to Bubble & Bake, Frankie keyed in Daryl George's phone number. She wanted to share information about the bird studies and pick his brain. She was walking a tightrope with the foundation chief since Fern's coded journal questioned his integrity.

Daryl picked up quickly. Frankie could hear the echoing drone of background noise.

"This is Daryl George."

"Hello, Daryl. This is Frankie Champagne. It sounds loud where you are. Do you have time to talk?

"I'm at the airport. I have to fly to DC for a weekend meeting with some of the wildlife big wigs." He sounded tired and unimpressed about the trip. "Go ahead. I'm not going to board for another hour."

"I've been reading Fern's past studies, along with Dominic Finchley's and Naomi Travers's. I talked to Robyn, too, just today. I'm wondering if you can shed some light on a few things." She instantly regretted making the call while on the run instead of waiting to get home with her notes next to her.

"Fire away. I'll see if I can fill in any blanks." Daryl must have walked to a quieter locale, wherever that was in an airport.

"What's going to happen to the martin study now?" She figured she'd ask the same question she just posed to Robyn to see if their answers jibed.

"That's not up to me. The foundation partnered with Dr. Fredrich on the study. We have a huge interest in completing it, but the funding goes through the university. Her decision carries the most weight. I can offer serious input, but without Fern's field journal, my input won't mean much."

"Can't Robyn testify about the study? She worked in the field with Fern. She must have her own data." Frankie needed clarification on the process.

Daryl's tired voice answered. "Robyn reports her data to Fern. As the lead scientist, Fern calculates the data into findings. Robyn's data is incomplete without Fern's, so no conclusions can be drawn."

The topic was a dead end in Frankie's mind, since Dr. Fredrich would decide if the study would proceed. "Okay, new subject. Do you know anything about a study on revitalizing habitat in Arizona for the thick-billed parrot? I think it was a recent study." Again, she cursed herself for not having note access, but she'd increased her pace and was almost back to the shop.

"Yes, I know about that study. It's a pretty big deal in the birding world. Anytime Uncle Sam wants to reestablish a wildlife habitat, people in my world pay attention."

"Do you know the status of the project? Is Arizona going to reintroduce the parrot to its mountain area?" Frankie hoped she could get an easy answer. The study was complex, involving many agricultural entities and environmentalists.

Daryl sighed. "It's still in the works as far as I know. Might even be in limbo. I think the birders on the study couldn't draw solid statistical evidence, if I remember right."

Frankie bypassed the kitchen entrance and headed up the outside steps that landed her on her apartment deck, fishing for her house key. She grunted as she juggled the phone, her purse, and turned the key in the little-used lock.

"Did you know Naomi Travers assisted in that study?"

"No, I don't remember that, but I'm sure I read the list of names. It was a huge study with a lot of players."

Frankie dropped her purse, headed to the bedroom, and pulled her notebook off her desk. For once, she was happy she'd taken Abe's advice and wrote things down longhand.

"Can I read you the names of the other bird scientists on the study and see if you know anyone? Dr. Kelley, Dr. Vance, Dr. Moody."

There was a long pause of dead air while Daryl considered them. "Sorry, I don't know them. Are there any identifying abbreviations next to their names? It might help."

Frankie took notes like a scholar. "Yes. Dr. Kelley is 'DG of Bot. at Cal Tech,' and Dr. Vance is 'D.Z. at So. AZ'. Dr. Moody is listed as 'BOU. '"

Daryl offered a mirthless chuckle. "You know, I need a glossary of terms in order to decipher all these pretentious abbreviations." He seemed to openly scorn the highly educated, making Frankie wonder what his background was. Surely, he must have a degree in order to head the wildlife foundation.

"I jotted them down while you were talking. Dr. Kelley is a Director General of Botany at California Institute of Technology, which bodes well for the findings in the study. Cal Tech is top notch. Dr. Vance is a zoologist at Southern Arizona. I can't comment on whether that's good or bad. And Dr. Moody is the ornithologist in the group, representing the British Ornithological Union, which is curious. Usually a U.S. study is headed by

Americans, but maybe Moody was hot to be on the study. Anyway, you could ask Naomi for information."

Except Frankie didn't trust Naomi. No, she'd be looking up those names for herself and see if there were dots to be connected.

"Anything else, Frankie? Are the investigators making any progress on Fern's murder?"

"It's slow going, I think. I'm sure they have details they're not sharing with the public. By the way, are you coming back to Deep Lakes? There's a memorial ceremony at Bountiful Fruits on Sunday at six p.m. if you're around."

"I won't be back anytime soon. Unless, that is, the police want me in town for questioning." Daryl's voice was dry and impassive.

"Haven't they already questioned you? Everyone associated with Fern who was in town when she died was questioned."

"They did, but they had no reason to find anything amiss. Why? Am I on your suspect list, Frankie?" His voice was lighthearted now. "You don't have to answer that. I just hope they settle the case and find her journal. I need that journal, and so do the purple martins."

Frankie wished him safe travels and ended the call. She believed Daryl was cleared from the suspect list on her crime board, but she didn't understand why Fern questioned his trustworthiness. Since Daryl didn't have control over the funding of the study, how could he be on the take?

# Chapter 17

*It is a thorny undertaking, and more so than it seems, to follow a movement so wandering as that of our mind, to penetrate the opaque depths of its innermost folds, to pick out and immobilize the innumerable flutterings that agitate it.* — *Michel de Montaigne*

Downstairs, Tess was in the kitchen, checking the baking board for next week. She seemed happier than she'd been in months since moving into the apartment above Rachel's Bead Me I'm Yours craft shop next door. Tess and Rachel had much in common and were near the same age, so they became fast friends.

"Hello, Frankie," Tess spoke musically, elongating the last syllable of Frankie's name. "You look frazzled today." The comment was an observation, not an accusation. Tess was intuitive and methodical. She didn't jump to conclusions but was gifted at reading people.

"Hi, Tess. You read that right. I'm being pulled in many directions today. It's still Friday, right?" Frankie pulled a ready-made flatbread from the cooler and several ingredients to top it off.

Tess had a smile that illuminated the kitchen. "You're always this way when you're working on a crime case. I can see the bees flying around your brain when you talk."

Frankie spread a little fresh tomato sauce on the flatbread, smoothing it out with artistic strokes. "Hmm, yes, I suppose you're right. What are you up to today? It's Friday night in Deep Lakes. Any big plans?" The small town didn't offer much on Friday nights once the tourists left town.

Tess automatically joined Frankie, cutting up mushrooms for the pizza while Frankie grated Asiago and Provolone cheeses. "I'm going to help Rachel set up for the workshop on Sunday afternoon. I'm going to teach people how to make twisted bracelets from fire opal beads." Tess was proud of her Ethiopian heritage and excited to bring the gems to Deep Lakes. "Rachel found a supplier for the opals, and we have a full house for the workshop."

Frankie was thrilled for Tess and happy that Rachel, typically a loner, had gained a friend, too. Deep Lakes certainly had its share of designing women, something the community frequently highlighted. Aunt CeCe would be leading a workshop tomorrow with Meredith Healy at Shamrock Floral down the block. Autumn wreath-making with wild grapevines, bittersweet, seed pods, and dried herbs and flowers was on the docket.

"I'm excited you and Rachel had so many people sign up, but I'm not surprised. Your own fire opal jewelry is just beautiful." Frankie finalized her pizza and slid the metal tray under the oven broiler. "I suppose you already ate lunch, huh?"

"Yes, thanks. I just wanted to have in my mind what I'd be making tomorrow. I like to have a plan for the day." Tess winked. "I learned that habit from my boss." She waved goodbye and pushed through the swinging doors that led to the lounge, so she could check in with Carmen, too.

Minutes later, Frankie sat at the counter, savoring bites of basil, mushrooms, and fresh cheese perfectly browned over a crispy crust. Her cell was tucked into her purse upstairs. It was the quietest moment of her day thus far, and all she wanted to do was turn her mind off and enjoy the repast. She couldn't resist checking her fitness watch. Really, was it possible only five minutes had passed? She wasn't accustomed to sitting still lately.

Her mind wandered to the evening ahead and whether or not the wine lounge would be busy. The Friday after Labor Day weekend was typically as lifeless as a bitter January day. Lifeless. Poor Fern and her family. Would the case be solved, and could she do more to help the investigation? For starters, she decided she'd better level with Shirley and offer her details in trade.

Then there was Abe. How much time could she set aside to sit in the bowels of the library doing research? What about her vineyard? The next harvest was slated for Monday. There were still two more varieties to pick after that. The Frontenacs. Would Manny have any luck finding more Frontenacs to add to her dire harvest?

'Grapes of Wrath': what did it mean? Maybe her mother had some insights beyond Frankie's concrete thoughts about the message. Someone was carrying a grudge, but who and why? What did the cat face mean? Was it one of the people who adopted a shop orphan and now regretted it, what with clawed-up furniture and cat puke around every corner?

So much for a relaxing meal. But the pizza was gone anyway, consumed under the influence of stress. She hopped down from the stool and retrieved iced tea from the cooler. The mix, prepared by Aunt CeCe, was an herbal blend of mint and hibiscus infused with blackberries from the countryside. She took a couple of sips and let the cool liquid refresh her body and mind as she leaned into the counter.

Carmen bounced through the swinging doors. "Hey, Frankie. Someone out front wants to talk to us about adding wine to our inventory. Did you call someone to stop in?" Carmen stood with both hands on her hips, looking partly confused, partly perturbed.

"Not me." Reluctantly, Frankie left the cold glass on the counter and followed Carmen out. "Might as well see what this is about." In their experience, the two figured it was much easier to deal with sales reps as they came, because they were usually relentless until someone listened to their pitch.

A tall, slender woman waited by the walnut bar in the shop. Dressed in a sophisticated red blazer and skinny black slacks, she tapped one patent leather pump against the bottom rail of the bar as she surveyed Bubble & Bake's decor.

Frankie and Carmen slid in place behind the bar, setting up a barrier between them and the salesperson.

The willowy woman turned away from her view of the side seating areas and presented a plastic business smile. She reached out a well-manicured hand to shake Frankie's.

"Lisa Carson. I'm with Wine on the Vine Distributors. We have the largest selection of wines in Wisconsin. We're known for our upscale vintages from California, Washington, and New York, as well as South America and Australia." She passed her business card across the bar top.

"I'm sure you noticed that our wine stock is locally sourced. In fact, you're looking at the vintner right here." Carmen spoke in a professional business tone that was meant to sound patronizing.

"Frankie Champagne. Owner of Bountiful Fruits Vineyard." Frankie softened her tone to try to make up for Carmen's don't-waste-our-time attitude.

Lisa nodded deferentially. "Of course. I just took over this territory, and I wanted to introduce myself. I wasn't sure if you carried other wines and wanted to be sure you knew about our company. If you wish, we could arrange a time for me to come and present a tasting for your staff."

Frankie found no reason to be rude to the young woman, but she felt the need to educate her from a Bubble & Bake point of view. "Ms. Carson, I imagine your wine selection is exquisite. But, as you can tell from looking around our shop, we cater to those who want a homey atmosphere." She spread her arms wide to indicate the shop decor. "I don't carry any other wines but my own, at least not now.  Our customers are happy with what we offer."

Lisa nodded slowly. "Yes, but it's always advisable to diversify your product offerings. In today's business world, it's the savvy thing to do."

Frankie was finished with her explanation and ready to dismiss Lisa, but Carmen leaned toward the woman, perhaps a little closer than necessary to ask, "Do you supply wines to Nearly Napa?  Is that why you're stopping? " She blew out an exaggerated breath. "We've been here five years, you know," as if a statement on their longevity and expertise would suffice for dismissal.

Lisa looked apologetic. "I'm so sorry. I didn't mean to offend your business. It's very charming." She might have croaked a little on the word "charming." "Yes, I distribute to the new wine bar."

Something about the shift in Lisa's tone made Frankie curious. "We're not interested in competing with Nearly Napa. We like who we are. It works very well for us. And, I'm sure Nearly Napa's identity and offerings work well for Rina Madison." Frankie watched closely to gauge Lisa's reaction.

The distributor swallowed hard, and her perfectly made-up face twitched. "Yes, well, I'm sure Ms. Madison will figure things out. She's new to the business world."

A light went on in Frankie's head. "Have you known Rina Madison very long?"

Lisa pursed her lips and her plastic smile slid downward. "We used to work together. She was the Wine on the Vine rep for this area." Lisa whispered, a breathy, petulant whisper.

Carmen arched one eyebrow. "How does one go from being a wine sales rep to a wine business owner, offering high-end wines, no less?" Carmen made 'wine sales rep' sound like garbage collector.

Lisa scowled at Carmen. "Apparently," she enunciated each syllable as separate words. "Rina landed a windfall somewhere. One week she barely has enough sales to pay rent. The next week she announces she's buying a shop to sell high-end wines."

Lisa huffed, remembering the conversation, and had lost her professional persona. "She keeps a very expensive wine inventory. And, she left the company high and dry, which means my territory expanded until they can secure a replacement." She pouted.

Carmen relaxed and pulled a bottle of Spring Fever Riesling from the chiller. She fetched a long-stemmed wine glass from under the bar and poured a glass for Lisa. "Here, try one of our Rieslings. It looks like you've had a long day."

Lisa went through the motions of pre-tasting, then took a sip, followed by a longer drink. "This is quite good for a Wisconsin wine," she pronounced.

Carmen and Frankie exchanged glances, smiling at the comment together.

"Did Rina say how she came by the money to purchase the shop and inventory?" Frankie knew commercial property ran high, especially in a downtown tourist spot. Besides, the building had undergone a remodel from the hair salon it had been, another costly expense.

Lisa took another luxurious sip. "From what I can remember, she said she has an uncle or something who is a vineyard manager in *the* Napa Valley, and that he backed her business." Lisa was impressed with the Napa region, for sure. "But she told someone else at work that her brother was her backer. So, I don't know for sure."

That was the second time today Rina's brother had come up in conversation. Frankie recalled her disappointing beauty salon venture in which Kris conveyed that Rina's brother introduced Rina and Lars. Who was this brother, anyway?

Lisa finished the last swallow of the Riesling, looking naturally pink and acting much more personable. Carmen held the bottle aloft. "Care for another glass?"

Lisa shook her head emphatically. "I'm on the clock and shouldn't have had the first glass. But thank you. I'd like to purchase a bottle to take with me." This time her smile was genuine and matched Carmen's.

By seven o'clock the wine lounge had a few groups of customers settled into the various alcoves, enjoying snacks, imbibing in wine, and holding light conversations. Cherry was making routine trips around the seating areas at a leisurely pace, mostly bringing fresh bottles of wine.

Carmen and Frankie had little to do in the kitchen, just constructing pizzas here and there. Jovie had prepared the charcuterie boards that afternoon and set them in the cooler, having come and gone like a phantom nobody saw. She bragged she could prepare the boards in her sleep.

The shop owners logged around a dozen tastings between five and seven o'clock, not a bad evening for the time of year.

"I think you can probably go home, Carmen. We're only open two more hours, and I just don't think it's going to get any busier. Go enjoy a Friday night at home."

Carmen brightened. "Ryan and I have been talking about going to that new Sandra Bullock movie. Maybe we can catch the late show."

"Great idea. I know. Garrett and I want to see that movie, too. It looks like loads of fun."

Carmen scrolled her phone and held it up to show Frankie the movie times. "Hey, look. The last show is at 9:40 p.m. You and Garrett could meet us out there."

"I don't think we'll be done cleaning up in time to go. Besides, are you forgetting about the bird walk in the morning? Going to have to get up before the worms!" Frankie taunted.

"Suit yourself. What about Sunday night after Fern's farewell ceremony? We could double-date with a movie and ice cream drinks afterwards." Carmen suggested.

Frankie nodded. "That sounds fun. Flying Fish Supperclub has the best grasshoppers. I'll run it past Garrett. He'll be in before we close."

Carmen gathered her belongings to leave just as Pom entered the lounge by way of the kitchen.

"Pom! You're not working tonight. What brings you here?" Carmen gave the woman a hug, hoping to see a glimmer of the old Pom—carefree and smiling. Pom looked worn with worry and lack of sleep.

"I was over at the parents'. Ash and Ivy are going over Fern's financial documents with Mom and Dad before they meet with the estate lawyer next week. It's all just too much for me." Pom wrung her hands in front of her like a woebegone granny.

Carmen smiled encouragingly. "Go keep Frankie company. It's quiet here, so I'm leaving early. I'll feel better knowing you're here to help in case we get a rush."

Frankie waved at Pom. "Nothing to do on a Friday night? I mean, there are so many options."

Pom laughed. "Well, there's always the high school football game. Go, Lakers!" She pumped her fist in the air, making Frankie giggle.

Up until Fern's death, Pom still retained much of her cheerleader youth from high school. Nobody would guess she and Cherry were over 30. Both were fit and still participated in community sports. Now Pom's gait had lost its buoyancy, and she slumped when she sat down, carrying the weight of the world.

Suddenly, Frankie felt an overwhelming desire to hug Pom tightly, like a sister would. She moved out from the bar to envelop her friend in a deep squeeze. "Oh, Pomelo." Almost nobody called Pom by her formal name, but Frankie weighed the moment and felt it fit.

Pom's tears covered Frankie's shoulder. "Tough times, huh?" Frankie whispered. Pom just nodded and continued hugging her. After a long moment, she sat up straighter and wiped both eyes.

"Thanks. I needed that." Pom looked down at the tasting menu, even though she had it memorized. "I hope I'm ready to teach next week. I don't want my students to see me when I'm not myself. Then, there's Ash and Ivy."

Frankie peered at her. "What about Ash and Ivy?"

Pom shrugged. "They're not the same without Fern. It's like they're missing a limb. You know, they were a balanced triangle, but now they have no base to stand on."

Frankie would have accepted Pom's view had it not been for Ash's own words ringing in her ears. He had called the three a tragic trio. Not exactly a balanced triangle. "I'm sure they will have to adjust in their own time, Pom. Have you noticed anything unusual about either of them?" If Frankie hoped to get to the bottom of Fern's death, she had to ask the hard questions eventually.

Pom looked up, searchingly. "What do you mean by *unusual*?"

Frankie didn't want to plant any ideas in Pom's head, so she didn't answer.

"They're both still in shock, like the rest of us, I think. Grief makes people act strangely."

"Who's acting strangely?" Frankie followed up quickly.

"I think Ivy is angry. She and Ash fight a lot about little things. Well, and big things, too, I guess. I heard Ash tell Ivy she should move out of the house and find another nursing job. He said they needed a break from each other."

"How did Ivy handle that?"

"Not good. She was mad, ranting, insisting they should continue their lives as Fern wanted." Pom sniffed and blinked back fresh tears. "I had to get away from them because they're going through Fern's finances, talking about her money, her insurance, how the house is paid off since she died. It was so impersonal. I couldn't stand it."

"That's it!" Frankie's outburst made Pom jolt upright, blinking in surprise. "Sorry, Pom. It's possible that Fern's financial statements might reveal something to help solve her murder. Can I come over after we close and take a look at them?" Frankie walked on thin ice with her request.

"Well, I don't know. I guess, if you think it might help," Pom began. "Should I call Ash and Ivy to ask them?"

Frankie took advantage of her hesitancy. "No. I think I'll just come in with you and Cherry, and we can explain why we want to see the documents. A united front?"

Pom shrugged. "I'll go talk to Cherry and see what she thinks. This is family business, and I don't mean to be rude, but I'm not sure that you should be looking at Fern's finances."

Inwardly, Frankie agreed. She wouldn't like it if an outsider wanted to see her finances either. "I'm not going to scrutinize every detail, just check for something untoward. Maybe you and Cherry can do the looking, and I'll be there in case you find something."

Pom nodded, tentatively. "I'm going to talk to Cherry right now."

The two sisters chatted on the bakery counter side of the shop, while Frankie checked in on her customers, bringing a fresh bottle of wine here and there. A couple of groups purchased wines and called it a night, and no other tasters had arrived. Closing the shop tonight would be a breeze, Frankie thought.

No sooner had the idea of an easy night cemented in Frankie's mind, when the shop door jangled and in walked Rina Madison, looking under the weather. Cherry and Pom shot Frankie matching shocked expressions.

Rina strutted past the sisters and headed straight to the walnut bar, where Frankie stood, uncertain how to greet the woman. Rina's face was flushed, making her bright eyeshadow, lipstick, and fake tan look more pronounced. She was dressed in her wine lounge garb, a tight black dress with pearl jewelry, and knee-high,

black boots with spiked heels. Either the boots or
something else was making her totter unsteadily.

"Hello, Frankie. I'm here for a wine tasting." Each
word came out more slowly than necessary, causing
Frankie to surmise Rina had already tossed back a few.

"Thank you for coming in, Rina. It's nice to see you.
Isn't your shop still open, though?"

"Yesss," she slurred. "But, Daria can handle it. It's a
quiet night for business." She surveyed the Bubble &
Bake lounge. "Just like here," she said brightly.

Frankie bit back a snarky remark and placed a tasting
list and pencil on the bar in front of Rina. "Here you go.
We offer six tasting samples of your choice. You can read
the descriptions and mark the wines you want to taste.
Just let me know when you're ready."

"How much?" Rina spoke from behind the wine list as
she held it up tightly toward her face to read it.

"Tastings are free."

Rina stared for some time at the wine list. A couple
of times she tried to maneuver the pencil, but it didn't
seem to cooperate in her current state. The kind thing to
do would be to offer Rina some coffee or tea, Frankie's
mother would say.

"How about if I bring you a palate cleanser before your
tasting, Rina? I have a refreshing tea blend that works
wonders, or I can make coffee for you." Maybe Peggy
Champagne was rubbing off more than usual.

"I don't see how coffee could be a pla, palate cleanser.
So, I guess I'll have some tea."

Cherry was within earshot and signaled to Frankie she
would retrieve the tea. She brought a large mug a couple
of minutes later and placed it in front of Rina.

"Is there anything the matter, Rina? You seem out of
sorts." Frankie prodded the buxom blonde.

Rina took a sip of tea, smiled serenely, and took another sip. "I don't usually drink, but the past couple of days haven't been the best."

Clueless, Frankie wasn't sure where to lead the conversation next. "Lisa Carson stopped in today." Based on Rina's ugly expression, that topic wasn't the best choice.

"Are you going to start carrying Napa wines so you can drive me out of town?" Rina's bitter accusation raised a few eyebrows.

Frankie shook her head and responded quietly. "No. Bubble & Bake has its own brand. High-end wines are fabulous, of course, but not our cup of tea, if you know what I mean." She hoped the explanation would put Rina at ease. The two businesses could coexist, and there was no need for animosity.

"Well...Leave it to Lisa Carson. That witch would do anything for sales." Clearly, the two women had not worked well together.

The next few minutes passed in silence as Rina drank her tea, relaxing and sobering up somewhat. Frankie cleaned the bar top and put away wine glasses that Cherry brought from the dishwasher.

"I want to say I'm sorry, so very sorry, Frankie." Rina had dropped the comment like a bomb and was about to cry. Frankie was speechless. What was Rina talking about?

Before either woman had a chance to utter another word, the shop door opened, announcing the arrival of Lars Paulsen, who looked ruffled. Taking long strides, he was beside Rina in seconds. Rina was miffed, pouted, and turned her body away from Lars. All was not well in paradise.

Lars placed one hand over Rina's, but she stubbornly pulled it away from him. Meanwhile, Frankie stood behind them at the bar watching the spectacle unfold.

"Rina, I'm so glad I found you. Though I have to say, this is the last place I expected you to be!" Lars placed his arm across the small of her back, presumably to help her off the stool. Rina sat back roughly against his arm, forcing him to remove the offending limb.

"How did you know to look here, Lars, if this is the last place you expected to find her?" Frankie interjected.

Lars looked at Frankie, as if seeing her for the first time that evening. "Oh, well, her car is parked around the corner. That narrowed things down." Lars was churlish.

Frankie couldn't conceive that Rina was fit to drive, even the short distance from shop to shop. Her eyes widened, and she motioned for Pom to come over. "Will you please check to see that Rina's car is legally parked around the corner?" Frankie met Pom halfway and whispered the request in her ear.

"Please go away, Lars. I don't want to talk to you." Rina still faced the opposite direction and began to sniffle.

Frankie handed her a tissue from behind the bar and glared at Lars, who was not easily swayed. Pressing his body against Rina's back, he tried to nuzzle her neck and ear. Frankie thought she might slap him herself if Rina didn't.

"Excuse me, Frankie, but this is a private matter, so if you could give us some space..." he let the comment dangle.

Abruptly, Rina turned to face Lars and spat out a rebuke. "Go away. You're being despicable, and I don't want to be around you."

Lars gripped Rina's arm, unwilling to relent. "If we could just go somewhere else to talk," he began.

By now, one of the groups nearest the bar area
had ceased their own conversation to eavesdrop on
the activity at the bar. Pom and Cherry stood nearby,
mouths agape, staring from Lars to Rina and back again,
dumbfounded.

With the shop's hygge reputation in jeopardy, Frankie
had a choice to make. She scooted out from behind
the bar and placed herself firmly between the unhappy
couple. Lars relinquished his grip, barely controlling his
indignation.

Mustering her best prison guard imitation, she
addressed Lars directly. "I will make sure Rina gets home
safely. Whatever is going on between you is going to have
to wait. Rina needs some sleep, and it wouldn't hurt you
either to sleep on whatever this is, Lars."

It was a stalemate. Neither Lars nor Rina moved nor
spoke. As long as they were immobile, Frankie had to be
part of the standoff, too. Cherry walked behind the bar
and stuck her head into the mix.

"Come with me, Rina. I'm going to take you home."
She shot a warning look at Lars, daring him to defy her.
He didn't, but he remained rooted to the spot at the bar,
looking out the window, until he saw Cherry drive away
with Rina in tow.

Meanwhile, Frankie cleaned up around Lars and
checked out the departing groups, now that closing
time was on the horizon. Frankie painted on her
best customer service smile, exchanged pleasantries,
and assisted guests with wine selections, all the while
pretending that Lars wasn't there. Finally, after Cherry
returned, Lars stalked toward the door and left.

The last group of customers, who were locals, lined
up at the register to check out. One of them was retired
teacher, Ken Medgers. Ken had a summer cottage on
Lake Joy that he shared with his siblings. He enjoyed

taking his turn at the cottage when the tourist season wound down.

"That was Lars Paulsen, wasn't it, at the bar, I mean?" Ken leaned down from his lofty height to ask Frankie the question.

She hesitated. Did she want to go there, to discuss a customer with another customer? Technically, she reasoned, Lars wasn't a customer.  He hadn't been there tonight as a patron, nor did he buy anything.

"Yes, I'm afraid it was." Deep Lakes still cared deeply about its history, including its founders, and the community would be protective toward the descendants of those founders, too.

Ken shook his head. "I thought he'd have grown up by now, but I guess time doesn't change everything."

"What do you mean by that, Mr. Medgers?" Since Ken had been Frankie's teacher, too, she couldn't bring herself to address him by his first name.

Ken smiled intelligently. "Lars was a naughty kid. His parents were beside themselves trying to get him to change his wily ways. He used to shoot rocks at birds and run old people off the sidewalk with his bicycle."

Frankie thought that the bicycle part sounded a lot like typical kid behavior to her.

Ken continued. "When he was in junior high, he broke into Smart's grocery store, stole cigars, cigarettes, and soda pop to share with his gang. Of course, because he was a Paulsen, he got away with it. Nobody wanted to press charges." Ken picked up the wine he had purchased and headed to the door.

After the final customers departed, the three women allowed their pent-up concerns to escape. None of them could believe what they'd witnessed.

"I've never seen Lars act that way. I can't imagine what they were arguing about," Pom said.

"I've never heard the story Mr. Medgers just told you, Frankie. That doesn't sound like the Lars we know." Cherry shook her head in disbelief.

Frankie needed time to process the information, and her attention turned toward viewing Fern's financial information at the Parkers' house.

"Let's finish closing up, so we can go to your house, Cherry. If that's still okay."

Cherry texted Ash and Ivy that they would be there in twenty minutes; then she called her parents to let them know, too. The Parkers didn't need any surprises, Cherry decided, and she couldn't be certain how the next scene would play out.

Garrett stopped in just as Frankie was turning out the shop lights. He looked worn out. Clearly, Fern's case was grating on him. Frankie knew the department enlisted him to help with problem investigations.

Garrett squeezed Frankie and kissed her romantically in one of the alcoves.

"I'm sorry to tell you this, G, but I'm going over to the Parkers from here. I want to take a gander at Fern Mallard's financial statements." Frankie swept her fingers through Garrett's windswept hair as she spoke.

Garrett smiled, a tired smile. "This case has everybody involved muddled up. I keep going over the same information with Lon and Shirley. I was hoping you'd offer me a distraction."

Frankie took him by the hand and led him into the kitchen. "When's the last time you had something to eat? I can make you a flatbread pizza."

Pom and Cherry followed them into the kitchen, gave one last look around the area, and announced they were heading out.

"It's okay if you don't come right away, Frankie. In fact, it will give us a chance to reason with Ivy and Ash, in case there's a problem." Cherry's practicality made sense, and Frankie decided a little time with Garrett wouldn't hurt.

"Okay," she said simply, "I'll see you in a little while."

Garrett pulled Frankie into his embrace and the two danced into the cooler together to retrieve flatbread and fresh ingredients, giggling as they bumped into each other on purpose.

It was well past ten o'clock when Frankie pulled into the Parker driveway. Heavy dew hung in the air where crickets chirped ferociously, making the night feel thick and unforgiving. The front lights were off, and she wondered if everyone had gone to bed, deciding it would be better to tackle finances freshly in the morning.

A whining creak cut through the darkness when Pom opened the front door, startling Frankie.

"Come in," Pom said, switching on the porch light. "We're in the dining room, and my parents have gone to bed, so we need to be quiet."

Frankie followed Pom's footsteps to the large dining table where Ash sat with his head bent over folded arms. Ivy had been crying, Frankie could tell; her red-rimmed eyes were bloodshot, and her face was swollen. Cherry sat stone-faced with documents in front of her, sober as a judge ready to announce a verdict. Pom took a chair next to Cherry and gestured toward an empty chair at Cherry's other side, placing Frankie dangerously close to Ivy.

Frankie waited, holding her breath. The silence was unbearable, and the weight of grief hung heavily about the room. She felt like an intruder stealing something valuable from Fern's family. "I'm so sorry about all of this, the intrusion into your lives, especially since you're all grieving Fern," she blurted out, unable to help herself.

Pom reached over to grab Frankie's hand, and Cherry turned to offer a faint smile.

"We know you're trying to help." Cherry pointed the remark toward Ivy, who must have balked at an outsider reviewing Fern's finances.

"I know everyone must be worn out here, so let's get right to it, shall we?" Frankie suggested, unwilling to prolong the suspense and agony surrounding the scene.

Cherry glanced at the document in front of her, particularly at the items she'd just highlighted in yellow. "You were right to be concerned, Frankie. I've highlighted these payments that were made to Fern." She gestured toward the paper.

"Fern received bonuses for the Townsend's warbler study, the hummingbird study, and the purple martin study. All three bonuses came from Dr. Sarah Fredrich at Riverwood with this notation: honorarium paid for beneficial findings from Stewards of the Heartland Group (SHG)."

The bonuses were substantial and contributed to Fern's ability to pay for the large house in Chicago's suburbia and health care for Ash. But the notation was perplexing.

"What does this group consider to be 'beneficial findings' regarding these studies?" Frankie assumed that Stewards of the Heartland must be an environmental group seeking to help wildlife.

"What are you saying, Frankie? Do you know something we don't know about these studies?" Ivy's voice held an edge of antagonism that made Frankie wonder what she missed when the finances were being discussed.

Aware that she was in the know because of her library research, she explained. "The Townsend's warbler study was unsuccessful, so the protected lands set aside for the warblers were sold to the almond industry for almond groves. The hummingbird study was a disaster in Costa Rica. All but a couple of birds abandoned the nesting grounds. A year later, the land was sold to the coffee industry."

The group exchanged dismayed expressions.

"What about the purple martin study?" Ash asked. "Fern wasn't done with the study. How could there be beneficial findings?"

Frankie couldn't answer the question. "I don't know, unless Fern did preliminary findings. I think Robyn said the study was wrapping up. She and Fern were just recording data from our area to conclude the study. Of course, we don't know what the findings are without Fern's field journal. Ha!" It suddenly dawned on her that if there were preliminary findings, Daryl George should have known or even received a copy of them.

"What is it, Frankie?" Pom asked.

"There's a rotten apple in the barrel, and it might be Dr. Sarah Fredrich. Don't tell anyone I said that." Frankie didn't elaborate. "I know it was difficult for you to share these personal documents. Thank you, Ash and Ivy. This was important."

Cherry and Pom followed Frankie to the front door. In hushed voices they shared the reason Ivy didn't want them poking around.

"Fern paid Ivy a lot of money for taking care of Ash. A lot of money." Pom seemed rattled by the dollar amount. "And with the grant money payments plus the bonuses, Fern was able to buy a huge life insurance policy that paid for the house in full, and then some."

Cherry elbowed Pom to prod her further. She bit her lower lip. "And Ash and Ivy are Fern's beneficiaries."

Frankie expected Ash would certainly be a beneficiary, but now it appeared he and Ivy both had much to gain from Fern's death.

No wonder Ivy seemed to relax when Frankie suggested Dr. Fredrich could be the person behind Fern's death.

"Wait a minute. Grant monies? Why would Fern be getting the grant monies? Those should go to the university." Something ticked in Frankie's brain.

Cherry left and returned with the documents. She started paging through until she found the items on the statement. "Here. These are sorted by types of payments. There are three payments made directly to Fern from Stewards of the Heartland. All are labeled 'study expenses.'"

"I'm not an accountant, but I do keep business books. I should think expenses associated with a study would be submitted to the university or to the wildlife foundation for reimbursement. These are considerably large payments." Frankie admitted she didn't know the protocols associated with the studies. Maybe this was normal, but she doubted it.

"I'll take photos with my phone as soon as Ivy goes to bed and text them to you," Cherry whispered.

Sitting in the driveway, Frankie punched in Abe Arnold's personal number. At least the man was savvy enough to possess a cell phone.

"Abe Arnold. What's up Champagne, besides you?" He sounded sharp, ready for action.

"Abe, can you meet me at Bubble & Bake? The game's afoot." She'd been waiting a few years to say that.

# Chapter 18

*Funny how "question" contains the word "quest" inside it, as though any small question asked is a journey through briars. — Catherynne M. Valente*

Abe was sitting on the back steps when she pulled in the SUV to park. His messenger bag was strapped over one shoulder, and he wore a light nylon jacket to combat the damp air.

"Where's the fire?" he asked before Frankie had both feet out of the vehicle.

"I've been looking at Fern's finances over at the Parker house. I know I'm not going to sleep, and two heads are better than one, so let's go inside, and I'll show you what's going on."

Frankie turned on the kitchen light, promised to return with her laptop and tablet, and scrambled upstairs for the tech equipment.

She found Abe staring in bemusement at her espresso machine. "I thought I'd start some coffee, but I can't make heads or tails out of this contraption."

Frankie laughed uncontrollably. "You sound like somebody's grandfather, Abe. Geesh, do you own anything from this century—besides a cell phone?"

She made a double-shot latte for Abe, opting for a single, instead, for herself. "Here, this should curl your hair." She sat down opposite Abe and logged into her laptop, turning it around after doing so to face the editor.

"Here you go. I'll use the tablet. It's smaller, and you're used to a computer, so this should work for you." Frankie shared the texted document with Abe after downloading it to her documents. She explained the bonus and expense payments Fern received.

"We're going to look up Stewards of the Heartland Group and snoop around their website for starters. Look at their officers or governing board and see what their mission statement says. That kind of stuff."

Frankie picked up her cell phone. "I'm going to make a late night call to Robyn." Frankie pressed Robyn's name from her contact list and waited. The phone rang a few times and went to voicemail, but Frankie intended to keep calling. On the second round, Robyn picked up.

"Hello," her voice crackled on the other end. Robyn looked at the screen. "Frankie? What's going on?"

"I'm sorry to wake you, but this is important. When you get paid for your work on studies, where do those payments come from?"

Robyn needed some time to process. She took a gulp of water to clear the cobwebs. "You mean the studies I did with Fern? The payment for our work comes through the university, of course."

"What about expenses that you incur during the course of the study?" Frankie prodded.

"We have to submit receipts to the university for reimbursement. Just like any other job, I imagine." Robyn said, yawning.

"Have you ever heard of Stewards of the Heartland Group?"

Robyn had. "They're a nonprofit organization that funds numerous studies related to wildlife preservation." Robyn sounded like she was reciting it from a brochure.

"Wow, how do you know that?"

"SHG is well-known at the university. Every time a new study proposal is posted, it's common knowledge that SHG will probably be one of the big sponsors. Why?"

Frankie declined to explain, opting to do more brain picking. "Robyn, if I wanted to talk to Dr. Fredrich, who would I have to go through?"

Robyn snorted. "You have to start with a phone call. That means you need to butter up Marla, who always sounds like she has a cold, or Tori, the shrill-voiced squawker. They are Dr. Fredrich's personal assistants."

Frankie realized that the next business day, Monday, was a whole weekend away. "What if it can't wait until Monday?"

"Got a pen and paper? Here's their personal numbers. Marla and Tori are on call, even on weekends. I hope you have a convincing plan ready if you hope to talk to Dr. Fredrich before Monday."

Frankie's plan was to work on the next plan. "Thanks, Robyn. Goodnight."

The SHG website was professionally crisp and vacant. The mission statement advertised platitudes about being partners for a better world, sharing the planet with our wildlife, yada, yada.

Frankie clicked on the board of directors and found dashing middle-aged men, clean cut, wearing tailored suits. They didn't look like the type to get their hands dirty. She imagined Daryl George would find them pompous and tiresome.

Abe tried to dig up information on L.P. Riggs, the CEO and organization president. "There's no photo of Riggs on the website. I can't find anything on him, not even a background description. Usually these people want the world to know why they decided to start their foundation."

Frankie shrugged. "A lot of these ultra rich people want to keep a low profile. It limits public access. Keep the riff raff out of their business. If SHG has as much money as I think they do, they're probably swatting away a lot of beggars."

"Try searching for Riggs or SHG along with wildlife studies in the search bar, Abe. I'm going to do the same." Frankie determined Abe needed the skills of those with at least a modicum of tech knowledge.

"Got any goodies laying around?" Abe asked. "I could use a snack,"

"Sure, just a minute. Wait, wait, wait. Here's something!" Abe looked up, expecting to see cookies or a donut, but Frankie hadn't moved. She was staring at the tablet in front of her with great interest.

"This is an article from the *Journal of Biodiversity Management.* It discusses SHG's funding of birds in forested regions and specifically mentions Costa Rica. They interviewed one of the directors, Vincent Ponti." Frankie buried her head in her hands, willing her memory to access a file. "I know that name. I know that name. Why do I know that name?"

Abe started tapping the keyboard. "Vincent Ponti. Director of Field Studies at SHG. You already knew that. No college degree listed, but this says he's a graduate from UW-Madison."

Frankie bounded to Abe's side. "Let me see that. No photo. Too bad. But, look. He graduated the year before I did. Maybe our paths crossed somewhere."

Abe chuckled skeptically. "Sure, sure. How many environmental science classes did you take with your liberal arts major?"

Frankie kicked his shin. "Not funny, Abe. My major was communications, and I had to take 12 credits in science, so there. But, you're right. Most of my time was spent in the Mass Comm building, working on the college newspaper and at the local radio station." The memory triggered something, but she couldn't grasp what it was.

"I think that's enough for now. Here's the plan. Tomorrow, I want you to call Dr. Fredrich and pretend you're Vincent Ponti or someone on SHG's board of directors." She shared Robyn's information about the personal assistants. "I want you on speakerphone, so I can listen in. We're going fishing for a trophy catch tomorrow."

"I still don't understand why you can't make the phone call, Frankie," Abe grumbled, lacking confidence in his ability to speak egghead lingo. "And you're sure that Marla or Tori will answer the phone at this ungodly hour?"

It had been a very short night for both of them. Abe had agreed to meet Frankie at five o'clock at the newspaper office, away from the Bubble & Bake crew, and before Frankie had to meet Carmen at Spurgeon Park for the morning bird walk.

"Because I'm a woman, and all the directors at SHG are men. Besides, there's a chance Dr. Fredrich will recognize my voice. We met at Fern's visitation." Frankie

handed Abe a bakery bag filled with pumpkin scones and
cranberry chocolate cookies.

Whether or not Marla or Tori would answer their
phones at 5 a.m. was another matter. The planned
conversation with Dr. Fredrich couldn't happen without
them; they had the necessary access to the doctor.

Frankie's knowledge about the dedication of personal
assistants was gleaned from the film *The Devil Wears
Prada*. "I'm sure any dedicated assistant will answer a
call no matter what time it is. If you met Dr. Fredrich,
you'd know she'd expect her assistants to answer. She's a
demanding woman."

The two discussed the plan at length one more time.
Frankie agreed to place the call using her cell phone,
since she knew how to use the speaker feature, and Abe
did not. She insisted Abe perform vocal exercises and
coached him until he was able to present himself as
self-absorbed and outraged.

Sometime during the night, Frankie had decided his
identity would not be Vincent Ponti, as Dr. Fredrich
might be accustomed to doing business with him.
Instead, he would be Morris Simon, a director who
attended Michigan State for a degree in climate science.
Frankie hoped Dr. Sarah hadn't had the pleasure.

Abe reached inside the waxed bag and pulled out a
scone.

"Uhn ah, no eating until you finish this call," Frankie
snatched the scone and bag away and set it on
Rance Musgrove's desk. Unlike Abe's hit-by-a-hurricane
desktop, Rance's was neat as a pin.

The editor took several deep breaths and cracked his
knuckles. "Okay Champagne; let's get this over with."

Frankie pressed Marla's number first, a 50-50 chance
she'd be the one on call. The call went straight to

voicemail. While the prompt to leave a message ran, Abe gave Frankie a look of panic.

"What do I do now? Leave a message?"

Frankie shook her head emphatically and hit the end call button. "We'll try Tori. If she doesn't pick up, leave a message, and make it urgent and upset."

Abe blew out a stream of air, took another deep breath, and waited for the next call.

Tori picked up quickly but sounded groggy, exactly what the two were hoping for.

"Hello, this is Tori Wells. Can I help you?"

"Tori, I'm glad you picked up. I need to speak with Dr. Fredrich immediately," Abe sounded like Clark Gable on steroids.

"Who is this, please?" Tori was awake enough for the automatic routine question to kick in.

"Dr. Morris Simon from SHG. This is urgent business, Miss." The patronizing term "Miss" had been part of the rehearsed repertoire, although it made Frankie cringe.

"Did you say SHG? Which study are you calling about, Sir?" Tori's alertness was accelerating. Time for Abe to pick up the intensity.

"I'd rather not say, Tori. I prefer to discuss that with Dr. Fredrich. This can't wait." Abe took a breath, then softened his tone. "Look, I appreciate your professionalism, Miss Wells, and I'm sure you're a huge asset to Dr. Fredrich, but I'm in a bind here, and I need your help. Can you kindly hook me up with her?"

Frankie face-planted at Abe's words, although she was certain he didn't know there was more than one method of "hooking up" in this century. Abe turned away from her disapproving look. He was on a roll now and didn't need a distraction.

Tori giggled, making Frankie relax. "Okay, Mr. Morris or Dr. Morris. I'm going to connect you with Dr.

Fredrich, but you have to tell me the subject of the call, or I'm likely going to lose my job."

"Very well. The purple martin study." Abe didn't correct Tori's slip of the tongue about his name, and he hoped Dr. Fredrich would be off her game at the early hour, too.

"Hold please." The two held their breath as the call went silent.

"This is Dr. Fredrich, Dr. Morris. Who the hell are you anyway?"

"Dr. Fredrich. This is Dr. Simon. Dr. Morris Simon. I'm a director at SHG. I know we haven't had the pleasure, and frankly, I don't have time for chitchat this morning. I need to know the status of the purple martin study. This is a mess!" Abe managed to roll from polite to fuming without interruption.

Dr. Fredrich tapped her knuckles on the desk in her home office. "Yes, it certainly is a mess. Nobody could have predicted Dr. Mallard's untimely death. Let me assure you that the study's findings will be presented to the right people." Her conciliatory tone suggested Dr. Fredrich was practiced at ensuring others.

Frankie raised her hands in the air as if conducting an orchestra. Now was not the time for Abe to lower the temperature.

"I'm afraid that's not good enough, Doctor. My people want more specifics. I have to talk to them this morning!" Abe slapped his hand on the desk to punctuate the problem.

"Why isn't Vincent handling this? I've always dealt with Vincent where studies are concerned." Her question was warranted, and Abe needed to turn in a convincing performance.

He spoke scathingly. "Vincent is doing damage control with our people. Believe me, I didn't want this assignment. I'm supposed to be playing golf today." Abe added a couple of swear words in the mix for color.

"Just exactly what kind of reassurance does Berry Fresh want?" Dr. Fredrich's tinny pitch showed her irritation.

Frankie shrugged, made a rolling motion with her hands for Abe to keep her talking. Meanwhile, she wrote down 'Berry Fresh,' likely the name of the company connected to the study.

"As I said, we're wondering how the study will proceed. What's the protocol, Doctor?" Abe's irritation matched Dr. Fredrich's.

The long pause on the other end of the call made Abe wonder if Dr. Fredrich had disconnected, but finally the heavy sigh of exasperation gushed from the speaker. "There is going to be a delay, so your people are going to have to be patient. I have a replacement in mind for Dr. Mallard, but she's not prepared to come aboard for another few months." Each word sounded like the prick of a needle.

Frankie passed Abe a note with " name of replacement" written on it. She discovered it was impossible for her to sit quietly as a bystander during their charade. She jabbed the note with her finger while Dr. Fredrich spoke.

"And just who might this replacement be? Why can't she come aboard for months? You really expect my clients to just wait around?" The outrage in his voice had a dark silkiness to it. Frankie was impressed.

Apparently, Abe hit a nerve with the doctor. "Naomi Travers has done some marvelous work on previous studies and is on the same page as SHG and its clients. She will have her PhD in December and will be ready to take the lead in this study." She paused for emphasis.

"And in many studies to come. Worth waiting for, don't you think, Doctor?"

Abe couldn't think of anything to add or ask. His mind was already stewing with the information Dr. Fredrich had just spilled. Still, he wanted his deception to end with a satisfying conclusion. "Well, you've given me something to offer my client at least. I'll do my best to smooth things over. Thank you for your time. Goodbye."

Frankie didn't give Dr. Fredrich a chance to say more. It was past time to cut the call. Visions of imaginary agents in dark vans listening in, ready to pounce on Frankie and Abe, knocked in her mind. Maybe Tori had been tracing the phone call the whole time. Didn't professionals only need a minute to locate a cell tower?

She and Abe sat back in their chairs, as nervous laughter filled the office. "That was remarkable, Abe!" Frankie congratulated the editor, who was wiping sweat from his forehead and face.

"Don't tell me that was the first time you ever staged a phone call!" Frankie was dumbfounded.

"Yes, first time. I don't operate that way, Frankie. I find sources to do the shifty stuff. Then, they call me with the information they uncover."

"I can't believe it, Abe. When you're in the investigating biz, you have to get your hands dirty once in a while." Frankie took pride in using deception at times, if it meant she could get to the bottom of a crime. Still, she understood that deception was a double-edged sword, and she felt suddenly squeamish.

"Well, it's too late to cork that bottle now," Abe said. "It actually was exhilarating, making that call, discovering secrets firsthand."

Frankie agreed. "More importantly, we have to call the police and share everything we just heard with them. I recorded the call, but I don't think it can be used as evidence because it was done without Dr. Fredrich's knowledge. But it cements the details in place."

'Wait a second. Can that recorded call be used against me? I don't need fraud charges or a lawsuit on my hands, Champagne!" Abe protested.

"Let's say we came by it, anonymously?" Frankie hadn't figured out the details to keep them out of trouble just yet. She hoped their gift to the police would help the investigation, and they could remain anonymous sources.

She texted Alonzo and Shirley and called Garrett. They would meet at Abe's office as soon as they could get there. By 5:40, everyone was in place, including Officer Pflug, whose riveted stare held hostility for the pair.

"This better be good, Frankie. I haven't even had my morning joe," Alonzo, however, looked fresh-faced. Garrett and Shirley had the good sense of carrying in travel mugs of brew. They all eyeballed Abe's bakery bag, so Frankie passed it around to appease them.

Bravely, Frankie told them about the recorded phone call and played the exchange between Abe, as Dr. Simon, and Dr. Fredrich, as the scheming swindler.

Pflug rose immediately after the call ended. "I've heard enough. I'll be heading into the office from here. Might I suggest the rest of you join me?" He looked pointedly at Alonzo and Shirley.

Then he jabbed his finger toward Abe and Frankie. "Not you two. No press allowed." Pflug was making Frankie feel like a bug about to be squashed again. His gaze locked onto Garrett, who looked with amusement at the officer. "I don't think you need to come in either.

We'll call you if we get a dead body." Pflug harrumphed loudly and slammed the door on his way out.

Alonzo and Shirley followed the professional courtesy of not commenting.

"I'd like to hear the call again. I want to double-check my notes." Shirley, who was part of the Abe Arnold generation, preferred to rely on written notes and verification of the facts. Alonzo nodded his agreement. It couldn't hurt to hear it again for the sake of processing the details.

"Well, let me just say: great work, you two." Shirley applauded their undercover schtick.

Alonzo sighed. "I don't like the way you came by this information. You know it probably can't be used in court. And you took a big risk. If Dr. Fredrich would have called you out, this whole thing could blow up our case." He shook his finger at both of them but mostly stared at Frankie.

She was used to being scolded by Lon, so she filed it away as more of the same, ready to move into the next phase of solving Fern's death. "What's next? Do you think this points to Naomi Travers? What about Dr. Fredrich? Could she have been part of the plot to kill Fern?" Her head was spinning with the new information, and she needed to go home to visualize it.

Lon interrupted her questions. "What's next is for us to go to work. We need to place this into the narrative of our investigation and proceed according to the law, Francine Champagne." Lon emphasized the word *law* and shoved his hat on his head. Then he grabbed the bakery bag and walked to the door.

"Shirley, I assume I'll see you shortly. Don't be long. There's work to do." The sheriff knew full well that Shirley was likely to share the direction of the investigation, and his speech was meant as a warning to keep it brief and routine.

To everyone's surprise, Frankie announced she was leaving as well. "I'm in a rush this morning. I'm meeting Carmen at Spurgeon Park, where Tasha is leading an honorary bird walk in Fern's name."

"Are you going back to the shop first? I'll tag along and pick up more baked goods for the office. Looks like it could be a long day," Shirley spoke in an ordinary manner, but Frankie suspected she had an ulterior motive.

Garrett looked at Abe. "I might as well go fishing. What are you going to do, Abe?"

The editor scratched his head. "Why don't we go to Dixie's for breakfast, Coroner? I feel like celebrating my first undercover job. The fish were biting earlier, and I think I snagged a trophy."

Frankie took the steps two at a time, up to her apartment deck. Shirley was directly behind her. Frankie had asked her to follow, since she had just enough time to add the morning's evidence to the crime board in her bedroom.

She retrieved the board and carried it out to the kitchen breakfast bar, where Shirley waited. The two studied it together, as Frankie added notes about Dr. Fredrich, Stewards of the Heartland, and Naomi Travers. The name Vincent Ponti still itched her brain matter.

"Okay, Shirley. Now you know what I know. So, how about a trade?"

"This is good data, Ace. After we talked last, I connected with Cherry, and she gave me the information you decoded from Fern's pages. There's still some puzzles there, though."

Shirley took a file folder from her briefcase. "If I were Naomi Travers, I'd be securing representation. Oh, wait a minute. I think she already has."

Shirley conveyed that Naomi's aunt and uncle are the prestigious Tate and Travers law firm out of Chicago. "Get this. They represented the almond growers in the acquisition of the protected lands in the Townsend's warbler project. The firm was also part of the legal team in the thick-billed parrot study."

"I smell a rat," Frankie speculated, as she added to her board. "I'm assuming you're going to see if they are connected to Berry Fresh, the company mentioned in the phone call."

Shirley nodded. "We need to find out just what kind of business Berry Fresh is and if they're after any of the purple martin lands."

"What about the Costa Rican coffee growers? " Frankie wondered. "I know it's outside the U.S., but could a U.S. law firm be involved somehow?"

"Pflug is looking into that. International matters are his territory."

Frankie raised an eyebrow. Donovan Pflug was still a man of mystery. For now she switched topics back to the case before them.

"I still don't understand if or why Fern would be part of fixing studies, and why is a group named 'Stewards of the Heartland with a mission to preserve wildlife' involved?" It appeared SHG was the money behind the martin study, and likely, other studies. It distressed and perturbed Frankie.

"Maybe Fern got in over her head. She needed the money to take care of her brother and pay her cousin. It might have started off as a one time thing, and then the company used it against her. Maybe threatened her in some way." Shirley theorized. "It's probably what got her killed."

Frankie thrummed her fingers on the counter top, back and forth, back and forth. Something was brewing in her mind, but the ideas were floating around elusively. She captured one thought.

"Fern had feathers stuffed in her mouth, Shirley. That's a personal attack. If she was killed because someone wanted her out of the way or because she knew who was behind the fixed studies, wouldn't they just send a hit man? SHG and the university both have the money to hire one."

Shirley laughed. "You watch too many crime shows. But, you could be right. However, your board says right there that Naomi had a grudge against Fern. She wouldn't hire Naomi to be an assistant on any more studies."

Frankie took up the narrative. "And without the studies, Naomi couldn't get her piece of the pie. I mean, supposing she's in on the corporate land takeovers with her aunt and uncle's law firm. Still, that doesn't explain SHG as a player. Why pretend you're an environmental steward if you're not?"

"You heard it on the phone call. Obviously, SHG is partnering with at least one big corporation to acquire land currently under protection by federal wildlife agencies. Fern's financials show a clear connection between SHG and the other foiled studies." Shirley was almost salivating. "We just need to get concrete evidence from the university or from the corporations involved. Crap."

"What is it, Shirley?"

"This is going to end up turned over to the feds. I'll bet my pension on it, Frankie. We might get to solve the murder if we hurry, but the feds are going to swoop in like vultures and make off with all our files." Shirley sounded as disgusted with federal law enforcement as Daryl George did with the federal bigwigs he called "suits."

Frankie's phone sounded off in her pocket, showing Daryl as the caller. Maybe Frankie was on the same wavelength as the wildlife foundation chief. She answered with a small laugh. "Good morning. You just crossed my mind. I was talking with a friend about federal authorities."

Daryl grunted before getting down to business. "Glad you're up early. When I got into DC yesterday, I did some checking on the Arizona parrot study. The powers-that-be tell me the mountain land slated for possible parrot habitat was subdivided into parcels for livestock ranchers."

"Isn't it difficult to have cattle running around mountain areas? When I picture cattle ranches, I think of nice flat grasslands." Frankie was skeptical.

"Well, modern ranching tactics include using drones to move the cattle. The rancher can manage his herd from the bottom of the mountain," Daryl instructed.

Frankie groaned. "Another win for industry. Another loss for wildlife. Thank you, Naomi Travers, and Dr. Moody, whomever you are."

"Yep, and there's more. I hope you're sitting down." Daryl paused for effect. "Your Dr. Moody on the parrot study is Dr. Sarah Anya Moody, which is the maiden name of Dr. Sarah Fredrich. She uses that name in all of her published works."

Frankie's grin couldn't be contained. "You have no idea how helpful this is. I owe you big time. Thank you."

Frankie added to her board and Shirley's notebook. Before parting ways, they went downstairs to the Bubble

& Bake kitchen, where Frankie loaded a box with assorted pastries, including a few butterhorns.

"Good luck today," Frankie chirped.

"You too, Ace. I'm sure you've got a plan. Just do me a favor. If you come up with something new, call right away.  Don't try to confront a killer by yourself."

Tess had witnessed the exchange from her station, where she was slathering icing on cinnamon rolls destined for the gathering of birders later that morning. "I hope you're going to listen to that wise woman, Boss." Tess's usual cheerful expression had been replaced with a warning look.

# Chapter 19

*Truth has to be given in riddles. People can't take truth if it comes charging at them like a bull. The bull is always killed. You have to give people the truth in a riddle, hide it so they go looking for it and find it piece by piece; that way they learn to live with it.* — *Chaim Potok*

Frankie could see a huge fray unfolding near the Spurgeon Park lot before she even drove in. She selected a spot on the perimeter, making for an easy exit if she chose not to stay.

Two groups of people appeared to be in a face-off. She recognized Tasha Rivers in the forefront, trying to defuse the situation, whatever the situation might be. Many other members of the bird club were standing near Tasha, also trying to talk to the other side. Oddly, the other group appeared to be led by Dawn, the attention-seeking newcomer in the bird club. She carried a sign that proclaimed "Fern Mallad = bird killer,", as did a few others in the group.

Carmen stood on the sidelines, waving Frankie over. She bypassed the gaggle of noisy sign carriers, some of whom were honking bike horns, literally sounding like geese.

"What did I miss?" Frankie shouted above the din.

Carmen pulled her further away from the crowd, back toward the parking lot.

"This is nuts, Frankie. The protestors are claiming Fern killed the baby martins on purpose. They've been circulating this video—I found it online." Carmen handed her cell to Frankie. The video was a short clip showing someone who could be Fern or a million other people (the face wasn't visible), releasing baby martins from a house that might have been located anywhere on Earth. Unable to fly, the birds immediately fell to the ground

Frankie shook her head. "Who organized this fiasco?"

Carmen pointed at Dawn. "The birders are saying she contacted everyone in the club who planned to come for the walk today, except for Tasha. Apparently, she was trying to change their minds about doing the walk in Fern's honor."

The throng of protestors amounted to around thirty people, but they made a lot of noise. Frankie counted around thirty more birders there for the walk, not including herself and Carmen. They, along with several others, chose to stand apart, watching cautiously.

"Has anyone called the police? Someone needs to before this gets out of hand." Frankie pulled her phone out, but Carmen stopped her.

"They should be here any minute. Tasha's husband called." Carmen suddenly looked around the crowd and panicked.

"Where's Tia? I told her to stay put over there on that bench." The bench was vacant.

Frankie and Carmen each looped around one of the two groups looking for Tia, who shouldn't be difficult to

spot since she dressed in bright clothes and walked with
two canes.

Frankie spotted her dangerously close to the cluster
of protestors. One of them, a man Frankie had seen
volunteering at Fall Migration Days, was wildly waving a
sign around depicting cartoon angry birds dive-bombing
humans.

Before she could reach Tia, the woman stumbled over
the man, tripped him with one of the canes, then landed
on top of him. The man was too dumbstruck to move
as he lay beneath a woman spewing a stream of Spanish
and swatting him over and over again with her sun hat,
a giant wide-brimmed straw accessory with oversized
bright flowers sashaying around the brim. Tia's canes lay
abandoned nearby.

The accident drew attention away from the shouting
match between a couple of protestors and a couple
of birders. One protestor dropped her air horn and
helped Frankie pull Tia Pepita off the man. The woman
retrieved Tia's canes and, together, they escorted her to
a nearby park bench.

"Thanks so much for your help," Frankie hoped this
was the beginning of a truce between the groups.
It seemed silly to Frankie. They were on the same
side when it came to protecting bird populations. She
wondered where the video clip came from and how it
came to Dawn's attention.

"Are you okay, Tia?" Frankie looked the woman over,
saw scrapes on her hands from where she had landed in
the dirt. "Can you move your arms and legs?"

Carmen scurried over to the bench. "What happened?
People said someone fell. Was it you, Tia?"

Naturally, the police arrived about the same time.
Officer Green stood between the two groups, while one

of the summer recruits, Officer Haley, came over to check on Tia. She opened a medical trauma kit.

"I'm going to check your blood pressure. What is your name?"

"Pepita Martinez." Tia fanned herself with her hat until Carmen tugged it away so the officer could do her job. Tia fumed. "Don't worry about me. You should check on the man I fell on. He probably got hurt worse."

The officer laughed, checked Tia's extremities, pronounced her blood pressure to be a bit elevated, likely from the fall, and left her in Carmen's and Frankie's capable hands.

"Here comes Ivy. Did you see Pom or Cherry in the birding group? This demonstration is going to upset them." Resentment was rising in Frankie at the thoughtless reaction from fellow birders. Did they even check their facts before taking sides?

"I'm glad to see you, Frankie. I was hoping to apologize for being upset with you last night, but this situation here is making me upset all over again. Do these protestors know anything about Fern?" Ivy was red-faced, as she scanned the crowd and the parking lot.

"Are you looking for Pom and Cherry? I can't imagine how you all must feel about this situation." Frankie scanned the area to look for the sisters, too.

Ivy blushed deeply. "They're supposed to be here, but I'm not sure where they are. I was supposed to meet Lars here."

Frankie looked at her phone. It was just past seven o'clock. The bird walk was being delayed indefinitely with the ongoing conflict. Officer Green was trying to mediate between the two sides. She recalled that Lars had a haircut scheduled downtown and wondered if he stood up Ivy intentionally. Should she say something?

"I heard Lars was quite a handful when he was a kid," Frankie began.

Ivy's brows knitted in confusion, as she wondered what Frankie's angle was. "He was; that's true. He got into some trouble here and there, but then we adopted him into our secret club. That was Fern's idea. She felt sorry for Lars. She always chose to see the best in everyone."

Frankie felt new respect for Fern, but at the same time she was bothered by the payments Fern received from grant donors.

"Why would she feel sorry for Lars?" Frankie found it difficult to have sympathy for a spoiled kid from a wealthy family.

Ivy raised her chin stiffly. "He had the legacy of two founding families to live up to. And as the only male to carry on those traditions, so much was expected from him. Around us, he could just be the neighbor boy." Ivy smiled in memory of those days.

"Two founding families?" Frankie was only aware of the Paulsens, one of the original founders of Deep Lakes.

Ivy nodded. "Lars's grandmother was Fiona Riggs, a foremost environmentalist in Minnesota."

A 100-watt light bulb switched on. "Riggs?" She hoped Ivy would elaborate.

"Yes, that's right. And in the end, Lars did both families proud. He founded two nonprofits. The Scandinavian Founding Fathers of Wisconsin and Stewards of the Heartland."

There it was. Lars was the common denominator. He must be the mysterious CEO L.P. Riggs; no pictures, no information about him anywhere on the SHG site. "Did Fern know this?"

Ivy wrinkled her brow once more, unsure if Frankie was talking to her or to a phantom. "Of course Fern knew. She bragged that Lars's organization sponsored some of her work."

Frankie pulled the coded journal pages from her pack and motioned for Carmen to join the conversation.

"Can you two look at these drawings in Fern's journal, and tell me what you think they could mean?"

Frankie pointed at the last entry in the journal. "What do you make of this bee drawing? Ivy, do you think the bee wearing the crown is a cryptic reference to Lars?" Cherry and Pom had shared that Lars's symbol in the Sensational Six was a crown.

Ivy shrugged. "It's hard to tell. I don't understand the bee drawing. I can't imagine how the bees would be related to Fern's work."

Carmen studied the drawing of the two bees, one crowned, one not, arrows connecting the two bees. "I think the crowned bee is the queen. This bee connected to her is a drone. Queens can't survive without drones. They live to serve the queen. I remember this from working with Carlos on his middle school project about bee hives." She shrugged at Frankie's surprised expression.

"Okay, genius. What about the flying robin followed by the words 'NO NO' and double exclamation points?" Whatever the flying robin and bees meant to Fern, it clearly disturbed her.

Carmen stared hard at the entry. "And none of you think it has to do with her assistant, Robyn?"

Ivy and Frankie shook their heads. "She cleared Robyn earlier in the journal as someone she trusted. But maybe this entry means that Robyn's in danger." Ivy wanted to be helpful.

Frankie added her two cents. "And Fern wasn't part of a robin study, so it doesn't seem to refer to birds."

Ivy smiled, as another memory surfaced. "Fern used to say we would never have to worry about robins. They were as common as sparrows, tough and resilient. That's why Lars always played the robin when we played bird tag. That, and because it was the only bird he could ever remember." Ivy laughed quietly.

Frankie went pale, as clues began to click into place. "The Ent Circle."

She grabbed Carmen's hand and yanked her aside.

"Come with me, Carmen. We need to go check on something. I'll explain in the car."

Carmen shook Frankie's hand away. "We can't leave Tia here. She has to come with us."

Carmen lifted Tia off the bench, where she was quietly sipping water from the bottle Officer Haley had given her, watching the two groups interact as if in a movie.

"Come on, Tia, let's get you out of the sun." Carmen handed her one cane and took her by the arm. Frankie picked up the other cane, and the three walked to Frankie's SUV, leaving Ivy confused as ever.

The two deposited Tia in the back seat and set her canes on the floor out of the way.

"Could you please drive, Carmen? I need to text Lon, Shirley, and Garrett." After her first sleuthing escapade, Frankie created a text group of the three to share important news.

"If you tell me where we're going, I'd be happy to drive. After you text them, would you mind filling me in? You just figured out who killed Fern, didn't you?" Carmen tensed, and a combination of excitement and fear gripped her.

"We're going to Pine Avenue Park. The Sensational Six used to play there in a grove of trees they called the Ent Circle. That's where we found Fern's journal. I think Fern might have hidden something else there, too, and we missed it the first time." Frankie sent a text alerting the officers to come to the park.

Lars finally arrived at Spurgeon Park, fresh from his haircut, and found Ivy still hanging outside the two groups. Most of the protestors had scattered. Some had rejoined the bird walk group, convinced the video clip was either doctored or wasn't Fern.

Officer Green had escorted Dawn to his squad car to cool off after she poked him with the sign she carried.

It wasn't clear if the bird walk was still going to take place, but Ivy had stopped paying attention, clearly distracted by her thoughts and the discussion she just finished with Frankie and Carmen. It appeared Frankie had drawn some important conclusion about Fern's journal, and somehow it was connected to something Ivy had said.

"Hi, Ivy. Sorry I'm late. It's nice you waited for me." Lars surveyed the bird club walkers, who were debating something, and pondered why they hadn't already started down the trail. "Is the walk over already?"

Ivy punched Lars in the shoulder. How could he be so oblivious, she wondered.

"Seriously, where's Cherry and Pom? On my way out here, I passed Frankie Champagne going the other direction like she was heading to a fire. Isn't she in the bird club?"

Chasing thoughts around her head, Ivy stared vacantly at Lars. "I haven't seen Cherry or Pom. I don't know where Frankie and Carmen went, maybe to take Tia home." Ivy stopped herself, returning to the conversation she just had. "No, Frankie said the Ent Circle."

In a flash, Lars was flying across the parking lot, Ivy hot on his trail. She started her car and followed Lars's black truck. Ivy had not worked out the puzzle but somehow knew the answer must be waiting at the Ent Circle, and Lars was somehow involved. She shivered. Could Lars have hurt Fern?

Frankie opened the back passenger door to retrieve Tia Pepita's walking canes. "Stay here, Tia. Carmen and I need to check something out, and we need to borrow your canes to do it."

Nobody was at Pine Avenue Park, so Carmen parked in the first space nearest the brick path that led to the tree grove. Frankie had hoped to see an official Whitman County squad there when they arrived, or at the very least, Garrett's car. She was anxious to share her latest hunch about Lars Paulsen.

Leading the way, the two veered off into the trees, when the brick path ended. "This way, I'm pretty sure."

She retraced the steps Pom and Cherry had taken among the scattered stumps and stones. Soon, the copse of lindens emerged, covered by the green vining curtain. Frankie parted the vines and motioned Carmen inside the large circle.

"Wow, what a fun spot for kids to play. It really is enchanting!" Carmen stood, looking upward at the tall trees and tiny piece of sky that served as a ceiling.

Frankie handed one of Tia's canes to Carmen. "This is Penny Loafer, the tree where we found Fern's journal. You can see it's hollow. Jab the cane into it, and see if anything else is hidden there."

Meanwhile, Frankie looked at the other trees for hollow spots, finding one next to the tree known as Uncle Wart. She shoved the cane upward, creating a shower of small pine branches, the perfect cushion for the object that fell out next. It was a drone.

"Ha, found it!" Frankie exclaimed.

Carmen turned away from the linden and skipped to her side. "A drone? I don't get it."

Frankie turned the drone over to examine its bottom enclosure. "Ha again! This is made by Flying Robin."

"Which is what, exactly?" Carmen's impatience was showing.

"A drone company, I imagine. The one Fern coded in her journal. It was something Daryl George said." Frankie paused to gather her thoughts and calm her thudding heart. "One of the bird studies ended with selling the protected lands to the cattle industry. But the land was in the mountains, where it would be hard to manage cattle. Daryl said the ranchers would use drones to move the herds around. So, I thought, if drones could be used to move cattle, why not birds?"

"And maybe drones were used to drive away the birds from the protected areas in the wayward studies," Carmen ventured.

"Exactly. But I don't know how the Flying Robin manufacturer is connected to the study sponsors. Somehow, it involves Lars. I just know it does."

"Do you think Lars killed Fern?"

Carmen's words were barely uttered, when a ruckus ensued with vines being torn apart, exposing Lars Paulsen holding a pistol.

"Drop the canes on the ground, ladies." Lars looked pleased with himself. "Well, do you, Frankie? Do you think I killed Fern?" Lars stared at the drone Frankie held.

Where in the world were Lon or Shirley or Garrett? Frankie's cell was in her front pocket, but she hadn't heard a notification sound and wondered if she even had a signal in the wooded circle. Wisely, Carmen began to inch away from her. It would be harder for Lars to keep track of both women if they could physically separate.

Frankie conjured a law enforcement showdown from a recent movie. She remembered the officer under threat kept the gunman talking as she waited for reinforcements.

"You came cross-country to Blackbird Pond that day, on an ATV, didn't you?" She began with the easy assumption.

Lars only smiled, waiting, just like the fat cat Frankie saw perched under her bird feeder.

She spoke quietly, carefully, soothingly. "You just wanted to talk to Fern, right?"

Lars threw his head back and laughed. "Wrong. I was already at the pond when Fern arrived. She found me at the martin house."

Frankie gasped. "You let the baby birds out. You killed them all." Her voice was a hoarse whisper, but her pulse drummed a loud roar in her ears.

Lars smiled. "Bingo."

"You wanted to convince Fern to throw the study. Somebody was getting a payout. Somebody wanted the land, just like in the other studies." She was trying to work through her own discoveries, still sorting the pieces of information.

"But, SHG, your company, was already paying Fern bonuses. Why?" Frankie still hoped Fern would be exonerated.

"It was easy to convince Fern that she was being rewarded for doing the best work she could do under unusual circumstances. SHG paid her for her expertise.

I guaranteed Fern we would protect her unblemished reputation." Lars relished in his trickery.

Frankie pressed on. "And Fern's expenses were reimbursed by SHG. Why was that?"

Lars gestured with the pistol, making the two women squirm. "Oh, that. I wrote those checks personally as advances. I told Fern I didn't want her to accumulate expenses, knowing she would be strapped financially in taking care of her brother." He paused, and his voice became bitter. "Of course, I expected her to go along with what I wanted in exchange. She owed me for my support."

Understanding was dawning. "But she wouldn't go along. She wouldn't fake information on any studies. Once she found the drone, she knew that you were behind the sabotage in the other studies."

Lars paused again, waiting for Frankie to elaborate.

"Flying Robin. Your drone company, right? The same drone company that disrupted the hummingbirds? I'm guessing the martins on Buena Vista were also evacuated by your drones."

Lars wanted to applaud Frankie's revelations, but the pistol prevented it. Instead he simply grinned. "Very good, Frankie. One of our drones crashed at Buena Vista, and I suspected Fern had found it, but I didn't know where she'd hidden it. Until Ivy said you were coming to the Ent Circle."

"It's strange. I thought killing off the babies on Blackbird Pond might convince Fern to go along with changing the findings. She hated seeing her feathered friends die needlessly. But, she refused to see things my way."

Frankie wanted to vomit. "I hope she fought back at least. So you must have Fern's field journal."

Lars nodded. "I didn't want her findings published. It would be best for everyone if the study was buried. And I thought there might be incriminating information in it about me."

Carmen had managed to move a few feet away from Frankie by this time, but she needed a few more feet to be in Lars's blind spot. A loud snap under her feet alerted him, and he waved the pistol at Carmen. "No, no. Where do you think you're going? Get back over there by Frankie."

Carmen purposely stumbled over a pretend tree root and lunged directly into Lars's leg, throwing him off balance. The pistol shot wildly then fell to the ground, just as Ivy charged into the Ent Circle, wielding her walking stick. She cracked Lars in the back, while Carmen leaned her weight on one of Lars's arms, hooked her arm around his neck, and placed her bent knee meaningfully between his legs. Carmen had learned a few wrestling moves from her sons.

Frankie retrieved the pistol, holding it gingerly.

"It's good to see you, Ivy. Thanks for coming." Frankie smiled, and Ivy smiled back, but she stayed poised over Lars with the walking stick, just in case.

The report from the pistol led Lon, Shirley, and Garrett racing to the Ent Circle. Lon and Shirley had guns drawn as they entered.

"Okay. You can get up, Carmen. We've got him." Lon spoke with serious calm.

Shirley took Ivy by the arm and led her several feet away, then reached her hand out to Carmen to help her get off the resentful Lars. Alonzo kept the gun trained on Lars, as Shirley cuffed him and read his rights.

Everyone left the Ent Circle then, Garrett and Frankie hand-in-hand. Alonzo shoved Lars into his cruiser, as Shirley took the drone and pistol into evidence.

"Thanks for texting us this time, Frankie." Shirley clapped her on the back.

"Don't thank her, Shirley. What you should have done is called us to come out here, and we could have looked for the drone. Right, Frankie?" Alonzo spoke harshly.

Frankie gave him the side-eye. "But, that's what I did. I mean, I didn't call, but I did text you to meet us here."

Frankie called Violet to tell her lunch would have to wait, since she was being unavoidably detained at the sheriff's office. There would be a lot of information to sort through and questions to answer.

Carmen volunteered to have lunch with Violet in her stead. "I don't think they're going to question me for long, Frankie. You're holding all the cards." She stuck her tongue out at her friend.

Frankie didn't mind. "That would be nice, Carmie. Violet would love to have lunch with you. Be sure to let me know how that new bistro is."

"I'll do one better than that. I'll bring you take-out." Carmen laughed playfully.

# Chapter 20

*You plant before you harvest. You sow in tears before you reap joy. — Ralph Ransom*

*Truths are first clouds, then rain, then harvest, then food. — Henry Ward Beecher*

The universe thwarted Frankie's Saturday plans. Thrilled she wouldn't be called as a federal witness, she was dismissed from questioning after providing a lengthy statement to Officer Pflug, then to a federal agent.

Shirley was right in saying the feds would act quickly; four of them swooped in with voracious appetites in under an hour. The questions were over for her, so now all that was left to do was to wait, and that was something foreign to Frankie Champagne.

Frankie watched the federal agents through the conference room window, laying out papers like a game of solitaire. The four black suits stood on one side of the table; Pflug, Shirley, and Alonzo stood on the other side. They took turns pointing to papers, picking them up, making gestures and excited decrees.

Although she leaned forward in the waiting room seat and strained to hear, she could only pick up the loudest words: "ethics, fraud, money laundering, wildlife crimes, and murder." All the pieces added up to a big victory for the feds, and a goose egg for Fern and the birds she cherished.

Garrett's input was needed sporadically, and he was instructed to stay in his office. During his trek to the conference room, he brought Frankie a cup of coffee and a granola bar.

She grimaced when he handed her the cup.

"Don't make that face, Miss Francine. I went into the sheriff's private stash and used the single brew machine." Garrett pressed a kiss to his fingers and touched her cheek, then leaned in as inconspicuously as possible to deliver a message.

"Carmen called. She's working the afternoon with Jovie and Tess. Your mother and Aunt CeCe will come in later to work at the wine lounge just in case Pom or Cherry can't come in tonight."

Carmen had been dismissed from questioning, while Frankie was still giving her first statement. She hadn't seen Ivy and suspected she was sitting behind a closed door in one of the conference rooms, while Lars was cooling his jets in a jail cell. There was little likelihood he'd be out on bail or bond before Monday, if at all.

Another hour passed while Frankie waited for the verdict. Garrett emerged from the interview room and told her she could go. She let out a prolonged groan and checked the time.

"I'm not sure what I'm going to do first. The list is extensive." She smiled weakly at Garrett, who wrapped his arms around her in the hallway outside the department office.

"Might I suggest a rest? You've been wrung through the wringer, so it's okay to take a nap. Then maybe we can go out to dinner tonight?" He searched her face and could see the wheels spinning in her mind.

"Dinner sounds good, but my mind is too busy to settle down. I've got a couple calls to make. What about you, Mr. G.? Are they finished with you yet?" Frankie noticed the lines around Garrett's smile had deep creases, and the gold flecks in his caramel brown eyes had turned muddy.

"Who knows? I haven't been dismissed, so I'm just hanging around to see if they need more information. Anyway, in case I haven't told you enough times, I'm glad you didn't get hurt."

She kissed him softly. "Why do you think Lars killed Fern with a stone and her binoculars? He had a gun and was prepared to use it on us."

Garrett smiled in spite of himself. Frankie was still in news reporter mode, trying to make sense of the details. He answered carefully, not wanting to taint the federal case.

"I don't think Lars intended to kill Fern. I think Lars figured he could intimidate her to throw the study. He could either bribe her with money she needed, or he could threaten to ruin her career. Besides, a gunshot wound is easier to trace to a suspect than a rock is."

Frankie smiled at the idea that Fern wouldn't cave in to Lars' demands. Somehow, it made her feel better to keep Fern on the pedestal where her family placed her.

"Fern wouldn't agree, though. She must have innocently taken the SHG money, thinking that Lars was an honest man."

Garrett wasn't certain it was that black and white. Maybe Fern just saw an opportunity to get her hands on money she needed, but regretted it later. He kept the notion to himself, leaving Frankie to draw her own conclusions.

"I'll check in with you before five o'clock, okay?" He checked the time. "That gives you about four hours to get into or stay out of trouble. Got it?"

Frankie didn't waste a minute. She pressed the call button for Violet, hoping they could meet for a bite or at least a conversation. The granola bar she'd eaten had no staying power.

"Mom, are you okay?" Violet sounded stressed. "Auntie Carmen assured me you were fine, but she told me a little about your morning, and I've been worried."

"I'm fine, just a little tired from sitting around and repeating my statement a hundred times." Frankie made light of the situation. "Where are you? I could use a hug from my daughter."

"Oh, Mom. I wish I could. I'm already on my way back to Point. I have a lab exam I need to study for, so I booked some time in the micro lab to practice before Monday." Violet sounded sad.

"That's great, Honey. You're doing what you need to do. We'll see each other next weekend, right? How's the mead coming along?" Frankie was immensely proud of Violet's mead project and wanted it to be successful.

Violet slipped easily into scientist mode. "It's progressing. Zane and I checked the specific gravity this morning, and we think it will be ready for a first tasting on Friday, depending upon whether or not it's still burping. So, I'll be down early Friday morning. I'm going to ride down with Zane and stay all day." She paused and proceeded in a disappointed tone. "Of course, nothing we do will make the mead ready for the harvest festival. I don't think it will be ready before Halloween."

"No worries, Vi. We'll launch it at our own special event at the shop. We haven't hosted a Halloween party at Bubble & Bake before. The shop name practically screams Halloween.  Let's talk next week. Good luck on your lab exam. Love you, Sweety."

For the third time that week, Frankie parked the SUV and went up the back stairway that led to her apartment deck.  She wasn't ready to discuss her morning with her bakery crew, and she definitely didn't want to see people from the bird club, or any other customers for that matter.

Entering through the sliding glass doors, she set her backpack on the counter and scrounged around her refrigerator. She still had a couple of deli salads in plastic containers, so she pulled out a tub of mixed greens and placed a generous portion into a shallow bowl. Then she topped it with Italian veggie pasta salad, satisfied that it would suffice until dinner. A  headache was still knocking around her forehead and sinuses, a reminder of the dreadful morning. She poured an extra large glass of water and downed a couple aspirin.

Sitting at the breakfast bar, she pressed the call button for Daryl George. Boy, did she have news for him. A robotic voice told her the number was no longer in service. Thinking she hit the wrong contact on her list, she tried again with the same result.

She logged into her laptop and went to the Midwest Wildlife Foundation site. Everything looked to be in operating condition. She clicked on the list of officers. The photo of Daryl George was gone, as was his name under the title of chief. In its place was a photo of a dark-haired middle-aged man with a trim beard:

Lawrence Abrams, acting president. *You bet he's acting. Where the heck was Daryl George?*

A general search yielded a corporate financial director, a college football player, and an Australian baseball player. Suffice it to say none of them would make the cut. She tried narrowing her search to his name plus "wildlife." Nothing. Then his name plus "ornithology." Nothing again. Her Daryl George had evaporated, for lack of a better term.

She shut the laptop with a huff, headed down her outside steps, and climbed into the SUV. A visit to Nearly Napa was in order. Whether it was to console Rina, confront Rina, or at least find out why Rina had apologized to her the night before, she wasn't certain. But she suspected Rina could cough up some answers about Lars and the Frontenacs. Now that Frankie knew Lars was capable of murder, he scored a place at the top of her list for vandalism in the vineyard.

She was surprised to see several open parking spots in front of Rina's business. She was even more surprised to find the shop was dark and empty. A sign tacked to the front door read "permanently closed."

Frankie walked down the alley to look behind the building. Rina's vehicle wasn't there. No lights were on in the apartment above the store, either, as far as she could tell. That was two evaporations in one day. She wondered what time would be appropriate to call Shirley for some answers.

Back at Bubble & Bake, Frankie slogged through the back door into the kitchen, a few early fall leaves swirling in with her. The day was dragging on, and she avoided calling Magda at *Point Press*, because she was too tired to file an article today. She needed more time and official answers first.

She tiptoed through the swinging doors to peek around the corner toward the wine lounge bar and seating areas. It was quiet. If the bird club hikers had been there at all, they had dispersed.

Carmen instinctively swiveled from her post at the walnut bar. "Who's lurking over there? It's safe to come out, Frankie."

The bar was empty, but a couple of sitting areas were occupied with guests. Peggy was talking to a group of seven and suggesting wine varieties for them to enjoy. Aunt CeCe poured glasses for a group of six that had ordered two bottles to share: one red and one white. Business as usual at the wine lounge on a quiet Saturday afternoon.

"Did the bird club come in?" Frankie wondered about the extra platters of cheese and veggies prepared for their consumption.

Carmen nodded. "Jovie and Tess managed them. They were scattering when I came in from the sheriff's office."

"The walk?" Frankie asked.

"Canceled. They decided they'd had enough excitement for one day. Besides, it was getting too late in the morning to find birds."

"Any news on the protestors?"

"Nothing new. The cops hung around until everyone from both groups left. Jovie said she overheard Tasha say that Dawn was arrested. Did you see her at the police station? I know I didn't see any protestors." Carmen made a skeptical face.

Frankie shook her head. She hadn't seen Dawn or any protestors either. "But I never saw Officers Green or Haley, so they might have still been at the park or on patrol."

"It's been a long strange trip today," Frankie laughed, as she conjured the Grateful Dead reference. "Daryl

George is missing. So is Rina Madison." She was about to explain, when Carmen produced a business envelope from underneath the bar and extended it to Frankie.

"I wouldn't go that far. Rina Madison stopped by a few minutes after I got in. She wanted to see you, but when I told her you were indefinitely indisposed, she asked me to give this envelope to you."

Frankie sat down on the bar stool and opened the envelope. She unfolded the letter and cash spilled out of it onto the floor. She and Carmen exchanged questioning looks, then Frankie read the letter aloud:

> *Dear Frankie,*
>
> *I know you don't remember me, but we were both in the communications program at the university in Madison. We competed for a radio internship, which you won. At about the same time, I hoped to pledge in the Zeta Phi Eta sorority. You were close friends with Catherine (or Cat as she was known), who was the president. Needless to say, I wasn't able to pledge as you took the last spot. Finally, I tried to convince you to go on a date with my brother, Vincent, but you wouldn't go, and the snub upset him terribly.*
>
> *Fast forward to now. I came into some money, and when I found out you owned a business in Deep Lakes, I saw my chance to open a business, too. It's funny that we both started in communications but ended up in the wine business. You were always in my way, so now I had the chance to get in yours.*

*Honestly, though, it was Lars's idea to vandalize your property. I just wanted to leave you a note as a clue that you had to figure out. Even my last name, Madison, was a clue, since that's where we went to college. I wanted to make you feel guilty because you always came out on top. But, while I was spray painting your shed, Lars cut open the net and pulled it off your grapevines. After that, I didn't want anything to do with him anymore. He has a mean side that many people don't know about.*

*WIthout Lars, I won't be able to keep Nearly Napa going. Yes, he was my main backer and funded the remodel of the store. So, I'm closing shop and leaving town for a fresh start.*

*I'm enclosing $400 in cash from the register and hope that will compensate you, at least in part, for your lost grapes. If for any reason you are looking for me, I'll be changing my name— again.*

*Sincerely, Rina Madison or as you knew me, Sabrina Ponti*

"Well, Frankie? I don't remember you being a high-society sorority sister. Any comments?" Carmen held an empty wine bottle toward Frankie as a microphone. "Knock it off, Carmie. Honestly, she didn't look familiar to me whatsoever. She must have changed considerably. Yes, I did compete for a radio internship between my junior and senior years, but I think there were a number of us who auditioned for it." She paused to review the letter before going on.

"I was never a sorority sister. I knew Cat from being in some of the same classes, and I actually baked cookies and muffins a couple of times at her request for sorority events. But, I was never asked to pledge, and I never applied. So, Rina's got her wires crossed there."

Frankie closed her eyes to conjure the memory of Vincent Ponti. She knew the name had sounded familiar when she saw it on the SHG website, but she couldn't place him.

"I wish Rina was still in town. The shop was already closed up when I stopped there to see her. I wish we could have talked this out instead."

"So, you don't remember breaking the guy's heart your junior year of college? How many men did you turn down that year, Frankie?" Carmen snorted.

Frankie's cheeks suddenly colored a deep red. When she spoke, she leaned toward Carmen to steady herself, keeping her voice hushed. "I remember. Oh, gosh."

It took minutes before she could go on as a flood of painful memories rushed through her. "I had been seeing Rick on and off during my junior year, and I had just found out that I was pregnant with Sophie. I didn't want anyone to know."

Frankie remembered how lonely she felt, hiding the secret from her family until she and Rick figured out what to do. She remembered her mother's disapproval and worse, her father's disappointment. Years later, Frankie understood. She was supposed to set the world on fire with her passion for journalism. Instead, she was a young mother desperate to complete her college degree.

Carmen pressed her face against Frankie's, forehead to forehead. "It's okay. That's ancient history. You can't believe you're responsible for Rina's brand of crazy."

Frankie blinked back tears. "It was a difficult time for me, but I guess it was a difficult time for Sabrina, too. Sometimes we just don't know what others are going through."

Frankie excused herself to return to her apartment. She needed to shake off the past and its clinging shadows, something she thought she had reconciled years ago. She made a stiff iced chai, willing her senses to be consumed by invigorating spices, and called Shirley. It was almost three, so maybe there was a chance she'd answer.

"Shirley Lazaar. Is this an official press call or something else?" Shirley chuckled.

"Do you have a few minutes, because I have questions," she spoke seriously and business-like, throwing Shirley off.

"Fire away. I'll answer what I can. The feds are still here, but we're taking a food break. I'd call it lunch, but it's too late for that." Shirley took her three- meals-a-day regimen to heart.

"Can I report on Lars's arrest and preliminary charges? I'm confused between whose jurisdiction is whose. But can I assume the murder charge is a county charge?"

Shirley grunted. "Once the feds take over, the charges tend to get bundled together. The feds will probably take over the murder charges. For certain, Lars is going to be housed at a federal site until trial." She took a large gulp of something. "Unless he pleads guilty, that is." She slapped the desk and laughed.

Frankie assumed Lars would have a team of lawyers working to get him released quickly. What can't money buy?

Shirley returned to the first question. "The sheriff plans a press conference tomorrow or Monday. I'd wait to see what information is released from that before you file a story."

"What about Vincent Ponti? Where does he fit into this?" Frankie had her pen poised and ready over her notepad.

"He's the face of SHG and chief negotiator on funding the wildlife studies. Lars wanted to hide in the shadows, hoping Ponti would take the fall. I'm sure that's still the plan he'll be working on with his defense team."

"Has Ponti been arrested?"

"The feds picked him up early this morning, not long after you and Abe turned over your recorded phone call. Before you ask, yes, the recorded call helped. And it's a gray area regarding the use of a one-party consent recording."

The thought of Ponti led Frankie down another path. "Rina Madison? Do you know where she is?"

Shirley grunted and tilted back in her office chair in surprise. "Let me ask you something. What do you know about Rina Madison?"

Frankie confessed the contents of Rina's letter to her. "I think she's left town. At least, that's what her letter suggests. She's Vincent's sister and Lars's former girlfriend, so she must know things."

Shirley grunted, paused, grunted again. "You didn't hear this from me or anyone in our office, got it?" Another grunt. "Sabrina is in federal custody. She's a material witness, and I think you know how those are handled."

So Sabrina hadn't actually disappeared. It occurred to Frankie that Sabrina's confession letter may have been a ruse to make her look innocent in taking Lars' money.

Heck, the money may have come from Vincent since he was the front man at SHG.

There was still one more burning question in Frankie's mind. "What about Daryl George? I tried to call him today. His number is no longer in service. I looked him up online. He's a ghost." Frankie's words brought an epiphany. "Let me guess: he's in federal custody, or he's a federal agent himself."

Shirley laughed. "You're getting savvy, Frankie. No comment."

Frankie perused her notes. "Let me see if I've got my facts straight." She smiled to herself after using another phrase borrowed from a television detective. "Were the drones used to disturb the birds in those protected areas?"

"Affirmative. The drones were a factor, as far as we know, in the almond grove area, the Costa Rica coffee area, the Arizona mountains, and the purple martin refuge areas. But all of that has to be substantiated yet, Frankie."

"Who wanted a piece of the purple martin territory?"

"Unofficially, it's a perfect place for cranberry bogs."

Frankie scribbled fast to keep up. "What's going to happen to Dr. Fredrich and Naomi Travers?"

"Both of them are under investigation but now that investigation belongs to the feds. Dr. Fredrich will certainly be suspended, pending the investigation, and I'm not sure what sort of fines or reprimands the university will face. It depends on how much they sanctioned."

Frankie blew out a long sigh. "Okay, that's all from me for now. I know Magda's going to be on my case to get this pieced together." Thinking of Magda brought Abe to mind. "Has Abe called to talk to you or Alonzo about this?"

"He did, but Alonzo told him a press conference would be coming soon, and he'd have to hang tight until then." Shirley let her words sink in. "So you know all of this is off the record for now, right?"

# Chapter 21

*Many times the light seems to go out. But another light, one held by a stranger or friend, a book or a song, a blackbird or a wildflower, comes close enough so that we can see our path by its light. And in time we realize that the light we have borrowed was always our own. — Joan Borysenko*

Bubble & Bake was blessedly quiet on Sundays, almost like a sanctuary. Entering the lounge in solitude, Frankie soaked in the residual fragrances of coffee, spices, vanilla, citrus, dough, and wine corks. Every scent contributed to the space that was hers.

It was mid-morning and the wine lounge wouldn't open until noon. Sun filled the enclaves and spilled over the seats, where Cherry and Pom settled in next to Frankie, Carmen, Tia, and Aunt CeCe. Peggy was absent, attending her standard Sunday brunch date with the church ladies.

The women were enjoying a fruity virgin sangria tea on ice, accompanied by savory cheeses, herb scones, and fresh fruit.

Since Fern's case was riddled with more holes than Tia's current crochet project, a granny square afghan, everyone had their hands up to quiz Frankie. The alcove looked like a one-room school.

"I just don't want to believe that Lars could be capable of hurting Fern. He was like family. I thought he loved all of us." Pom, like Fern, saw the best in others.

"Money and power are good companions of corruption. The Flying Robin drones were similar to ones used by the military, so they had the capacity to disrupt wildlife. Lars had many agricultural customers who purchased the drones to scare off flocks of invading birds and critters that would decimate their crops." Frankie stopped a minute to gather her thoughts. She could guess at tying pieces of evidence together, but the ideas were still conjecture.

"I think Lars saw an opportunity to make a lot of money by inserting his nonprofit company into wildlife studies, especially in the ones with protected lands under scrutiny. Maybe those lands didn't need to be protected because wildlife wouldn't thrive there."

"And once the lands lost their protected status, they could be sold to companies who wanted to use the land for agriculture or business." Cherry picked up the threads.

"I want to talk about your grapevines, Frankie, and CeCe's dreams." Tia Pepita cared about wildlife but was more interested in CeCe's connections to the dream world.

CeCe put an arm around Tia and gave her a loving squeeze. "I guess the alley cat running around the vineyard was a mixture of Rina and your college friend, Cat?"

Frankie laughed and shrugged. "I don't know how to interpret dreams, but I think your dream about all different types of birds falling from the sky seems to point to the drones chasing the birds away in all those different studies. You're a whiz, Aunt CeCe."

Pom frowned. "And Lars seems to be the reason your Frontenacs were ruined. I just don't understand how he became so, so ugly." Cherry grabbed her sister's hand and held on tightly.

Frankie's face brightened. "The Frontenacs were not ruined. We still have a crop to harvest, and there will be more next year. At least the vines are still thriving. There could have been a lot more damage." It was high time to lighten the mood, if possible.

"I wish you could have seen Carmen's wrestling moves. I don't think Lars expected a takedown." She sent Carmen a high-five wave.

"And Ivy coming in to clobber him with that walking stick," Carmen laughed, hoping that Pom would find a little humor in the women getting the best of the villain with the gun.

After a weak smile, Pom dropped her eyes once more. "Poor Ivy. I think she's had a crush on Lars her whole life. He betrayed her, too."

By now Tia Pepita was wiping away tears, and Aunt CeCe had a faraway look that took her somewhere sorrowful. Carmen and Frankie exchanged questioning looks.

Cherry rose, pulling up Pom with her. "We're going to have to set our sadness on a shelf until later. The shop's opening soon, and we can't greet customers who want wine tastings with these sad faces. Pom, you and I need to figure out what we're bringing to the farewell ceremony later."

"What exactly are we supposed to be doing at this ceremony anyway?" Carmen's skepticism was rising.

Robyn was waiting at Bountiful Fruits when Frankie's SUV arrived. Carmen, Peggy, Aunt CeCe, and Tia rode along with Frankie, hoping they had brought along appropriate offerings for the ceremony. They had relied on Aunt CeCe's understanding of the farewell ritual, based on the Samhain Celtic ceremony of honoring the dead.

"Where's your robe and hood?" Tia blurted out when she saw that Robyn was dressed in everyday field clothes for working outside.

Carmen stifled a giggle and elbowed Frankie. Aunt CeCe's explanation had wandered into the stories of druids and lore from a variety of cultures, leaving Tia thoroughly muddled.

Thankfully, Robyn smiled brightly at Tia. "The Samhain takes place around Halloween, and it's meant to honor those who died without anyone to mourn them. Part of this tradition is to welcome in the harvest season. That's why the vineyard is the perfect place for us to gather and say goodbye to Fern."

Robyn asked Frankie to lead the way to the flat area below the vineyard where the ceremony would take place. Peggy volunteered to wait in the parking lot for the rest of Fern's friends and family to arrive.

Robyn was satisfied the fire pit would make an adequate hearth to light a ceremonial fire and burn some of the tributes to Fern: a wishbone, pine cones, acorns, and one of Fern's stuffed animals from the Parker house. Robyn offered an embossed certificate from an award she and Fern had won together, and Ash placed Fern's favorite childhood book, *Harriet, The Spy*, on top of the kindling. Even Alonzo hesitantly tucked a tail feather into the pile from a tom turkey he had bagged last spring.

Tia Pepita, showing her Catholic devotion, placed a palm frond, blessed by a priest, onto the fire. "I don't want to bring down God's wrath," she murmured.

After Robyn ignited the fire, Fern's loved ones shared a fond memory about her, followed by prayers and well-wishes for a peaceful afterlife. Aunt CeCe, who felt deeply connected to the natural world, offered a poem to Fern:

*"I hope I can be the autumn leaf, who looked at the sky and lived. And when it was time to leave, gracefully it knew life was a gift."*

She recited it and placed the paper into the fire. Then, she took a handful of flower

petals and tossed them into the air, where they danced with some windswept ashes.

Garrett and Alonzo had thoughtfully purchased prepared fried chicken, potato wedges, cole slaw, and cut-up melon for a welcomed feast in the gazebo away from the fire. Food and beverages elevated the mood, while the low-burning fire acted as a comforting reminder of light, hope, and eternity.

As the food was passed around, people began emerging from their reverent contemplations, and conversations flowed freely. Sitting beside Garrett, Frankie squeezed his knee, and he drew her closer to him. She dropped her head on his shoulder, a warm comforting place.

"Thank you for bringing food and, well, just for being you, G." Frankie lifted her face for a kiss. "I love you," she confessed. It seemed like the appropriate time to tell Garrett what her heart wanted to say.

Garrett's smile curved upward, reached all the way to those caramel eyes she loved, and he breathed in a meditative breath. "Thank goodness, Frankie, because I wouldn't want to be in love alone." The moment lingered in the autumn air as they kissed again.

A somewhat sharp clearing of the throat intruded in their dream world and brought them abruptly back to the gazebo. Only a few faces were staring at them and smiling sedately. The source of the interruption, Peggy, was standing above Frankie's shoulder.

Frankie wriggled out of Garrett's hold and, wearing a broad grin, turned to look at her mother.

"Oh, oh. Am I in trouble, Mom?"

Peggy dropped her pretended disapproving look. "No, you're not in trouble. I'm glad to see you looking so happy, Dear. May I just have a word?" She inclined her head away from the gazebo, and Frankie followed her down the steps toward the herb garden.

The garden made Frankie smile in memory of creating it with Garrett earlier that summer. They had done all the landscaping and planting together, and it was a sanctuary for butterflies, honey bees, and humans. The two women sat on one of the cedar benches.

"The grapes of wrath," Peggy began. "I never got back to you about that. Now that you know it was Rina who wrote the message, does it ring any bells?"

Frankie smiled. It was typical of Peggy Champagne to leave no stone unturned. Her meticulousness was sometimes like a feeding frenzy. Even now, she could see the little piranhas swimming around in her mother's head.

"Honestly, I'm guessing it doesn't go any deeper than Rina having anger toward me, blaming me for things in life that didn't go her way. She told me in the letter that the cat was supposed to be a clue to her identity. A reminder of our mutual friend, Cat. But, I didn't get it." Truthfully, Frankie stopped caring about the message and the vandalism. What's done is done.

"There, there, Dear. You're a busy woman. You didn't have time to figure out every clue. Besides, she might have done a better job at leaving a clearer hint." Leave it to Peggy to criticize a vandal's technique.

"Now, don't laugh at me, Frankie. I just think that Rina may have decided she had the right to play God. You know the phrase 'grapes of wrath' has many references, including biblical. The grapes symbolize evil in the world, and they are crushed under God's anger with his justice."

"So, you think Rina was warped enough to see me as an evil person? Giving her the right to destroy my grapes? Rina said that it was Lars who cut the net to expose the grapes. He was capable of a lot of ruthless things." Frankie didn't want to think about it anymore, though. She knew she'd have to review every detail about Fern's death in order to write the news article. But today was all about reflection and restoration.

"And, what about Dominic Finchley? I see he's not here today, and he was the prime suspect for quite a while in Fern's death." Frankie wondered if her mother was keeping a scrapbook of Frankie's investigations. She stifled a giggle, imagining the proper Peggy Champagne, who represented high society in Deep Lakes, proudly displaying her daughter's crime boards like sports trophies around her house.

"So, is Dominic Finchley a hero or villain in this story?" Peggy pressed through Frankie's musings.

"He's no hero, Mother. Robyn organized the ceremony and invited people. There's no love lost between her and Dom. Besides, the evidence suggests Dom never came to Fern's aid at the pond. If you want to know what I think..."

Peggy nodded emphatically. "I do, actually, want to know what you think. I trust your instincts, Frankie. You should know that." She squeezed her daughter's hand when she spoke, and a sense of pride rose within Frankie.

"I think Dom came to the pond to reunite with Fern because he needed her. She'd written all of the published studies from Dom's notes. Dom was no scholar and a poor writer. He relied on Fern and couldn't afford to lose her professionally, so he glommed onto her personally." She was charged up now and advancing full speed to a conclusion.

"If Dom had tried to save Fern, he would have been wet up to his knees at least. Some of that pond water would have been present in her vehicle, yet there wasn't a trace of pond water in it. I think he saw her, panicked, and thought of the one thing that could save his professional rear end."

Peggy clucked her tongue. "Don't be crass, Dear."

"As I was saying, he needed Fern's journal. Professors must have a required number of articles published to retain their positions. If he could take over Fern's study; well, the work was already finished. All he would have to do is put his name on it, perhaps get Robyn or even scummy Naomi to write the article. That would buy him a few years in his profession."

Peggy gasped. "Good thinking, Dear. Have you told any of the Parkers your theory?"

Frankie shook her head. "No, and I won't either, unless it becomes critical to do so. The truth may come out anyway at the press conference or after the investigation concludes, whenever that may be."

Impulsively, Frankie hugged Peggy. "Thank you for supporting my wily ways, Mom. Now, let's get back to the celebration."

Walking back to the gazebo, Frankie noticed Ash and
Ivy staring into what remained of Fern's farewell fire. She
separated from Peggy to speak with them.

"What's next for you two?" she dared to ask the
question that had been hanging over them since Fern's
demise.

Ivy smiled, her hand on Ash's shoulder. "We've had
time to talk these past few days, especially after looking
at Fern's finances. I'm going to look for another position.
It's time."

Ash nodded, looking encouragingly into Ivy's eyes.
"And I've already applied to a college program
for counseling youth with disabilities. They're on a
trimester schedule, so I could begin in October."

It was hard to believe how quickly things had
transpired. "I'm surprised, but I'm happy for you both for
taking a leap of faith. Where will you live, Ash?" Frankie
thought of the house that Fern had paid off, wondering
if it was a legal deal.

"We're pretty sure the house is going to be
seized, probably all of Fern's assets, too." Ash spoke
nonchalantly, wrapping himself up in the cloak of
pretense again. "We met with the lawyers. They told us
everything would be scrutinized in the investigation. It
could take years."

Ash grabbed Ivy's fluttering hand to calm her. "But
we'll be okay. The college has housing made just for me."
He laughed. "And Ivy can get a job anywhere. There are
people lined up for miles waiting for a personal nurse."

Ivy punched her cousin. "You make it all sound like
roses and unicorns, Ash." She turned toward Frankie.
"But Ash is right. We'll be okay. And thank you, Frankie,
for finding out who killed her." Ivy choked on her words.

"I couldn't have done it without your help in more ways than one. You came in like Gandalf the Grey, reading to cast down the Balrog with his staff."

Ivy snickered. "That was Fern's walking stick, so I'd call it poetic justice."

# Epilogue

A week and a day after Fern's farewell ceremony, the Bubble & Bake kitchen had resumed a semblance of normalcy. Following a peaceful night's rest, Monday morning ushered in brilliant sunshine and cool, crisp temperatures. The kitchen windows were open to the fresh fall air, and the crew had manned their stations in pastry-making fashion.

Tia entrusted her emotions to mashing yams for muffins and scones. She sniffed audibly as a tear slid down her cheek. "I miss that big bobcat, Piper."

Frankie paused in rolling out scone dough to smile encouragingly at Tia across the countertop. "I do, too. But he's going to have an exciting adventure with his new keeper, Ivy."

Ivy decided to adopt Piper in Fern's honor and had picked up the giant Main Coon on Saturday. She also shared her news that she would be leaving the country in two months, heading to Honduras to be a nurse at a mission clinic. She was embracing her chance at a fresh start.

"Speaking of a new start," Carmen cleared her throat thoughtfully, "isn't it time one of us had a heart-to-heart talk with Cherry? She can't stay at her parents' forever, and I don't think her relationship with your brother is helping matters.

Frankie openly agreed. "Let the dust settle another week or two, then you and I will talk to her together, Carmie."

Turning her focus back on Tia, Frankie reassured her. "Don't worry. Dr. Sadie has a lineup of new kitties for the shop. It always seems to be breeding season in the cat world."

Satisfied, Tia returned to smashing yams in rhythm with an up-tempo rendition of "Autumn Leaves," while Tess hummed and added a bebop here and there. She was dumping ingredients in the floor mixer, the first step for tart and quiche crusts. Carmen swayed her hips as she stirred the bubbling apple-cinnamon filling for fritters and kringles.

Such was the musical scenario that Garrett and Peggy encountered when they entered the back door of the shop, each carrying a rolled up paper. To Frankie's surprise, each simultaneously planted a kiss on either side of her face.

Peggy unfolded the latest edition of *Point Press* and laid it on the countertop next to her daughter. The article about Fern's murder filled half of the front page, above the fold.

"Isn't it remarkable that Frankie and Abe Arnold have learned to work together on the same puzzle?" Peggy commented above the music to everyone.

Meanwhile, Garrett unfolded the latest edition of *The Whitman Watch*, revealing the front page article with the shared bylines covering all of the space.

"Three cheers to you, Miss Francine, for some top-notch investigative work. And I echo your mother's sentiment. I'm glad you and Abe buried the hatchet without burying it in somebody's heart." Garrett chuckled at his joke.

All work ceased in the kitchen, while everyone gathered around to read the articles and give Frankie kudos for solving the crime.

"I'm glad that awful Dr. Fredrich and Naomi, that glittery harpy, were both suspended from their universities and programs. Serves them right." Carmen spat the words out in satisfaction. "You helped make that happen, Frankie."

Frankie smiled, accepting their praise and high fives. "Thank you, but I couldn't have solved the case without Cherry, Pom, Ivy, and Abe. Not to mention Garrett and Shirley. I'm lucky to have so much support." She scooted over to give Carmen and Peggy hugs. "Including both of you. You're my rocks. But, to tell you the truth, I'm thinking of bidding adieu to journalism and taking up a safer hobby."

Peggy and Carmen scoffed, while Garrett produced a doubtful grin, but Aunt CeCe sweetly asked, "And what would that be, Frankie dear?"

"Oh, I was thinking about cliff diving, maybe, or race car driving."

"I hear Space X is looking for volunteers," Carmen quipped.

# The Newspaper Article in Point Press

### *Autumn Harvest: The Dire and the Divine*
*by Francine Champagne*

Autumn at Bountiful Fruits, as in any vineyard, is the busiest season. We harvest our grape crops; press them; remove the extra stems, leaves, and pomace; and the wine crafting begins.

During vinification, work continues in the vineyard to prepare the vines for the brutal onslaught of a cold climate with months of winter weather: snow storms, ice, below-zero temperatures, and days without a ray of sunshine. But, let's not dwell on that. Because now is the time to enjoy the fruits of our labor.

I grow four grape varieties on my small farmland acreage. If you know anything about grape production, it takes at least five years of tending vines before grapes can be harvested for wine.

I've been giving TLC to my Frontenac vines for seven years. I watched them grow from bare root, to producing canes, glossy-leafed vines, and finally, clusters of flowers and berries. Patience may be a virtue, but it's barely a visiting guest in this personage. Still, while the vines were cultivating maturity, I was cultivating patience.

The payoff for all that nurturing was about to come to fruition in a few weeks. I had plans for the Frontenac harvest. A Bountiful original wine was about to be conceived, a beefy red that would hold up to Midwest charred steaks on the grill. I could hardly wait to taste the notes of cherry, currant, and sweet spices on my tongue. A small portion of the pressed juice would debut in our fortified port this year as well. It would be my immeasurable pleasure to bring both varieties to all of you.

Then, the unimaginable happened. The grapes survived the hurly-burly of weather extremes, survived pestilence and plagues of crop diseases, and survived critters whose aim is to burrow or devour—well, almost.

What my lovely Frontenacs couldn't survive was a man-made assault. A vandal in the vineyard came under the cover of night, cut open our netting, and invited birds to breakfast on our Frontenacs.

We lost about a third of the Frontenac crop, meaning there wouldn't be enough from our own property to produce a wine of origin, from vineyard to bottle, so to speak. It's a badge of honor to include the abbreviation W.O. (wine of origin) on a wine label. From roots to vines to grapes to vintage, the wine is yours, as precious as a child.

So what, you might be thinking. Just accept it, go buy some Frontenac juice and move on until next year. Sure, but it's not that simple. Vintners order harvested grapes or pressed juices well in advance from year to year. Many vintners have standing orders with cultivators or producers, so ordering juice requires advance planning. Furthermore, many cultivators will not ship juices.

When the juice cannot come to the vintner, the vintner must go wherever the juice lives. This isn't always practical, case in point: I could get juices from Australia. If only.

Before you shed tears for me and my vineyard: stop. I leaned on my brilliant vineyard manager, Manny Vega, and we connected with a—drum roll, please—grape cultivator near Lake Pepin, just over the Wisconsin border in Minnesota.

I'm thrilled to announce our collaboration with Three Sisters of the Vines grape growers. As fortune smiled upon us, Erica, Kay, and Christy (the Three) had a small plot of Frontenacs that were unclaimed. The sisters were certain the grapes would need one more season before they were ready for vinification. But the auspices of the weather gods cheered the grapes into maturity, albeit leaving them orphaned in the harvest. But not for long. It truly does take a village to make a vintage.

Now, it's your turn to cultivate patience. As we labor away in the winery for the next several months, by this time next year, you will be enjoying Well-Red Women, a pure Frontenac vintage, brought to you by Bountiful Fruits and Three Sisters of the Vines.

Meanwhile, we invite you to Deep Lakes to celebrate the season of thanksgiving at our harvest fest in October. Bountiful Fruits will feature two new white blends made from our Edelweiss and LaCrescent: Let's Be Riesling-able, a traditional bright, crisp vintage reminiscent of fine German wines, and Tiger Lily, featuring flavors of orange and kiwi ending in an herbal finish. This wine sports the loveliest of burnt orange and green hues, like a fall campfire. Be sure to stay tuned for our first ever Bewitching Bubbles and Halloween Bakes on October 31st featuring a new spirit: Bountiful's first mead—Golden Desire.

# Recipes

## Kiss My Acropolis Quiche

Saute the following in a little olive oil until tender:
- 2 thinly sliced shallots

- 1-3oz bag sun dried julienne tomatoes

- 4oz fresh baby spinach (tear in half if large)

- Greek spices: ½ tsp each - oregano, basil and mint (dried)

- ¼ tsp of pepper or more to taste

- ¼-½ tsp orange peel

On the bottom of your go-to pie crust (9 inch or 10 inch dish):
- Place ¼ cup chopped black olives

- Place cooled sauteed mixture

-

Top with crumbled feta to taste (½ to 1 cup). *If you don't like feta, use mozzarella.*

Mix 5 eggs beaten with 1 ⅔ cup whole milk - pour this over the ingredients layered in the pie crust.
Bake at 420° for 15 minutes to brown the crust
Turn the oven down to 340° for 25-30 more minutes
It's important to let this rest for 20 minutes to blend flavors and it is even tastier the next day.

# Cherry Rhubarb Crumb Bars from Aunt Sally

Grease or generously spray a 9 x 13 baking dish
For Crust and crumb topping:

- 1 cup plus 4 TB butter, melted and cooled to just warm

- 1 tsp vanilla (or try any other flavored extract you like)

- 1 cup sugar

- 2 large egg yolks

- 3 ½ cups flour

- ¾ tsp salt

Mix melted butter, sugar, egg yolks and salt with a spoon until smooth and pale yellow in color. Add in flour in three portions, stir until combined after each addition. Use about 3 cups of this mixture and press it onto the bottom of the greased baking dish. Set aside the rest of the crumb mixture. Cover it and keep it at room temp.

Freeze the baking dish/crust for about 45 minutes. Meanwhile, make filling.

Filling:

- 1 ½ cups chopped rhubarb (fresh or frozen)

- 1 ½ cups tart cherries, halved (fresh or frozen)

- 1 tsp vanilla or almond extract

- ½ cup sugar

- ½ tsp salt

- 1 tsp lemon juice

- 1 Tbl cornstarch mixed with 2 tb water, shaken in small container (You may need more if you have extra juicy fruits)

Combine fruits, sugar and salt in a saucepan. Heat to a boil. Reduce heat and simmer, 8-10 minutes. Mash fruit into smaller chunks with a spoon as it simmers. Add cornstarch mix and bring back up to a boil to thicken. Remove from heat and add extract and lemon juice. Cool to room temp.

Bake chilled crust at 325° until pale brown, about 20 minutes. Remove and increase oven temp to 350. Spread fruit mixture on top of warm crust. Sprinkle top with leftover crumb topping (you could add any spice of your choice to the crumb topping first - I like a little cinnamon). Bake for 25-30 minutes. If you serve this warmed with a scoop of ice

cream, people will swoon.

# 1960's Potato Chip Cookies (with a twist)

- 1 cup granulated sugar

- 1 lb. (4 sticks) butter, softened

- 1 Tbl vanilla

- 3 cups crushed potato chips (Kettle chips work well. The key is not to use a baked chip.)

- 3 1/3 cups all-purpose flour

- 1 teaspoon Kosher Salt

- 1/2 teaspoon Sweet Paprika

- 1 package Heath Toffee bits (1 1/3 cups)

Heat oven to 350°F.

Mix sugar, butter, and vanilla with a hand mixer in large bowl until fluffy.

Mix in crushed potato chips.

Stir in flour, Kosher salt, and paprika by hand. Stir in Heath Bits.

Chill dough until firm/stiff, about an hour.

Use an eating teaspoon-sized spoon; scoop into a loose ball. Place on parchment or silpat-lined sheet about 2 inches apart.

Bake about 10 minutes or until light brown (centers will be soft). Cool on wire rack.

Makes about 90 cookies.

These will make you feel like a kid again. Just ask my grandkids - they love them!

As a reader of this book, you will find more of Frankie's fall recipes at
https://joyribar.com/deep-dire-harvest-additional-recip
es/

# Acknowledgments

Thank you, readers, for your continued support of Frankie and friends and life in Deep Lakes. Thank you, too, for supporting an indie author and indie bookstores.

This book would not be possible without the guidance and wisdom of many. I owe a debt of gratitude to my editor extraordinaire, Kay Rettenmund, and beta readers; Katie David and Janelle Bailey. You are the triple threat that made this book fly!

Thank you to my early readers: Laurie Buchanan, Jeannée Sacken, Maggie Smith, and Jacqueline Vick. Your time is priceless, and your generosity immeasurable.

Thank you to my husband and comfort counselor, John. You've taken on a tiger by its tail and lived to tell the tale! I love you.

Thank you to Tom Heffron, the cover designer who invites readers into the book, and who has been on the front line of creating a Deep Lakes brand.

Thank you, Daryl Christensen, for all you do in the birding world as a field scientist and conservationist.

Did you know that Purple Martins used to be very common in the U.S. but that their populations have declined almost 40% since 1966? Reasons for this decline include use of pesticides in the 1960's (which has mostly been curbed), and competition for nesting sites from invaders like European Starlings and English Sparrows.

But, there's a man-made reason for their population decrease as well. Before America was even a country, native people offered hollowed-out gourds to attract martins, and we learned from their appreciation of nature. Since the early 1800's, Americans have built colony houses on poles for the martins, who live and nest in large groups. During modern times our population has changed, and many martin houses have been abandoned or uncared for. Never fear, though; there's been a resurgence in the construction of martin condominiums, thanks largely to the Purple Martin Watch, Purple Martin Conservation Association, and Purple Martin Society of North America.

These organizations are working to make us aware of the importance of the martins, who help control the insect population. These members of the Swallow family eat at the Flying Food Court, literally: they reportedly consume 2,000 mosquitos per day. Martins catch all their food on the fly and drink the same way, skimming the surface to scoop up water in their bills. Their population has become stable once again, thanks to those who build and maintain the colony houses that the martins rely on for nesting. Our own local Muirland Bird Club erected four martin houses in our small area, keeps track of resident martins, and maintains the compartment dwellings.

During the summer months, you can find many martin houses situated near the shorelines of ponds, rivers, and lakes. I hope you stop to watch them, especially when they are feeding their young. Their musical concert alone, with their mellifluous trills, is quite charming, but their acrobatics across water surfaces to retrieve bugs are a real showstopper.

If you love bird watching and want to be part of bird conservation, I encourage you to visit the Cornell Lab of Ornithology online and/or join one of the many organizations that help protect our bird populations: the National Audubon Society, the American Bird Conservancy, the Bird Conservation Alliance, or the National Resources Foundation. Or, you can participate in one of the annual backyard bird counts (see the Cornell Lab site or eBird.org for more information).

I hope that, like me, you discover there's more worthwhile tweeting in your backyard or neighborhood park than on social media. Happy birding!

Joy

# I'd Love to Hear From You!

Please **leave a review** where you purchased your book, or on one of these sites:

- Goodreads

- BookBub

You can also **follow me** at:

- Facebook
  JoyRibarAuthor

- Instagram
  authorjoyribar

- Or sign up for my periodic **newsletter** at
  https://joyribar.com/signup/

# About the Author

Joy Ann Ribar pens the Deep Lakes Cozy Mystery series in central Wisconsin. Joy's life history is a cocktail of careers including news reporter, paralegal, English educator, and college writing instructor. Her hobbies include baking, exploring the outdoors, and wine research. Joy infuses this mixture into her main character, Frankie Champagne, adding a special blend of sass and humor. Her writing is inspired by Wisconsin's four distinct seasons, natural beauty, and kind-hearted, but sometimes quirky, people.

Joy holds a BA in Journalism from UW-Madison and an MS in Education from UW-Oshkosh. She is a member of Mystery Writers of America, Sisters in Crime, Blackbird Writers, and Wisconsin Writers Association. Joy and her husband, John, can be found traveling the country and Canada in their Winnebago, spreading good cheer and hygge!

If you'd like to see Joy in person, send her a message via email, on Facebook or Instagram, to see if she's coming to your neck of the woods.

f facebook.com/JoyRibarAuthor/

BB bookbub.com/authors/joy-ann-ribar

g goodreads.com/author/show/19312175.Joy_Ann_Ribar

instagram.com/authorjoyribar/

Made in the USA
Coppell, TX
07 February 2023

12361860R00184